TOUCHED

SEAN MOONEY

MOONEY BIN ENTERTAINMENT

Credits

Published by Mooney Bin Entertainment

(formerly Mad Moon Rackets)

www.MooneyBinEntertainment.com
www.facebook.com/MooneyBinEntertainment
MooneyBinEntertainment@gmail.com

Please check out other ways we can entertain you!

Written by Sean Mooney

Editing by Alexandria Croxford-Page

Layout and further Editing by Tiffany Lewis

Cover Photo by Andy Goth

Contents

Prologue

"Power," The Suited Man repeated. "What is the most desirable trait to possess when seeking power?"

The Man in White's eyes nervously darted to and fro. He delayed for a few seconds to ponder, eventually settling on a shrug as his response.

The Suited Man loved nothing more than a good discourse, something he would not get here. He wasn't surprised at the task of dragging his companion through this particular dialog, especially given the current circumstance. After all, while The Man in White had come here willingly, it wasn't exactly by choice.

"Machiavelli once said," The Suited Man continued. "There is nothing more difficult to take in hand, more perilous to conduct, or more uncertain in its success, than to take the lead in the introduction of a new order of things. Bearing that in mind, let's explore the question."

The Man in White watched in silence as The Suited Man took a sip of coffee. The cup was set down by manicured hands made pristine by a lifetime absent of hard labor. He curled his fingers into his opposite palm, resting his forearms on the table before he proceeded with the one-sided conversation.

"Perhaps it is money. Money can buy friends, equipment, and open doors that are shut to the general populace. Furthermore, it is easily attainable given the right set of qualities. So maybe the answer is money?" He lifted his coffee to his lips again, attempting to give his partner a chance to respond. When the coffee was back on the table and the deer-in-headlights look was still plastered to The Man in White's face, The Suited Man continued. "Cash, while a fantastic resource to have at your disposal, can have its usefulness directly measured by the competence of its wielder. Have you ever heard the expression about a fool and his money?"

The Man in White's eyes shifted as he weighed his options and searched for the appropriate response. Before one could be given, The Suited Man waved him off. "Of course you have! I almost forgot who I was talking to. So you get the point. Money, while a great tool, is only good when properly applied." He stopped to take another sip of his beverage.

This man is painfully easy to manipulate, The Suited Man mused as he suppressed a grin his hubris begged him to display. The grin suppressed, he instead gazed out the window as if reflecting on the topic at hand. His handsome face and full head of dark brown hair reflected back at him ethereally in the glass, giving him someone to silently converse with as the Man in White tried to keep up.

I love this. They're so adorable at this phase. That Glimmer, the Glimmer of hope still sparkles on the horizon. They're sure it will lead them through the oubliette of terror. They'll do anything to seem like they're playing along, all the while chasing the ever-present sparkle. It's their hope, their salvation, their safe way out. But we all know about the Glimmer... The Suited man grinned internally at his little secret. *Though it is almost painful to keep up the pretense, breaking it to speak frankly would shatter the facade I've so carefully built. So, we continue.*

"If not money, then what?" The Suited Man leaned back, folding his hands on the table. Hawk eyes looked across the table, commanding The Man in White's attention with his presence. "Force? Strength has always been a favored attribute of any superpower. One can't impose their will on an opposing entity without the proper application, or at least the threat, of force."

The Man in White maintained his shaken composure, realizing full well his input was not needed in this conversation.

"But, if we learned anything from Foreman-Ali, or the United States and Viet Nam, the application of force without the proper finesse or guidance will be wasted, and in the end, trivialized."

The Suited Man leaned forward, pointing a finger. "My father, by the way, lost a fortune on that fight."

"Viet Nam?" The Man in White ventured.

The Suited Man raised an eyebrow, using a look of distain in lieu of a verbal retort.

The Man in White remembered silence was his best weapon.

"I digress; the point being that force is fortunately not the answer." He leaned back again, taking the time to stare intently at The Man in White over another prolonged sip of coffee. He gauged the conviction of his conversation partner, finally deciding the last hour had broken him down enough to get to the root of their conversation. "The key to power, the ability to enforce one's will over another, is will itself. Without the determination to accomplish your task, and the knowledge that you will succeed, all of your other resources are useless. Think about that for a moment." The Suited Man paused, swirling his coffee idly in the cup as he imagined The Man in White's thoughts spinning in a similar manner. He enjoyed a few lingering seconds of watching memories flash behind his companion's eyes. Satisfied, he continued, "I see you catch my grift."

"Drift," The Man in White corrected.

"What'd I say?"

"Never mind." He hushed himself.

"Regardless," The Suited Man continued, concealing his grin again, "Power is about control. Control over people, events, or if you want to be poetic, destiny. But in the end, it is control. Maintaining that control takes drive, determination, or as I like to call it: Will. You can beat the richest, strongest and best-liked man. You can cheat him out of his wealth, outmaneuver his strength, and drag his reputation through the mud. Unless he has the drive to brave being ruined again, he will never again take the chances needed to get back up, and will be of no use to anyone who matters." The Suited Man pursed his lips and furrowed his brow at his own words. *Look frustrated at the topic, but not at the weak delivery. You have him now, so don't oversell it. Let's just get to the point.*

"S-so... what you do you want me to do?" The Man in White stammered out.

Fine, make yourself look like the impatient one. The Suited Man laughed to himself. *Here I thought I lost ground, and you give me another hilltop. Maybe you're not good enough for this after all. Maybe you're not the right one. Wait, who am I kidding? That's already been determined. You know, some of the fun is taken out of the match when you get to see the other team's playbook during pregame.*

"Eager to get to work, then? I can respect that." The Suited Man finished his coffee, then slid out of his seat and brushed his suit down to clear any wrinkles. He watched as The Man in White got up in kind, throwing his untouched beverage into a nearby waste bin. The Suited man gave a smile like a shark. "Let's take a walk, shall we?"

1

H ale rolled to his other side, letting one eyelid pry open to glance at his alarm clock.

11:00 PM

A sigh forced its way through feathers as he shoved his face back into his pillow. Light brown hair stuck out in tufts from the billowing white folds of fabric, creating small stalks of waving wheat in a snowy field of cotton. A frustrated groan escaped his lips. "Hour one complete," he mumbled. "Seven more to go."

The restless man let his eyes droop closed again, trying to clear his head. Thoughts were walled away, barricaded back in an effort to keep his overactive mind from preventing the sweet embrace of sleep.

A drop of random thought turned into a trickle of curiosity, widening into a rivulet of questions, which eroded holes in the dam holding back Hale's thoughts. With no Dutch boy in sight, the mental barrier collapsed, making way for a river of ideas to flood his mind.

Don't forget to submit the electric bill.

Change the cat's litter before you leave.

Get your oil changed before coming home.

Buy chips, you're out.

You missed your deadline, don't forget your extra online work.

Mail the DVD back.

He sorted through his mental list, ensuring it was complete and well organized so he could comfortably finish his agenda over the next 24 hours.

"I suppose the good thing about insomnia is I get so much done during the night." He informed the empty room.

Hale laid still, slowly rebuilding the mental wall in an attempt to let his mind settle. With a little luck, the wall would hold and sleep would take him. His body felt heavy. Exhaustion after a long day and little sleep the night before pulled him away from consciousness. Little by little, his muscles relaxed as his breathing slowed to a comfortable rhythm.

Time passed.

Despite his efforts, thoughts bubbled back up to the surface, returning his mind to a state of high alert.

He risked another look at the clock.

11:03 PM

Hale grudgingly sat up in bed. He hunched over and rubbed his face to pull out of the half-trance brought on by his insomnia. The musty smell of his apartment filled his nostrils, mixed with a bit of stale exhaust fumes from a pair of cars passing by outside, and... something else. He pulled out of his hands, shook his head and leaned back, taking in a deep breath. Cigarette smoke?

> *. . . Red nails clicked the flint down on the*
> *matching colored lighter . . .*
> *. . . . . . Menthol covered a night of tequila*
> *shots on her breath . . .*
> *. . . . . . . "Don't give me that! I gotta*
> *have one after a good romp."*

The contrast of clarity from the unexpected insight was jarring in his disoriented state, giving the real world a surreal quality. Hale shook his head again, clearing the string of invading images from his mind. The last thing he needed was to Wander at this time of night. The dirty little secrets in his neighbors' lives could keep him up till dawn.

In spite of himself, his brow furrowed as he struggled to remember. *When did Mrs. Dowling start smoking... or drinking tequila, for that matter?*

"Let's not, please..." he asked himself out loud. "At least do something productive with your time instead of Wandering."

Hale pushed himself out of bed, idly scratching his stomach as he walked out to his living room. Living room was the official term for it. Crawlspace with a wall divider was more appropriate. The kitchen opened directly into the main living area, all of which was crammed into what could have been two large closets. There was a kitchen pass thru generously labelled as a 'bar' by the leasing office, though it only served to limit the amount of space Hale had to walk between his bedroom and the main living area. He navigated through with practiced ease, yawning as he turned sideways and bent back to avoid either tripping on the couch or clipping his side on the jutted-out ledge.

The fridge bathed the kitchen in weak, incandescent light. Cool air greeted Hale as he bent down to examine its contents, "Soda... caffeine, bad idea... OJ... still too much sugar... eh, don't want water..." Hale continued conversing with himself as he picked through his options. "Moo juice it is."

He grabbed the milk and opened a cabinet. A glass clanged on the counter as he twisted off the plastic top of the milk with his other hand.

> . . . Alex twisted the plastic top off with
>> his right hand as indistinct words were
>> spoken
>>> . . . . . . Alex slid out of bed, wiping his
>>> right hand on the sheets vigorously
>>>> . . . . a damp spot was left on the
>>>> sheets next to a laptop emitting
>>>> moaning sounds

"Goddammit Alex!" Hale dropped the cap, nearly knocking the jug all over the counter as he did. He turned on the sink and washed his hands, scrubbing at the imaginary residue left by his somewhat damaged friend. "It's bad enough you didn't fucking shower before coming over. Wash your goddamn hands at least."

With the milk in the trash, Hale plopped onto the couch with his bottle of water. He grabbed for the remote as his laptop booted up. If he wasn't going to get any sleep, he could at least get some writing done. He was already a day behind deadline. Fortunately, an abundance of stories were available due to the local surf tournaments and city hall elections. Mr. Ockerman, Ockie to Hale and a few others around the office, had let him slide due to the excess of opportunities. It helped that ol' Ockie liked Hale. As newsroom editors went, Ockie was not the strictest of bosses, but he definitely knew how to make you feel like an idiot when you screwed up. Over the past year and a half, Hale had performed admirably enough to earn a rapport with Ockie that gave him certain leeway, like missing the occasional deadline.

The TV came alive in the background.

"*–ahm is a top notch skater with the potential to go pro.*" The narrator said over the skating video. "*He's, like, totally the next Tony Hawk or Rodney Mullen. He was born and raised in Orange County, and now lives right here in Long Beach with his sister and girlfriend–*"

Hale chuckled. Local Public access channels always entertained him. The stations featured all local talent... well, local at least... and were about as good as anything else broadcast during the twilight hours. Plus, he occasionally got lucky and heard about some local goober with enough public interest to fill a quarter page article. One of his favorites involved a family that had paid to put out a 30 minute special on their father. He was turning 85, and they wanted to honor him by putting on a show featuring his close relatives and friends. The group went on about how great he was, and how much he had achieved in his long life.

The story captivated Hale. The man was a WWII vet, an entrepreneur, and raised four kids on his own after his wife died during childbirth. A true hero, through and through. When Hale took the story to Ockie, who was a Vietnam Vet himself, he damn near got carte blanche to fill half a page in the local section. Just thinking of the story made him smile.

Despite his personal investment, he never followed up with the family after showing them the article. He kept his memory of them stagnant. There would be no tainting his memories with family drama, the death of the elderly hero, and especially no dirty secrets from his mind Wandering.

No, better to leave them be. Happy. Whole. Perfect.

He opened up the 'Investigations' folder on his C:\ drive, reminding himself to change that ridiculous name. Granted, one could consider journalism a type of investigative activity, though his current work hardly qualified as what the folder was created for. That had been a time of naivety and false hope. A time when he believed Wandering could be put towards a proactive cause. Something he could use to make money, a comfortable living even, instead of just a random stream of information.

That dream died quickly.

A Private Investigator is no good if you learn more about your clients than their targets. It's also no good if you aren't trained in actual investigation techniques and instead choose to rely on your 'natural talent'. Not knowing how to work a high grade camera, or even owning one, being unable to hack accounts, and lacking the knowledge of stealth techniques were a recipe for dismal failure. Finally, clients wanted real proof, not just information. 99% of the time, they already knew what was happening, they just needed to see it to close the book and move on. A testimony of information with a 'trust me, this is true' as a guarantee only made for angry customers.

He backed out of the folder and single clicked, highlighting the word 'Investigation' to rename it. His fingers hovered over the keys as he thought of what to type. As if responding to a dreaded task, his brain wrestled over the various suggestions that rose to the surface. He inwardly challenged his own intelligence as each new suggestion was conceived, leaving his finger quivering over the 'Delete' key.

"Stupid nostalgia…" he muttered after a long pause. He hit Enter, keeping the name as is.

"–*broken 24 bones over his career, but hasn't broken his spirit. He's out there every day–*" The announcer continued to chatter on as the young skater ollied off of a staircase and ground down a railing, landing in a front manual.

"Impressive, Hawk Jr." Hale sipped his water and focused back on his laptop. "Now back to the wonderful world of local politics."

IF HE doesn't stop yelling at me, I'm going to fire him. He will never work for me again. I'll replace him with a younger, more talented worker. One who appreciates their job and understands the delicate tact of the workplace. And one that doesn't use such repetitive, annoying chirps to get my attention–

Hale's eyes opened to sunlight coming through the drapes. High pitched, mechanical chirps emanated from his room in a steady beat. The position of absolute authority and confidence evaporated with the dream, replaced by recognition and panic as the chirping was identified as his alarm clock.

The TV is still on, and my laptop is lying sideways on the floor. I definitely fell asleep on the couch.

He reached down, picking up the laptop and looked at the clock in the corner.

7:16 AM

"Fffff–" He bit his lower lip to prevent a string of curses from reverberating through the apartment complex. Hale liked his neighbors, and he was reasonably certain the contractors who built the community had used cardboard and papier-mâché instead of drywall for the interior dividers. Anything above a loud whisper was unlikely to be muffled.

Having been tormented by insomnia for decades, Hale jumped into his 'I woke up an hour late' routine with fervor. He spread toothpaste across bristles as the shower warmed up, flung the day's polo shirt and khakis onto a hook outside the bathroom, and massaged shampoo into his hair as a breakfast burrito rotated dutifully in the microwave. Hale diligently brushed his teeth with his left hand, lathering up his hair with his right, an awkward process perfected through practice and necessity.

Within 9 minutes of waking in a panic, Hale was standing on his front doormat. His laptop bag dangled from one hand as he fumbled with his keys in the other, leaving his breakfast burrito to dangle out of his mouth. The lock clicked into place and Hale turned on his heel, and marched down the walkway towards the stairwell.

He passed the Dowling's door. Mrs. Dowling's empty plastic chair sat against their outside wall, her newest romance novel resting on the seat. He usually saw her on his way out. She liked to spend her mornings reading and watching the small neighborhood wake up from her elevated walkway. A friendly smile and a 'Good Morning' generally saw him off to work. Their acquaintance was a friendly one despite having little further knowledge of each other.

He slowed a step as he passed the seat, remembering the cigarette smell that set him off Wandering last night. He bit a chunk off his burrito and pulled it from his mouth, giving him an excuse to pause as he shuffled his keys to his other hand.

"Don't do it," Hale whispered to himself through a mouthful of egg and hash browns. "Let it be."

Even as he spoke the warning, he found himself turning around. He set down his laptop, pocketed his keys, and reached for Ms. Dowling's book. He let his fingers run over the smooth cover before picking it up. It was still crisp and new. He brought the book up to his face, flipping through it quickly with one hand, letting the pages fan crisp air across his skin.

. . . Mrs. Dowling removed the book from

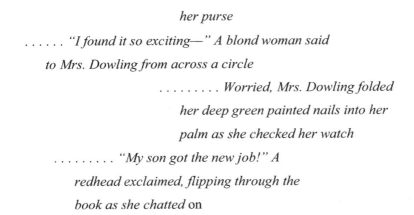

her purse

. . . . . . *"I found it so exciting—" A blond woman said*

to Mrs. Dowling from across a circle

. . . . *Worried, Mrs. Dowling folded*

her deep green painted nails into her

palm as she checked her watch

. . . . *"My son got the new job!" A*

redhead exclaimed, flipping through the

book as she chatted on

Hale returned from the moment of insight, tossing the book back down onto the chair. The Wander had going completely off topic, revealing nothing important... as he had come to expect. "You don't want to know, just leave it."

And with that, he did.

2

Hale rushed through the doors of the bustling newsroom of The Crest. Hale always thought the name sounded too much like toothpaste, no matter how much the owner of the privately owned newspaper explained the irony of the title.

'It's a subtle connection to the beaches of the fine city we report on,' he once said in a quarterly Town Hall meeting. He proudly talked about how he had built the company up from scratch to its current grandeur. What he didn't say is 'from scratch' included a large inheritance and a desire to be in a position where he might be bribed by public officials.

Jerkoff.

Regardless, Hale didn't have to worry about him. He only stopped in to make an appearance and feel important once or twice a month before retreating to his beachside resort. He'd look through up and coming stories, praise random people for their dedication, and make demands on changes that would be completely overruled after he turned around. Everyone knew he was there for show, and only threw fits when the business slowed down. The real person Hale worked for and had to worry about was–

"Ockie!" Brandon yelled out, running past Hale with a manila folder clasped in hand. "Ockie! I got that surf special for you right here. It's good to go on our online feed as soon as you give the go ahead."

Herbert Ockerman turned from his passing comment to another journalist, striding towards both Brandon and Hale. While his 64 years showed in his thin grey hair and defined lines on his face, as well as a pair of light tan pants that were hiked up a bit too high to seem fashionable by today's standards, Mr. Ockerman's mannerisms and demeanor exuded confidence and authority. Ockie was someone you listened to and respected because he had been more places than you, seen more than you, and learned more than you. The occasional upstart would try and call Ockie out in a playful social sparring match, or even worse, start some talk behind his back. The former situations always ended with a borderline politically incorrect verbal beat down, leaving the other person's pride bruised and bloodied. They'd recover; they'd just learn who the greater social predator was between them. The latter ended with more humiliating encounters. Ockie knew everyone and heard everything, putting him in a position to prepare proper retribution for such petty office politics. One such co-worker logged into his PC to find his background splash screen had been changed to Mr. September 2009 in a thong. Serendipitously, Ockie just happened to be walking by as the man logged in, giving him the perfect opportunity to declare the inappropriateness of lewd pictures on one's work computer loud enough for the next few rows to hear.

Ockie reached out for the proffered folder, not breaking stride as he moved past them. "Thank you, Brandon. I'll look at this now. Hale, follow me." Ockie smacked him on the arm with the folder as he passed. He continued speaking to Hale as he opened the folder and scanned over its contents. "I see we've adopted a new work policy to not only miss a deadline, but show up over half an hour late the day after. I can only hope our competitors embrace this as a new trend and implement it across the board immediately."

"No sir, Mr. Ockerman. I–" Hale followed behind the man, beginning to explain.

"Jennings," said Ockie, cutting Hale off to speak to another man as they passed. "My wife is a teacher; 6th grade English. Wonderful lady! You'll love her! I promise to get you a seat in the front row next semester if you turn in another story with more than four commas in a sentence."

"Sorry, Mr. Ockerman." Mark Jennings blushed, chuckling nervously to himself.

Hale marveled at the sight for a moment. The man had such a delicate balance. His words should cut and wound people, but his tone and expression somehow softened the blow. He delivered the message clearly, but kid-gloved the impact with his dry sense of humor. It was almost like a grandfather saying, 'Ya mucked it up, boy... but I know you can do better.' You didn't like hearing you screwed the pooch, but you attacked the issue again with renewed confidence knowing you could improve while getting another chance to impress the old codger.

Ockie approached his office, smiling to his secretary. "Mrs. Williams, radiant as always. My compliments on those stunning shoes. You put the rest of the office to shame."

"Oh, Mr. Ockerman..." Mrs. Williams waved an embarrassed hand, grinning and looking away. Mrs. Williams looked to be a bit older than Ockie, and was undisputedly the nicest person in the company. She took the job after surviving her late husband, hoping to fill the days with something other than TV and lounging on her porch. She'd bring in homemade cookies and sandwiches at least twice a week, passing them out with smiles and warm wishes. She enjoyed the looks on people's faces, the warm "thank you's" in their eyes. It reminded her of her husband.

She didn't advertise that last part, Hale just Wandered into that tidbit during one of her charitable rounds.

"Come on in, Mr. Langston."

Hale hated when Ockie used his last name, but that was just the old man's way of addressing people.

"Please close the door."

Hale shut the door behind him, immediately turning and resuming his explanation. "Again, my apologies, Mr. Ockerman. I slept through my–"

Ockie held up a hand and winced, "Please, please, it's Ockie. And sit down, Hale, the show's over."

Hale looked confused.

"I can't have you walking in 30 minutes late a day after deadline and *not* dress you down in front of everyone. People will think I'm favoring you," he

grinned, then adopted a more serious expression. "Or worse, that I've gone soft..."
He allowed his raised eyebrows and somber frown to mock the severity of his
words. He broke back into a soft smile after a few moments, motioning to a chair
across from him. "Sit."

Hale grinned and shook his head, sliding into the seat. "Thanks, Ockie.
Seriously though, I'm sorry. I screwed you bad enough with that massive ball drop
yesterday. I just couldn't sleep last night, and it made me sleep right through my
alarm. I did get that piece finished though, since I was up." He pulled his laptop out
of his bag.

"Email it to me." Ockie waved again, dismissively. "I won't be able to use it
'til tomorrow's run anyway." He paused, leaning back in his chair and folding his
hands. "So what's with the sleepless nights, kiddo? You feeling alright?"

Hale shrugged, frowning. "I've never really slept well. My mind goes into
overdrive at night. I start thinking about all the stuff I have to do during the day, get
ideas for projects, new stories I could pursue." He sighed, letting his hands flop
down. "I swear, by two in the morning I could develop a cure for cancer."

"I'm gonna call you on that when this California sun catches up to me."

"I'll start reading medical journals before I go to bed." Hale let a grin sneak
passed his worried expression.

"Alright then." Ockie sat forward again, resting his arms on his desk. "If you
need anything, you let me know. All the same, I hope you understand yesterday's
flop and today's fashionably late entrance have placed you firmly in my pocket,
mah boy."

"Absolutely, Ockie." Hale grinned, standing up and slinging his bag over his
shoulder.

"Have a good one, Hale. And don't look so happy walking out of here! I just
chewed you out, remember kiddo?" He smiled, tapping his desk twice with his
palm before grabbing the manila folder and leaning back in his chair.

. . . "—remember kiddo. Do us proud over there."

Ockie's proud face masked the fear in his eyes
...... "He's fine, Harriet. He only
missed one letter, you'll see."
.... muffled sobs from Harriet emanated
from his chest as he hugged her close . . .
.... the soft feel of a folded flag
in his hands . . . "We'll always
remember, kiddo..."

Ockie's memories carried a deep undertone of sadness. The image of the news editor in his younger years speaking to a man that could only have been his child did not soften the vignette at all. A lump tightened in Hale's throat as he walked out of the office. Now he felt as if he unintentionally manipulated Ockie's emotions. Did he get close to Ockie so quickly because Hale reminded Ockie of his lost son? Guilt washed over him, making it easy to appear somber as he walked out of the office and over to his desk.

———

HALE COULDN'T quite see the sun setting on the ocean from the section of 7th Street he took home. Almost to add insult to injury, he did get a nice blast of sunshine in his face from over the lip of the asphalt hill hiding the horizon. He flipped the sun visor down to shield his eyes, rolling through the traffic past Long Beach University to get home. The drive was only a few miles, and all side streets, though this time of day these streets were packed with students and tired office workers coming home for the day. This meant each mile took at least 5 minutes to cover, turning a short 4-mile commute into a twenty minute trek across town. It fit the So Cal stereotype: 20 minutes to everything.

The chirping of a digitally-produced Beethoven song along with vibrations on the dashboard drew his attention to his phone. The face display read 'Alex'. He swiped the phone open and put it to his ear.

"'Sup man."

"What's goin' on, boss?!" Alex said, overenthusiastic as always. While overbearing at times, it couldn't be denied his general excitement for life was contagious.

"Not much, contemplating riding my bike to work from now on. I could use the exercise, and this traffic is ridiculous."

"Not me, dude. I love AC too much. Plus, I get plenty of exercise rollin' off your mom every weekend."

Ah, good, the 'your mom' jokes have started. "Well, I guess low standards do yield some positive byproducts."

"Huh?"

"Never mind," Hale chuckled. "So are you planning on forgoing banging my mom for the night and invading my apartment instead?"

"You know it, boss!" Alex was derailed easily and his confusion was quickly replaced with his usual jovial excitement. "Hey, I know these chicks that live near you. I worked on replacing some drywall in their apartment complex earlier this week and got their numbers. Sophomores, dude, and hot as shit! Want me to bring them over for a little house party?"

"And scare 'em away with my 500 square foot palace? No thanks, dude. Plus, I really don't want to entertain tonight. It's been a long week."

"Alright, homo. I'll be over in an hour. You better get that gay porn hidden away before I get there. Wouldn't want you to out yourself accidentally."

"And ruin my chances of slipping you a Roofie-Colada? Never."

Alex laughed on the other end of the phone before hanging up. Hale grinned to himself. Alex had a way of cheering him up with his infectious good moods. And while getting laid with no strings attached with some young co-eds, hot co-eds, knowing Alex's standards, sounded good in theory, there was more to the situation than Alex realized. It shattered the mood when all too often, her mind was full of anything but Hale. Apparently intimacy inspired Wandering, and Hale had been treated to images of his date in a threesome with two football players, or a much more energetic and enjoyable session with a female partner. That one had initially been kind of hot, but eventually the unwanted insights just become just a blow to his pride.

Damaged self-image was one thing, but it was by far not the worst he had born witness to. Hale's most jarring Wander resulted from a playful smack on the rear, resulting with a memory of an abusive ex beating her up. The sudden empathy of fear and helplessness destroyed any chance of staying in the moment, which sent a very unintentional message that he was not interested in his partner.

Hale didn't know what caused these little flashes of insights. A little research had led him to a similar ability called Psychometrics. Hale didn't like that name, and it seemed the descriptions of the ability weren't exactly what Hale had experienced. So he'd created his own name for his ability. He called it Wandering. He liked his title better, as it was if his mind simply wandered from topic to distantly related topic. It could start from the touch of a door handle, the smell of a fragrant perfume, the taste of chapstick on a girl's lips, or sometimes even the sound of a voice. It was random most of the time; stuff he didn't care about or even want to know. But without fail, the information gleaned was never wrong.

Certain activities always seemed to make Wandering come on stronger and with heightened clarity. A bad fight with a loved one, a physical altercation in a bar, a mourning relative at a funeral, and almost always, a moment of passion with another woman. It was as if sex acted as an amplifier, flinging secrets he really didn't want to know in his face. It made one night stands difficult, and relationships with any woman that wasn't inexperienced and wholly faithful damn near impossible.

This was a subject he hadn't broached with Alex. He let his friend think him a bit of an introvert, which was true, and a bit of a coward when it came to women, which wasn't completely false. Explaining his... insight... without sounding like a complete psycho was just not something he knew how to do. Fortunately, Alex was easygoing and a loyal friend. He brushed away what seemed like social quirks with his comrade and accepted Hale as he was, or at least how Alex perceived him.

This worked well for Hale.

Hale was still weighing the pros and cons of calling Alex back and taking him up on the offer to bring the girls over as he walked up the stairs to his apartment. He pulled out his keys as he judged the probability of the girl having issues that would inevitably set off some horribly mood-wrecking Wander. The pros and cons continued to tip on the scales as he passed the Dowling's door. A noise caught his attention, and he paused to listen. Mrs. Dowling was speaking to someone. Her husband, Hale surmised. Her voice didn't sound pleasant, but she wasn't yelling. He leaned in toward the door, trying to make out the words. His hand rested against the door to ease in closer...

> . . . a woman laughed as her back slammed
>
> against the door, his hands exploring her
>
> body
>
> . . . . . . a hand of red, manicured nails
>
> pulled the door shut

Hale pulled away, coming back to himself.

"Hale." Deep breaths centered him as he spoke to himself. "You don't want to get involved." With that, he closed the rest of the distance to his door, unlocked it, and walked inside.

Hale closed his door and set his laptop down on the counter. A regal feline greeted him upon turning into his cramped apartment. Commodore sat, back straight, eyes narrowed as if sitting on a throne. His fur was black going from his tail, up his back and wrapping the top of his head, giving way to white cheeks, brow, and muzzle. Three white splotches decorated his chest like an officer's medals with ankle high white boots to match. He stared Hale in the eyes from his position on the bar like a disappointed parent.

"Good afternoon, Commodore," Hale said to the cat, giving him a mock salute. "Glad to see me home, I see..." He stopped, sniffing at an odor that caught his nose."... smell, what the hell is that smell?"

Hale looked around the floor to find a neat pile of Commodore's latest achievements on the entryway carpet. The carpet around it was all leaning towards the masterpiece, showing that the cat had attempted to cover it up with the non-existent surrounding litter.

At least he'd tried.

Hale looked back up at the cat with a frustrated look, who returned the stare with that same gaze of condescension and disappointment.

You brought this on yourself, human, Commodore's eyes said.

"Yeah, yeah, I know. I forgot to clean your litter again... but seriously, can you give me a better warning?" Hale griped as he grabbed a handful of paper towels and hunched down to the floor. "Maybe some meows, or even a bite on the ankle as I walk by your litter box?"

The cat stared down at him with careless eyes. *I won't stoop to such base behaviors, human. Your lackluster performance as my servant does not merit extra work on my part.* His expression communicated more than Hale could hope to with simple words.

Hale balled the paper towels up and walked into the bathroom. Commodore jumped from the counter and marched behind him. His white boots marched in perfect rhythm, following his soldier to the battlefield known as the Litter. He leapt up to the hilltop, known to some as the bathroom counter, so he could look down on the field and ensure his squad defeated the enemy properly.

Scoops of litter were sifted, removing the land mines from the battlefield, and summarily disposed of safely into the toilet. The day's undertaking was topped with the balled up wad of paper towels. Hale brought the litter bag out from under the cabinet, pouring a fresh layer of pebbles and crystals, then mixed it around with the scoop. He slid the bag and scoop back under the sink, then looked up at Commodore from his hunched position.

"How's that, sir?" He asked, raising his eyebrow and giving the cat a sardonic grin.

Commodore's ears perked and round green eyes relaxed into pleased slits. An affirming chuff, more like a bark by Hale's estimation, escaped his lips. *You've done well, grunt. Now pet me.*

Hale chuckled, scratching the cat on the head.

"Spoiled beast."

He wished he could understand what was going on in that cat's mind. He was sure he ranked lower on the social ladder than he should.

The front door flew open, banging on the wall. "Hey homo, the beer is here!"

Commodore's brow flattened, converting pleased eyes back to their narrow, discontented slits.

Hale stood and walked out of the bathroom, greeting Alex with a shit eating grin. "Hey Pooky. Aww, you brought me cider!"

Alex held forth the six pack in his left hand. "Yeah, well, I figure since you don't like pussy anymore, we might want to start weaning you off the hard stuff. Wouldn't want any hair to grow on that chest, now would we? Might upset your first boyfriend."

Hale took one of the ciders out of the six pack, leaving Alex holding the rest. "Don't get mad 'cause my drink of choice has more alcohol and better taste than your 'manly' beer. I like to enjoy what I drink."

"You are correct, it is important to enjoy what you swallow." Alex set the rest of the cider down on the bar, sliding over the top of the couch into a sitting position. His six pack of stout was placed on the floor beside him. He obviously didn't expect them to be out long enough to get warm.

Hale laughed off the last of the traded blows, taking a seat on the other side of the couch. He twisted off the cap of his cider and tilted it back. He had the sudden inclination to ask Alex to wash his hands after last night's milk episode.

"Seriously dude, what gives?" Alex pulled out the bottle opener attached to his keys while he spoke. "I mean, this is like, the third time in the last couple months I've had fucking smoking hot women ready to donate their panties to your floor space, and you just brush it off. You having trouble getting it up or something?"

"Fuck you, man." Hale laughed and backhanded Alex's shoulder. "It's not like that. I just got a lot of stuff on my mind. Tired from work, you know." He sipped his beer, looking over at his friend. It wasn't hard to put together how Alex had a steady stream of women flowing in and out of his bedroom. Aside from the steady stream of sexist and homophobic comments that tumbled from his mouth, he was a jock in college, had a body built for sports, a confident personality that enticed women to say yes, and a good head of hair that was naturally highlighted by the sun from working outside all the time.

Hale remembered him back in high school, talking about gunning for the NFL as soon as he hit college. He was good. He played hard, had the heart, skill, the whole works. Regardless, every year recruiters came and went, giving him a pass each time. There was no tragic story. He didn't blow his knee out at the big game. He didn't have a baby that forced him to stay home. He was just a couple inches too short and a couple steps too slow. Fortunately, Alex retained his positive outlook, despite spending four years in college to earn an Associates degree, and moved on with his life.

"It's one thing to be tired, dude, but nothing tops off a bad day like a good top off, you know what I mean? And it's not like these girls are looking for deep conversations or some shit. They're here for the same reason we are."

"Maybe I'm not looking to catch Hep C from one of your guttersluts, or even better, get one of 'em knocked up so I can be paying out child support for the next couple decades." Hale raised his bottle, toasting the freedom from STD's and being a baby's daddy.

"Fuck that, man. Seriously, I've been doin this shit for years. You just have to play it safe." Alex counted out his safeguards on his fingers to accentuate each point. "I wear a condom, I make sure she's on the pill, I pull out, and I punch the bitch in the stomach when I'm done."

Hale spit cider all over the table.

Alex laughed.

"And you wonder why women think you're a misogynist?" Hale wiped at his chin with his sleeve. "There's something wrong with your brain."

"Like I'd ever lay hands on a woman! People know I'm just fucking around. The ones who don't take life too seriously anyway." He grinned and waved Hale off. A silence hung for a moment before Alex adopted a more somber expression. "Speaking of crazy feminazis, you're not still hung up on Amy, are you?" he asked with a wince.

"Naw, man. No." Hale shook his head as he took another sip of his drink. *Wait, take that back. If you're still pining over your ex, he'll rag on you and tell you to move on, but it will close the subject. Get that look of embarrassment on your face, and then pretend to own up.*

Alex eyed him, sensing a follow-up was coming. "You sure...?"

. . ."You sure Hale won't be mad? I mean,

he's over me, but–"

. . . . . . Amy put both hands on the mirror, watching
Alex's reflection. "Oh god! Fuck me!"

Initial rage born from betrayal quickly shifted to annoyance and frustration. *Goddammit Alex,* Hale cursed internally. *You have to put your dick in everything, don't you? I don't care that you slept with my ex, we broke it off clean almost six months ago, but this is damn inconvenient timing. Now if I use the lie it makes my best friend feel guilty, which isn't worth avoiding an uncomfortable conversation. Huh, come to think of it, this entire conversation was probably geared to lead to this single question. Bravo, Alex. Bravo. That's a level of social manipulation I didn't credit you with.*

Hale looked back up at his waiting friend. "Are you gonna keep eye fucking me, or are you ready for me to school you in the Shipyard for the next hour?" *If he drops the topic here, he was just fishing about Amy.*

"You talk a lot of shit for someone who ends up at the bottom of the scoreboards every time." Alex picked up the game controllers under the coffee table, tossing one into Hale's lap. "I seem to remember doubling your frags last time you tried to step up."

"And I remember someone spitting beer all over me when I had a sniper bead on him during sudden death. Screen watching whore."

"All's fair in love and war..." Alex grinned, looking over at Hale. Something caught his eye, causing him to look over his shoulder.

Commodore sat with his regal posture on the bar, looking down at Alex with disapproving eyes.

"What the fuck's with your cat, dude? I mean, it kinda freaks me out when he does that."

Hale glanced back at Commodore and shrugged. "What can I say, man. The cat can sense evil."

3

Drive-Thru Java was a pleasant sanctuary for Hale. The establishment prided itself on serving primarily as a drive-through coffee bar, meaning the vast majority of its customers never set foot in the building. This was important to Hale. The less foot traffic, the less likely he'd stumble on something that would make him Wander. It took many failed attempts before he found this ideal retreat. He quickly learned that dark corners of popular coffee houses, 24 hour diners, obscure areas of a library, and secluded spots in public parks generally flooded him with romantic encounters of teenagers with no place of their own and exhibitionist couples trying to spice things up. It was one thing to have a good book interrupted by the frustrated feelings of a student studying for their Finals, or a business exec sweating over a speech outline. Those he could accept in small doses. However, nothing derailed a good story like a sudden flash of a girl quietly having an orgasm on her boyfriend's fingers.

His favorite table sat on the east side of the building within a gated patio. There were two important factors of this location: the building blocked the breeze and sunlight from the ocean, and passerby would not just walk by and sit down to relax. In order for another person to enter the gated area they had to walk through the coffee house, thereby ignoring the awe-inspiring and conveniently located drive-through on the west side of the building.

It was as secluded a public environment as Hale could ask for.

Hale enjoyed these moments of public solitude. It gave him the feeling of being a social, outgoing, and normal person, all the while avoiding all human contact and thereby eliminating the risk of Wandering like a completely antisocial, abnormal person.

He flipped the page of his book, idly sipping from his coffee as he devoured the words on the page. The plot was thickening. After the hard boiled detective had finally won over the girl, the killer exploited this perceived weakness by kidnapping her. Now he held the hero in a moral quandary; does he go to save his love, or does he follow the trail of the killer and save an innocent life?

Mysteries were his favorite. In the pages of a book, there was the element of surprise. There were unknown variables, which would only be deduced by critical thinking, or by turning to the next page to see what came next. There were no sudden Wanders. No insights to spoil the secret. It was an enigma until the end. The only time this did not hold true was after a particular book signing. Hale decided to buy the last book out of a trilogy he was enjoying at an event featuring the author, who conversed with fans as she signed copies of her newest release.

"I've loved the series so far. I'm looking forward to seeing what you do with the disease," Hale had commented as his book was being signed.

The author picked up the book, flipping through towards a section in the back. Eyes peered over the rim of the book as she flashed him a mischievous grin. "You'll love it…"

> . . . she grinned mischievously at her
> husband, "You'll love it, I've got it all
> planned out!"
>
> . . . . . . He handed the book over. "Hon, no one
> will guess it's a psychosomatic condition. It
> made the story!"

Hale's expression had dropped, managing a half-polite thank you before storming out of the store.

No more book signings until after the book was devoured, Hale had decided. This book had not been ruined. And the author knew how to grip her reader.

He felt the anguish of the protagonist as he pored over his choices, knowing either one would have tormenting results, and neither would feel rewarding in the end. The question was: did he choose to be the selfless hero, or the romantic savior?

"Is this seat taken?" a voice asked.

Hale didn't even look up. He was fixated on the paragraph. The back of his mind deduced that out of the four chairs at his table, the voice was not likely to take the chair he was sitting in, or the one on which he rested his feet. Figuring it was safe, he quickly muttered, "Uh uh."

He managed to maintain his grip on the imagery of the story, focusing on the pained expression on the hero's face as he toiled alongside him through the moral dilemma.

"I'm sorry, was that a no that it was not taken, or that I couldn't take one?"

The detective's harrowing decision was interrupted at its cusp, shattering as Hale was yanked out of his fantasy to see a portly man standing across the table from him. The man looked confused. No, wait, that wasn't confusion. He was nervous. The crooked tie must have exuded the air of confusion.

It's a frickin' chair, jackass, just take it and leave me the hell alone!

"Yes, I mean, no, it's not a problem. Go ahead and take it." Hale tried to cover his irritation with a smile.

And fix your tie, you look ridiculous.

"Thanks, sorry to bother you." The Portly Man fumbled with the chair, banging it against the table on the way up. The table shook and jerked, launching Hale's coffee into the corner of the patio. Visible nerves shifted to embarrassment as he put the chair down. It would be more accurate to say he inadvertently slammed it down and, flustered, started reaching for his wallet. "I'm so sorry! I'm a mess right now. Here, let me pay for that."

"No, it's really not necessary." Hale leaned back as the man flattened a wrinkled bill between his hands.

Please don't get near me. I'm so close to having a peaceful afternoon. Last thing I need is to Wander about whatever chaos is going on in your life.

"Please, I insist." The Portly Man proffered a five dollar bill to Hale.

Awesome. I've politely declined, which means I can now be the asshole who completely brushes him off, possibly inviting more and more offers and apologies, or I can be gracious and take the bill. Hale took a moment to weigh his options. With a sigh, he reached out. *Please don't. Please don't. Please don't.*

The man handed the bill over. Hale took the corner between his index and thumb, gingerly taking the money. "Thanks, it really isn't necce–

... "–ssary, but I appreciate it, Susan," The Portly
Man smiled as his female friend hugged him.
... "–name is Cass, and she–"
... "–at Drive-Thru Java," Sue
smiled to The Portly Man.

"–ssary…" Hale felt himself stumble over the word as he Wandered. Now feeling like a moron, he just smiled and raised the bill to the man as an appreciative salute. "Thank you… I appreciate it."

The man just nodded. His own insecurities seemed to outweigh the strange behavior of the man whose coffee he had just catapulted. He picked the chair up, more carefully this time, and moved to the other side of the patio. He sat down in the opposite corner, facing the newly acquired seat. With the empty chair and lack of a drink, he continued broadcasting 'I'm waiting for someone' with the occasional look around the building and surrounding sidewalks.

Hale allowed his attention to linger on The Portly Man.

Damn you for making me curious.

It was a side effect of Wandering. The information he gleaned was always accurate, but only a small piece of the puzzle. It was like trying to play one of those games that revealed the picture piece by piece, and walking away after the first two pieces are shown. As a naturally curious person, the suspense would drive him crazy.

The Portly Man pulled out a pack of smokes, setting them on the table in front of him. Hale compared the gestures to a violent nicotine craving as the man jumped and shifted, until he saw him adjust the pack left, right, then back to its original position.

Obsessive compulsive? Hale pondered, watching the man fiddle with the pack again. *What the hell is wrong with you? What are you doing here? And fix your goddamn tie!*

The back door to the patio jingled, drawing both men's attention. A pair of long legs hugged by denim and shin-high black boots stepped out onto the patio. Hale's eyes were drawn upwards over a black baby doll top covering a slender torso, which transitioned beautifully into pale skin and a cascade of fiery red hair. The outfit had a pleasant mix of appearing dressed up while still remaining casual enough to fit in at a coffee shop.

Hale allowed himself to gawk, saturating himself with the beauty's profile for a moment.

The Portly Man straightened in anticipation, smiling hopefully.

The woman gave a polite smile back.

Mystery solved. Hale thought, pulling his eyes away before he was caught staring. *Blind date. Let's just hope they keep the chatter either quiet or short. Actually, let's hope for both.*

Annoyance fading, Hale scanned back a few paragraphs, attempting to immerse himself again before reaching the point he left off. It was hard for him just to jump back into an intense part of the story. It seemed to lose momentum, robbing him of the emotional empathy he shared with the characters. How was he supposed to enter a violent fight or a tearful parting with a blasé attitude or, more relevant to his current situation, an annoyed one?

Now where were we? Ah, here we are. Moral quandary... chase the killer or save his girl... he's driving up the freeway... northbound ramp takes him to the killer, southbound to his girl... Hale took a moment to chuckle at the obvious symbolism between the 'north' and 'south' choices. The book's religious undertones liked to make heaven and hell references frequently to accentuate the righteous versus sinful and selfish choices. *He gripped the wheel until his knuckles were white, sweat beading on his forehead–*

"Is this seat taken?" a voice asked.

Hale let the book fall forward onto the table, pursing his lips in frustration as he looked up. A rush of intrigue and delight collided with his irritation, leaving him conflicted as he gazed at the face of the woman who had just walked out onto the patio. Hale's mind did some quick mental calculations. She was standing over here, suggesting he was wrong about the blind date, or something had gone seriously wrong within the last 10 seconds. He risked a glance past her to The Portly Man.

Suspicious eyes were fixed on the woman and Hale.

Nope, not wrong about the blind date. So what is she doing here? A waft of vanilla perfume caught his nose...

> . . . "—rather use vanilla, Sue. It's
> softer."
> . . . . "—appreciate it. Remember, back
> patio, pack of cigarettes on the table."
> . . . . Susan hugged her vanilla scented
> friend.

She smiled in an attempt to entice an answer out of him, bringing him to the realization he'd be sitting dumbly for god knows how long.

"Uh, no, it's n–"

Before he could finish she had slid into the chair. She propped her elbows on the table and looked at him over her interlocked fingers.

Hale paused, regaining his foothold on reality and attempting to sanely address the situation. "You realize I don't smoke, right?"

No Hale, that's not sanely.

"Neither do I." She cocked her head at the odd opener.

"No, I mean…" Hale stumbled. Aside from being caught off guard, the woman was striking. She didn't have the stereotypical facial structure of a cover girl, but her beauty was undeniable. To add to the mystery, she displayed an exotic mix of high cheekbones, pale complexion, and pouty lips that made it difficult to assign a specific ethnicity. Hale centered himself, attempting to re-enter the conversation like a human being with a decent grasp on the English language. "I think he was waiting for you. That pack looked like a signal of some sort."

"Maybe he was just getting ready to smoke." She offered.

"He's waiting for someone, and smokers don't generally wait after bringing their packs out."

"You're observant."

"You're dodging the issue."

Hale? Hey! It's me, down here! Something stirred beneath his waistline. *She's beautiful! Why are you trying to scare her away?!*

"Perhaps I'm simply deciding my afternoon is better spent at this corner of the patio." She leaned forward as she spoke.

She's blocking her cleavage with her arms. This means she either sucks at the seduction game, or she's trying to keep my attention on her words and not her tits. "Not to be rude, but, I'm kind of busy." Hale raised his book.

HEY! I'm talking to you! The voice below his waist shouted again.

"You're suggesting a bound stack of paper will be more interesting than a stirring conversation with a total stranger?"

"I love a good story."

I can make your life difficult if you choose to ignore me!

"I have a great story."

"I don't think we have enough time."

I'm warning you! I can make any standing moment an embarrassment!

"What if I bribed you with a drink?" She offered.

"I have plenty of chai over there if I get thirsty." He gestured to the corner containing his spilt cup.

"You have a girlfriend." It was a statement, though not disappointed.

"No."

"Boyfriend?"

"No?" Hale took a moment to gauge whether his mannerisms came off gay.

"Live with your parents?"

"No!"

His confused expression asked the question of 'Where are you going with this?' *She doesn't look dissuaded at all. If she was just trying to throw off the pudgy guy, she's done it by now. Why is she still here?*

She smiled at him, a curious glint in her eye. "You're amusing. I bet you enjoy being mysterious."

Okay, let's try something a little reckless. Hale adopted a knowing look on his face. He spoke softly to ensure their eavesdropper wouldn't be able to listen in. "Tell you what, in the spirit of mysteries and keeping prior commitments, I'll make you a bet. If I win, we say our goodbyes and you take your chances with the smoker. If you win, I'll put my book away and actually contribute to this conversation."

"Ooh, that sounds interesting. And with the cynical tone to your voice, how could I refuse? What are the terms?"

She's genuinely enjoying this. I'm being an asshole on purpose, lady, go away.

"I'll bet you I can guess your name with no hints."

She eyed him suspiciously, calculating her odds. "He didn't tell you he was waiting for me, or spill my name to someone on the phone?"

She's good. You were curious about Porky's nerves over there, and aren't curious at all about the beauty with a brain sitting across from you?

"Nope. I've never heard anyone speak your name, nor have I seen it written down."

"On your honor?"

Hale held up two fingers in the 'Scouts Honor' fashion. *Technically that's true... Wandering isn't really hearing or reading, right? Meh, I'm going to say it's true.*

She regarded him with suspicious eyes for a few more seconds, "Deal."

He grinned. "I'd say from your complexion that your ancestors liked to stay out of the sun. Your red hair suggests Ireland or Scotland, both of which tend to be proud of their heritages. This suggests you were given a name in line with your ancestry. I've got a 50-50 chance between the two islands, so I'll go with Irish decent. Going through some of the more common names gives me a short list of possibilities. I'm going to go out on a limb and say... Cassandra." He waited for the shocked expression so he could play up the mysterious angle and shoo her away.

It never came. She maintained the same look throughout his entire charade. She was not so much looking at him as dissecting him. Each word seemed to be individually gathered, analyzed, and pulled apart as he spoke. When he finished, she maintained the quizzical expression as if she was still expecting the ending. Staring at him over her interlocked fingers, she leaned back and rested her hands on the table.

"I have a counter offer, double or nothing," she said after a long pause. "I know you love a good story, so if I can legitimately surprise you and become more interesting than that book, we continue our conversation."

"And how do you plan to double my winnings?" Hale asked with a chuckle.

"Not only will I leave you to your inferior story," she said, glancing at his book, "but I will do more than just go back to Phill over there. I'll give him a legitimate chance instead of the mercy date that our mutual friend begged me to give him."

"Phill annoyed the piss out of me ten minutes ago. That's not a great prize."

"But you seem like a decent person under that anti-social exterior, and I'm sure you'd like to see a fellow man have a chance on a blind date instead of completely wasting his time. Or you could go with the selfish reason," she grinned.

"What's that?"

"It's killing you to know if I'll win."

She's right. Hale thought, the muscles at the corners of his eyes tightening to suppress a grin. *She was intriguing. It wasn't just her looks, nor her ridiculous persistence. It was the way she spoke, her mannerisms. Something intelligent was behind those eyes, and he couldn't help but be curious to see what she would produce.*

Hale took in a long breath, signifying his surrender with a belabored sigh. "You win. Let's see if you can surprise me."

Her grin was cocky, as if she'd finally been given the opportunity to move the final piece into a perfectly constructed checkmate. She sat up again, folding her arms in a way that still managed to obstruct casual glances down past her chin. "You're not only here alone, but you live close by. Close enough to get here without your car, I'd gather."

It was true. The shop was only a block from his place. "What makes you think I even have a car?"

"If you don't, it's by choice. Your clothes are new, and reasonably fashionable. And if you have the money to spend on them and $5 chai teas, you have enough to afford a motorized transportation. Returning to the topic of clothes for a moment, while they are nice, they aren't *too* nice. You haven't shaved for a day, and your hair is well kept, but not styled. You'd be a prime candidate for Queer Eye. Plus, with the multiple attempts to see past my arms…" She glanced down to the blocked view to accentuate her point. "It's clear you're either not gay, or desperately trying to distance yourself from the local stereotypes."

Hale could not hide the blush in his cheeks. "Hey, I've had gay friends that were scruffy!"

"Shh," She winked. "It's not your turn."

He pursed his lips to hide a grin while she continued.

"You've chosen to sit outside a drive through coffee shop to read. Most people read in quiet places like libraries, or at least inside the aforementioned java establishments. Your presence here means you really don't want to interact with anyone, and you're willing to suffer the noise of passing traffic to do so.

"I'd say you're just anti-social. However, when you regain your footing from being verbally ambushed, you're witty and insightful. You've demonstrated not only the ability to maintain a conversation and keep someone orally engaged, but the ability to look past the basic meanings of simple words and gestures. This leads me to believe you have a defensive wall you've put in place. This could be due to recently going through a bad breakup, or possibly a string of unsuccessful connections for one reason or another.

"Which brings us back to your previous 'victory'. You are smart and perceptive, but a horrible liar. While I am a quarter Irish, I'm primarily Russian and German. My hair is naturally black, though with the proper chemicals I've accomplished a wonderful shade of natural looking red. And finally, Cassandra is a Greek name with which I share no ancestry with whatsoever. My mother simply thought it was pretty.

"However, when you delivered your completely asinine assessment of my heritage to achieve your end result, you did so in an attempt to prove how you reached the goal. The only requirement to win would have been to say the name and move on. But you didn't, which means you were trying to trick me into believing you accomplished your 'victory' in another way than your actual means. This suggests one of two things: you either lied about Phill over there telling you my name, thereby nullifying your victory due to cheating, or—" She trailed off, letting the moment hang.

Hale's breath caught in his throat. Could she have possibly deduced how he really knew her name? Even if she didn't, had his reckless display compromised him into revealing his ability? Was that a bad thing? What if he was forced to explain and she thought he was crazy? It would drive her away.

I thought that was the point.

It bothered Hale when even his own mind seemed against him.

"—you've been stalking me." She ended the assessment with a suspicious raise of an eyebrow.

Hale stopped for a second. *She's too smart to think I'm actually stalking her.*

Is she mocking me?

"That emotion you're feeling—" She leaned in, wearing a wry grin— "is called surprise. Now, which story are you interested in learning?"

She is mocking me.

Hale paused, truly floored. He looked into the eyes of Cass, who was sitting with that cocky grin of victory across from him. She had done her part. She had taken him completely off guard, and intrigued him enough to make him want more. He let his eyes stray over her shoulder to Phill, who was still watching them both intently.

Screw you and your crooked tie, Phill. You interrupted my book.

His eyes returned to the woman across from him. Hale slowly reached out, setting his book on the table. "Alright then. Tell me your story."

4

"**S**witch the backdrop to blue, please," Jeremiah said. "Imanu'el wishes for the backdrop to contrast and exhibit a heavenly color."

"Este, si?" the man holding the brown sheet asked.

"No, no." Jeremiah shook his head, trying to think of the correct way to deliver the instructions to the man. Despite having lived in Southern California for most of his life, he had never been skilled with Spanish. This was crippling from time to time, such as when he hired a few migrant workers from outside of a home improvement store to help set up a studio. "Uh... this." He pointed at the brown sheet. "Not brown. Blue."

"No marrón?" The man asked, confused.

"Uh... blue..." He wracked his brain for the word. Spanish class had been a long time ago, but colors were definitely something they went over. He started repeating rote phrases they went over in his head, trying to jog his memory. *Something about playa, or mar... 'The ocean is blue' was the phrase... what was it.* Suddenly it snapped to him. "Azul! Azul, si? Blue?"

A look of recognition crossed the man's face. "Ah, si. Lo siento." He smiled and nodded, moving back over to the table of items to switch out the sheets.

Jeremiah looked over the makeshift set. The fold out table had been covered in cheap white cotton, the plastic lawn chair draped with gold, and soon the gaping holes in the walls would be obscured from view by a hanging blue sheet. Sure, it was a broken down studio, but no one else would know that. And you had to start somewhere.

Jeremiah moved over to the camera and fiddled with the tripod. *The shot will be too high from here. The throne should be the center so the viewers can focus on him easier. It will help accentuate the message.* His train of thought was interrupted by a sound behind him. It was a familiar hum, low-pitched and constant. It betrayed his approach a moment before he spoke.

"Jeremiah." A voice called out from behind.

Jeremiah turned immediately, and there stood Imanu'el. He was a short man, standing at 5'7", but he exuded such an aura of conviction and confidence that it overcame any social drawbacks of his size. His short brown hair was neatly combed back, his face clean shaven, and his white linen clothes hung straight on his body, pressed and cleaned for the event. Jeremiah proudly predicted Imanu'el's pristine image would project well for his speech.

"Yes, Imanu'el?" Jeremiah folded his hands in front of him and bowed his head.

"I have a task for you."

"Of course, what is your will?"

"While we will need zealots for our cause to promote the message and further the mission, it is important we gather all who can be a focal point for the faith to ensure the belief of our zealots remains strong and pure. This will be my message tonight. I will reach out to the Touched."

"Imanu'el," Jeremiah spoke, hesitant to offer even a small challenge. "Do you think it is wise at this juncture? We are still small, and while the message is powerful, this revelation will not only create exposure unlike anything we have done before, but may very well dissuade some from the cause."

"You speak from a place of truth, Jeremiah," Imanu'el spoke warmly, a small smile adorning his face. "In the past, others who have attempted to spread their message with such claims eventually brought about their own downfall. The cynical nature of humanity today demands that such miracles be observed, lest they be disregarded as a simple ruse."

"You understand my concern perfectly, Imanu'el."

"But Jeremiah, think of your own experience." His face glowed with pride as he spoke of his zealot's history. "When His will brought us together, did you think of me as anything more than a man? Did you think of yourself as anything more than a street urchin?"

"No, Imanu'el." The words brought back memories in a flood. Imanu'el was not wrong. No more than six months ago, Jeremy Higgins walked the streets of Long Beach with no more direction or purpose to his life than any other vagrant who claimed alleys and park benches as their homes. Now he bore a different name.

"You survived day by day through acts of sin," Imanu'el spoke softly, and held his tone to remove any insinuation of judgment or condescension. "You traded your conscience for money that did not belong to you. You sold your flesh for a warm bed and shelter. You clouded your mind with poisons to ease the pain. Through all this, you clung to reality to ensure you maintained a grip on every advantage you had. You refused to have any of your good fortune taken from you by an act of subterfuge. Talks of His will or your divine purpose would have fallen on deaf ears, would they not?"

Jeremiah hung his head, cheeks red with shame focused on the floor.

"Yet here you stand." Imanu'el dipped his own head to catch Jeremiah's eyes again. "Dressed in the grays of the penitent, and serving selflessly, tirelessly, to promote a message that you once would have discarded as trash. I have Him to thank for bringing me such a valuable zealot, as without your help, we surely would be lost."

Pride bubbled within Jeremiah and surfaced in the form of tears brimming his eyes. Imanu'el's words acted as a salve to the wounds the memories had reopened. At times, he could not bear the shame of his former life. He was sure, however, that his faith and vigorous pursuit of the cause would absolve him of his previous transgressions. He would pay with loyal service for his former life of debauchery and sin.

"And why, Jeremiah? Why did you cast off your rags, your life, even your name to stand before me here today? Why did you give up a life that you had come to understand and practice with ease for one of hard work and struggle? What could turn Jeremy Higgins, the street urchin who lived in the shadows, into Jeremiah, the zealot who would lead others to the light?"

Jeremiah's eyes, brimming with tears, rose to meet Imanu'el's once more. When he opened his mouth to speak, his breath caught and his voice threatened to crack. He gulped, steadying himself so he may speak without losing control. He had cried enough to Imanu'el. It was time he set that weakness down and move forward with his new purpose. "It was you."

Imanu'el smiled. "Yes, Jeremiah. Through His will, I have been gifted with the ability to prove to others that miracles do exist. Prove that His love is with us, and that we have a chance for salvation in this world of darkness. My gifts aside, it is with your help, and your gift alone, Jeremiah, that those who are Touched by His great cause will be brought together."

Jeremiah managed a smile and nodded, blinking back tears. "Thank you, Imanu'el. For everything, thank you."

Imanu'el smiled warmly, moving forward to embrace his zealot. "No, Jeremiah, thank you."

———

WHETHER THE conversation had risen to volumes Phill could hear or not, the pair decided Drive-Thru Java would not be the best venue to continue their impromptu date. Avoiding Phill's venom-filled stare, and his crooked tie, Hale followed Cass back through the coffee shop and out to her car.

The modest sedan had paid for its time on the road. The white paint along the driver side was interrupted by a large dent on the door, scrapes moving up in thick gashes to the driver side mirror, which seemed to have been completely torn away.

"Trouble gauging the distance to the center divider?" Hale nodded in mock understanding. "I have that problem, too. Parked cars get in the way, too, but I figure if you just keep driving you won't have to worry about leaving a note."

"I see I've broken past the outer shell of the cynical hermit and now get to meet the sarcastic asshole." She stuck out her tongue. "I count myself lucky."

"Let me guess," he offered as he opened the door and slid into the passenger seat. "Parked on the side of the street and got tagged by a passing car?"

"Car is not the word for it!" Cass left the keys in the ignition, animating her hands as she flew into the description. "It was massive! I swear, someone must have converted a dump truck and decided to try and crush the first redhead's car they came across."

Hale grinned. The fiery redhead was cute when she got animated.

Her hands lowered, the mock hysteria of her voice returning to a more serious tone. "So maybe it was more of a family-sized SUV and their murderous intent just happened to coincide with me slowing in front of them to pull into a spot on the side of the street." She turned the car on. "They still should have seen my brake lights." She frowned, bitterly. "They didn't stop to leave a note, either..."

Hale chuckled. "So, Mrs. Earnhardt, now that I have nothing but the utmost confidence in your driving skills, where are we going?"

"You live a regimented life, don't you?" She pulled out of the parking lot and merged onto the main road.

"Not really..."

"Then let's not concern ourselves with the destination, and focus on who is taking the trip."

"Fair enough. So, about that story you owe me."

"I think a bit of quid pro quo is in order, don't you think?" Cass smiled. "After all, I told you a summary of my background back at the coffee shop, let's hear yours."

"Ah ah, that was told to me to win your double or nothing bet." Hale waved his finger. "I hardly count that as telling your story, more like whetting the appetite."

"And how am I supposed to hold you to telling me your tale, hmm? I lose my bargaining chip if I lay out my life now. You first."

Hale rolled his eyes. "Fine, fine, keep me in suspense. So what do you want to know?"

"Surprise me. Tell me your story, and make it interesting."

"So embellishment and fabrication is encouraged?"

"Only if you remain consistent. I don't want to bring up a favorite story to my friends and have you not remember."

"I suppose that's fair." Hale leaned back, trying to find a starting point. "Well, I work for The Crest."

"Like the toothpaste?"

"No, no not–" Hale laughed in spite of himself. "The newspaper. I'm a journalist."

"Ahh!" She looked over, eyebrow raised. "I assume that's just your secret identity to cover for your true profession as a superhero crime fighter."

"Huh? Wha–" *Hale, she's referencing Superman, not you. Calm down.* "Oh, no. Heh. I'm not that interesting, unfortunately. I saved my neighbor's cat once, though."

"See, you've been holding out on me. I bet there was a fire involved."

"Insightful as always. Mrs. Hackett was smoking like a chimney while I climbed the tree to pull little Jenny down. Little bastard scratched the hell out me, too."

"Jenny?"

"Yes. Atrocious, isn't it?"

Cass contorted her face in disgust. "How can someone name their cat Jenny?!"

"I know, I know..." Hale nodded his head in apprehension.

"That's something you'd name your daughter."

"A daughter you didn't like!" Hale agreed.

"Hey, I have a friend named Jenny."

"Sorry, name of an ex, bad association." Hale shrugged with a grin.

Cass stopped herself from going on the tangent and veered back to their sub-topic. "Seriously, how do you name your cat Jenny? A cat is far too regal for such a base name."

"I completely agree. Their places in the world must be properly acknowledged by title and name to fit their grandeur." Hale realized he was smiling. He couldn't remember ever having a discourse like this with anyone. Alex was his best friend, but sarcasm and intellectual humor weren't his strong suits.

"So you're a cat person, too?"

"I am the proud servant of Commodore," Hale beamed.

"Ooh, good name," Cass complimented. "But does he fit his title? I mean, one does have to live up to the standards they have set before them."

"He goes above and beyond. You'll see when you meet him." Hale stopped, immediately watching for a reaction.

Nice going, jackass. Hale kicked himself internally. *Way to be presumptuous. Then again, this will give me a good indicator whether she'll start problems over small things, or if she can roll with an awkward, somewhat presumptuous comment.*

"The challenge is on, then. He better measure up." She turned off 7th, guiding them south.

Interesting. Scorekeeper! Mark another one for Cass.

Hale took advantage of the pause. "So you've heard of my heroic exploits and my indentured servitude, what about you?"

"I'm not horribly interesting, to be honest."

Hale pursed his lips, tilting his head down to give her his best glower.

"I'll tell you," she laughed. "I just wanted to warn you beforehand. I'm a business analyst for an independent consulting firm. I am sent into firms to analyze processes, examine productivity, and come up with solutions to make sure they generate the most income per hour of labor possible."

"So you're the person they call in right before they fire a bunch of people?"

"It would be fitting, wouldn't it?" Cass glanced over at him, a thoughtful expression adorning her features. "You being the secret superhero, and here I am, the villain who sabotages people's lives by removing their jobs and giving them to robots."

Hale went through a short list of sexual jokes involving appropriate punishments for a villainess, and wisely decided to remain quiet. He thanked his will for maintaining the courtesies of his upbringing despite Alex's bad influence.

"Truth be told, we try to redistribute work more than remove jobs. There's always more work to be done, and companies are generally happy to improve their productivity. They are able to offset their costs rather than hand out pink slips to a dozen employees to save on salary." She sighed. "And though I'm a lackey under the true 'efficiency experts' who manage the projects, I do get more face time with the grunts in the office. That means they know me better, which means more likely to place blame, or even to clip someone's car and rip their mirror off after you leave their building on your last day." She shrugged and gave a bitter grin.

Hale cocked his head. "Really? Someone was that pissed at your company they took it out on your car."

"And you thought I was exaggerating about the 'trying to crush the first redhead's car' thing?" She rolled her eyes. "Okay, maybe I embellished a little, but it's what's suspected. Someone lost their job and happened to drive out on their last day in their red SUV, the same color as the one that sideswiped me four blocks away when I pulled off to the side of the street. The company gave me a couple thousand dollars to settle the matter, which I put into bills and savings. I honestly don't care that my car is ugly, it serves its purpose to transport me to and from work. I have more important things to worry about than my vehicle's cosmetic status." She made another turn, bringing them along the shoreline and rolled the windows down to let the fresh sea air in.

"That's practical. Though I could wager a guess that while the appearance of your car doesn't bother you much, you do take pride in other appearances." Hale gestured to her outfit. He shifted his body sideways and leaned his cheek against the headrest.

. . . she pressed her face into the headrest,

staring down at her phone

. . . . . . a sob escaped her lips, and tears ran down

her cheeks

. . . . the phone lay on the driver seat.

"Cassandra? Cassie, are you there?"

"–treet, but my personal appearance is a completely different matter. What you project when you meet people is important, in my mind."

Shit, I started Wandering in the middle of our conversation. How much did I miss?

"Are you okay?" She eyed him, quizzically.

And she's perceptive. He thought.

"Yes, fine, sorry." Hale shifted back to his original sitting position. "I like to face people when I talk, but I just made myself uncomfortable."

"Looked like I lost you for a second." She made another left turn. Hale realized she was taking them in a large circle, and would soon be back at their starting point.

"So what was the deal with the blind date?" Hale asked, attempting to shift topics.

"Ugh, I'm in trouble for that one." Cassandra laughed in spite of herself. "Phill and I have a mutual friend. I've known her for a few years, and Phill has known her since high school. He has this pathetic, quasi-platonic relationship with her, meanwhile anyone who watches them together can see he's hopelessly in love. She, well… she has other ideas about their associations."

"So how did you get wrapped up in the mix?"

"Well, she found out through one of his friends that he was going to throw caution to the wind and finally ask her out, and decided to head him off at the pass. Like a true friend, she called her female acquaintances to see if anyone was available, desperately trying to set him up to derail his plans."

"Of course, since confronting him would be the coward's way out."

Cass rolled her eyes. "So I get the call. She begs me, calling out some recent favors she did for me, and like an idiot, I agree. 'No promises', I told her. I agreed to coffee and a conversation, that's it."

Hale couldn't suppress a smile.

"Yeah yeah, I know. I'm a bitch."

Hale let himself laugh, trying to pick his words carefully to make sure his comments were comical and not insulting. "A little, yeah. But you got put in a bad situation. I mean, Phill is not just going to forget Sue, and she should know that sooner or later a reckoning will be at hand. If she's really the guy's friend, I think she owes him an honest conversation."

Cass' breath caught for a moment, though she quickly recovered and smiled, looking at him knowingly. "Thanks for confirming that for me."

"No problem. Don't want you beating yourself up over someone else's cowardice." He paused as they neared 7th street again, letting silence fill the car. Unable to resist, he added, "It was a pretty bitch move to leave him hanging like that."

"I blame my accomplice," she grinned, and then nodded to the road. "You're going to have to direct me from here. I'd drop you off back at DTJ's, but Phill might still be there sharpening those daggers in his eyes."

The conversation slowed as they turned onto 7th and headed back towards their starting point. Hale's mind raced, knowing that he was now directing them back towards his place. His imagination wandered to the straps on her baby doll sliding off her shoulders, her lips pouting as he leaned down for a kiss. His mind did a quick mental comparison of the other women he had been with. There wasn't an extensive list. Well, not compared to some others he knew. The number of Hale's conquests fit in the teens, while others who frequented his apartment with beer and homophobic insults claimed somewhere in the triple digits. It still boggled his mind how Alex hadn't become a father or contracted something horrific in his time.

Well, maybe he had. That's not something you advertise.

Hale snapped back to reality when he realized his street was coming up. "Here, turn left."

Cass maneuvered into the left turn lane, flipping her blinker on and stopping at the light. She idly reached back and fished a bottle of water out of the back seat.

Hale wrestled internally for a moment before allowing his hormones to make a decision. Seeing the opportunity to see his first clear shot of cleavage, he risked a glance down, only to look back up into the waiting eyes of Cass. Apparently she could find the water just fine while watching to see what he'd do with his opportunity to peep.

"Here." She casually offered him a water. "You seem a little anxious."

Hale's face flushed as his breath quickened. *Way to go, Hale. Why don't you avoid trying to fuck her in your imagination so you don't ruin all your chances in real life? Maybe this is why Alex goes for the dumb ones, he doesn't like being kept on his toes.* Annoyed with himself, he simply nodded in thanks, blushing heavily, and took a heavy gulp of water. *I think I like being on my toes.*

Cass pulled the car out front of the apartment complex Hale directed her to, sliding the car into park. She leaned back against her door to look at him.

The car is still running, her body language screams 'don't try it'. You messed up this opportunity, Don Juan. Just thank her for a good conversation, and try to set up date #2.

Hale cleared his throat, capping his water bottle. "Well, thanks for the tour around Long Beach and a pleasant conversation."

"Thank you for rescuing me from a painful afternoon," she added with a smile. "And for sacrificing time with your precious book to do so."

Hale chuckled. "Yeah, no problem." He looked down in his lap.

Why are you still embarrassed? Get over it or you're going to lose your chance!

Before Hale could overcome his self-imposed blocks, Cass spoke. "Well?"

"Well?" Hale perked up, hope mixing with confusion.

"I don't want to be presumptuous, but I don't think Commodore would approve of his person gallivanting around town with someone who he has not had the privilege of meeting, and you did promise me that he would measure up to his name."

She takes my own presumptuous question and throws it back at me like it was expected. I think she's playing with me, but I can't say I'm not enjoying it.

Hale laughed. "Fair enough, let's go see if you measure up to Commodore's standards." Book and water in hand, Hale slid out of the car while Cass threw her keys in her purse. Hale took the moment he was out of sight to knock on his forehead, trying to bring himself back to the place he was 20 minutes ago.

Don't lose it, this girl is a keeper.

Her door closed. "Lead the way," she smiled.

"And you can see here on the left," Hale spoke in a tour guide's voice, "the infamous apartment raided by the DEA last year for storing more than a ton of pot in hermetically sealed bags. And here on the right, the alleyway that featured the short lived car chase last month. I believe the suspect got as far as the second dumpster before wrecking his car and getting lit up by his pursuing officers."

Cass looked where he was pointing, giving morbid laughs where appropriate.

"So this is the ritzy part of town, you're telling me."

"Nothing but the best for me. I spare no expense when it comes to safety and comfort. But, just to be safe," He patted his black over shirt. "Gotta be sure to wear neutral gang colors."

"You're serious?" She eyed him.

"Nah, it's not that bad. I mean, the DEA and car chase really did happen, but people will leave you alone here." He stopped, looking at Cass. "To keep my conscience clear, make sure you do have someone with you at night."

They walked up the stairs to the walkway, moving past apartments as they closed the distance to his 500 square foot palace. Hale looked to see Mrs. Dowling sitting outside, reading her book.

"Good afternoon, Mrs. Dowling," Hale said with a smile.

The woman looked up from her book, transitioning her surprise to a genuine smile. "Good afternoon, sweetheart. And who is this beautiful young woman you have with you?"

Has she been crying? Her eyes... it's probably the book. Those trashy romance novels always have ridiculously sad endings. Hale dismissed the thought.

"This is Cass." He paused while Cass reached her hand out to shake Mrs. Dowling's.

"It's a pleasure."

"The pleasure's all mine, dearie," Mrs. Dowling smiled.

"Cass was nice enough to give me a lift from the coffee place down the street."

"Well, that was nice of her." Mrs. Dowling gave Cass another smile before returning to Hale. "Well, don't let me keep you two. It was nice seeing you again." She reached up and patted Hale on the arm.

. . . "Tony, please." She patted him on the arm
    again.
      . . . . . . "—paranoia. Leave me be,"
     his gruff voice snapped
         . . . . Mrs. Dowling
          huddled in the bathroom,
          thick tears rolling down
          her cheeks

"—to meet you, too," Cass said.

Hale snapped his gaze over to her, meeting another quizzical look as she turned away from Mrs. Dowling. He smiled and turned back towards his apartment as if nothing had happened.

With a click, the door opened.

Hale quickly realized his apartment was a bachelor's pad. Dishes piled in the sink, cups and bottles littering the coffee table, and a pile of laundry on his bedroom floor.

He grinned at Cass, "Gonna have to fire that maid."

"I'll say." She wandered in, taking the room in. Though the place was a disaster, she didn't look visibly repulsed. She turned back to face him. "So, where is the king of the household?"

Hale motioned to her right. "Right there on the ledge."

Cass turned to see the motionless figure of Commodore perched on the corner of the bar. He sat in his regal pose, scrutinizing the new visitor to his domain.

"Hello Commodore," Cass spoke with a smile, taking a step forward. "My name is Cassandra Voss. I've come here to petition your approval, post facto, to drive your person around in a large circle while conversing with him about small portions of our meager lives. Do I have your blessing?" She gave a short, mock curtsey.

Hale held his hand over his mouth to cover his grin. *Alex makes fun of me for talking to my cat like he's a person. If he ever saw this...*

Commodore regarded Cass for a few more moments, sniffing the air about her. Finally, he let his eyes relax and gave a soft 'chuff' of approval. He leaned his head forward a bit, inviting a pet.

Cass grinned, reaching out and scratching the noble beast on his scalp. She turned to Hale. "I think we're safe this time." She retracted her hand.

Commodore, unsatisfied with the paltry tribute, shot his eyes open and swung out, batting Cass on the still outstretched hand.

"Well, my apologies," Cass giggled, resuming Commodore's petting. "I wasn't aware you weren't done with me yet."

Commodore purred loudly, standing up and moving back and forth on the bar to guide Cass' hand up and down his body. Then, after a couple passes, he jumped from bar to couch and flopped into the corner.

"I think I've been released." She shrugged to Hale.

"It's a good thing he gave his approval," Hale warned, taking a few brave steps forward. "I think he can exercise a court martial at his rank."

"Well then." Cass took a step to Hale's side, removing him from her pathway to the door. "We better not push our luck."

Don't push it, just get her number and follow up later.

"Agreed," he grinned. "Wouldn't want to test his patience. However…" Hale looked over at the couch suspiciously, then dropped his voice to a secretive whisper. He leaned in to look Cass in the eyes as he spoke. "He does have a short memory, and I'm sure it won't take him long to forget this little indiscretion. Once we're in the clear, I'd like to call you, maybe take you out for dinner. I can't promise spoiled blind dates, drug raids, or disgruntled employees attempting vehicular manslaughter, but I can provide some more good conversation, and I might not even get overly embarrassed after falling into one of your traps to get a look 'past your arms'."

"That was mean of me, wasn't it?" She grinned mischievously.

She did set me up.

"It was," he smiled back.

"Sorry, I had a vindictive moment."

Why? Did I do something? Don't ask, let it drop.

"Truth be told, in hindsight I'm kinda thankful you did," Hale grinned.

Cass bit her lower lip, staring up at Hale.

Kiss her!

Don't. You'll scare her off.

You're already in close! She's biting her lip, that's like shooting off a flare.

You like this girl, it's worth waiting. Don't risk it.

"You're intriguing." She broke the silence, interrupting his internal struggle.

"I love a good mystery." He shook his book again. "Maybe I'm just projecting."

"I hope not." She paused again, continuing the stare. Finally, she broke her eyes away, digging her phone out of her purse. "Well, there is one problem."

"What's that?" Hale cocked his head, curious.

"'Hey You' and 'Cute Guy' are already taken in my contacts list." She looked up at him. "So what should I put you in here as?"

A wave of realization washed over Hale. "Wha–, I mean, wow." He grinned like a fool and smiled. He realized he had never bothered to introduce himself properly. He didn't know what threw him for more of a loop, the fact he had forgotten or that she was finally bringing it up now. "Hale. Hale Langston."

Cass extended her free hand, which Hale took gingerly.

"Pleasure to meet you, Hale Langston. I'm Cassandra Voss."

5

"I pray that you absorb this message and act on the faith that I know rests within you. Please, contact us." Imanu'el gave a final nod and smile to the camera. "God be with you." He held the pose as Jeremiah counted down from five on his fingers.

"We have finished," Jeremiah confirmed, stopping the recording. "It was incredibly moving, Imanu'el."

The man's serene image drooped a bit. He stood slowly. "I hope it was enough, Jeremiah. While the miracle the Lord has gifted me is spectacular, it unfortunately does not improve my oratory skills. I can only pray that His gifts, along with the blessing of you and the other Zealots, will be enough."

"I have no doubts that it will be, Imanu'el."

Imanu'el crossed the distance between them, taking Jeremiah's head gingerly in his hands. He was shorter than his Zealot, so he had to pull the man's face down, tilting his own head back to place a kiss on Jeremiah's forehead.

Something stirred in the Zealot. Survival on the streets had demanded many things from him. If he wished to feed his appetites for food, shelter, and the blissful embrace of narcotics, he had to earn his keep. As the nights grew colder, his stomach groaned louder, and as his blood itched for relief, the spectrum of tactics by which he was willing to employ to satiate those appetites grew more and more broad.

He knew it was wrong. He knew it was sinful. While Jeremiah never had strong feelings towards any member of the same sex as he grew up, as his willingness to compromise his values expanded, the details of his survival became less and less important. Selling your body was easy and lucrative, and Jeremiah had quickly learned that the vast majority of one's clients would be male, regardless of the sex of the prostitute. While his natural attractions did not change, any reservations due to social upbringing or thoughts of the act being taboo were removed. Jeremiah realized he was attracted less to the sex of the body, and more to the person within.

I must remain resolute. He demanded to himself. *My life of sin is over, and I will not poison such a great man, nor his good work with such temptation of debauchery. His trials are already great, and if I maintain my loyal service, perhaps the Lord will absolve me of my previous life's indiscretions.*

"I thank myself every day for having a Zealot such as yourself devoted to the cause, Jeremiah. I would be blessed if more were to join our ranks with even half of your devotion." Imanu'el glowed. "Doubt is a poison that will cause any movement to rot from within, and it is good to stamp it out with fervor whenever it rears its head. Thank you, Jeremiah. Thank you for keeping me on the righteous path."

Jeremiah nodded as Imanu'el released his face. Tears brimmed in his eyes, some from pride, others from shame. He refused to let such a great man fail. He would not let his own weakness poison Imanu'el's purity.

"Thank you, Imanu'el." His voice wavered. "It means so much to hear you speak those words."

Imanu'el smiled and nodded to him. "Please, plug the camera into my laptop so I may perform the necessary work on the footage before it is broadcast. The time draws near."

"Of course, Imanu'el." Jeremiah bowed his head and turned away. A pain he could not identify as guilt or longing gripped his heart. He prayed silently to bolster his faith, using the words to salve his emotional wound.

———————

HALE LET out a soft grunt and shifted his weight. Warm breath passed over his neck as lips kissed softly down to his shoulders, sending chills from his side to his ankle. Exertion showed visibly as sweat beaded on his forehead. Hale's hands slid up Cass' smooth sides, traveling past the curves of her hips with his fingers and walking up the ladder of her ribs. His palms caressed the sides of her breasts as she ground back and forth on top of him.

A gasp of pleasure echoed in his ear, causing a small jolt of excitement down his body. His hips responded with counter thrusts, causing a wave of escalation to rise between their bodies. As they touched each other, pleasure washed over them and promoted new reactions, which were returned in kind, encouraging each touch, kiss and thrust to be accentuated even more.

"Don't stop." She whimpered, arching her back and rolling her hips to and fro.

Hale moaned, his own hips moving back and forth in rhythm with her own. He felt his legs tingling and his breath getting shorter. His muscles tensed as he watched Cass' beautiful form writhe on top of him, an expression of ecstasy on her face that matched his own.

A digital rendition of Beethovan's Fur Elise played in the distance. Maybe from a car outside. A techno remix, no doubt. Hale's attention shifted, pulled towards the music.

Almost in response, Cass moaned loudly, blissfully shouting at the ceiling as if to pull Hale's focus back. His eyes shot back to her perfect form, feasting his gaze on her bare flesh as his body resumed its previous ascension.

The digital piano notes were supplemented by a violent rattling. The walls themselves seemed to reverberate with the music, vibrating on cue at the end of each half-bar.

Hale's bliss rose to a peak as his attention fractured.

His eyes pulled open to see his phone rattling on his nightstand, vibrating along to the tune of Fur Elise. Realization hit him from multiple angles, as did a shudder of pleasure as the images of Cassandra Voss echoed in his mind. The interrupted sequence of dreams confused his body at the last second, causing it to deliver all of the expected physical outputs, while shattering his nerves' broadcast of sexual elation.

"Ah... fuck, FUCK! You've gotta be kidding me." Hale sat up, looking under the comforter in disbelief. Disbelief was trumped by visual confirmation, and he dropped the blanket in a mixture of disgust and disappointment.

The rattle brought his attention back to his phone.

Hale growled, picking up the phone and pressing it to his ear. "What?!"

"Whassup, homie?!"

"Goddammit, Alex," Hale grumbled. "Your timing is fucking impeccable."

"Dude, did I interrupt something?" Alex's voice switched from curious to elated. "Dude! You got a chick with you? Put me on speaker, I'll cheer you on!"

"You're a dick."

"Come on, man, don't say you couldn't use the encouragement," Alex laughed.

"What do you want, man, it's almost midnight."

"Like you ever sleep anyway," Alex scoffed. "So you got someone with you there or not?"

"Not really."

"Huh?"

"No," Hale answered bitterly, cursing Alex silently again.

Something shifted on the bed, drawing his attention to Commodore. The cat looked up at him through displeased eyes.

Human, what you dream about on your own time is your business, and I can't stop your association with the loud mongoloid, though I do expect my slumber to go uninterrupted. Is that clear?

Hale reached over and scratched his cat's head, who only seemed to get more annoyed and pulled away.

"I figured you deserved a day off tomorrow. Play hooky and come out tonight. I found this bangin' bar right off the ocean. There is some fucking talent here tonight, too. Speaking of– Hey!" Alex's voice pulled away from the phone.

"I'm Alex. Hang out for a sec, I gotta get my lame friend here to get his ass out of bed, then I'll treat you to another one of those Hypnotic Martinis."

"You're an asshole," Hale sighed.

"What was that, Hale?" Alex's voice pulled back to the phone.

"I said 'where are you at?'"

"This new place called Bourbon Street. It's the shit, dude, seriously. Frozen drinks with Everclear, and they even hand out beads at the door. It's like Mardi Gras in So Cal! How hot is that?!"

"I gotta work tomorrow, dude."

"Hale, don't be lame." Somehow Alex delivered this in a tone of warning, as if deciding against his invitation could somehow violate the karmic balance of the universe.

"Alex, I have to be able to think at my job."

"That's not my fault!" Alex laughed, and his voice became distant again as if his attention was being pulled away. "Seriously boss, you're gonna be sorry if you miss this."

"Thanks for the invite, dude, but I'm gonna pass."

"Your loss."

Alex must have missed the End Call button, as Hale could still hear the muffled chaos of the bar in the background as Alex's voice sharply faded out. He listened for a few more seconds at the shouts and squeals over the blaring rock music before hanging up with a chuckle and a shake of his head.

Hale tossed the comforter off of him, eliciting a growl from Commodore as the cat jumped off the bed. He carefully slid off the mattress, stripping off his boxers and tossing them in the corner as he wandered over to his bathroom and blinked the sleep out of his eyes.

While a good portion of him wished that Cass had stayed after they traded numbers, she did end up taking her leave shortly after. Whether she had just wanted to scope out his place, drag out the last bit of their first date, or was legitimately just interested in meeting Commodore, Hale did not know. One thing was for sure:

65

Cass had left an impression. Her looks aside, Hale felt an extraordinary attraction to the woman. She was intelligent, frighteningly perceptive, and possessed a dry wit that appealed to his sense of humor.

And she's ridiculously hot, Hale reminded himself.

After washing himself up and donning a clean pair of underwear, Hale wandered out into the living room. He knew from experience that the attempt of sleep would be wasted at this point. Being woken up from a nap, much less deep REM, meant he would not be visited by the Sandman for some time. Sometimes a little fantasy and some hand lotion did the trick; however, given the circumstances of his rude awakening, Hale doubted that little trick would work tonight.

Following his usual late night ritual, the TV clicked on as his laptop whirred through its startup sequences. Hale rubbed his face in attempt to focus. As a cruel irony, his mind wouldn't let him rest, but it had no problem clouding his thoughts with the lie of exhaustion. He had to force his brain back to attentiveness in hopes of actually tiring it out, after which he'd have a chance at sleep again.

"–dark times we live in, yet He has reached out once again to give us all hope."

Hale looked up at the TV. A young, clean-cut man with white linen clothes was speaking. He sat at a table with a gold cloth over it and a dark blue backdrop. A local phone number was fixed to the bottom of the screen.

Hale looked closer. *Yep, that's a foldout table covered by a thin sheet,* he confirmed. *Way to splurge on your studio set, preacher.*

"I have been gifted with a miraculous ability, one that simply cannot be believed unless viewed in person. The tricks of modern day video would taint any who saw His work through me. Your mind would be forced to disbelieve, and His message would be lost."

Whoa there, we have stepped out of the realm of quiet preacher and into supernatural evangelist. Hale chuckled, logging into his laptop. *What's the price of your salvation, preacher? And let me guess... you prefer cash to fuel your miracles.*

"My words will paint me as insane to most who view this, and I apologize

for such reckless claims that surely damage your will to believe. Perhaps if I was more cautious, I could earn your trust through a more standard sermon, one that you have already accepted as the comfortable truth." The man spoke clearly and confidently, cool blue eyes fixed on the TV. His stare reflected a measure of sorrow as he spoke.

"Mr. Preacher," Hale said, cocking an eyebrow. "Me thinks you really believe this yarn you're spinning. Go you."

"But time is of the essence, so I must risk temporarily breaking your faith in me in order to rally those who can bolster it tenfold to my side. So now, I am no longer speaking to the majority of God's children. I am reaching out to the Touched."

The cursor on Hale's word document blinked expectantly, but Hale found his attention focused elsewhere.

"There are those in this world Touched with gifts beyond the comprehension of common man. Gifts that science cannot explain. Gifts that could be generated by only one source: His divine will. It is the few chosen amongst the flock who I reach out to now. You are blessed, my brothers and sisters. You have a talent that cannot be taken away, explained, nor disproven. You have a gift that can change the world."

Hale was transfixed on the television. *This isn't happening. I'm still dreaming. Never once in all of my life, or in any of my Wanderings, have I ever even suspected someone else to have anything close to... whatever it is I have. This has to be a con.*

"If you are Touched with one of His holy gifts, I beseech you, reach out to me. I can assure you, there are others like you in this world. And while I am sure you have put your gifts to good use on your own, imagine the difference we could make in the world by combining our efforts." The preacher opened his hands, gesturing to the number at the bottom of the screen. *"While your hesitation at hearing this is completely understandable, know that I will expect nothing of you until you see with your own eyes that I speak the truth. Call this number, brothers*

and sisters. Call this number and we will meet. There I will show you my gifts, and I pray that you will bless me with an opportunity to speak with you about yours."

Hale found himself slack jawed. With half a thought, he typed the number into the blank, waiting page of his laptop.

"I pray that you absorb this message, and act on the faith I know rests within you. Please."

He clasped his hands again. *"Contact us."*

6

"No, you really fucked me on this one."

"Sue, come on," Cass sighed, slumping against the wall. Her head slid down an inch, pulling her hair up slightly. It was a subtle tactic she had learned as a child. Apparently it made her look more pitiable, and her father had never been able to deny her when she used it.

'Stop being cute, I'm trying to be angry,' her dad would say.

'Sowwy daddy,' would be the typical response. Any argument they had was generally averted immediately and replaced by a trip for ice cream.

"Come on?" Sue contorted her face to give an incredulous look.

I really wish you wouldn't do that. Cass thought. *It's not only annoying, but it really reminds me of the face that animated dog made. God, what was its name? It was the smart one from the movie where he saves the girl from the speeding train. Come to think of it, Phill kind of looks like the conductor... maybe the two of you are destined for each other.*

"Are you even listening to me?" Sue chided, her lips curling, nose scrunching and lower jaw jutting out, accentuating the canine resemblance that Cass hated.

"W–Yes!" Cass straightened. *Damn it, went off into my own little world there. What did I miss?*

"So..." Sue raised an eyebrow expectantly.

Damn. Maybe a general response will cover me... "Isn't it self-explanatory?" Cass offered.

"You standing up Phill on a date that was supposed to save me, and leaving with some other random guy right in front of him is self-explanatory?!" Sue's voice picked up in pitch as she continued, entering into the realm of a small shriek. "This really fucked me, Cass!"

Why does she have to swear like that? Oh yeah, she traded in a pleasant personality for that glamour-mag look. I may not be the cover girl you are, but I can hold my own. You're in for a rude awakening when you turn 40. Cass did a quick mental check of Sue's mother's picture. *With your genetics, make that 30.*

"Look, I'm sorry. Really, I am." Cass leaned on her elbows, hands out and waving to accentuate her words. "I just... couldn't. You know? I have no idea who he is, nor did I have any interest. On top of that, I felt horribly guilty, because I was basically sent as a countermeasure for you."

"A what?"

"Counter—" Cass allowed herself a short pause to suppress a frustrated sigh. "Diversion. You know, throw him off of you. The whole reason I was doing this was because he was going to finally ask you out on a real date, and you wanted him to forget you."

"And now he's not only not countermeasureded," Sue tried to throw the word back at Cass, who in turn bit her lip to halt the laugh in her throat. "–but now he's totally pissed. He not only thinks I set him up on a bad date, he knows you set up that guy to be there."

Cass cocked her head and furrowed her brow. "Hold on a moment... what?"

"He talked to the guy before you got there." Sue bobbed her head and crossed her arms. "He said the guy was all nervous, like he shouldn't be talking to Phill. Apparently he even tried to wave off money Phill offered for spilling his drink."

A wave of comprehension crossed her face as Cass put things together. Making connections in a mystery always made her feel better. She was always the kid in the front row while a magician performed, and though she'd be wide eyed at the end of the performance, she'd be too busy in her mind figuring out the mechanics of the trick to utter any verbal praise. "And he told the guy who he was meeting."

"Why do you look so pleased with yourself? Are you happy for backstabbing me?"

"No, just figured something out, is all." *Hale, you owe me... you cheated. Can't say I didn't enjoy the end result, though.*

"You're just figuring out how bad you screwed me?" Sue challenged. "Phill is going to be heartbroken for a few days, and then he's going to come right for me!"

"No, not that, I just…" Cass winced, waving off her statement. "Sorry. I didn't realize Phill had told Hale my name before I got there. I wasn't talking about me completely blowing your plan."

"Why would Phill tell some random guy your name? He's not an idiot."

Sue, you're my friend, but if you keep looking at me like I'm a moron, I'm going to prove which one of us passed grade school without requiring extra semesters during the summer.

"He grabbed a chair from the guy and knocked over his coffee. He said he expected the guy to be mad, but he was too nervous to raise a fuss about it." Sue adopted a cavalier attitude. "Looks like your friend needs to learn not to blow his cover next time."

"But you said Phill talked to him."

"Yeah, for like, two seconds!"

There's that dog face again. Cass thought.

"He grabbed a chair, and then gave him money for knocking over his coffee. Phill's real perceptive, you know!" Sue became suddenly defensive. "He can read people really easily. He was going to be a detective, but decided to go into a field with more critical thinking instead."

Cass let her friend's last statement go unchallenged, as her previously solved mystery was exhibiting holes. She brought up a pointed finger to start a new thought, then paused with a thoughtful expression on her face. Connections were drawn as angles were analyzed. Vetting through a list of potential events that led to her current situation, she started to draw new conclusions. Moments later, her features melted into a satisfied smile and an accusing glare. "You set me up."

"What?!" Sue made the dog face.

"You sent Hale there to pull me away from Phill, because you want Phill for yourself, but didn't want to admit it." She smiled triumphantly. It explained everything. If Sue somehow knew Hale and sent him to the coffee shop to intercept her, he could have been prepped to present exactly what she was looking for, providing a perfect distraction from Phill.

"What the fuck are you talking about?!"

Cass' moment of victory faded. This wasn't a performance. This was real anger, though the panic on Sue's features confirmed she wasn't completely off the mark. This shattering of Cass' second airtight conclusion jarred her too much to respond to the accusation.

What am I missing?!

Sue grabbed her purse and slid out of the booth. "Enjoy your time with *Hale*." The name dripped off her tongue with venom. "Hope you don't mind sharing. With a name like that, you're probably just a beard." Sue jeered. With a graceful twist, she spun on her heel and stormed out of the bistro.

Cass sat in silence, reexamining the evidence in her mind in attempt to draw new conclusions.

———————

HALE STARED at his phone. The number from the broadcast last night sat dimly on the screen, the backlight off due to inactivity.

The entire day had been like this. Despite waking up on time for once, he had spent most of the night staring at his phone, dialing, clearing, and redialing instead of sleeping. His exhaustion was overwhelmed by curiosity and anxiety caused by the broadcast, making it easy to pull him back to consciousness as soon as his alarm sounded. He took a leisurely shower, standing under the hot water for over twenty minutes with a blank stare on his face.

The process of dressing and commuting blended in with the first hour at work. Hale's thoughts kept drifting back to the ad, each time screaming to call and talk to them, all the while simultaneously chastising him for being such a gullible fool.

It took Ockie shouting at him from three cubicles down to snap his focus back to his work, "Hale, until I put you on weather, get your head out of the clouds."

It shook Hale out of his daze for a bit, but still found himself drifting whenever he had a few seconds. The hours dragged by painfully slowly. Back at home, Hale sat on his couch, staring at the numbers on his phone. The TV was dark.

Commodore sat upright on the coffee table, staring at his servant with an analytical look.

Hale threw the phone down on the couch. "You're a moron." He slapped the cushions of the couch as if to emphasize his point and pushed himself to his feet. "Those guys make their money on this. They prey on stupid saps that think they are special and want acceptance. They show them a few magic tricks, then take their money. You really want to be one of those guys?"

He opened the fridge.

After looking over the orange juice, water and single can of soda for a full minute, he slammed the door and stomped back over to the couch.

Commodore glared at him. *You truly are a simple, indecisive creature, aren't you?*

Hale ignored Commodore's judgmental glare, picking up his phone and checking the number one last time. "I won't give them any money, I'll just go to hear what they have to say."

His thumb descended to the Send button.

The phone flashed an instant before with the message: "Incoming Call... Alex"

"No! Shit... Hey!" Hale recovered, throwing the phone to his ear.

"Dude!" Alex yelled, music blaring in the background.

"What's up, Alex?"

"So I got the perfect cure for your homo-itis." Alex's voice mixed with a girl's laugh. From the proximity, it sounded like she was hanging off his shoulders. "Last night's party was shit in comparison to this one. I'm telling you dude, you have–"

"Sure man, where's it at?"

"Dude, don't be a bitch. Come out of your hole and have fun with us."

"I said sure, where you at?"

Alex paused for a few moments, gathering his wits from the shock he just received. "Don't mess with me, Hale." Alex warned. "I swear man, if you flake on me I'll bring an armada of drunk hotties right through your apartment and party in your cramped ass living room till the cops come arrest us."

"Alex, I need a frickin' drink, just tell me where to meet you."

"WHOOO!" Alex pulled the phone away as he howled in triumph. "Come down to The Sandy Clam man. We're just getting started."

"The Sandy Clam?! Is that a strip club?"

"WHOOOO!"

"Alex? Alex?" Hale sighed. "Alright man, I'll see you there." Hale hung up the phone. "Just a couple of drinks, then I'll call them. Probably."

Hale grabbed his jacket, shoving his phone in his pocket, and walked out the door.

"No, THAT won't be necessary. Thank you." Jeremiah hung the phone up.

"Any progress, Jeremiah?" Imanu'el asked softly.

Jeremiah turned, a dejected look on his face. "Only a dozen calls since the message was put out, Imanu'el."

"You don't seem pleased." Imanu'el made the statement a question.

Jeremiah drew his courage, responding softly. "They are mocking you,

Imanu'el. None of them wish to see the truth. At best, they call to joke and play, and at worst, claim you are a blasphemer."

Imanu'el's face did not register any disappointment, nor deterrence. He spoke calmly, "Jeremiah, the road will not be easy for us. It will be filled with trials and pitfalls. We will be mocked, scorned, and mistrusted. What is important, Jeremiah, is that we remain resolute in our faith." He smiled, giving Jeremiah a comforting nod. "We will succeed, Jeremiah. You must remain strong."

Jeremiah nodded, feeling Imanu'el's words as a salve on his spirit. The aura of serenity from the man calmed him. His despair seemed to lift, and the knowledge that the righteousness of the cause merited the heavy burden. "Thank you, Imanu'el. Your words are always there to bolster me in my moments of weakness."

Imanu'el sat next to Jeremiah, attempting to strengthen the broken man with his presence. "You are loyal and dedicated, Jeremiah, and I thank you for that. What's more, your time is being wasted here. I have come to relieve you of this work." He gestured towards the telephone. "While it is necessary, we have much better uses we could be putting your talent to."

"But what if one of the Touched call?"

"I am not beneath picking up a phone. I have work to do here anyway, and it will not provide significant interruption to pick up the phone every few hours."

Jeremiah nodded. He straightened his posture a bit, but still kept his head at a shallow bow in reverence of Imanu'el. "What would you have me do?"

Imanu'el smiled, bringing his palms up to Jeremiah's cheeks so he could look him in the eyes with pride. "You are going to go on your first Pilgrimage."

CHAOS POURED out the doors and onto the street from The Sandy Clam. House music reverberated off adjacent buildings as the doors opened to release a small crowd into the night. One drunk couple laughed as they stumbled and fell onto the hood of a parked car next to the curb. A small group of people on the sidewalk started cheering them on as the couple pushed themselves further up the hood to make out.

Hale allowed himself an amused daydream of a bodybuilder storming out and defending the chastity of his car. The fantasy died when the pair slid off and ran to their respective doors, pulling themselves in and peeling out into the street.

Hale walked through the small crowd of people as they lit up cigarettes and laughed.

"Man, they better not get pulled over!" The Muscular Guy said.

"No shit, huh? Jay's breath could sanitize an operating room!" The Scrawny Guy laughed.

"Wait, what does that mean?" The Stumbling Blond giggled.

"You know, the alcohol on his breath." The Scrawny Man tripped over his words. "Sanitizing, you know."

"That's pretty stupid, dude," The Muscular Guy said.

"I thought it was funny," The Brunette Attachment said as she hung off The Scrawny Guy's neck.

"I still don't get it." The Stumbling Blond looked confused.

"Because it wasn't funny," The Muscular Guy commented.

"You just don't appreciate intelligent humor." The Brunette Attachment snuggled into The Scrawny Guy as she grinned. "Don't worry, we'll get visual aids next time."

The Muscular Guy grumbled.

What the hell am I doing here? Hale berated himself. *There is a reason you don't follow Alex to these shitty clubs.*

"ID please," The bouncer asked.

"Huh? Oh, right." Hale fumbled with his wallet, pulling out his license. "Here you go." The bouncer took the ID, ran a blacklight over it, bent the opposite corners together, then handed it back to Hale. "You're good, go on in."

Hale took the ID back, looking at its warped shape. "Seriously man? Why?"

The bouncer gave him a look, "You wanna get bounced before you step inside?"

Hale shook his head and bent the ID back a bit, trying to reset its shape.

. . . the bouncer bent the

ID.

. . . . . . "Sure, if you want to let every 17 year

old with a fake in, you could bend it like a

fucking fairy."

. . . . "—to God, if one more

underage kid is at my bar you'll

be ou—"

"Yo, you going in, or what?" The bouncer asked. His lip curled up a little, clearly aggravated at the inexperienced club goer.

Hale looked up at him for a moment. Despite the fact the man was massive, and looked like he could yawn during a gunfight, Hale had felt something. Whatever that conversation was that he Wandered into, the man was scared. Maybe not scared, but upset. Maybe worried? Regardless, Hale said, "Yeah, thanks. Oh, and sorry about the ID thing, man. I know you're just doing your job. It's been a bad day, ya know?"

The bouncer regarded him with a skeptical look for a moment. Judging him sincere, he nodded, "No problem, hoss. Enjoy your night."

Hale nodded and walked in. To his relief, it wasn't a strip club. Rather a dive bar owned by a man who liked swimsuit models. Various centerfolds were posted around the walls, taped up behind plastic, or sometimes framed with an autograph and a mark of lipstick. There were also hundreds of Polaroid's of previous patrons tacked up around the magazine postings, telling every man who walked by that any of these hundreds of beautiful women could walk in at any moment and be his prize for the night.

Hale doubted his reasons for being here again. *There's a liquor store across the street from my apartment. I'll just get a bottle and drown myself in the peace of my own home.* He laughed to himself and began turning around.

"Holy shit! It's the hermit in the flesh!" Alex's voice cut through the music.

"Goddammit," Hale cursed to himself. He turned around to meet Alex with a semi-enthusiastic smile. "Hey man, how's it going?"

"I swear, I must have passed out on the bar, cause this shit can't be real." Alex unlinked himself from the smiley blond and embraced his friend. He gave him two slaps on the back to ensure the hug was still masculine, and then released him.

"Hello, hello," Hale said, awkward nerves sneaking into his voice as Alex hugged him. The bar was already not his scene, now he had his drunk friend hugging him. Hale was not in his comfort zone.

"Come on, boss, I'll buy you your first drink."

"Who's your friend?" The blond asked. She swayed and leaned on Alex, eyelids drooping.

"Oh, right. This is Hale. We go way back. Seriously, this dude is fucking awesome, you're going to love him."

Hale recognized the pattern of speech. Alex didn't introduce her, and immediately launched into something outside the standard ice breaker, meaning he had no idea what her name was. *Fine, Alex, I'll save you.* "Hi, what was your name?" Hale shouted over the music.

"Kimberly," she said, giving a small wave in greeting. "So, like, Hail like the weather?"

"Yeah, pretty much."

The trio maneuvered through the crowd to the bar and were greeted with shouts of welcoming. Hale didn't recognize anyone who seemed to know Alex personally, yet from the cacophony of shouts he may well have befriended them all earlier in the night. A flurry of introductions was exchanged, followed by waves and head nods. Hale thanked his luck that this group wasn't big on shaking hands, as it saved him from some potential Wandering.

A beer slid in front of Hale. "There you go, bro! You got next round!" Alex smiled.

The crowd circled around the area of the bar, shouting and laughing. The topics seemed to shift from Bryan's fat assed wife, to Robert's awesome job editing porn all day, to Geoff's mom, sister, or dad depending on the tone of the joke, to Alex's dick and comparisons of its size and almost-mythological feats of conquest, to Kimberly and her impending operation to get her legs out of the air. Bryan would shake his head and drink, Robert would say 'hell yeah' and smile until someone brought up the fact he worked on gay porn, Geoff would say 'fuck you guys', Alex would give pointed glances to Kimberly until someone would bring up his record level of STD's, and Kimberly would flip off the group and threaten to leave. Everyone would always laugh when they weren't the targets, and everyone would always manage to forget they'd already made similar jokes after each 20 minute rotation.

Hale got through his fourth beer. He wasn't a good drinker, and he didn't normally like crappy tap beer from a dive bar, but the distraction it provided was welcomed. Despite being far out of his element, Hale laughed with the group, drank with the group, and in the end, had fun with the group.

He almost wrote off the vibrations in his pocket to the bass beat until Kimberly leaned over and yelled, "Your pocket is glowing!"

Hale slid out of his chair, pulling his phone of his pocket to see 'Cass V.' on the face. Quickly, he swiped the phone open and threw it against his ear.

"Hello?!"

There was a pause. "Hale? Hale!" Cass tried raising her voice the second time.

"Cass! Hi!"

"Can you turn the music down?"

"Uh... no. Sorry, my buddy Alex dragged me out to a bar."

"You're drugged out on X in your car?" Cass asked, surprise heavy in her voice.

"No! No... Uh, I'll text you, one second, okay?"

"Sure." Cass felt stupid for needlessly yelling on her side of the phone, and was glad to hang up.

Hale opened up his text message window, fingers flicking letters onto the screen. 'At bar, friend dragged me out tonight.' He moved towards the door as he waited for the response.

'Fun. Want company?' displayed on his phone.

A jolt went through Hale's body. She wanted to see him again. And just like his luck, he was half drunk and at a dive bar across town. 'Crappy bar, meet somewhere else?' He sent it off, hoping to have some time to sober up.

'1st Date – You're interesting. 2nd date – Meeting friends is good. What bar?'

Hale passed through the doors and stood on the sidewalk. He realized she passed up another golden opportunity to start something with him to put him on the defensive. She could have easily said he was deliberately trying to keep her away from his friends. "Have I been dating the wrong women?" He asked himself aloud.

"Yes! Yes you have!" a woman's voice answered loudly.

Hale looked over with a startled expression.

The young girl was falling over, and being dragged off by her smiling friend who mouthed 'I'm sorry' as she walked. "Come on, you, let's get you home."

"But heee's haaaawt!" she whined.

. . . "-hot, but displaced through the heat
sink-"

. . . . . . "Kristen, you've had your face in
Engineering books for months. Come o-"

. . . . "Okay, fine, we're doing shots,
but don't let me go home with anyone
tonight."

Hale shook out of his Wander, covering his moment of insight with a nervous chuckle before turning back to his phone.

"Still time," a deep voice rumbled behind him.

Hale turned to see the bouncer, standing by the door with his arms crossed.

"Chase her down, and she'll annoy her friend 'til she lets her go. Easy catch."

Hale smiled. Apparently his apology had endeared himself to the man enough to earn a little nudge of encouragement. "Nah, it's cool. She just wanted a night to decompress." He just waved the phone at the bouncer with a smile. "Plus, mine's better."

'Sandy Clam, on PCH, come on down', he texted back.

———————

JEREMIAH GOT off the bus and stepped out onto the sidewalk. The fresh smell of sea breeze filled his nostrils as the waves crashed in front of him. A sandy volleyball court, a well worn basketball park, and a thin stretch of beach were all that separated the street from the Pacific Ocean. He gazed out at it for a few moments, losing himself in its tranquility.

"Hey man, you got a dollar?"

Jeremiah turned to see a man in rags with a gloved hand out.

"I'm really hungry, man." He smiled a toothless grin. "Can you help a veteran out?"

"You're not a veteran, you're an ex-con named Lawrence," Jeremiah said flatly. The surprised look on Larry's face showed Jeremiah that Larry didn't remember him. Either Jeremiah's transformation in Imanu'el's care had been that significant, or Larry's mind had begun failing him. After letting the man gape for a moment, he pulled a crumpled dollar bill out of his pocket and extended it to him. "Take this, Larry, and try not to buy poison with it. There is still a chance for you. Turn to Him for answers." He lifted his eyes up to denote who he referred to, then patted Larry on the shoulder and walked past him.

This will be a good night. Jeremiah decided, taking his first steps up the hill of Pacific Coast Highway.

7

"You're fucking with me, right?" Alex demanded, his temple pressed to Hale's as they both looked towards the door. Alex gripped Hale around the shoulder, keeping his friend close as they both stared forward. At the end of their tunneled vision, Cassandra Voss smiled and handed her ID over to the bouncer.

"I'm really not."

"Dude, you better not be f–"

"I'm not fucking with you, Alex," Hale forced a snap into his response, as he was only able to be half-annoyed. His other half reveled in the jealousy and praise from his friend.

"You bang her yet?"

"Second date, dude. I told you that."

Alex paused, eyes locked on Cass as he slowly processed his response. "You bang her yet?"

"Dude, goddamn it," Hale protested, pulling away. "You're going to scare her off."

"Hale, I ain't gay," Alex said, eyes still fixed on the redhead who had tentatively stepped into the bar. "But I will start necking with you right now if it'll scare her off of you and give me even half a chance."

"Alex, serio– Alex!" Hale pushed Alex off of him as he made kissy faces and jokingly pawed at Hale. Alex continued laughing hysterically even after a final punch to the solar plexus made him pull back. Hale lingered on Alex a second longer to be sure he was done before judging it was safe to turn back toward the door.

Cass stood mere feet away with a wry smile on her face. "Am I interrupting something?"

Hale flushed, "No, no... he just, uh, you know, being an asshole."

Cass' grin did not fade as she nodded at Hale. She glanced over at Alex, then back at the blushing man in front of her.

"Oh, right. Cass, this is my asshole friend, Alex."

Alex smiled broadly, extending his hand. "A pleasure."

"Likewise."

"Alex, this is Cass." He gave Alex a strained smile as if to convey 'Don't fuck this up for me.'

Alex winked at him in an attempt to give reassurance, then turned back to Cass and gestured at the blonde. "Cass, this is Kimmy."

"Kimberly," she corrected, and shook Cass' hand.

"Who said it wasn't?" Alex smiled as if he had made a joke. "So what are you drinking, Cass?"

"I suppose a Citrus Vodka would be a good way to start off a Monday evening."

"Alright," Alex nodded to her. He leaned over to Hale as he turned to the bar. "Good job, man, I like her so far."

"Seriously, don't fuck this up for me..." Hale murmured back to him through a smile.

"Citrus Vodka, and another round of the shit that keeps coming out of the tap." Alex called out to the bartender. He spoke back over his shoulder to Hale, "Don't worry, Boss. I got you covered."

Hale leaned back forward to address Cass. "So, uh, welcome."

"Thanks." Cass adjusted her purse, looking around. "So this is one of your preferred hangouts?"

"Oh yeah," Hale said, nodding and pulling his lips down. "Gotta love this place. I come here at least four, maybe five times a week. I figure the quality drinks and fine ambiance really put things in perspective after a long day at work."

Cass grinned, but played along. "Yeah, I thought I saw you in one of those Polaroids as I walked in. Was that you lifting the two girls up, one in each arm?"

"The wha–? Oh, that one. Yeah, that was back in my lifting days. I had to cut back, you know, give a little bit of hope back to the competition."

"You're ridiculous." She allowed a small laugh.

Hale smiled, but was cut off as a pair of drinks was shoved between them. Alex winked at Hale and then shot a smile over to Cass. "There you are, Citrus Vodka and piss on tap."

Cass' eyes shot up and sparkled with wonder. "They have piss on tap here?"

Both of the men were struck dumb for a moment.

"Oh my god." She was suddenly serious. "I have searched everywhere, up and down this strip, in every restaurant, bar, and liquor store, and I have never been able to find piss on tap."

The two startled men stared for another moment before Alex broke the silence. He turned to his friend and spoke calmly. "Hale, where did you find this woman?" He turned back to Cass. "You are fucking awesome!"

"I guess I'll be in the ladies' room," Kimberly said from just behind Alex, a disgusted look on her face.

Cass ignored the woman's pointed look. Hale had seen the subtle, and not-so-subtle, power struggles ensue when Alex's previous conquest came up against competition and he noted, for the second time in as many dates, that Cass wasn't interested in that. Instead, she continued the conversation as if nothing happened. "Why thank you." Cass saluted him with her drink and took a sip. "And what is it you do, Alex?"

"Construction," Alex answered, a hint of pride in his voice. "I spend my days building stuff with my bare hands, or knocking the shit out of it until it comes down."

"Your family?"

"Nearby. They live in OC."

"Friends?"

85

Alex backhanded Hale on the shoulder. "Aside from this asshole here?"

"Would you need more?" She shrugged.

"Hell no!" Alex took the bait with gusto, becoming wildly animated again. "Hale is the man. I mean, when I can drag his antisocial ass away from his damn apartment and fucking evil cat."

"Hold on now." Cass cocked her head and pointed with her free hand. "Commodore will not appreciate that kind of talk, especially when you think he cannot hear you." She nodded solemnly.

Alex paused, a dumb grin on his face. His head swiveled comically to Hale, back to Cass, and then to Hale again. The same goofy smile stayed plastered across his mouth as he looked them over. "Hale, I–" He put a finger up as if to accentuate a point before his eyes fell on Cass. He pulled the finger in, placing it over his own lips as if to cut himself off. He dropped his finger from his lips and retrieved his drink. "Very well, I approve."

"Excuse me?" Cass asked, wearing an amused smile of her own.

Hale sighed, shaking his head before taking a long swig of his beer.

"I approve," Alex restated, saluting his drink as if to accentuate his point. "You may have sex with my friend."

Hale spat beer all over the floor.

"Excuse me?!" Cass repeated. To Hale's surprise, while clearly shocked, she looked more entertained than offended, and her choked laughter supported his assessment.

"Oh Jesus Christ..." Hale cursed.

Alex pushed himself up onto two chairs, speaking down at them and gesturing reverently like Moses to the Israelites. "You, Cass, may have sex with my friend! You have the right, nay, the privilege, to kneel and worship at the altar of this man's cock!" He ended his sermon with outstretched arms, soaking in a wave of laughter and applause from every barfly who could hear him over the music.

Hale slammed his forehead into his palm, but couldn't help laughing himself.

"Bravo, Reverend Alex." Cass set her drink down so she could applaud lightly. "Bravo. I can see you're the shy one of this group, and appreciate you breaking out of your shell to give your blessing."

Alex jumped down, his ear to ear grin back on his face. Kimberly appeared behind him again, tugging at his sleeve and whispering in his ear. Alex's eyes lit up, and he backed away as she tugged. "If you'll excuse-a me–" His voice became that of an evangelical minister. "But I have another sermon I need to attend to in mah-ya private quarters. Pr-AISE Je-he-sus!" He disappeared through the side door with Kimberly.

Hale lifted his head back up and looked over at Cass, unable to suppress a grin on his face. "I'm sorry, he's a dick someti—"

"Hale." She regarded him with a raised eyebrow. "I'm not made of glass. I can tell the difference between a guy who likes to push buttons for comical value, and an asshole with respect issues towards the fairer sex. I grew up with both types of men saying inappropriate things to me all the time, and I was raised by a single father."

"Really?" Hale's inebriated judgment did not catch the second part of the question in time. "What happened to your mom?"

Cass paused, biting her lip. She inhaled deeply, then proclaimed. "This won't work."

"Huh?" A chill shot up Hale's body. *What'd I do?*

"I'm far too curious about you, yet I can't just grill you all night and have you dodging every question, so we're going to have to work out a system." Her eyes narrowed as she plotted.

Hale grinned, relieved his initial fear hadn't come to fruition. "May I propose a solution?"

"I'm listening."

"We pour shots. You ask a question. I ask a question." He leaned in closer, using the excuse to talk rather than shout as he moved into more intimate space. "And we have to answer honestly, or drink to avoid responding."

"I don't think you'll survive this," Cass smirked.

Hale raised an eyebrow, giving her a quick look up and down. "You're what, a buck ten? You sure you can last past the first round?"

"Buck twenty five, thank you, and I'll remind you I have a strong Russian heritage and was raised by a single man. That should give you an idea of the first round to pour."

"Da," Hale answered with his best Russian accent.

———

CROWDS SEEMED to avoid Jeremiah. Not only was he walking alone in a peculiar mix of gray jeans, gray sweatshirt and a grey t-shirt, but he seemed to move towards people's path as they walked by. Those that regarded him with suspicion made no attempt to hide it when he moved almost close enough to slam into them as they passed. Occasionally someone would shout a warning,

"Watch it, buddy."

"Move it, asshole!"

"What's your problem?"

Jeremiah paid them no mind. He was concentrating. Listening. With each step, he renewed his confidence knowing that he was one step closer to progress. He remained vigilant, ignoring the shouts when he could, apologizing profusely when it was necessary. After each encounter, he continued on as he was.

"Imanu'el," he whispered to himself. "I will find them."

———

THE SHOT glass was overturned on the table.

"You suck at this," Cass mocked.

"I can't say I was expecting an opener of that caliber."

"It was an honest question."

"It was a bullshit question." Hale raised an eyebrow, giving her a knowing look.

"It was a little bullshit," Cass admitted with a grin.

"Then how about we start with real stuff?" Hale signaled for another shot to be poured. "The get to know you questions, you know. After we get past the surface we can get into the cheating questions to force each other to drink."

"'How do you usually seduce a woman' is a fair question." Cass straightened and pouted out her lower lip.

"It was a bullshit question," Hale repeated as he fought back a smile.

Cass grinned.

"Alright cheater, it's my turn." He pondered for a second. "When is your birthday?"

"May 25th," she answered immediately.

"And?"

"You said day, you said nothing about year."

"You're making this difficult." Hale pursed his lips and narrowed his eyes, trying his best to act frustrated.

"No, I'm making this fun."

"Your turn, cheater." He held his gaze of mock judgment.

"Where were you born?"

"A hospital."

"See?" She patted him proudly. "You're learning."

"Alright, let's see." Hale chose his words carefully. He had intended this as being a quick and fun way to learn some facts about Cass, but it quickly evolved into a battle of wits. *Fact learned, she's intelligent and quirky.* He grinned to himself, unable to deny he was enjoying the spin she'd placed on the game. "What college did you graduate from?"

"UCSB. I moved up to Berkley for college, then came back down here."

"Volunteering info, are we?"

"Call it charity for the pitiable."

"Ouch, not only a cheater, but a mean one," Hale held his hand over his heart, a look of pain on his face. She gave her mischievous grin again, forcing a smile out of him. She had a way of biting the tip of her tongue when she did that, giving it almost a childlike innocence. It was the kind of look he expected a kid to give a parent after they'd been caught making birthday macaroni art to surprise them.

"What city were you born in?"

"Garden Grove, but I lived in Orange 'til I was five." Hale gyrated the shot glass, swirling the liquid around the edges as if to remind the pair of the stakes at hand. The chaos and noise of the bar seemed to fade into the background as their game continued. "Where, besides California, have you lived?"

"New York, Illinois, Texas, Florida, and Louisiana." She rattled off the states with an eloquence earned through practice.

"Jesus, why did you move around so much?"

"I don't think it's your turn," she smirked. "What did you want to do as a career when you were growing up?"

Hale chuckled, flushing. "A, uh… private investigator." He almost took his shot just to avoid looking at her.

Cass arched an eyebrow, but said nothing.

"So, uh, yeah, why did you move around so much?" Hale was still flushed.

Cass silently lifted her shot and drank it down, raising the glass for the bartender in the same motion. After a wince to help the alcohol down, she continued, "Why did you give up the glamorous dream of being a PI?"

Hale pondered drinking, fidgeting with his glass for a moment. *How can I word this without outing myself?* He chewed on his tongue as he thought, absorbing Cass' curious glare. "Long and short, I am no good at investigating people, or finding things. I have some natural talent I thought I could develop off of, but it never went anywhere. Plus, I feel odd invading people's lives and stalking them."

Cass seemed satisfied with the answer, but no less curious.

Alright, let's see if I can get to my last answer in a roundabout way. Hale thought for a second. "What do your parents do?"

Cass scowled at him and drank again.

"Damn, I'm two for two." Hale sat up and smiled as pride beamed from his face.

"Don't think you're going to win that easy." She held up the glass for another refill. She set the freshly filled glass on the table, leaning in to speak. "The day we met, you spoke to Phill. I know you did. Did he mention *any* names during your conversation? Think before you answer."

Defcon 5! We have a red alert! Alarms were going off in Hale's brain, and a voice in his 'Oh Shit' section was screaming at him in a tone that reminded him of General Patton. *Do not, I repeat, do not answer this question, sir. This is a trap. The answer is too obvious, and she is too crafty. Do not answer the question! I repeat, pick up the drink and toss it–*

"No, he didn't," Hale said, confidence waning in his voice.

Cass' grin pulled up a little.

Bring up the memory databanks, screen all previous interactions. We're missing something!

"You're sure? Wouldn't want to break our code of honor, now would we?"

Hale furrowed his brow, replaying the conversation with Phill to the best of his recollection. *What am I missing?* After a few moments, he shook his head, "Honestly, I can't think of a single one. He asked me for a chair, knocked over my drink, and demanded I take money–" Hale trailed off.

Shit! Shit! Patton yelled from the back of his head. *Prepare appropriate counter-intelligence measures. The leak has been found. The Sir has done fucked up!*

He had Wandered. The money had changed hands and he had Wandered to the setup of the date. Phill had talked to a woman, thanking her for doing him the favor. He wracked his brain, trying to remember it.

Now what, Sir? You are in a corner. You can either start lying your way out, or you can come clean. Silence is no longer an option!

Wait! The logical side of his brain chimed in. This voice was much more collected, cool, and soothing. *Why does this even matter? Even if you did get a name of a friend from Wandering, how is this even relevant?*

If The Sir wishes to continue to ignore our perfectly rational paranoia, The Sir may continue suffering the consequences of his recklessness.

Cass' triumphant grin remained, watching his features as his mind tore through details and possibilities. "Did you forget something? A minor detail you failed to mention in the past?"

Hale's expression returned from the confusion and pondering, and he decided to stick with the truth, "Honestly, he did not mention a single name."

Cass pursed her lips, her own mind clearly racing. After a long moment of staring between the two, she released the lock on his gaze and leaned back. "Your turn."

"How old are you?" Hale ventured, attempting to bring the questions back down to a comfortable level. He didn't like feeling ambushed, even when a good ambush was the point of the game.

"Twenty six," Cass answered immediately, transitioning seamlessly into her next question. "Do you know Sue?"

Impact. We have impact!

"Sue?" Hale asked innocently.

"It's not your turn."

"Just trying to clarify" He was flailing, and he knew she saw right through it.

"Answer to the best of your ability."

A metal song started over the house speakers; Something grungy about bodies hitting the floor. Hale found it oddly appropriate. "No, I don't know Sue. At least, I don't know the Sue I think you're referring to. I've known a Sue and or Susan or two in the past."

Cass' expression didn't change. She was akin to a cat playing with a small mouse.

"Uh, what did you want to do for a living when you were growing up?" Hale's tone carried a bit of desperation, trying to regain a semblance of control over the game.

"Trial attorney." Again, her answer was immediate, transitioning smoothly into her next question. "You mentioned Sue's name as we drove around after leaving the coffee house. How did you know her by name?"

The perimeter has been breached! The Sir's obstinate decision-making has caused the enemy to breach the main perimeter!

Hale looked at her dumbly. She had avoided a direct line of questioning for what she really wanted to know: How he knew Cass' name. She led him to believe she was walking him down a safe path, all the while pushing him the completely opposite direction. Now he found his alternate destination trapped, and linking right back to the treacherous path he was originally trying to avoid. After several more moments, he simply picked up his shot and drank.

"Interesting." She smiled at him, the curious glint in her eye sparkling brighter.

What is she thinking now? Maybe that I'm a stalker, or I was some kind of plant at the coffee shop? Does she think I lied to her? If any of those are true, why is she still here? What makes this girl tick?! Hale shifted in his seat, putting the glass on the bar to be refilled. He remained locked in Cass' gaze, trying to figure out who was more intrigued by the other. "You are a very interesting person."

"I could say the same for you, though I don't think my mysteries hold a candle to yours."

"I–" *Don't fuck this up.* Hale tried not to pause too long, lest he sound more shaken than he was. "I don't want you to be scared of me. And I really hope that didn't sound as stupid to you as it did to me."

"I have a knack for picking out men with unhealthy behaviors," Cass said as she leaned forward. Her curious stare had lowered, but still hovered behind her eyes. "You can generally tell if a man needs distance and medication rather than affection from a good conversation and observation of mannerisms. I haven't picked up any bad indicators from you, yet. Some of the warning signs are there, but I think they're misplaced."

"Warning signs?"

"Is that your question?"

"No, no." Hale had forgotten they were even playing. "Uh, what was your major at Berkley?"

"Psychology, with a minor in criminal justice."

"Ah." Hale pursed his lips and nodded. *Way to go there, Sparky.*

"I have a proposition." Cass motioned to the bartender with two fingers, then pointed at the still full shots.

"What's that?" Hale wondered if this is what a punching bag felt like.

"I derailed your little game," she said, organizing the shots in front of them. "So let's backtrack. Call it a 'Speed Round'. We'll each ask the first three questions that come to mind, little things, the get-to-know-you stuff, then take our first shot. Three more questions, same harmless topics, then the second shot. Then we pay our tab, leave this shitty bar, and see where the night takes us."

"I think that's a bargain given the circumstances."

"You'll learn quickly I'm not a pushover." She smiled.

"As much as it freaks me out sometimes, I'm glad."

"Okay," she said, placing her hands flat on the table, both of her shots between her forearms. "Ready?"

Hale mirrored her pose. As his hands descended, he remembered a piece of advice Alex had given him. 'Break the touch barrier, dude. Harmless shit, a hand on the shoulder, small of the back, a touch of the fingertips. It gets 'em more comfortable with you, mentally and physically.'

His fingertips rested on the table, lightly touching the tips of Cass' fingers. She didn't move.

"Ready," he said, the small gesture building his confidence.

"Are you an only child?" she began.

"No. How many siblings do you have?" He fired back.

Cass twitched at his superior wording of the same question. "None. And you?"

"A younger sister." Hale thought about asking more about her parents, and decided against it. "Did you like moving around as a kid?"

"Yes and no. Hated new schools, loved my father. Where did you graduate?" Cass picked up her shot glass, using the hand that did not touch any fingertips, and downed it before Hale answered.

"Cal State Long Beach, Bachelors in English Lit. Do you live on your own, now?" Hale followed suit, downing his first shot. He left the fingertips touching, but didn't have the moxie to connect the second pair of hands as he replaced it on the table.

"Since I was 20. Where do your parents live?"

"Oregon, they moved after I went to college. Do you like living in So Cal?"

"It's nice, but overpriced. There's better out there." Cass shrugged. "What would you like to be doing in five years?"

"Journalism is fun, but I think I'd like to do something else. Maybe teach, or write a book. Do you have a five year plan?"

"Own my own consulting firm. I've seen what my boss bills out, and I realize how little I make." She picked up her shot glass. "Do you like Thai food?" She downed her shot.

"I would eat curry every day if my body would let me." *Last question, what do you want to know? Eh, might as well search common ground.* "Do you like video games?"

Cass slid out of her seat, ensuring her footing was true before leaning all of her weight down. She motioned to Hale's shot. "PC games, sometimes. They're far superior to console."

"That's an argument for later." Hale downed the shot and stood. He swayed, then righted himself.

"A dancer, are we?" Cass noted playfully.

"I do like dancing, and what I lack in quality I make up in quantity."

Cass laughed and pulled her wallet from her purse.

"Oh, come on," he pleaded, reaching for his own wallet. "I dragged you out to this shithole, I can get the tab." He nodded to the bartender, handing over his ID to let him know which tab to close.

"Well, I suppose I shouldn't shoot down an act of chivalry, though I will claim responsibility for the cab."

"Cab?"

"You're not driving, and unfortunately, neither am I."

"Ah—"

"Let's discuss this outside," Cass cut him off. "If you can walk better than I can, we'll renegotiate."

Hale retrieved his card, scribbling on the receipt before putting his wallet away. "Very well," He swept his arm towards the door. "Lead the way."

'—the small of the back.' Alex's voice rung in his head.

Cass took the lead. Hale walked half a step behind her, sliding his hand up to the small of her back. She leaned back against it, angling herself towards him.

That's a good sign, right?

Yes, the softer voice from earlier responded. *She likes you, Hale.*

The two walked out of the doors, the bouncer giving Hale a nod of approval and a 'not bad' look at the sight of Cass on his arm. Hale managed to give him a nod and a wink bank, acknowledging the compliment and accepting the camaraderie that had somehow built since the beginning of the night.

They stopped out on the sidewalk.

"Seriously, I have a thing about drunk driving," she said, turning to him.

"I really don't feel that bad." He was telling the truth, but he also knew he had just drank two shots that were going to hit him shortly.

"Cab. On me. Call this a learning experience. Next time we'll plan drunken outings a bit better so we don't have to rush home on a work night."

"Next time?" Hale smiled. A figure walking up the sidewalk behind Cass caught his eye, but he dismissed it. "So I graduate to date three?"

Cass rolled her eyes and sighed, "I suppose. I mean, you are cute, and I guess you're interesting enough to give one more shot."

"Oh you suppose?" Hale said, confidence bubbling up inside him. He let his hands slide onto her hips as he stepped close. Her face registered a hint of surprise, though she didn't pull away. Excitement forced blood to jolt through his veins. *You can do this. She likes you, show confidence, lean in and seal the deal.*

Flushed, he gently pulled her against him at the waist. He cracked a small smile as his right hand drifted up to her cheek, sliding gently down and over her shoulder, cradling the back of her neck in his palm. Cass didn't breathe, though her slightly upturned head and parted lips invited him to continue. He leaned his head forward, gently guiding her with his hand into their first–

"Excuse me, miss. Do you have the time?" a voice came from behind her.

Cass' face pulled sharply away in surprise.

You have got to be fucking kidding me. Hale looked over Cass' shoulder.

"You have got to be fucking kidding me," Cass said over her shoulder.

I want to keep you, a voice said from the back of Hale's mind.

"I apologize for interrupting," The Gray Hooded Man's eyes were wide and anxious, as if her answer was of dire importance. While the immediate suspicion was drugs, he was too clean to be strung out. His hair was groomed, he was freshly shaven, and despite his all gray outfit being odd, it was washed and pressed. "The time?" he asked again.

Irritated, Cass held up her right arm, looking down at her watch.

Quickly, The Gray Hooded Man leaned forward as if to study the watch himself. At the last second he turned his head and grabbed Cass' hand, pressing his ear to it. His face was rigid with concentration as he appeared to listen to the back of Cass hand intently.

"Hey!" both Hale and the nearby bouncer shouted in unison.

Hale pushed between them, grabbing Cass' captured wrist with one hand, and straight armed The Gray Hooded Man in the cheek with the other.

> *. . . a man in white stood over The Gray*
> *Hooded Man with a smile. . .*

Hale's equilibrium wavered as he recovered from the Wander. The images were so clear, the voices so precise. Without question he recognized the Man in White from the TV the other night. He allowed himself to deprioritize the physical conflict in front of him, focusing instead on how these men could be connected.

Startled, The Gray Hooded Man stumbled back, transfixing a similar anxious look on Hale. With lightning speed, he jumped forward and took Hale's head in between his hands. He pulled forward and pressed his own cheek up to Hale's ear, tilting his head so his own ear rested against Hale's temple. There he latched on, unmoving.

Hale thrashed, attempting to dislodge The Gray Hooded Man from his body. The initial shock he received from a Wander with surprising clarity was pushed to the back of his mind to allow room for self-preservation. He could hear the bouncer shout a warning, and then movement became difficult.

It feels like the bouncer has hands on the guy, Hale thought. *Just get this psycho the fuck off of me.*

As suddenly as he was grabbed, the man was pulled back. Though inches of distance been put between their bodies, The Gray Hooded Man still had Hale's head in a vice grip. The bouncer stood next to Hale with one hand locked around The Grey Hooded Man's throat, forcing him away from Hale and Cass.

The Gray Hooded Man kept his eyes locked with Hale. He kept their faces as close as he could despite the bouncer's resistance and spoke in a strained voice. "You are Touched."

Hale's world stopped. The night's distractions had been for nothing. The initial purpose of his escape had found him. He knew immediately what the man was referring to, and deep down inside, knew this was not some elaborate con. The setup was too great, the execution too perfect. They'd have no way of knowing he had even seen the broadcast, much less contemplated a call. The odds of this being a coincidence had to have been astronomical, and Hale just didn't buy this being a ruse.

In shock, Hale attempted to piece together something intelligible to say to The Gray Hooded Man. He should ask questions. He should confirm his suspicions. They should go somewhere private and talk, discuss, and reveal the mysteries that had been weaved in the broadcast last night. He needed to know who the man on the television was. He needed to know who the man holding his face was. He needed to know there was other people out there just like him.

And that's when Alex cold cocked The Gray Hooded Man.

8

Hale was frozen as his brain wrestled over half a dozen responses. The Gray Hooded Man lay unconscious on the ground, having hit his head on the bumper of a parked car while falling. Alex was shouting and bouncing on the balls of his feet. The bouncer was standing between all parties involved, ensuring the conflict escalated no further. Cass was simply staring, though not at the scene as Hale would have expected, but rather at him. She had that intuitive look in her eyes as she studied his reaction.

"What's up, bitch?" Alex threw his arms out. "Step up to my homey now, fucker! I'll knock your bitch ass out again."

"Alright man, he's down and out." The bouncer had one hand pressed against Alex's chest, keeping him back. He kept one eye on Alex, the other on both Hale and Cass. "Just walk away, it's over."

"Yeah, that's what I thought," Alex yelled at the unconscious body over the bouncer's shoulder.

"You got 'em, man, now back the fuck off." The bouncer was clearly irritated.

Hale pondered helping The Gray Hooded Man up. He had said 'You are Touched'. He was certainly referencing the broadcast that had been plaguing Hale's mind over the past few days. If Hale could just talk to him, he could figure out what was going on. He could set up a meeting for later. He might be able to get some answers that had evaded him his whole life.

Then again, if he went to him, that would open up some uncomfortable questions with both Alex and Cass. Alex, he could handle. Cass was too smart for some bullshit explanation.

If he left, he may never see the man again. He may lose his opportunity to find some meaning for his gifts. Hell, the man might be arrested and taken god knows where, which would remove any possibility of Hale tracking him down again.

Cass regarded him with narrowed eyes and a curve at the corner of her mouth.

Dammit, this is not helping. Hale chided himself. Then he came to a realization. *The phone number! Why didn't I think of that! Just get out of here before Cass gets any more suspicious. You can call them later.*

"Are you okay?" Cass asked, her curiosity bleeding out into her voice.

"Yeah, sorry!" Hale jumped a little, pulling back from the scene. He realized his finger was still intertwined in one of her belt loops when she moved with him. "Let's, uh, let's get out of here."

"Yo, dude!" Alex pointedly didn't use Hale's name. "You rolling out?"

"Uh, yeah, thanks man. I'll catch up with you later." Hale thought he saw The Gray Hooded Man stir on the sidewalk. It wasn't until now he realized Kimberly, Alex's latest conquest, was standing a few feet away from her champion with a frozen deer-in-headlights look.

"Yeah, fucked you up good didn't I?!" Alex taunted the unconscious Gray Hooded Man again, backing down the sidewalk in the opposite direction. He grasped Kimberly around the waist, pulling her along with him. Still a little shocked, she stumbled along.

The bouncer made sure the two groups were well on their way before he knelt over the unconscious figure to examine the damage.

Cass and Hale walked swiftly up the sidewalk. Hale absently kept his palm pressed on Cass' lower back, as if guiding her along his own aimless direction. Cass had her arm draped over Hale's, her hand resting on his shoulder. This gave her the ability to easily look back to ensure they were not being followed, and to continue studying Hale's face as they walked.

"You know, that gets kinda annoying," Hale said, meeting her gaze.

"What?"

"The whole psychoanalysis thing." He grinned at her, trying to temper his discomfort. It hadn't bothered him when she'd turned those inquisitive powers on him at the café, or even inside the bar, but now his mind raced with questions and he couldn't hope to come up with answers for his strange reactions to The Gray Hooded Man. "You're staring at me like I'm a word search puzzle or something."

"Don't be silly, you're much more interesting than a word search. Perhaps a Rubix cube, or at least a crossword."

"Funny."

"I try." Cass paused, giving Hale a moment to finish off any jokes before she continued onto the real subject on her mind. "So will I have to keep drawing my own conclusions, or are you going to tell me what happened back there?"

"We got attacked by a crazy homeless guy and got saved by Alex?" Hale ventured. "Well, technically I got saved by Alex, I did save you first."

"Yes, you're a regular Lancelot." She gave a wry grin. "But while that was no Black Knight, he was no petty bandit either."

"Interesting choice of metaphor. Tell me more, Guinevere."

"The man was clean shaven, groomed, and wore freshly washed clothes. He didn't smell, or at least I couldn't smell him in the moment before he grabbed me."

"Okay, so crazy, but not homeless." *How is she so calm after that? My heart is beating out of my chest, and she's still in Sherlock Holmes mode. Wait, does that make her Irene Adler? If so, am I Sherlock?! What parallels does that draw for our relationship?!*

Hale, a calm internal voice chided. *Shut up and listen to her.*

"He had that desperate, frantic look in his eyes, but he was lucid a moment before," Cass spoke as if she was leading Hale by a leash. "Nervous? Sure. Troubled? Most definitely. Though the type of psychosis that would cause someone to commit random acts of violence on strangers would likely have had a different buildup, and certainly a different execution. He showed too much emotion during the act to be any type of sociopath, and he didn't actually hurt either one of us."

Hale paused, giving a frustrated sigh as they walked. *Where the hell are we? We've been walking without direction for how long?* "We should call a cab." He stopped on the sidewalk, looking around. Of course, there were no cabs were in sight.

She paused, staring up at Hale as if weighing the pros and cons of continuing her list of observations and deductions. It was frustrating, and her cool visage began to crack and let that frustration show through. There was a mystery here. There was a problem to be solved. She had the knowledge, training, and ability to pick through it. That wasn't an issue. The question was the social ramifications.

Hale looked down at Cass, his eyes a mixture of wonder and worry.

Cass reached into her purse, pulling out her phone. She came to the conclusion that Hale had the decency to cut his line of questioning at the bar when he saw her resistance. She would let this drop.

For now.

"I have a company saved on my phone for instances like this."

"Ah, cool," Hale said. Relief replaced the worry, but not the undercurrent of wonder.

"It's late, and after that experience, I think I want to take a hot bath and rest," she continued before Hale could get his hopes up. "I'll call two cabs. That way you don't get home too late, either."

Hale nodded.

That knave! The calm voice came from the back of his head again. It sounded like the General with a blunted edge to its tone. What's more, the word choice didn't match his mental figment of the tough man that gave him warnings. *He could have at least had the decency to wait ten seconds. He could see you were having a moment. It would have been your first kiss with that beautiful woman! A magnificent kiss, too! She's breathtaking. She's brilliant! She's a little frustrating with the Sigmund Freud impersonations, but one could argue it almost makes your interactions more interesting.*

Fuck the kiss! No no... this was the General. The bearing was a clear opposite to the calm, passionate voice from before. *The woman can wait. That Gray Hooded Man had intelligence the likes of which we've never seen! He could provide valuable information regarding the nature of our operations and how they function!*

It's still a matter of respect. Hale liked this softer voice. He decided to name it The Poet. *Knowledge or no, he should exercise common decency. Plus, it is not as if we don't have a number to get in contact with his organization.* Not that he knew that, but it just goes to show you shouldn't act with haste.

Hogswallow! The General roared. *He had an objective, and he ran full bore into it. He attacked with ferocity to ensure his cause wasn't kept from him by chance or unnecessary delays.*

In fact that is exactly why his cause was kept from him. The Poet replied smugly.

Pacifist pussy.

Pompous windbag.

"Thank you very much," Cass finished, clicking her phone closed. She looked up at Hale to speak, stopping to eye him upon seeing his expression. "What's so funny?"

"Oh, nothing." Hale realized he was grinning. "It's stupid, really."

Cass cocked her head, giving him a sideways glance.

Hale gave an embarrassed smile, holding up his hands defensively. "Alright, you know how you sometimes have an internal monologue with yourself?"

"Are you suggesting you can read my mind?"

She's kidding, right? Hale smiled to give himself a moment to properly gauge her expression.

Yeah, she's kidding.

"Not yet, but I'm working on it." He winked. "Well, when I'm going over something or weighing pros and cons, I give the different sides different voices. It makes it easier to separate issues in my head. It can also be kind of amusing when I let myself go with a train of thought."

"You're odd," she smiled. "I used to have thoughts in different voices growing up. A warning fatherly voice when I was doing something stupid, a teacher's voice when I went against something I had been taught, et cetera. Over time they all just became one internal voice."

"Nah," said Hale, waving dismissively. "Thinking to yourself is much more fun this way. Trust me, the world is much more interesting inside my head."

"I'll take your word for it," Cass' grin was warm, and without reservation. She peered as lights topped the hill behind Hale. "We got lucky, there was a cab that got a no-show at that new club down the street. You can take it."

"And leave you here alone on the street?" Hale gave a comical look of condescension. "After all, it's in my best interest to ensure someone doesn't steal you away and put you in their pocket. I do want to have date number three."

The cab pulled up slowly, pulling over to the curb as Cass waved. She turned back to him. "Fair enough. And date number three you shall have." She leaned forward, standing on her tip toes to breach the gap between them.

Hale's breath caught.

Her lips passed by his and planted a peck on his cheek. She could tell he hadn't shaved. Short stubble poked her soft lips, tickling her skin as she pulled away. "Good night, Hale."

"Good night," he managed to speak in a tone slightly above a whisper.

Their arms extended as she backed away, allowing interwoven fingers to slowly become undone, remain touching at the tips, and finally break away.

———

"A COMPLETE failure, obviously. The subject cannot even walk." A voice spoke.

Why can't I move my hands? Are they stuck? What is on the ground that could possibly be that sticky? I can barely move my body, much less stand up and walk.

"A degenerate and a failure," another voice responded. "Likely too drugged to be of any use."

That's not right! I'm clean now! Where did these doctors come from?

"Shall we dispose of it?" A third voice asked.

Dispose of it? It?! What is going on?! What is keeping me stuck down here?! Panic urged him to mentally check for physical restraints, or the telltale wooziness of sedatives.

"It is the logical next step. Roll it over and begin adding pressure."

Who are these people? What are they going to do to me?! I need to get free. I need to get out of here!

"On three, two, one..."

They moved me! I can... I can't move. If they rolled me over, I should be able to move now. I shoul– OW. My head! Who are these people? I can only see shadows.

"Press harder. His skull is too thick."

They're trying to kill me. I am going to die here in this place. I don't even know where 'this place' is.

"Add rhythm."

It feels like they have a boot on my head... why are they pressing back and forth. It just makes the pain throb, but it doesn't do any more damage... How am I going to get out of here?

"I said how many fingers am I holding up?"

That doesn't even make sense! How can I see when they have me blindfolded? Wait a second, that wasn't one of the same voices.

"Stay with me, count the fingers."

It's a deeper voice. I recognize that voice. He was just yelling at me about something.

"You can do it, man. Look at my hand and count the fingers."

Jeremiah's vision cleared of the blotted hallucinations that had been standing over him. The sick swirl of confusing images receded, and the boot he had imagined pressing against his head disappeared, though the throbbing pain he had imagined it inflicted was very, very real. He blinked, and the sight of the bouncer came into focus. He held his hand up, fingers extended.

"Three," Jeremiah said, relieved the hallucinations of doctors had been dispelled.

"Alright, can you stand?"

There was a small crowd around them. Jeremiah realized he had created quite the spectacle. Someone was talking to a nearby friend, confirming the body laying out in front of the bar was indeed still living.

"I... think so," he grunted in response, attempting to prop himself up. His legs were wobbly, though with the bouncer's assistance, he managed to get on his feet.

"Alright man, I'm glad you're alright." The bouncer used a practiced tone conveying warmth and warning. "But we don't like people starting shit here. I recommend you get to an ER to get that head checked out, and don't come back around here unless you can play nice with others. You understand me?"

Jeremiah looked around at the gawking spectators, trying to remember why he was here. As he looked from face to face, ending his canvas of the area with the name of the bar and the bouncer's stern expression, memories came back.

"Yes, of cou— wait!" He stopped, the pain in his head forcing him to slow down and speak softer. "Where did that man go?"

"It's better you leave him alone, capiche?" The bouncer warned.

"No, no. I must talk to him." Jeremiah was frustrated. He was also off balance.

The bouncer tightened his grip. This served the dual purpose of keeping Jeremiah upright, and accentuating his next point. "You need to go to the ER. You need to stay the hell away from that guy and his girl. You've caused enough trouble tonight, understood?"

Jeremiah couldn't believe it. He had found one of the Touched. He had his first chance to pass on the message. And instead of bringing back what could have been a new Zealot for the cause, he had instead failed Imanu'el.

———

SHEETS RUSTLED with a rhythmic tempo. Hale leaned his head back, his eyes squeezed shut and his breath held tight in his chest. The events surrounding the Gray Hooded Man and the Public Access broadcast occasionally invaded his mind, though the powerful images of Cass helped push them aside. He imagined her pale skin, her mischievous smile under hungry eyes. He flashed back to the moment outside the bar when he pulled her close, feeling her hips press against his. Their eyes were locked, and he could feel the warmth of her body as he leaned forward to kiss her.

Images swirled, and the subsequent events were rearranged to fit his purposes. They locked in a passionate embrace. Their lips pressed together, parting slightly to allow their tongues to flit out and touch. Hands moved freely over each others' forms, and suddenly, the venue changed from street-side to Hale's bedroom. Reminiscent of his dream the previous evening, he imagined Cass' nude form writhing beneath his.

He inhaled again, holding the breath as he felt himself nearing climax. The fantasy of Cass looking over her shoulder at him while grasping the headboard with both hands sent him over the edge. His arm pumped furiously, and a strained moan pulled through his throat.

After his ecstasy peaked, breath evacuated his lungs with a deep sigh of relief. Hale laid back, drawing in deep breaths as his body settled down. The images of Cass faded from his mind, and his muscles wound down, relaxing and growing warm. When his eyes finally drifted open, he saw Commodore laying at the side of the bed, glaring at him through narrow slits.

You are a disgusting creature, human. The cat's face said.

"You know, Commodore," Hale said to his cat. He didn't expect him to understand, but it made him feel better to make the attempt. "It's kinda disturbing when you watch me like that."

Don't try to make me the villain, pervert.

Hale slid out of bed, holding his right hand out a bit as he moved over to the sink. Hale's mind drifted as water shot out of the faucet over his lathered hands.

Alright Hale, The Poet said calmly. *You've had time to think, time to procrastinate, and time to... relax. It's time. You can't avoid this opportunity, you'd never forgive yourself.*

Like hell! The General spouted. *You have a perfect defensive position, which will be compromised if these cultists find out who you are. Making that call pushes you down a one way street, which you shouldn't be ready to commit to yet.*

Hale, you're not a coward. Careful, methodical even, but not a coward. You know you cannot avoid this. Pick up your phone and make the call. The Poet's voice was soothing.

Time is your ally right now, and picking up that phone makes it your enemy! The General bellowed.

Weren't you just arguing to pursue and confront The Gray Hooded Man not an hour ago? The Poet asked.

Do not blame me for my hypocrisy, The General responded defensively. *He's the one who assigns the voices. It's not my fault he assigned me to this side of the debate.*

Hale sighed. Knowing what he had to do, and knowing delaying the inevitable would just torment him for another day, or two, or however long he dragged this out, he walked back into his living room. Both the Poet and the General knew he was a procrastinator, and all three of them were in agreement that it would be now or never. He picked the phone up off the bar.

He had a new text message from Alex.

'Dude, call me' was all that it said.

Shall I make the argument for procrastination now? The Poet asked.

Hale hit the send button, calling the source of the text message.

I can call them after, Hale justified. *I should talk to Alex about what happened anyway.*

"Dude?" Alex answered.

"Sup Alex."

"Dude!" Alex's voice raised an octave. "I totally fucked that guy up, huh?!"

Despite the ridiculous string of events and Alex's base understanding of the evening, Hale laughed. He found the irony amusing. "Yeah you did, man. Thanks, by the way. I wasn't really enjoying the guy all up on me like that."

"No worries, boss. What was with that, anyway? What happened before I rolled up to make that guy get in your face like that?"

"Honestly, I have no fucking clue," Hale lied. "He interrupted Cass and I right as we were about to have our first kiss–"

"Did you kiss her?!" Alex interrupted.

"Uh, no. Like I said, he interrupted."

"Fuck that guy! I don't care if he was opening fire with a machine gun, that chick is hot, dude. Ignore his bitch ass and get your mack on!"

Hale cringed at the 90's Gangsta lingo that Alex slipped into. The manner of speech annoyed him, but he let it go. "Trust me, I wanted to, but the guy grabbed Cass. He gripped her by the wrist and wouldn't let go."

"No shit? Just like that?"

"Kinda. He asked her for the time first, but then just grabbed her before she could respond."

"That's fucking weird." Alex was, with good cause for once, genuinely confused.

"So I push the guy off, right? Next thing I know, he's wrapped around my face like a barnacle."

"Yeah, I came around the corner right as he jumped at you," Alex said. "I just couldn't figure out what led up to that. I mean, you had some drinks, but I'd never seen you start shit with someone before."

"Trust me, I would have been fine staying out of 'the shit'. Fucker ruined a good night with Cass." Hale's bitterness crept through his voice.

"What? You didn't pick up where you left off afterwards? I figured you guys went home after we parted ways."

"Nah, she was pretty shaken up. She called two cabs. After she left, I walked back down to my car, waited a bit to sober up, then just drove home." Hale rewound the night in his mind. "Speaking of going home with someone, how did you come up on the fight? Didn't you go home with that blond chick?"

"Ha, nah, we just went out to a dark spot on the beach. I figured I'd give respect to the bar and give her its namesake." Alex chuckled.

"That's pretty nasty, dude," Hale grimaced.

"She loved it man. So much that after watching me wreck that dude she wanted more. She's passed out in my bed right now."

"I don't know how you get away with this shit, man."

"Years of practice and a gift from God, boss."

Hale knew from experience not to clarify what the gift from God was. Alex liked to talk about his penis, and would take any opportunity presented to brag. "Fair enough. Well, thanks again, man. You came through in a clinch. And thanks for dragging me out. Despite the rough end, it was a good time."

"No problem, man. Seriously, you need to come out more. Getting out of that hole will do you some good."

"I'll try," Hale promised. "You know me, I just like my space most of the time."

"True true." Alex pulled away from the phone for a second. "Gotta go, blondie is stirring. I think we're up for round three."

"Go forth and conquer, my friend."

"Oh, Hale, hold up." Alex said quickly, then lowered his voice. "Do you remember this chick's name?"

"Un-fucking-believable." Hale slapped his forehead with his palm. "I should leave you hanging on this to teach you not to be such a douche."

"Seriously man, that shit is awkward. Don't leave your knight in shining armor hanging!"

"You owe me," Hale laughed. "Kimberly."

"Thanks boss! Peace." The call quickly clicked off.

Hale looked at the darkened screen on the phone, realizing his reasons for procrastination had run dry. He'd relieved his sexual tension, clearing his mind of any lust that would cloud his judgment. He'd caught up with Alex, answering some of the questions that had been left hanging. He'd had time to think, giving himself to opportunity to ensure this was the right move. There was no other reason to delay.

Hale dialed the number he had copied onto his laptop and hit Send.

———————

IMANU'EL GENTLY dabbed the cloth to Jeremiah's wounds. The blossoms of blue and green flowered around bright red caverns in Jeremiah's skin. The split on his forehead was bad, though the deep purple and green bruising on his opposite cheek did not look pleasant either. "Tell me what happened," Imanu'el said gently.

Jeremiah winced as the cloth passed over the cut. Pain registered across his face, hiding the shame that welled up beneath. "I was walking down Pacific Coast Highway. I had passed a few hundred people, none of which showed any promise. Their souls were quiet. While I garnered many a strange glares for attempting to hear their potential, I knew it was a necessary inconvenience to advance the cause."

Imanu'el nodded silently, dipping the rag back into the bowl of hot water.

"I pressed on, taming my frustrations with the knowledge I was on the right path, and that perseverance would win the day." He pursed his lips. "That's when I saw them."

"Them?" Imanu'el asked. "There were more than one?"

"Yes… well, no," Jeremiah corrected himself. "There were two individuals I spotted, and while I had initial suspicions upon approaching them, I was incorrect. I heard... it is hard to describe. It changed, like a wave." He let his hand flow up and down slowly.

"Oscillating?" Imanu'el offered.

"Yes, I think." Jeremiah cleared his throat, embarrassed at his lack of vocabulary. He had tried to emulate Imanu'el's method of speech and diversity of words since they met, but he was still learning. "Normally it doesn't do that. It almost sounded like two of the Touched were standing next to each other. I had never heard something like it, and since I've never heard two Touched next to each other, I had to assume that's what it would sound like."

"But it wasn't two?"

"No." Jeremiah hung his head in shame. "I approached the woman first. I was too excited, too anxious. I grabbed her wrist so I could listen closely. I wanted to hear which tone was hers. It might have helped me in talking to them." He shook his head fervently, immediately regretting the sharp motion due to the wave of fresh pain it brought. "Ah! Sorry." He winced and regained his composure. "In my haste, I scared her, and the man. As I listened to her life pass through her veins, the man pushed me away. At his push, I knew I had been wrong."

"From his push?" Imanu'el looked confused. "You could hear from that far?!"

"Yes. Even as I was walking up I could hear him faintly. I thought the two of them standing together had made it, uh..."

"Amplified?" Imanu'el suggested.

"Yes, amplified. But I was wrong. When he neared me, I knew the... oscillating sound had come from him alone. I had never heard anything like it. Again, in my excitement, my anxiety, I acted rashly." Jeremiah flushed crimson with shame anew. "I frightened them, and he felt the need to defend himself. I tried to tell him! I tried to let them know why I was acting so strangely, but I was a fool to think I could make them understand."

"You doubt your ability, yet I believe it was the shock of success which rendered you incapable," Imanu'el reassured. "What happened then?"

"I... I held the man in my hands." Jeremiah strained. "I heard his life, heard his soul singing out. It was incredible, Imanu'el! From you, I hear a deep, resonant sound. It is constant, and ever present. From this man, it was like a symphony." Jeremiah caught himself, worried his enthusiasm over the other man's gift may offend Imanu'el. After all, Imanu'el's gift was divine.

Imanu'el looked at his devout pupil, urging him to go on with his eyes.

Reaffirmed in his place, Jeremiah continued. "His soul sang high and low, but I only had enough time to tell him he was Touched. Then... then I was attacked. It came from the side, and the bouncer later told me it was the man's friend who attacked me. I was knocked unconscious and thrown into a parked car." Jeremiah bit back tears, refusing to allow the memory of his failure to make him look even weaker to Imanu'el. "He would not let me follow, would not even confirm which way they went. Despite his warning that he'd call the police, I scanned up and down the sidewalks for over an hour. After I was sure the man and woman had departed, I made my way back here. I am so sorry, Imanu'el."

Imanu'el said nothing, instead dabbed at Jeremiah's wounds again. He examined the cut on Jeremiah's brow, pondering whether it would need stitches. "This may need more help than a warm rag. To prevent infection or the need of stitches, I cou–"

"No, Imanu'el," Jeremiah said firmly. "I will not let you sacrifice for my failures. I will heal over time, and the wound will remind me what price I must pay for haste."

"You are sure?" Imanu'el asked, concern carrying his voice. "My personal sacrifice is minor to reward such devotion."

Jeremiah shook his head, wincing again at the pain it brought. He wanted to agree, to stand witness to Imanu'el's miracle and feel the closeness between them but it had been his foolishness that caused his injuries and they were his pains to bear. "No, thank you," he responded softly.

The phone rang.

Jeremiah moved to rise, but was stayed by Imanu'el's hand. "Sit, Jeremiah. You have done enough this evening. Allow me to share your burden." He crossed the room to the ringing phone and answered it. "Hello? ... Yes, I am he... My followers call me Imanu'el."

Jeremiah looked up at Imanu'el, clearly waiting to support his mentor when the prankster unveiled his ruse.

Imanu'el returned the gaze, but did not return the disheartened expression. In place of disappointment was a glow of hope and pride, the beginning of promise. He continued with the conversation, eyes locked with Jeremiah. "I'm afraid so... Yes, it was nothing permanent, thankfully. My apologies for any fright this may have given you... Of course, we are still quite interested in meeting with you, albeit under much more peaceful circumstances... I'm sure you do, and we will have answers in return... This coming Saturday, noon."

Jeremiah's jaw went slack as Imanu'el rattled off the address to the caller. Disbelief mixed with joy as Imanu'el said a gracious thank you, gave God's blessing, and hung up. Frozen with anticipation, Jeremiah stared while waiting for a response.

"Jeremiah," Imanu'el said, his glowing smile filling Jeremiah with warmth. "Mr. Hale sends his apologies for the injuries you sustained at the hands of his friend."

9

"Mr. Langston, you didn't tell me you and Mr. Kent had teamed up over the weekend." Ockie smacked Hale's back with a manila folder as he walked by. "Good work, kiddo."

"Thanks, Ockie," Hale grinned up at him. The smile faded along with Ockie's footsteps. Relief and excitement from the previous night's call were the only thing overpowering Hale's exhaustion and discontent. The confirmation that The Gray Hooded Man was connected with the preacher on TV had demolished all but the last remnants of doubt from Hale's mind. Either this was the most capable, well researched, and luckiest con ever concocted by man, or these people legitimately had powers akin to the gift Hale himself possessed. Hale had promised himself that he would not give them one cent, nor would he show them what he could do, or even describe it, if nothing prompted him to Wander, until they had given him undeniable proof that they too had some sort of gift. Once Hale was sure they were 'Touched' like he was, then he'd be willing to hear what they had to pitch.

He'd still be hesitant on the money front.

Yet Saturday was a long way away. That left Hale with a lot of nighttime to lay awake through, and nothing productive to do except catch up on backlogged work. After the phone call to Imanu'el, the pitter patter of laptop keys resounded through Hale's apartment as he completed editing assignments, drafted a story on a local pet rescue, and threw together a list of outlines for potential stories that would require Ockie's final approval to research. The night's labors not only caught him up from his previous week's slacking, but propelled him ahead of the curve for this week.

Being ahead did little for the lead weights hanging off the ends of his eyelids.

Shaking himself back into reality, Hale tilted back the energy drink Mark had donated to him. He made a sour face as the vile liquid poured down his throat. It was reminiscent of the spoonfuls of thick cough syrup his mother had forced into him as a child. To this day he was not convinced the stuff had any actual effect on his infected system, other than his body naturally bolstering its immune system with the sole motivation of not having to digest more of the sludge.

"Mark, seriously, what is this stuff?" Hale shook the can at him. In his mind, the splashing liquid sloshed like oil against the sides of the can.

"You don't like it?" Mark shrugged at him, swirling in his chair. His lap became a makeshift desk with two of Ockie's handwritten edits laid across his thighs. Despite the present technology, Ockie would occasionally have a flashback and handle business the old fashioned way. Printouts with comments in red ink would then fly out to various desks. It didn't happen often, which gave it a certain charm when the hard copies did make their way out to the floor rather than annoyance at the antiquated practice. "I live on the stuff, man."

"I could caulk the cracks in my wall with it," Hale grimaced.

"Keeps you wired all day, though," Mark smiled.

"With a name like Heavy Metal I would hope so." Hale looked at the can with distain, wondering if he could brave another draught of the swill.

"So why are you so wiped out? Can't sleep again?"

"That, and my buddy decided to drag me out to this shitty bar last night."

"Sad you went?" Mark asked idly, only half paying attention to the conversation as he went over Ockie's gouts of red ink on his work.

"Nah. I'm not much of a bar goer, but it was a good time. Plus, I converted it into a date," Hale said with a grin.

"A date?" Mark's eyes lifted back up to Hale, his interest renewed. "Who's the lucky man?"

"Your dad didn't break the news yet?" Hale looked puzzled.

"Nice." Mark's eyebrows shot up at the unexpected delivery.

"You've met Alex," Hale reminded him. "That man fires off more shit talking than you can comprehend. Taught me to keep on my toes."

"Fair enough. But seriously, a date? Who with?"

"It's random as all hell," Hale admitted. "I was at a coffee shop reading a book. Long story short, a guy grabs a chair from me, spills my coffee, and then waits on the other side of the patio. There I am, minding my own business when this girl comes in, sees the other dude, then walks over to me and starts up a conversation. Turns out her friend put her up to a crappy blind date, and she chickened out at the last second."

"So you were the lesser of two evils?" Mark grinned.

"I'll take it, man. This girl is amazing." Hale's grin grew past his normal smile, happiness beaming through his exhaustion. "She's stupid smart–"

"Stupid smart?" Mark jabbed. "You must be tired..."

"Don't be a jackass. You know, like 'Bill Gates makes a stupid amount of money', or 'That house is stupid big.' Don't pretend you don't understand my lexicon." Hale playfully glowered at Mark before he continued. "Anyway, she's smart, got a good set of wits on her–"

"Those are always important," Mark nodded.

"Not–" Hale shushed himself, looking around to make sure no co-workers were eavesdropping. The last thing he needed was a meeting with HR. "Wits, dipshit. With a 'W'."

Mark stifled laughter.

"But yeah, she's got a good pair of those too," Hale smirked.

"So I'm waiting for the 'she's got a great personality' or 'and then I took her back to the sanitarium...'"

"Heh, nah. She drove me around a bit, then dropped me off at home. The date last night at the bar was date numero dos." Hale held up two fingers to translate his sudden break into Spanish.

"So, back to your place after date numero dos?" Mark asked, biting his lower lip and shooting his eyebrows up and down. The comical gesture reminded Hale of a bad 80's flick.

"Eh, almost."

"Pfft! Almost!" Mark threw up his hands in dismay, rolling his eyes to accentuate his disappointment.

"Couldn't be helped, man," Hale chuckled. "This hobo ended up jumping us outside the club. Kinda killed the mood."

"You're shitting me."

"I shit you not, mah friend." Hale leaned back in his chair. "I pushed him back, the bouncer helped, and then Alex jumped out of nowhere and clocked the guy." He felt a twinge of guilt that he couldn't give full context to the story, but he suppressed it. At least he was making his friend out to be a hero. Still, his journalistic integrity tugged at him.

"Jesus." Mark took a moment to digest the event before launching into his next jibe. "You couldn't play the role of the savior and turn that to your advantage?"

Hale shook his head and smiled. "That was the night, man. We went our separate ways afterwards. It's all good. I have high hopes for date number three." Hale's expression paused as he drew a connection from Mark's last comment. "Hey Mark, side question, you ever heard the name Imanu'el before?"

"The Spanish version, or the Hebrew version?" Mark responded quickly, abandoning the previous topic and pouncing on the opportunity to show off his hard earned knowledge.

"As one who has gone through a bar mitzvah, I was hoping you could help me with the Hebrew one."

"Pulling the race card, I get it." Mark nodded. "Your passive aggressive attack against one of God's chosen people has been noted."

"Alright, alright, my celestial karma has been damaged, I get it. Get to the point."

"It's a combination of two words," Mark's features perked up as he capitalized on the opportunity to relay information from his years of religious upbringing. "Immanu, which means 'with us', and El, meaning 'God'. There's some significant religious debate over Imanu'el in religious texts, but unless you want to walk down an argument over who the true Messiah is, we should leave it at that."

"No shit."

"None whatsoever." Mark shrugged. "The name essentially means 'God is with us', and has been attributed to potentially being Jesus or another idealized form of God. Why do you ask?"

"Random curiosity, really." Hale lied. "The hooded guy was yelling something crazy about Imanu'el being our divine savior or something, and it kind of stuck with me."

"That is random," Mark agreed. "To be fair, homeless crazies don't have to make sense. He was probably pulling information from an old Sunday school class and feeding it through his drunk, schizophrenic brain."

"Probably," Hale nodded, trying to drop the matter.

"So, now that we're done with your clever attempt to dodge conversation on your budding love life," Mark started.

Good, he's dismissing my question as an attempt to change topics. Hale realized with relief.

"What's the game plan now?"

"No game plan, really," Hale admitted. "I like the girl, and all I can hope for is a good third date."

"Zol zein mit Mazel!" Mark encouraged in his best Hebrew accent. "Try not to have any accidents, but if you do, name it after me."

Hale grinned, toasting Mark with his can of Heavy Metal before taking a swig. A sour look on his face exploded as his taste buds reminded him why he had stopped drinking the beverage. Mark erupted into a fit of laughter.

THE WEEK had crawled by. By overburdening himself with work and other meaningless distractions, Hale had made his way through it with the majority of his sanity intact. While the anxiety of making the initial call to Imanu'el had been alleviated, the new anxiety brought on by the anticipation of Saturday's meeting had forced the second hand to move slower on the clock.

Hale walked up his staircase as thoughts swirled around his head. A thousand preconceptions challenged his expectations for the meeting. The initial impression he received from the public broadcast was that Imanu'el was just one of many religious evangelists. Not being a man of any strong faith, Hale immediately discounted them as misguided at best, or at worst, outright frauds. However, this first impression was body checked upon stumbling across their alleged connection to the supernatural… how else would Imanu'el have found him?

Hale hated that word: Supernatural. If it was natural, super denotes an enhancement of an existing trait or ability. The ability to follow a pattern of information off an item or touch of a person wasn't something anyone Hale knew could do. This led him to believe it was unnatural, lowering the credibility of the word Supernatural. Maybe super-unnatural. That would be more accurate, but far less easy on the tongue. Unnatural would work, too, but sounded much less glamorous. The lack of the super made it sound like a casual deformity.

Regardless, the organization Imanu'el ran gained significant credibility when what's-his-name in the gray hood stumbled across him. Call it fate or an act of God, whatever you prefer, but Hale's reasons to discount the super-unnatural claims of their little club were getting thinner and thinner. Only a direct meeting would seal the deal and push him one way or the other. For now, he would limit their knowledge of him, keeping his last name and address a secret. Had he put more thought into it, he wouldn't have called from his cell phone. C'est la vie. Hopefully they didn't have caller ID at their office.

"Good afternoon, Hale."

Hale looked up at the voice, stuttering his steps as his thoughts left the rails they travelled on. He saw Mrs. Dowling sitting on her chair. Despite the familiar warm tone and the pleasant look she gave him, Hale sensed something was amiss. She usually wasn't sitting out here when he arrived home. She was an early morning reader, using the afternoons to occupy whatever errands or other items on her schedule that didn't involve a paperback. What's more, while her voice was pleasant, she wore a small smile that didn't reach her eyes. It was detached, and Mrs. Dowling was nothing if not an empathetic person.

"Good afternoon, Mrs. Dowling," Hale returned, his quizzical thoughts surfacing in his eyes. "Enjoying your afternoon?"

Her nod and lowered tone was one of resignation, acknowledging the true question behind the casual greeting. "Yes, everything is fine. Just enjoying the last hours of the day. I realized I don't watch sunsets anymore. I've become so accustomed to waking up early, I've lost half of the beauty that the sun gives us every day."

Hale nodded, still curious. "You going to enjoy the sunset from here?" He looked over his shoulder at the darkening sky. "We're east facing, after all. Maybe a short drive down 7th would get you a better view?" He offered, his tone still adding unspoken questions.

"I can't see the sun from here, but I can enjoy the colors it paints on the sky." She smiled, gazing up. "The shifting in the clouds is my favorite part. They are like an easel to the sun's rays, soaking up its colors and shining its brilliance, all without having to strain your eyes against its light."

Hale nodded, attempting a genuine smile. This was strange for his benevolent neighbor. Despite the situation, Mrs. Dowling always put forth a cheery disposition. Her smile was always radiant, her eyes shining with happiness, and her inquiries into your well-being always genuine. This was different. It seemed forced. There was something artificial about her current demeanor. Her words portrayed one thing, though her mood had clearly shifted to a darker temperament.

"I never thought of it like that," he replied. "But now that you mention it, it makes perfect sense."

She offered another empty smile. "I hope you enjoy your evening, Hale. Tell Cassandra that I say hello."

Even in the state she's in now, whatever it is she may be going through, she manages to keep other people in mind. She's amazing. "Thanks, Mrs. Dowling. I'll do that." He paused, stopping a half step ahead of his neighbor's chair. He turned back, doubting his words as he spoke them. "Mrs. Dowling, if you need anything, you just let me know, okay? I just… just want to make sure everything is okay."

She turned from the sky back to Hale, the empty smile allowing sadness to creep behind its illusory cast. "Thank you, Hale. It won't be necessary, I will be fine."

> . . . "I will be fine." Mrs. Dowling put the bundle in
>
> her purse.
>
> . . . . . . "–dangerous. Make sure you are properly
>
> trained in its–" A man's voice, unfamiliar.
>
> . . . . "–ust worry about you. You
>
> seem differ–" A woman's voice,
>
> younger.
>
> . . . . "Don't worry, I'll be fine,"
>
> Mrs. Dowling said with sad resolution.

Hale shook away from his Wandering. Mrs. Dowling wore a warm expression on her face. The previous sadness seemed to have been temporarily alleviated by a newfound hope, beaming out at Hale's confused face.

"I've always known you're meant for greater things, Hale." Mrs. Dowling's smile was genuine.

Unable to put together an appropriate response, Hale stumbled through his words and settled with a nod and a clumsy thank you. When Mrs. Dowling turned back to the sky with her warm smile intact, Hale judged his progress with the conversation had reached its pinnacle, and resumed his journey back to his

123

apartment.

───────────

CASS ROAMED aimlessly around her apartment. This was a common ritual when wrestling with a decision. Her mind liked to pick random problems and analyze them, keeping her in a constant state of activity even during periods of rest and recreation. If she wasn't focused on something, her brain used the idle time to process through her curiosities.

Unfortunately, certain conundrums resulted in internal arguments. Sometimes she didn't want to take a logical step forward in a problem. Sometimes she wanted her emotions to win over and do what felt correct, not what was statistically the best choice. The majority of her mind didn't work that way. While this did wonders for her professional career, it shattered most personal interactions, as relationships simply don't work on such regimented rules.

When conflicts such as this reared their ugly head, Cass paced. The pattern she took around the room was random and simultaneously repetitious. There was no purpose in her travels to the sliding glass door, across the rug to the hallway, and back across to the fireplace. The triangular pattern was simply the path of least resistance, allowing her to continuously move while her brain did the same. Fortunately, her employment allowed her the luxury of the extra apartment space to wander even with the ridiculous price hikes in Irvine.

The problem for this evening was Hale. The facts, which she recounted in her head, all led her down a very specific path. *He is completely unknown to me and my friends, meaning he can't be easily verified as 'safe'. He is introverted, which can be a sign of... no, not introverted,* She corrected herself. *He's quiet. I like that sometimes, though. The biggest issue is his knowledge. How did he know my name? How did he know Sue's? These are two crucial pieces of information he exhibited without explanation. There are only a few ways he could have learned those two tidbits, and none of them are pleasant. This means he is likely dangerous, and should be avoided.*

A heavy sigh broke the train of thought, and her passage to the hallway was diverted by the desire for something to sooth her irritated mind. Cass moved onto the cool tile floor of the kitchen, grabbing a bottle of water from the fridge. The variation in her physical repetition dragged her concentration away from the current issue, allowing her a moment of peace while she unscrewed the top and poured chilled water down her throat. With a gasp of relief at the completion of her swig, she re-capped the bottle. The pause in physical activity was just long enough to allow her mind to search for a new thought, ushering her back into the previous mental debate.

Hale is clearly not dangerous. He's timid, and evasive regarding the aforementioned sensitive information, but that doesn't mean he's dangerous. The chances of him stalking me and ending up in the same coffee house I was sent to on a blind date are almost nil.

Actually, quite the opposite. The opposing thought challenged her in a less exuberant, more scholarly fashion. *If he had somehow followed you, or god forbid, tapped your phone, he'd know exactly where you were going. This would be a perfectly reasonable explanation for him being there. He admitted to being a failed PI, but that doesn't mean he doesn't have any tricks of the trade up his sleeve.*

Reasonable for someone with extreme paranoia! He's not a stalker. Even if he was, I would have seen him tailing me at least once if he knew that much. I'm good with faces.

Your memory is not infallible.

No, but you know I'm right.

The logical voice in her brain continued to chastise her as she moved over to the phone. "You can shut up now. I'm not listening to you tonight." The verbal dismissal seemed to help ward off the internal warnings. The beeps on her cordless phone muffled the final protests, giving her peace and quiet when the receiver confirmed its connection via soft tones. She waited patiently, wandering over to the sliding glass door again as she counted off the rings. She was admiring the clear night sky from her 12th story view when the other line clicked on.

"Hello?"

Hale's voice was low and quiet. He was shaken. Something was wrong. It immediately threw Cass' momentum off, turning her voice into a timid schoolgirl for the opening of the conversation.

"Hale? Hi, it's me, Cass." She allowed herself a moment to be annoyed. She hated when people said 'It's me', especially when they followed it with a name. Doing it herself amplified her own annoyance. She bit her lower lip to bring her attention back to the call. "Our evening was derailed on Monday, and my week has been maddening. I was hoping you were free to meet up."

"I, uh…"

He was distracted.

What is going on?!

Maybe he is looking through your window and wasn't expecting the sudden call.

Oh will you shut up?!

Cass ventured a look out the 12th floor window in spite of herself.

"This may be a bad time," Hale ventured.

Cass, not being one to be easily thwarted when she had made up her mind, nor one with fragile emotions that would shatter at the implication of rejection, redoubled her confidence and returned her normal tone to her voice. "Well, it is Friday night. I expect you have plans, which I don't mean to alter. Perhaps I could be a tagalong again."

"Um…" He paused. The distance of his voice suggested the phone had been pulled away.

"Hale." The name was stabbed out as a warning, rather than a probe for his attention. While potential rejection did not slow Cass, rude phone etiquette was a hot button.

The response it elicited was not one she had expected.

"My next door neighbor has been murdered."

———————

RED AND blue flashing lights streaked across the community's walls. Hale's landlord skimped on basic repairs like light bulb replacements. It would take near half of the complex to go dark before he would finally go around and fix them up. This left the complex rather dim at night, giving all the more room for the police and ambulance to flood the courtyard with colorful, flashing lights.

Cass pulled up to the curb. She exited the car and slid through the small group of people gathered around the police line; Rubbernecks with nothing better to do on a Friday than see if they could catch a glimpse of some horribly mutilated corpse. There was always those kinds of people, no matter the neighborhood or tragedy. Cass held in her disgust, giving a polite smile and a lie about her apartment location to the police officer to allow her past. She maneuvered between the two patrolmen blocking the gate and walked down the path towards the second staircase. Another patrolman was at the bottom of the steps. Worried creases marred this younger officer's forehead as Cass approached. He held out a tentative hand, lacking the confidence to stop her with any real authority. Another friendly smile, appropriately sobered due to the surrounding events, and a mention of Hale's apartment number allowed her to pass.

She saw Hale as she crested the top of the staircase. He sat outside his apartment in the same chair she had met Mrs. Dowling in the other day. His face was a mixture of shock and disbelief. He didn't even register Cass' approach until another police officer standing at the door of the Dowling's apartment questioned her presence.

Hale's attention snapped up. "Officer, it's okay, she's with me."

The officer removed himself from Cass' path, allowing her to move the rest of the way to Hale. She moved over to him, kneeling down next to his chair.

This was the part she wasn't good at. Despite her gender's stereotypical strong connection with their emotional side, Cass was horrible at empathizing with people during times of pain. She tried to fake it as best as possible, putting a hand on his shoulder, "Are you alright?" It was a clichéd question, and she knew her false sincerity shone through. It wasn't as if she didn't care, she just felt awkward.

Hale didn't seem to notice anything forced in the question, or at least he didn't make mention of it. "Yeah, I'm alright. I'm just... surprised, I guess."

A stretcher bounced out of the apartment, surrounded by voices of coroners as they called out warnings to back away and clear the path. A black coroner's bag lay atop of the stretcher, its puffed out sides and center revealing it was not as empty as when it had been rolled into the apartment.

"I walked by her every morning," Hale continued. "She always greeted me with a smile and a few words of encouragement to start off my day."

Cass remained silent, trying to give support to Hale by just listening. She let her eyes wander away from him for a moment to watch the coroners carefully wheel the body downstairs. Each step seemed like a challenge, and the morbid side of Cass' mind imagined one of the men slipping, causing the stretcher to bounce out of control and throw its decomposing passenger over the railing. Reality was much less grim. No bad strands of fate caught either of the men's ankles, allowing them to expertly reach the bottom of the staircase and move towards their waiting vehicle.

A new sight drew both Cass and Hale's attention back to the doorway. Two police officers escorted the petite form of Mrs. Dowling out, hands cuffed behind her back. She stalled her steps as she crossed the threshold of her apartment, taking a glance to her right where Hale and Cass sat. The same sad, resigned smile that she wore earlier in the evening still adorned her features.

Hale's eyes returned more regret than Mrs. Dowling's... now technically 'Ms.' Dowling's. His expression pleaded with her to somehow take it back, to just go back to the way it was.

Ms. Dowling responded with a slight upturn of her smile to Hale. With the same warm tone he had always remembered, she spoke out to him, "I'll be fine, Hale, and so will you. Don't go disappointing me now."

Hale opened his mouth to say something, to offer her comfort or even to ask why, but nothing came to him and the moment passed. With that, the officers gently turned her away.

Hale's stomach churned, then clamped as if shut in a vice. His face flushed, and his eyes burned from tears that threatened to fall unchecked. Determined not to discard any more masculinity in front of Cass, he blinked back the tears and tilted his head back.

"You look sick," Cass commented. "Do you need anything?"

"More courage," Hale laughed morbidly.

"More courage?" Cass tried to sound supportive, but her curiosity edged through her tone. She couldn't be handed a portion of a new puzzle without getting a little excited, even in situations like these.

"I should have prevented this." His voice was defeated.

"This reaction is natural, Hale." Cass called on her years of academic study to comfort Hale with the facts. "You feel misplaced guilt, but the truth of the matter is you had no way of knowing what she was going to do."

"I knew," Hale countered. "I just didn't want to get involved."

"Did you hear arguing?"

"No."

"Abuse?"

"No."

"Hale," Cass said, a convincing level of reassurance in her voice. "You couldn't have known enough. You barely knew her, and you're not a psychic."

"Not exactly, no." The words were out before Hale could think to stop them. He expected a shockwave of regret and anger to surge up in response to his partial admission of his ability, but nothing came. The fear he had built up over his whole life did little but cower in a corner of his mind, overshadowed by the confidence grief provided. For once, self-loathing provided him some relief by forcing him down a path he would normally consider self-destructive.

"Not exactly?" Cass eyed him, her lips pursing speculatively. She had met people before who had claimed certain otherworldly powers to try to be special. She had made the decision long ago those people deserved no time in her life. Cass hoped Hale wasn't about to disappoint her.

That's selfish. She chided herself. *He told you it was a bad time, he obviously needs someone no matter how bad you are at playing that role. And didn't you just decide he wasn't dangerous? Give the man a second to explain.*

"I am not a psychic," Hale confirmed, much to Cass' relief. "But I know things I shouldn't."

Cass' relief spun into anxiety. Was she about to learn the answers to the questions that plagued her over the last couple weeks? She remained silent, remembering an old tactic her father had taught her.

"*Cassie,*" he had said. She hated being called Cassie by anyone but him. "*One of the biggest mistakes you can make when selling someone on something is to sell them out of it. Once they've come to a decision, don't meddle with it. Just stay quiet, let them stay convinced, and complete whatever deal you're arranging. Continuing to poke and prod after they've said 'yes' just gives them a chance to rethink and say 'no' again.*"

"I knew Mr. Dowling was likely seeing someone else on the side," Hale continued, eyes focused on the ground. The confession came forth easily, as if Cass was helping him remove the burden from his shoulders, and the welcome relief could cause no harm. "I knew Mrs. Dowling was suspicious. I knew she had unpleasant altercations with her husband about them. What's more, I knew Mrs. Dowling had gotten a weapon. It wasn't clear it was a weapon, but it was clear enough. But, like a coward, I decided not to get involved."

Cass decided a little guidance would be helpful. He was giving information, but not answers. While she realized it was callous to casually disregard the plight of the Dowlings in favor of personal curiosities, Cass felt her priorities were acceptable. After all, what was done with the Dowlings was done. She could only hope something good would come out of the tragedy.

At least, that's how she justified it to herself.

"Hale, you might have had suspicions, but how could you know all of that?" Cass asked. New suspicions revolving around spy equipment or a P.I. friend began evolving in the back of her mind.

"I'm Touched," Hale said with a sardonic smile.

Cass narrowed her eyes, trying to sort the meaning out of the cryptic answer before asking clarifying questions. It was important to her to figure out everything she could on her own. It helped to keep the questioning linear. Tangents only slowed the process.

It took her a few moments of searching for connections before she remembered their outing on Monday night. The vagrant's strange outburst as he grabbed Hale's head was 'You are Touched!' Cass had originally dismissed it, writing it off as the ranting of a madman. Was that strange man that attacked her connected to Hale somehow, or was Hale just babbling in his shocked pain?

"Hale?" Cass settled on the one word prod to attempt to let him explain himself, rather than fumbling with guesses.

Hale stood, finally looking back at Cass. "We should go inside."

10

"Beer?" Hale offered, opening the fridge.

"No, thank you," Cass declined. She sat on the back of the couch, facing Hale in the kitchen. Any hint of concern or support she had attempted to project a few minutes earlier had melted away. Her curiosities were forefront on her mind now, and her inquisitive eyes projected her questions.

Hale grabbed a cider for himself, twisting off the top and tossing it in the trash. He let it sit in his hand and bubble, staring absently at the floor again while he picked through what to say next. The desire to blurt out his secrets had been ever present throughout his life, but paranoia of being ostracized and branded as a madman had prevented him from plotting out a reasonable way to present the facts in a real situation. Now, with a real opportunity in front of him, he was lost.

He had mentioned it in an indirect way to his mother when he was young. It was around fourth grade, and Hale had been protesting a bad grade he had been given on an essay test. The subject was 'morality'. In retrospect, Hale had even less respect for such a subjective topic than the average child. Regardless, Hale's complaint of 'I got graded down because I said it's okay to lie to people you love if you want to make them happy' was met by a questioning look from his mother.

'Well, I'm sure Mrs. Stuckerman just values honesty, and wants you to value it, too,' Hale's mother had suggested.

'No!' Hale said triumphantly. 'Because her and Mr. Baxter spent time alone together after school, and she lied to her husband about that!'

The 'lie' was not received well by his mother, and the further protests of its validity and how he came to acquire such knowledge was met with a grounding and a firm talk about 'keeping his head out of the clouds.'

'Young man,' his mother had chastised. 'Making up stories about people can get them into a lot of trouble. And don't go pretending you're some type of loony psychic, either. Grownups that do that get a visit from the nice men in the white jackets and get to spend their life in a padded room. For now, you get to stay in your room to get a taste of what that would be like.'

Looking back, Hale could understand her confusion and worry, even if the execution was a little over the top.

"Hale?" Cass prodded him again. She was not trying to be impatient, but each passing second added to her growing mountain of anxiety. Her mind demanded satisfaction to the questions that had built over the previous days.

As if sensing the need for a distraction, Commodore jumped on the counter between Hale and Cass. Quickly gaining his balance after his ascension, the ruler of the household relaxed into an upright, regal pose. He looked over at Cass, then back at Hale.

Good, Human. You've brought the pretty one again.

Commodore looked back at Cass, narrowing his eyes into pleased slits and giving a small chuff to request attention.

Cass, distracted by the noble beast on the counter, allowed a small smile and reached up to pet the cat. The scratches on his head were met with cheek nuzzles against her hand and a deep, low purr. Lost in the rapture of the feline for a moment, Cass hoped in the back of her mind that Hale would use this as an opportunity to put whatever confession he had together, else she would have to beat it out of him with her shoe.

"You know how cats can sense some things?" Hale asked. "Like when they'll just freak out for no reason in a room and puff up, or growl at thin air. Some people claim they can see ghosts, or just have senses that normal humans don't have."

Cass looked up at Hale, releasing Commodore to remain on the counter without affection, much to the cat's chagrin. Cass gave a nod to Hale, propping herself up on the back of the couch to give him her full attention.

"Sometimes people claim to have similar senses. You know, like a sixth sense, or a mind's eye." Hale reached for words, coming up with some of the explanations he'd read in various New Age and occult books that he'd looked into back when he had first tried to find out about his own abilities. "They claim to be able to see things normal people can't. Whether it's reading palms, or talking to the dead, or telling your future through your psychic resonances."

Cass held back commentary.

"Since I was a kid I've been able to see things." Hale's beer bubbled in his hands, which shook slightly. The Fear in the corner of his mind had stopped cowering, and was now wrestling with his newfound Courage. "Th-things, that, you know, other people can't see."

"Like dead people?" Cass offered dryly. Her skepticism was at an all-time high at this point, and she knew she would be leaving disappointed after a few more answers.

"No, nothing stupid like that. Sorry, I mean, not stupid as in, like, you made a stupid suggestion. Just–" Fear wrapped Hale's tongue around its fist, causing his sentences to come out sloppy and disjointed. Meanwhile, Courage began renewing its assault to beat the resistance back. "Never mind. I mean, I don't know if I even believe in that stuff."

"Hale, you need to explain more clearly," Cass pressed.

"Sorry, this is hard." Hale admitted. He bought himself a few seconds and fed his Courage reinforcements by tilting the bottle back and taking a swig of his beer. He felt the troops needed higher proof ammunition for this conversation. "I haven't actually talked to anyone about this before."

"That's fine," Cass said, reassuringly. *If you're seeking attention with a special snowflake story, that's likely a lie. No point in making up super powers if you don't try to grab people's attention with them.* She calmed the thoughts, reminding herself she didn't know for sure he was going to claim anything unnatural yet.

"I sense things. Images, experiences, emotions. Weird, random stuff that doesn't have to do with anything. I can't control it. Sometimes it happens when I brush past someone, other times when I touch or smell something someone has been in contact with."

"You sense things?" Cass repeated. She felt something inside sink as a triumphant voice in the back of her head mocked her for ignoring previous warnings. Her face remained stoic, refusing to betray her dismay for fear he would see it and try to pretend he hadn't meant what he was saying, or that it had all been some kind of joke. She needed further confirmation he meant it, and then she would leave.

"Like with the Dowlings. There was someone with red fingernails that had been in their apartment. I saw them one morning when I passed their door. The image just jumped into my mind." Hale dredged the images from his memory, reminding himself of his failure to fuel his Courage. He had lacked the strength to help Mrs. Dowling when he'd known something was wrong. He'd told himself it was none of his business. Now a man was dead and a poor old woman would face jail time. The tides of the internal battle shifted as Courage pressed a barrage of attacks to ward off Fear's interference. Hale verbally strode forward, Fear being wrapped up by Courage with bindings of atonement. "I had a feeling it was something sexual, but nothing told me it wasn't Mrs. Dowling. Not specifically, at least. But I should have known. This woman smoked, seemed like a party girl, plus the red fingernails just didn't seem like Mrs. Dowling's style. Plus, Mrs. Dowling was clearly upset about something. The connections were all there, I just was too much of a coward to make them."

Cass had finally heard enough. Her eyes felt heavy, though she knew she was not upset enough to cry. Disappointment was rising up like a wave, crushing her budding hopes for the man she had stumbled upon in a coffee shop, along with any budding feelings she had for him. She was already on her feet, walking towards the door in an unconscious effort to obey her logical side's demands.

"Goodbye, Hale." Her voice remained firm despite a small choke on the first word. Apparently she had reached past dry disappointment and had entered into dismay. She couldn't even look Hale in the eyes as she said it.

"What? Wait!" Hale's realization caused Fear to surge back up, throwing off the shackles Courage had laden over it. A cold chill gripped him, realizing he had mere seconds to prove he was not crazy. If he didn't, he would live up to the fear of pushing away people just as he had imagined for decades. But what could he say? What, if anything, would be relevant enough to prove he had insights that no one else did? He wracked his brain for the Wanderings he received while at Drive Thru Java. Phill had given him some minor insights, as did Cass when she first sat across from him, specifically when he smelled her–

"Perfume! Vanilla, you like more natural scents! You said that to Sue before going on your blind date with Phill. Well, not with Phill, more with me, but you know what I mean. I'm right, aren't I?"

The information caused Cass a momentary pause as she opened the door as she recalled the event. She gave a halfhearted laugh, shaking her head. "So you do know Sue." She looked back over her shoulder. "That's the only way you could know that. Did she tell you to go to Drive Thru Java, too? Nevermind, don't answer that, I'll just find out from her." Cass turned to leave, a new anger for her friend blossoming. She disliked betrayal. She disliked lying more, especially when she couldn't discern it herself. She didn't like being the one left out, the last to know. Whatever their intentions had been, she'd been made the butt of their plans.

In a panic, Hale continued to reach. He had Wandered in the car with her. There was a phone call. She had been called something else. It was a pet name. It was a man's voice. He called her–

"Cassie!"

One foot out the door, Cass stopped dead in her tracks.

"Cassie," Hale repeated frantically. "The man on the phone called you Cassie, right? You were crying in your car. In the passenger seat." Hale pleaded with whatever karmic fate was guiding this series of events that Cass did not suddenly get offended that he had inadvertently spied on what had felt like an incredibly private moment.

Fortunately for Hale, that thought didn't cross Cass' mind in any serious capacity. One of the things that attracted him to her on their first date was her ability to separate important issues from ones that could be inflated to seem important. Unfortunately for Hale, Cass' mind still had trouble wrapping around his ludicrous claim of supernatural ability.

She stopped in the doorframe. This was something new. *How does he know about that?* Cass attempted to pick apart possible angles. *If he knew Sue, he could know about the conversation we had about perfume and Phill. It also explains how he knew my name. What about this? Sue doesn't know about it. No one does. Well, no one except Dad and, well, no one around here.*

"Cass," Hale said, desperation in his voice. "Please come back inside. I know it sounds crazy, but I'm not lying to you. Please, just let me explain."

Her father's voice reminded her about selling someone after they're sold. Apparently Hale didn't get that lesson.

If you leave now, you lose nothing. The internal voice coached her. *You have your answers. Who cares if he believes what he says or no. Who cares if it is real or not? He's obviously not safe.*

You like him, and he is very, very different from anyone else you know. Stay. The second voice pleaded from lower ground. The strong, logical voice was overpowering. Being in a position of no loss was enticing.

What is there to gain here? He's living paycheck to paycheck in a dingy, crime-ridden neighborhood with his fantasies anchoring him in place. This is a short-term investment of time at best. Do the smart thing. Leave.

"Cass?" The word was a question as much as a form of address. Hale remained still, waiting for Cass to make her decision.

Cass finally broke her gaze from the ground, disallowing any more internal arguments so she could clear her head and answer for herself. Her eyes met Hale's, her vision beginning to blur as tears of frustration and sorrow attempted to burst forward. In an even voice, she answered, "I need to go."

She let go of the door, leaving Hale holding the handle on the other side, and walked away.

––––––––––

THE NIGHT had not been kind to Hale. The flood of 'what if' questions had plagued him like a swarm of locusts, making any attempt at sleep an impossibility. Hale made attempts to lose himself in the comfort of his pillow, but visions of the talk earlier in the night would swim through his thoughts. Different word choices were used that changed Cass' inevitably poor reaction to one of warmth and acceptance, causing Hale to shake forth from his mental anguish with a fist slamming against the bed or a scream projected into the pillow.

Deep, darkened circles had formed under Hale's eyes. He wandered aimlessly around his apartment, Commodore watching him idly from his perch on the bar. Light crept around the curtains, proving Hale had lost all track of time and any desire to keep track of it. He had set an alarm on his phone for eleven, giving him plenty of time to shower and head out to the meeting with Imanu'el at noon. Unfortunately, the thought of the meeting he had been anticipating all week filled him with nothing but annoyance.

These bouts of self-loathing after what Hale deemed a dismal failure were generally followed by further acts of self-destruction. Last night Hale thought his self-destructive streak would result in a positive gain, as he'd finally have someone he could really talk to. Now he realized how foolish he had really been. Cass had her feet firmly planted on the ground, and he hadn't known her long enough to get a rapport that would demand she hear him out.

Stupid. Hale reminded himself. *Stupid stupid stupid.*

Mental flagellation was interrupted by the electronic notes of Beethoven's Fur Elise and the percussion of his phone rattling across the counter.

Commodore jumped to the defense of his post, springing to a battle ready stance after spinning in midair to face the noisy device which had encroached on his territory. Tail up and hackles raised, the furry warrior turned sideways and hopped three times down the bar, finishing the assault with a swipe of his front paw. The phone ejected from the ledge, bouncing on the carpeted floor.

Satisfied with the defense of his domain, Commodore settled, looking down at his fallen foe from his perch on the ledge.

"God damn it, Commodore!" Hale growled as he scurried over to retrieve his phone. He hunched over to pick it up, dodging a follow-up swipe from Commodore as he stood and lifted the phone to his ear.

Apparently Commodore didn't appreciate his victim being resuscitated.

Hale moved away, annoyed at his cat's normally endearing behavior, and spoke into the phone. "Hello?"

"–llo? Hale, you there?"

"Alex? Yeah, sorry. Commodore launched my phone off the countertop when it started ringing."

Alex paused. "Does he usually do that?"

"Eh, sometimes. Not often."

"That cat seriously has a hate on for me." Despite the words used, Hale could hear a grin through Alex's voice.

"Like I said, man, he can sense evil." Hale felt some of his hate for the world draining away at the humorous exchange. Alex's infectious happiness was helpful in times like this. It was why they'd stayed friends for as long as they had, through high school and college, and into their adult years. When Hale fell into one of his depressions, Alex was there with off-color humor and exuberance to drag him back out. "What's going on, dude?"

"Oh, yeah, so I got a free bottle of 20 year old scotch from my foreman last night. Apparently he's back on the bandwagon, and decided to give away everything in his liquor cabinet to help remove temptation. You want to help me demolish as much of this shit as we can tonight?"

"Yes," Hale responded.

"Wow, and with authority," Alex chuckled. "Will your lady be there to revel with us, or is this a private party? Cause if she's there, there's this skater chick I've been dying to nail. I'll bring her o—"

"Cass won't be there," Hale responded, unwilling to admit to Alex he'd been broken up with already. "She's not too happy with me. Feel free to bring the girl over. You can use my couch if you guys get too tanked."

"What happened with your girl?" Alex posed the question like an attack.

"Not a big deal, dude." Hale tried to push the issue off.

"Hale," Alex spoke with a firm tone of authority as if he was directing his child. "You're a serial monogamist with ridiculous standards I haven't been able to figure out after knowing you for a decade. This girl is cool as shit, and you like her. Plus, let's be serious for a second, she's fucking hot."

"Well, we can't forget the important details." Hales voice dripped with distain.

Alex ignored his tone. "Seriously man, don't let that one go. I don't want you being all mopey on me in a week when you realize you fucked it up."

"The vote of confidence is endearing," Hale muttered.

"Yeah yeah, so I'll cruise by later and bring the bottle. It'll be good times."

"See you then."

"Peace."

Hale hit the End button, but was immediately greeted by the phone vibrating and chirping. It was 11:00 am. The alarm clicked off with another push of the End button, and Hale began his routine to face the outside world.

11

The adrenaline of the upcoming meeting saved Hale at least two accidents. He was not a bad driver; however, driving while tired was not his specialty. He had heard it called 'road hypnotics' somewhere. He didn't know if it was an actual term, but it seemed accurate. On straight roads with nothing but painted lines flying by him at a steady pace and his body relaxed in a comfortable seat, his eyelids felt heavy and dreams drifted into his mind. He had considered setting up a chair in his room with a driving game on his laptop to simulate the effect on sleepless nights, but something told him encouraging his subconscious to associate sleep with driving would end poorly.

He fought the strong pull of sleep with loud music, dialogues with himself, and fresh cool air whipping in from lowered windows. Despite the variety of stimuli, the music would occasionally become too rhythmic and repetitive, his dialogue would fail to be engaging, and slower speeds would simply provide a refreshing breeze. During these times, his eyelids would droop and Hale would find himself tugged towards the dream world.

Luckily, the first time this happened he rolled over the reflecting plates in the center of the road, allowing a loud, reverberating set of bumps to travel through the car, throwing him back into an alert state with a fresh rush of adrenaline. The second time was at a red light. While sitting comfortably at a stop, the exhausted portion of his mind rationalized that it would be okay if he just closed his eyes for a moment. After all, he was stopped at a light, what could possibly happen? While he didn't roll into oncoming traffic, he did provide one pedestrian with a healthy shock followed by anger as they tried to cross the street. Fortunately, their yell of protest had shaken Hale awake, allowing him to clamp down on the brake before any contact was made.

Hale mentally fortified himself.

This is what you've been waiting for. Decades of wondering and dreaming will finally be answered. I finally have a chance to be around people I can truly talk to.

Surely Cass and Alex are a small price to pay for such a boon, The Poet commented softly.

Cass was a mistake. Hale gritted his teeth at the memory of last night. *I was not right in the head, and I let my guard down. I already know Alex wouldn't understand. I won't make the same mistake with him.*

I imagine this new club you are joining will have no impact on your personal life, The Poet reassured. *Surely your closest friend will not notice your new associations, what they stand for, or whatever activities they have planned.*

This is what I want! Hale fought back. *I don't want to be the outcast. I don't want to be the freak. I want to talk to someone who understands.*

Finding a small handful of people who may, and I stress <u>may</u>, understand you will provide some temporary relief. But are you truly so unhappy now? Do you not trust Alex with all things except your one dark secret? Is not every friendship plagued with at least one portion of one's past or present that they will take to their grave? He's hidden truths from you before; lets' not forget Amy. Your secret is unique, most assuredly, but is it truly so damning that you must risk ostracizing an individual that has known you and supported you as a friend for almost a decade?

I'm not going to let you spoil this. Hale tried to block out the argumentative portions of his brain. He could not tell if this was his emotions getting the best of him, or if the Poet was tapping into a more logical part of his mind. *Besides, I'm here now, so it's a little late to turn back.*

Hale parked his car in front of the dilapidated structure Imanu'el had given him the address to. The building certainly didn't fit the image Hale had arranged in his fantasies. When he was a child thinking about meeting others like him, he had always imagined a secret military base, or maybe a grand mansion with a brightly illuminated entrance hall complete with twin curving staircases and a crystal chandelier. Men in tuxedos and women in long dresses had greeted him, smiling and expressing their excitement at his presence. Chairs had been pulled out at a grand banquet table, or sometimes a room covered in maps and beeping computers, and handshakes were completed with 'Glad to have you aboard' and 'It is an honor to have you with us.'

What Hale had not imagined was a tiny, abandoned looking art studio decorated with fresh graffiti as the only paint not currently peeling from the walls. A window had been busted out and replaced with a plank of plywood. The roof tiles varied in color from the intermittent gaps in the original tiles and the recent patchwork fixes. The downtrodden status of the building and its location in this part of town sent a clear message that this was not a wealthy operation by any means.

Hale doubted they had room for a banquet table in the tiny interior.

"Well," Hale verbally coached himself, giving time for a sigh of resignation. "This is what you've been waiting for; let's do it."

He stepped out of his car with practiced gestures, pretending this was no different than walking into his office or apartment. To an outside observer, the new arrival to the old abandoned art studio was confident, and clearly on a mission. Hale's eyes focused on the front door of the building, taking deep breaths to steady himself as he walked. After a few steps and just as many breaths, Hale realized quick deep breaths were doing more to destabilize him than otherwise. He took a moment to lean against the wall next to the door, shifting weight off his feet to regain his equilibrium.

As the dizzy arrival to Imanu'el's meeting rested against the structure, a silver van pulled onto the gravelly parking lot. Hale kept his eyes closed for a couple more moments to ensure he did not risk falling over when he stood again, then lifted his head to take a look at the newcomer.

The glare of the sun on the windshield completely obscured the passenger, leaving only the driver to be seen through a break in the starburst of sunlight. Her initial appearance of mid-thirties was betrayed by treated blond hair and shiny, stretched flesh. She gave a skeptical look through her windshield at the ruins before her, as well as a quick, judgmental glance over Hale. Her lips began moving as her head shook side to side to her obscured passenger, clearly disapproving of both her destination and of the apparent drunk leaning next to the door.

Hale decided he didn't need any more negative factors to assault his convictions. He turned his back on the van, straightened his posture and opened the door.

The portal opened up to a dimly lit studio. A small foyer absent of any tuxedoed men or well-dressed women, more along the lines of a cubby hole, greeted Hale. The small area was perfect for a secretary's desk or a security table, though no such luxuries were featured here now. The space was bare, featuring only unattached cable wires extending from the wall, and nails yearning for a picture frame or motivational poster. The tiny waiting room was divided from the main room by only a drawn curtain, as it seemed the door that had once been its previous divider had been unceremoniously ripped off.

Hale stepped through the woefully spartan entrance, parting the curtain with his hand to take a gander inside the next room. This was clearly the main area of the studio. From a quick glance, the space easily took up the majority of the building. Aside from three doors near the back, which Hale assumed were offices, bathrooms, storage, or a combination of the three, there was nothing else to this building.

The room was furnished with three couches, two of which were set up near the center of the room facing towards a podium, the third was back in the corner with a small stack of crates acting as a coffee table. A large table sat between the couches and the podium, but it was too high to be a normal table for a lounging area. Its height made it too unwieldy to put ones feet up or provide any other apparent use, making it a bit out of place.

Hale almost completely missed a young raven haired girl that sat shyly on the back couch. She had been so unassuming he all but overlooked her. She eyed Hale as he came in, but looked down quickly when he turned his gaze to her. She folded her feet under her, leaning up against the armrest as she tucked her hands between her knees. Her white barrettes and black and white striped dress reminded Hale of a gothic comic character he had run across on the internet at one point. Some mopey girl with an evil-looking stuffed animal that prided herself on being an outcast. Aside from the clothes this girl didn't look like she was trying to make a statement. Her mannerisms projected the same inner conflicts Hale himself was feeling right now, so he refrained from any snap judgments.

Hale took another glance across the room. This time he noticed the large table was not the only thing out of place. All three couches were different styles and upholstery. One of them was an old and badly-damaged black leather couch. Tears were patched up by metallic silver duct tape, and the surface badly cracked from too many hours out in the sun. The second couch was a faded brown fabric, rife with cigarette burns complimented by beige stuffing pushing through. The final couch, where the Shy Girl sat, featured a strange, plaid-like design with a rough look. While the couch looked like it may not have been in the best physical condition, it also looked as if it could withstand a full charge from a fleet of tanks. It reminded Hale of a couch his grandmother had when he was little. But while the furniture was horribly uncomfortable to sit on, the bed folded up inside it was divine. Unfortunately, a spider hiding in the bed had bitten him on the cheek during an evening's sleep, scarring him from ever wanting to sleep on the pull-out bed again.

Matching the theme presented by the couches, the podium featured several chips in the wood, and one long crack down its face. Hale estimated at least a quarter of a roll of duct tape was holding the flimsy stand upright from the inside, and that the poor soul who actually leaned weight on it would quickly meet the floor below.

The Shy Girl's eyes averted as he looked over at her again. Figuring they were the only two people here so far, and he assumed they were all here for the same reason, Hale pursued the avenue he figured normal people would at this point: conversation.

"So, how many Goodwill runs do you think they made to drag all this stuff in here?"

The Shy Girl jerked her widened eyes up to him, frantically trying to find a response to such unsolicited social advances. She darted her eyes around at the items populating the room, then back up to Hale. She shrugged, unwilling to give a wrong answer.

Hale attempted a friendly chuckle, "I was just joking. It's just, yeah, never mind. I'm Hale." He offered his hand across the makeshift coffee table. He usually avoided touching others for fear of Wandering, but even that didn't seem a terrible idea here. At least there was the possibility he'd see her own version of being Touched.

The Shy Girl tentatively leaned forward, placing her fingers in the palm of Hale's hand and lightly squeezing. She responded in a timid voice, "I'm Brittany."

Hale smiled despite his sudden dislike for the name. He couldn't place it, but something about the name Brittany bothered him. Maybe it was the way she said it. Maybe he never noticed the sharp trio of syllables, each attacking the ears of the individuals listening to the introduction. He thought back to his ex-girlfriend Brittany, who by all accounts was a wonderful person. He found himself drifting into memories and completely forgetting the girl in front of him for a few moments before snapping back to the present.

"A pleasure to meet you," Hale nodded, withdrawing his hand. "So, what brings you here?"

"Um…" Eyes darted down, then back up to Hale. "Are you with Imanu'el?"

"No," Hale shook his head. "Not part of his, uh, group, or whatever you call this." He looked around a bit, trying to search for the name. Realizing it was irrelevant, he moved on. "But I did call him, and he's the one who invited me here."

Brittany smiled with a short nod, lowering her gaze back to the crates in front of her.

Hale stumbled a bit. The girl's lack of confidence gave him a boost of his own as the socially superior member of the conversation, he found himself drawn to less than appropriate topics.

'So, you have super powers too, huh?'

'Come here often?'

'Did you happen to beat up a guy to get an invite here, too?'

As each question played in his head, he felt more and more ridiculous. What's more, he was having trouble focusing on the conversation, despite this being the second Touched person he'd ever encountered. The first had grabbed him by his face, literally grabbing his attention. For some reason his mind refused to engage with this new subject. He eventually settled for, "Well, it was nice meeting you. I'm going to take a look around."

Brittany glanced back up at him and gave a nervous smile, then resumed her downward gaze. Hale turned to walk deeper in the room. He wasn't sure what his destination was yet. Perhaps he'd give a closer inspection to the podium, or if he really summoned his courage, see what was behind door number one.

The choice was made for him as the front door opened behind him. A halo of light shone around the curtain divider to the entryway, and Hale turned to see who would emerge through it. The ring of light dimmed as the door clicked shut. A few light footfalls enhanced the anticipation of both inhabitants in the main room. Hale and Brittany both fixated their eyes on the curtain, frozen in sudden trepidation as they waited for the newcomer.

The curtain swung to the side dramatically, revealing the new arrival. Of the swirl of emotions and thoughts that bombarded Hale's psyche, the expectations and interpretations of who and what this newcomer was, the first and foremost thought was:

Is he wearing a fucking cape?

No, it was not a cape. It took Hale a moment to digest the sight, but it was a robe. The thin garment was bright red with gold embroidery around the cuffs of the sleeves, base of the robe, and lining the neck and rim of the hood. The hood draped over the forehead of a tiny white male, though the cloth rested poorly causing it to fold over one corner of his face, leaving the rest exposed. Round rimmed glasses poked out from the uncovered side of his face, while the covered side made the fabric jut out oddly. The small amount of stubble gave the impression this individual did not have to shave often, reinforcing a boyish aura.

Hale gave another look up and down the robe as the figure took slow steps into the room. The fabric looked cheap, almost like a thin table cloth. It reminded him of a red version of the Gandalf costume his mother bought for him when he was nine. The hood had always annoyed him, because the slightest breeze would catch it and move it around his head, ruining his attempt to mimic the great Grey Wizard.

The robed figure clasped his hands in front of him and approached Hale. The hood failed to cover his face effectively as he approached, head lowered. Further ruining his gravitas and mystique, Hale could still see one dark brown eye peering up between the folds in the hood's fabric.

He extended his hand to Hale. His hand was small, drawing Hale's attention to the diminutive figure's height. He was noticeably shorter than Hale, hovering around five feet tall.

"Good afternoon," the robed figure greeted. "My name is Xarnon."

Hale took his hand, stopping mid-shake as the higher pitched voice and name registered in his brain. The name was simply too much for him to let go without a visible reaction. "I'm sorry, come again?" he asked.

"Xarnon," the man repeated. "With an 'X' at the beginning, not a 'Z'."

"Xarnon?" Hale repeated, disbelief shrouding his voice.

"Yes," the man said confidently, withdrawing his hand and folding it at his stomach.

"Is that French?" Hale asked, unable to withhold sarcasm.

"I don't think so…"

". . . I don't this so, Percival. This place

doesn't look safe..." the blond woman

in the van said.

". . . . . this to me, mom. I really want to

meet..." Percival/Xarnon said.

". . . . . time to go meet your new friends, are

you ready?" the voice called down to the

basement as Xarnon put away his new Dungeons

& Dragons book.

Hale shook away from the Wander. Despite the rush of information and potential questions, Hale found himself more curious as to what type of mansion Xarnon would have to live in to have a basement in Southern California. As he pondered the potential real estate options, one of the back doors opened. He spun away from the robed individual and looked at the newcomer. He recognized the man instantly. His facial features were partially obscured by a hand rubbing his forehead, but the gray sweatshirt and pants gave him away immediately.

Jeremiah walked through the room, rubbing around the stitched up gash on his forehead. He winced at a deeper pain, and risked a glance up as if the light of the room was akin to a threat of physical violence. Upon seeing Hale, Jeremiah's steps stuttered, a glint of fear in his eyes.

"Umm, Mr., uh, Hale, yes?" Jeremiah asked.

"Yeah, um, listen," Hale said, extending his hands as a gesture of peace. "I'm real sorry for what happened last week."

"Please, please, Mr. Hale," The lines thinned out in Jeremiah's face as a display of his relief. "That... situation was not caused by you. I–" Jeremiah cut off the sentence, wincing again. He cocked his head for a moment, and then spoke again in a strained voice. "I caused that situation with, ah!... with my own eagerness."

Hale watched the man in front of him speak as if he had his head in a vise.

"Are you okay? Do you need some painkillers, or something? I think I have something in my–"

"No, no," Jeremiah waved him off, taking a few steps back and reopening his eyes to look around at them all. "It's fine. I just… I'll be fine. I will be in the back office for a few more minutes. When I return, I'll assemble everyone so we can speak."

"Is Imanu'el already here?" Hale asked as Jeremiah retreated.

"We'll talk soon." Jeremiah turned, hand still extended back towards Hale as if warding him off from following.

Hale's temporary wave of remorse receded back to allow the ocean of irritation to resurface. Despite the temporary distraction little… Bethany… Brandy? What was her name… anyway, the distraction she had been, meeting 'Xarnon' and the odd exchange with Jeremiah simply fueled the ever growing bitterness that had been welling up within Hale since last evening.

The front door flew open, drawing Hale's attention back to the curtained divider. This newcomer had no intention of making a slow, dramatic entrance. The curtains flew back before the door even fully closed, flooding daylight into the poorly lit studio room.

Hale wouldn't describe the entrance as a walk, more of a swagger. The woman looked about Hale's age, and carried a certain air about her. It was an aura of a cocky youth, a rebel without a cause looking to prove something to someone. It may have been the way she set her jaw, or the way she burst into the room with such bravado, but the projection of her general bearing screamed 'Just try something.'

Hale remained quiet, watching the woman approach as she looked around the room. The metal hoops on her bondage pants jingled with each step, contrasting the immobility of the tight, sleeveless shirt she wore. Dark hair framed her face, kept from waving too freely by the product liberally applied through it. Shades of purple and black makeup complimented the dark veil of hair, giving her both an air of attraction and an aura of intimidation. When she had nearly crossed the threshold of normal conversational distance, she called out, "So is this the place? One of you Imanu'el?"

Hale realized this was not a person he could endure a conversation with, so he settled with a shake of his head. On his outings with Alex, he had met this person before. Sure she may have had a different name, face, body type, or even gender, but the person was the same. She would strut into a bar or other establishment and immediately try to assert her dominance. They might try to socially overpower a circle of people, physically match up with people twice their size, or even attempt to out drink the biggest guy there. They generally ended their nights of social competition sick off of alcohol or going home with a random one night stand who could help counter their hidden feelings of inadequacy. Alex had been that one night stand on at least a few occasions Hale could recall.

The Cocky Woman looked over Hale and Xarnon as if sizing them up, completely missing Blair… no, Brenda?... in the corner. She finished her estimation with a snort. With her internal assessment completed and accentuated by her external outburst, she moved past the standing duo and flopped down on the leather couch, spreading out to take up almost all of the seating space.

These are the people who share my unique place in life? Hale protested. *The cocky bitch, the game geek and the withdrawn girl? These are the people I'm risking Alex over? These are the people I'm considering confiding my biggest secret to? This is insane.*

"So what is it you do?" Xarnon's voice broke up Hale's thoughts.

Hale turned to him, re-centering himself in reality. "I'm a journalist." He gave strong consideration to ending the conversation there and simply leaving.

"No, I mean, what is it you **do**?" Xarnon asked, pointedly leaning forward on the last word to help its verbal emphasis.

Not ready to play along and tilt his hand, Hale played dumb. "I'm not sure I follow."

"Well, we are all Touched, as Imanu'el called it." Xarnon's voice was overdramatic, and his words clunky and out of place. "It suggests we all have powers of some type or another. For instance, I am a mage." He completed the statement by crossing his arms. Hale guessed it was meant to be impressive, but it missed its mark significantly. It was like watching Gandalf as a kid being physically overpowered by a Hobbit. The Cocky Woman gave a hard bark of laughter.

"A mage?" Hale asked, skeptically. "As in, you throw fireballs?"

"No, no. I unfortunately have not tapped into my power to that extent, yet." Xarnon seemed a little deflated. "Yet."

"Then…" Hale arched his eyebrow, allowing his expression to ask the question.

"I can move things."

"Move things?"

"Yes."

"I can move things, too." Hale kept his skeptical look. "What kind of moving are we talking about?"

"With my will alone." Xarnon clarified, his chest puffing back up a little. "I can reach out and move things with my mind."

Sir! The General bellowed from within Hale's mind. *Normally we would consider this an invalid and ridiculous claim, but given the circumstances of this meeting, it may be wise to lend credence to this little weirdo.*

"So, you can toss cars around and crush buildings with a thought?" Hale ignored the General's suggestion, allowing his feelings of annoyance to color his mood.

"No, um." Xarnon averted his eyes, clearly falling from the fairytale pedestal he had painted for himself. "Nothing that big."

"So, maybe a motorcycle?" Hale offered. When he received an embarrassed look as a response, he continuing. "A mountain bike? A skateboard? Maybe one of those miniature cars kids play with, what are they called again? They had that one fast taking guy advertise them?"

"I did move one of those!" Xarnon chimed in, a moment of pride causing him to burst with exuberance and drop the Gandalf voice for a moment. After the moment died, Hale's expression helped him realize the feat, while unnatural, was far from truly impressive. He immediately shifted posture from the strong and confident sorcerer to the weak and whiney wannabe. "But I'm still learning! I can't control it all the time, but I've moved plenty of things before!"

Any bit of Hale that would be impressed at the ability to exhibit supernatural telekinetic power was suppressed by the ridiculous costume and mannerisms of the individual. He felt like he was watching Urkel accidentally move an iron with his mind, causing a fire to break out in the living room. After the fire is put out and everyone looks at him with rage, he shrugs and says 'Did I do that?!' Hale, as the audience, was not impressed by the supernatural feat. He simply joined in with the rest of the crowd by laughing at the inane actions of a ridiculous character.

The lingering frustrations from the previous evening did not help his desire to belittle the world around him. Little Gandalf was spared Hale's razor wit when the back door opened right as Hale unpursed his lips to release more bile.

"Ladies and gentlemen," Jeremiah called out. His voice was strained, and his demeanor clearly shifted back to his pained expression as he moved into the room. He held his hand up to his temple, squinting and affixing his gaze on the floor. "Sorry to keep you waiting. I think we can commence our meeting."

The room turned their attention to him, but before Hale could speak, the Cocky Woman called out from the couch. "So you must be Imanu'el."

The Cocky Woman annoyed Hale. Granted, he was already irritable and on edge. Despite his current disposition, something about the brazen way the woman waltzed in, the look of superiority she gave to him as she passed, and now the condescending pitch in her voice as she spoke to Jeremiah only drove up the frustration slowly gathering since he'd walked in. His finely tuned powers of observation drew him to the conclusion that this woman was a bitch.

"Uh, no, I," Jeremiah stuttered, bumping into the podium as he clamped his eyes shut. He pressed the palm of his hand on his forehead, wincing in pain. "I'm sorry, no, he, Imanu'el, I am..."

"Well, spit it out!" The Cocky Woman snapped, disdain dripping from her voice.

"Will you give him a fucking second?!" Hale barked. The sudden surge of anger and verbal outburst took even him by surprise. Instead of tempering it, he embraced it and charged forward. He was not overly happy with Jeremiah's behavior either, however the current focus of his ire was this egotistical woman. "He's having a migraine or something, cut him some slack."

"And who the fuck are you?" She popped up from the couch, spinning to face Hale. Her right hand shot out a few inches to her side, opening up with the palm out towards Hale. The odd gesture drew Hale's attention for a moment, and he mentally compared it to her pantomiming a softball clutched in her hands.

"Please, calm – calm down." Jeremiah lifted his head up, stabilizing himself on the podium. The weak structure shifted to and fro at the introduction of his weight. Sounds of wood bending and duct tape snapping alerted the leaning man that this was not an implement he could use to actually support himself, and he straightened his posture.

"Are you one of the Touched, too?" Xarnon asked the girl. His original confident demeanor had cracked, and a timid weakling in a strange outfit had replaced him.

"Not by any of you," the girl scoffed.

Hale shook his head as if physically hit by the words. He finished reeling with an incredulous look. "What?!"

The girl jutted out her lower jaw in a sneer, as if daring Hale to say more.

This can't be happening. Hale thought. *I've let my mind explore almost every possible scenario of meeting others like me. I've imagined the best and worst case scenarios. Even in my nightmares I could never have come up with something this catastrophically bad.*

It might not be so bad, The Poet chimed in. *These people are likely as unnerved as you, and different people have different methods of defending themselves. Perhaps you just need to give them time.*

154

Maybe they just need a good slap, or a good kick in the ass in the case of that one hood-wearing weirdo. The General spoke up. *I'd be happy to administer the slap to the mouthy bitch, sir.*

They are people. Touched, like you. Give them a chance.

Fuck their chance. They obviously don't operate on the same level as you.

Wait to hear what Imanu'el says, The Poet said softly. *If he is half as charismatic as he was on the broadcast, he can hopefully calm this group so you can see who they truly are.*

"Uh, Imanu'el will not be here today." Jeremiah cleared his throat, practically choking out the words.

Sir, we have confirmation that the final straw has arrived. We are loading it onto the camel's back as we speak, The General shouted, his voice accompanied a numb feeling washing over Hale's face.

"What?!" Hale, the Cocky Woman, and Xarnon all asked at once. Hale thought there might have been a fourth voice chiming in, but he wasn't sure.

"I'm v-very, very sorry." Jeremiah held his hands out as if to quell them. "It was something last minute, something he needed to see to personally. He has asked that I sp–"

"This is bullshit!" The Cocky Woman said, eager to jump into a new conflict.

Hale felt his own perverse pleasure at the prospect of having a new target to vent his frustrations on. Despite his distaste for the woman and her actions, he found a budding kinship during this shared moment. Some voice deep inside him begged him to stop, though its inconsequential mewling was insignificant in comparison to the grand desire to rip someone down to his level.

"I was told very clearly that Imanu'el would be here," Hale barked. "Not just on that fucking TV broadcast, but over the phone when I spoke to him, too. Let me guess, he won't be here, but he'll be at the next meeting? Oh, and the next one will only cost $49.95, right?"

Pull out your forces, sir, The General goaded. *The loyal platoon is safe at home, probably with a six pack to assist with R&R. Let's withdraw and regroup.*

A second thought rose up faintly in the back of Hale's mind, one that muttered something about the improbability of a con. He brushed it aside.

"No! No, not at all. Please," Jeremiah moved away from the podium, taking a step around the wobbly structure and moving towards the group. His eyes, lively and open for a moment as panic set in, quickly snapped shut again. His hands shot back to his temples as he doubled over. "Ah! N-no... I can explain."

"Stop!" Xarnon shouted, raising both hands in the air. He seemed to find the character he had portrayed when he'd arrived, as his voice boomed off the walls rather than squeaking out of his throat. "We are all Touched, as Imanu'el has called us. We are special. We need to band together."

"We're all special?" Hale looked at him incredulously. A deep-seated wish to be rid of his 'gift' once and for all rose up for the first time in ages. "How in the fuck are we so special?"

"I am a mage." Xarnon crossed his arms and stood straight, regaining his composure fully. "One day my powers will grow, and I'm sure your–"

"Your name is fucking Percy and you live in your mom's basement." Hale spat. "You're not special, you're a fucking D&D geek who thinks his spells are real. And you! Superbitch." He turned to the Cocky Woman. "You better have a damn good PR guy if you go public with your Toucheded, Touchedness," Hale practically growled as he stumbled over how to refer to their inner talents. "Whatever the fuck Imanu'el wants to call it, cause people might bring back witch burnings just to justify getting rid of you."

Hale looked over the shocked face of Percival, the furious face of the Superbitch, and the mortified face of Jeremiah. The room was his, a reward for throwing the biggest tantrum. Hale's rage demanded more than just the awe of the attendees.

"And this place?" He motioned to the building and walked towards the podium. "Seriously, it's more likely that the fucking ROOF," Hale kicked out with all his might, shattering the podium into its various individual sections as it tumbled down to the floor. "Will cave in on our heads than us getting something productive done here."

He turned back to his captive audience to take a last look around the room. He spotted a girl in dark clothing and white barrettes that he barely recognized just before she disappeared through the curtain divider and out the front door with tears streaming from her eyes. Hale allowed a moment to ponder why he had not noticed she had been in the room before. The knowledge that he had hurt someone who, at least on the surface, seemed like an innocent gave volume to the muted voice in the back of his head.

Hale, leave now before you cause any more harm, The Poet pleaded.

Hale took a deep breath, clearing his throat before making his final, quiet proclamation. "I'm outta here."

With that, Hale left.

12

Contrary to the drive over to the meeting site, the drive home was not plagued by bouts of behind-the-wheel-narcolepsy. Hale drove with white knuckles and gritted teeth, mumbling curses both to and at himself.

Why did I even bother? They were a bunch of rejects and misfits, no one I would associate with under normal circumstances.

Since when are these normal circumstances, dipshit? You have something few others do, if even that. You may be alone with your talents. At least they could empathize.

I wish I hadn't even seen that TV ad! Then I wouldn't have wasted my time, and I might not have had the courage to tell Cass, which would have given us an actual chance at a relationship.

Sir! The General chimed in. *That meeting was akin to a monkey fucking a football! While amusing, nothing useful was going to come of it.*

You overreacted, Hale, The Poet cooed softly. *You raved like a madman, destroyed their property, and scared that poor girl.*

Better she wise up now than get caught up in that crowd, Sir. You did the little one a favor, whether she knows it or not.

Think of Jeremiah, too. He was obviously suffering, possibly due to the injuries he suffered from Alex, and yet you still attack him and his cause. You didn't even give him a chance to explain.

Jesus Christ, Hale! He pushed aside his manifestations of ego. *What were you thinking? What got into you? Yeah, it was a stupid meeting. Yeah, it may have been a scam after all. But at least act like an adult.*

The chimes of Fur Elise from the rattling device on his dashboard broke his train of thought. He suppressed his first instinct to throw the annoying piece of vibrating plastic out his window, and opted instead to just swipe it open and press it to his ear.

"Hello?"

"Hello, may I speak to Hale Langston?" an unfamiliar voice asked.

"Speaking," Hale responded absently, splitting his attention to look over his shoulder and change lanes.

"Mr. Langston, I'm calling about your digital cable service and internet," the voice continued. "We recently opened up a new package deal that includes internet, digital television, and digital phone service for a discounted price."

"Sorry boss, not interested," Hale responded flatly.

"Sir, if I may, what phone service do you currently use?"

"I don't."

"Excuse me?"

"I don't use a phone service."

The salesman paused on the other end of the line, trying to formulate his question in a way that did not sound insulting. "Sir, you are speaking to me on a phone now, correct?"

Swing and a miss.

Hale changed lanes again, speeding up a bit to breeze through a yellow light. "It's a cell phone. I don't have a home phone, no real point anymore."

"Oh, my apologies, sir." The salesman transitioned from apology right back into his pitch. "However, with our digital home telephone plan, you could enjoy a variety of features–"

"It sounds like a great deal, man, but I'm just not interested." Hale felt his standard issue polite responses waning. His morning had been aggravating enough, and while he usually didn't like hanging up on people, salesmen included, his patience was wearing thin.

"I'm sorry to hear that, sir. Are you satisfied with your current cable and internet services? Is there anything I can do for you while I'm on the line?"

"No, I think everything–" Hale drifted off at the sound of a siren's chirp. He glanced in his rearview mirror to confirm the red and blue flashing lights behind him. "Shit… Boss, I'm being pulled over, I'm going to have to go."

"Very well sir, please have a pleasant–"

Hale clicked the phone off and tossed it back on the dashboard. He twisted the wheel to the side, pulling off to the side of the road. His internal grumblings became external as he continued cursing his luck. Here he was, enjoying his Saturday afternoon by riding the wave of an adrenaline rush after meeting with a bunch of halfwits and wannabe's, and now he got to top it off by being pulled over for God knows what.

The officer took his time, which gave Hale a chance to take some deep breaths, relax, and calm his nerves. His senses began to clean out the taint of anger and frustration, minus the new addition of being pulled over, of course, and his body relaxed in his seat. The gentle thrum of cars passing mixed with the rustling of palm trees along the side of the road creating a soft white noise. The wind generated by passing vehicles rocked his car a bit, reminding him vaguely of the rocking chair his grandfather used to have. He could curl up in that chair and fall asleep in no time. Granted, if he didn't have a pillow to cushion the hard wood armrests or seat back, there was a good chance he'd wake up with a bruise from sleeping on such rough edges, but the deep slumber always seemed worth it.

A tap on his window brought Hale out of a dreamlike state. He had dozed off. Unsure of how long, Hale knew it was long enough for the cop to run his plates and walk up to his window. The officer looked down through aviator glasses, a look of suspicion crossing his features.

Hale sat straight and rolled down the window. "Can I help you, officer?"

"Did I interrupt a nap?" The officer asked.

"Sorry, sir. Was just trying to relax while I waited."

The officer leaned forward and sniffed at the air. "What's got you so tired? You been drinking?"

"Not yet, sir. I plan to make an early go at it after the way this day's been going."

The cop resumed his previous stance, simply nodding at what seemed to be a satisfactory answer.

"License and registration please."

Hale fumbled through his glove box, digging out the paperwork for his car from empty CD jewel cases, receipts, and crumpled up note sheets from various journalism cases. Eventually he found the correct document, just as crumpled and disheveled as the rest. He straightened the paper out with his hands as best he could, then handed it over with his license.

The cop took the documents, looking over them for a few seconds before continuing. "So Mr. Langston, are you aware it is illegal to drive while talking on a cell phone?"

Hale, surprised as he was, ran a few potential responses by his internal censors, allowing them to screen his words before they violently erupted from his mouth. The process took less than a second, and he settled on the respectful and politic response of,

"You have got to be fucking kidding me."

———————

HALE FINALLY got home at 1:00. The weary feeling in his body combined with Commodore's nod in greeting as he entered his apartment was reminiscent of returning from a long day at work. Hale decided he would continue his usual routine upon arriving home after such. He flipped open his laptop, powering it up while he groomed himself in the bathroom. A quick teeth brushing and a splash of water to the face made him feel a little more refreshed. His body yearned for sleep almost immediately, though Hale suspended the gratification of rest long enough to take a quick gander through his email and to enjoy a cider. Seeing nothing that required immediate attention, nor anything that could assist in his rather unpleasant day, he retreated to his room and flopped down on the bed.

Commodore hopped up and padded his way across the covers as Hale drifted off. The noble beast prowled up to Hale, took ginger steps onto his back, kneaded his flesh for a minute to ensure maximum comfort, then curled up and closed his eyes.

Hale's mind swirled. The weight of sleep was like an anvil pulling him down to the dark depths of a bottomless lake. Even through his descent, images of the previous 24 hours attempted to haunt him. The look on Mrs. Dowling's face as she was taken away by the police. The reaction Cass gave after he finally decided to reveal his secret. The look on Jeremiah's face as he greeted the group of Touched. The tears streaming down someone's face as they fled from Hale's fit of rage. Finally, the condescending words of the police officer who chastised him for endangering the public with his irresponsible use of a cell phone.

The images meshed into a strange sequence of thoughts, concocting a dream involving a police officer with a migraine attempting to arrest Cass for something involving discrimination while attendees of his earlier meeting watched with enthusiasm. The logic within the dream made sense, and the sense of camaraderie with the figments of Hale's imagination was palpable.

Hale felt at ease, as he knew that Cass was the minority in this situation. She was normal. Un-Touched. She had no abilities save that of a run-of-the-mill human being, remarkable mind or no. After the meeting he'd endured, she may well have been the best of them all.

Reality notwithstanding, in Hale's world, she was outnumbered. Hale started to understand the 'discrimination' after he looked around and saw hundreds and thousands of other people wandering the streets, each with their own special talents and abilities. He paused to wonder how he was able to distinguish their unique natures, and quickly dismissed it. Of course he could sense them. That was natural, was it not?

Hale felt at ease. He relaxed as the day-to-day tensions began to drift away. No pressure regarding his ability, or the attempts to hide it, existed in the slightest way. He was like everyone else. Well, mostly everyone else. And for this reason alone he could be happy. He could rest. He could feel…

…PAIN!

"JESUS CHRIST!" Hale's exclamation followed shortly after Commodore sprung from his bare back, using his rear claws to dig in for extra traction as he leapt. "Fffffuck! Commodore! Come back here, I'm going to make a boot out of you."

Hale stumbled up, still disoriented from being torn from a restful sleep. He took a moment to gauge his surroundings and get his bearings.

It's dark. Ok, so I've been asleep for a while. My back is probably bleeding. Stupid cat. Why did he freak out like that?

As if answering his question, a series of knocks sounded at the door.

Hale moved through his bedroom door, vaguely aware he was still only wearing pants as he maneuvered through his tight living space. Commodore perched on his standard spot on the countertop, watching the door intently.

"Really, cat?" Hale grumbled at the vigilant feline. "Was a couple of knocks really worth tearing up my back and running out here?"

Commodore looked up at his servant. *Human, if you are foolish enough to deign security as a useless endeavor, that is your folly.*

Hale ruffled the cat's fur on his head, which was answered by an annoyed look and a quick jerk away from the offending hand.

Crossing the remaining steps, Hale reached out, twisted the doorknob, and pulled it open.

Cass stood across the walkway from the door, leaning up against the railing. She had her arms crossed in a defensive posture, and she looked up at him through crimson bangs that flowed down over one eye. She wore a green bomber jacket to ward off the chill, and crossed jeaned legs at the ankle to comfortably stand on her calf-high boots.

Hale's self-confidence overrode any desire to take in the beauty in front of him. His hand immediately shot to his head, quickly smoothing over his hair, which seemed to be shooting out in three directions. He imagined it looked something like the Sydney Opera House, and suddenly wished he had taken a moment in his disoriented state to throw some water on it before answering the door. It wouldn't have been styled, but at least tamed.

The sudden chill from the night air reminded him he was also not wearing a shirt, leaving him both more exposed and with an embarrassing story to tell should she see the fresh claw marks on his back.

"Cass. Hi. I, uh, sorry, I just woke up," Hale stumbled.

Cass took a moment to pause, chewing her lower lip as she applied final revisions to preplanned words. "That phone call. The one where the man called me Cassie. When did it happen?"

Hale's eyes darted as he wracked his brain. The answer seemed important, so he wanted to give the right one. She was here, wasn't she? She didn't walk out of his life forever, and had apparently now given second thought to what were simply ridiculous claims less than 24 hours ago. The mantra of *'Don't fuck this up'* repeated in his head.

"Uh... I, well, I Wandered into it when you were driving me around," he said weakly. "I, I don't know when the call was. It doesn't really, you know, work like that."

"What was the call about?" Cass pressed.

"Cass, I..." Hale ran his hand through his hair, clearly flustered. "I don't know. It's not like watching a movie or anything. It's like getting a torn page from a book. I got a hint of what was going on, but that's it." He leaned on his door frame, nervously crossing his arms across his chest to offer some cover.

Cass simply stared at him, visibly torn on what to think.

"Would you like to come in?" Hale ventured, taking a step away from the doorway to give Cass passage.

Cass hesitated for a moment to mentally shed the final vestiges of her reservations, and then took a tentative step forward. She locked eyes with Hale, stepping across the threshold into his apartment.

Hale closed the door as Cass slipped past him and settled in the entryway of the kitchen. It was as close to outside as she could get while still being inside. She merely stepped in and to the right of the door, as opposed to walking straight through to the main living area. Hale figured it was also a way for her to avoid getting too close to him during this awkward moment. He silently wished he had not slept through the day, and instead had time to groom himself and be somewhat presentable for this unexpected visitor.

"Hale," Cass said, her tone matter of fact. "You understand what you are claiming is impossible?"

Hale nodded, "About as close as you can get to it, yeah."

"You understand why I'm having trouble believing it?"

Hale nodded again. "The same reason I haven't told anyone else."

Cass paused again.

Hale didn't immediately understand the shift in Cass' features. She wore a worried expression over her standard inquisitive persona. She had been studying him with narrow eyes, almost as if he was ready to lash out like a viper if she wasn't careful. He could understand that. She was scared, or at least had good reason to be.

But now, the gaze shifted. Her expression remained inquisitive, as it often was in one form or another, though now a measure of confidence had been restored. The cautious glint in her eye melted away in lieu of a predatory stare, and the corner of her lip curled up into a hint of a grin. Hale was not sure what to make of it until Cass took a step forward, wrapped her arms around his shoulders, stood on her tip toes, and kissed him.

The kiss was welcomed, albeit unexpected. After the initial shock of the physical contact and sudden shift in conversation passed, Hale reciprocated by sliding his hands around Cass' sides, leaning down to allow her to shift her weight more comfortably. Her lips, still chilled from the cool night air of Long Beach, were cold against his. The strange temperature pressing against his lips contrasted sharply with the warmth of her breath, which brushed his skin as they pulled away for a moment to speak.

... Cass walked in a triangular

pattern around her apartment.

...... "Our evening was derailed on

Monday, and my we–"

.... "You sense things?" Cass

asked Hale as he stumbled through his

explanation

Huh, I've never watched myself through someone's eyes before. Nor have I felt a pit in my stomach like the one she had when she was talking to me...

"I'd really like to expl–" Hale started, feeling Cass' disbelief and disappointment through his Wander.

"Shut up, Hale. Later." Cass pressed their lips back together, letting her tongue brush his as they took conjoined steps back towards the couch. She pulled away for another moment. "Why is your cat doing that?"

Hale's attention diverted to the source of her question as he sat on the back of the couch, pulling Cass closer to him as he leaned. He hadn't noticed, but Commodore had apparently taken offense to the aggressive invasion of his territory and the clear physical abuse of his servant. The feline had frozen his mouth in the open position, hissing wildly at the couple locked in a passionate embrace. He stopped hissing only long enough to take another deep breath, not even bothering to close his mouth between outbursts to conserve energy.

Cass pushed forward, causing Hale to fall backwards. He twisted his descent to set down comfortably across the couch. Cass followed his lead and used him as a cushion for a secure landing.

Settling in on top of him, Cass straddled Hale and pressed up against him, leaning down to start another passionate kiss. Their skin flushed in unison, both caught in the rapture of the moment. Hale slid his hands up Cass' sides, letting his thumbs brush against the sides of her breasts as he gently massaged his fingers into her back, encouraging her hips as they began to grind back and forth against his.

. . . Sue's hands clutched under Cass'

arms, pulling her forward into a tight

embrace.

. . . . . "It's alright, Sue..." Cass

consoled.

. . . . Tears ran down Sue's

cheeks as she buried her face into

Cass' shoulder.

"Hey," Cass said, touching his chin with her finger. "Where are you?"

Hale's eyes lowered from their wide, Wandering posture to the relaxed state he'd been in moment before. "Sorry, uh..."

Rather than try to explain his involuntary escape from the moment, he quickly thought of another excuse. Grabbing a small throw pillow from its fallen place the floor, Hale leaned up and tossed it at Commodore. The hissing guardian continued in his verbal protest, though he scampered from the countertop and raced across the floor into the bedroom. The hissing devolved into a low growl, followed by silence.

The throw pillow, having missed its target, flew through the open bar area and into the kitchen. The padded projectile slammed into the empty bottle of beer left over from earlier that day. The glass bottle clattered against the counter, rolled off, and shattered upon impact with the floor. Hale could not bring himself to care about the destruction in his kitchen, and was already refocusing his attention elsewhere before the sound of shattering glass ceased.

Ignoring the fleeing cat and the broken glassware, the two resumed their activities. Hale sat up, wrapping his arms around Cass' waist to keep them close. Fingers ran through his hair as he placed soft kisses on the exposed skin between the low cut fabric of her shirt. Not willing to press his luck and move a few inches lower, he instead pushed up and kissed her neck. The gesture was met with an arc of her back and a pleased moan. Cass' fingers intertwined in his hair, encouraging him to continue.

As Hale moved his lips up her neckline and to her earlobe, her hands explored his shoulders and chest. Eyes closed as she cooed in tandem with his kisses, letting her hands be her sight to take in his physique.

Cass allowed Hale to continue for a little while longer as she gyrated her hips against his, then slid her hands down his arms and guided his fingers around the base of her shirt. As his fingers curled around the hemline, she shrugged her jacket off and lifted her arms. He played his part and pulled her shirt over her head, tossing it on the floor next to the jacket.

Excited and filled with confidence from her encouragement, Hale leaned forward again, kissing back down Cass's chest until he buried himself in her cleavage. Trailing his fingers up her spine, he took her moans and the sudden rush of goosebumps across her skin as an indicator to keep going. He placed his fingers on the clasp of her bra, pinching it together to release with a satisfying snap.

Cass put her hands on Hale's shoulders, gently pushing him back into a laying position on the couch. With a mischievous grin she pushed her shoulders forward, letting the bra straps fall forward, and then the bra itself to slide off and down her arms. Hale grinned back up at the beauty in front of him, marveling at her form. Her slender torso transitioned into finely curved breasts, accentuated by a hungry smile on her luscious lips. He knew something had happened to spark this. Something had changed her mind and sent her back here.

Hale let his curiosity remain unsated, keeping himself in the moment with the confidence he would find out later.

Cass leaned back, looking down at Hale as she slid her hands down to his thighs. The motion left her completely exposed, and the arch in her back accentuated her figure. She smiled, enjoying his reaction as much as he was enjoying the visual gift. It was an intimate moment. Both of them were inherently defensive, guarding their own private lives cautiously, and intuitive about the world about them. Yet here they sat, half naked and exposed, allowing them to be both physically and emotionally vulnerable for the moment.

"What's up, homo?!" The door flew inwards. Alex stepped in, a broad grin on his face and a paper bag filled with clanking bottles under one arm. The other arm featured a thin blonde with an athletic frame covered by baggy pants and a tank top. The sideways cap and snakebite lip piercings completed the stereotype Alex had labeled her with. "I hope I'm not– HOLY SHIT!"

Cass and Hale responded with natural shock at the sound of the door flying open, both snapping their attention towards the entryway. As Alex made his grand entrance, the two rolled away from the door. Hale reached out to cover Cass with his own body but she reacted faster, rolling away from the intruder and sending herself sideways off the couch and to the floor.

"Fuck! I'm sorry! I didn't know!" Alex stumbled back out of the apartment, the bag of booze sliding down his side as he attempted to both hold his hands out and cradle the bag all at once.

"Alex, what the fuck, man?!" Hale shouted.

"Ow... that hurt..." Cass groaned from the floor.

"Dude, you invited me over!"

"No I didn't!" Hale protested

"I hit your table with my arm," Cass mumbled.

"Dude!" Alex stepped back through the entryway, swinging the door halfway closed to speak through the crack and cut off visibility. "Remember, drinking and crashing on your couch?"

"Uh..."

"Can he please leave?" Cass asked, face shoved into the front of the couch in embarrassment.

"Is that Cass? So you two are okay now?" Alex asked, a hopeful tone edging in his voice.

"Alex..." Hale's tone was a growled warning.

"Thank you," Cass moaned, clutching her arm.

"Right, I'm gone, no worries." Alex stepped away, closing the door.

Hale shook his head, unable to suppress a small laugh from escaping at the ridiculous series of events that had occurred since he woke up not ten minutes ago. He pulled his eyes away from the door to check on Cass when the door cracked open again.

"Uh, I do have to go, right?" Alex asked.

"Alex, fuck off!" Hale shouted.

"Right, see ya." Alex shut the door again.

After lingering on the door for a moment longer to ensure Alex had actually retreated, he turned around and looked to Cass on the floor.

"How you doing?"

"I think my pride took the brunt of the wound, though falling onto your table was almost as unpleasant." Cass kept her face buried in the corner where couch met the floor, one arm draped over her breasts, the other over her face.

"Sorry about that." Hale rested his chin on the edge of the couch. "You woke me up when you got here. I had no idea what time it was, and I kind of forgot that Alex was coming over."

"Mental note: we lock the door next time clothes have the potential to come off."

"Yeah, that took me by surprise, too," Hale grinned.

Cass peeked up at him from under the crook of her arm, then rolled on her back to gaze up at him. Her arms crossed over her chest to continue the conversation without the distraction of naked flesh.

"Well," she said with a smile, "I didn't exactly make my intentions known."

Hale chuckled, leaning his face against the couch for a second in an attempt to relax and enjoy the situation for what it was. After taking a breath he propped himself up with a palm under his chin and looked back down at her.

"So, can I convince you to join me back on the couch, or shall I slide down next to you?" He asked, a cocky grin plastered onto his face.

"I'm going to opt for door number three, actually."

"Oh?" Hale let his disappointment show. "Am I going to have to brutally murder my friend now?"

"No no, nothing that severe, tempting as it is." She assured him. "We should take advantage of this forced break and change venues to one with a bit more comfort and room."

Hale followed her gaze to his bedroom, and he helped her to her feet, only to chase her through his doorway. The pair collapsed onto his bed, giggles soon smothered by the heat met between their lips.

13

The two lay intertwined in Hale's bed. Cass rested her head on Hale's chest, her arm draped across his stomach, and her leg intertwined with his. She idly picked her index and middle finger up in a slow rhythm, counting up and down his ribs. A thin sheen of sweat reflected moonlight back at the bedroom window. The matched grins of contentment spread across Hale and Cass' lips accompanied the glow.

Hale rested his hand on Cass' shoulder, his head propped up by pillows so he could smile down at the woman in his arm. He enjoyed the moment, realizing that his horrific day had somehow ended here. It was a blissful experience, and he did not want to taint it. However, he knew questions were on both of their minds, and only hoped that the inevitable conversation would not steer the night away from its pleasant course.

"Did you want to talk?" He asked.

"Hmph." Cass buried her face into his chest to compliment the comical retort. She mimicked a child's whine. "I don't wanna…"

Hale chuckled. "Wait, hold on, Cass doesn't want answers… Who are you?"

She tilted her head slightly to allow one eye to peer up at him. Her grin confirmed he was right in his assessment of her curiosity. She rolled over to face him, keeping her head rested on his chest. She settled in again, pulling the covers around her shoulders. Now that they were out of the passionate moment, it seemed that modesty had made demands. Wisdom allowed Hale to smile inwardly at the suggestion that Cass could feel vulnerable without making his observations known.

"Alright smartass, let's talk."

Hale grinned back at her. "Why don't you start? Not that I'm complaining, but I have to say I'm a little curious as to why you are here. I mean, we didn't exactly part on a good note yesterday, so I didn't expect to have you naked in my bed tonight."

"It's a long story involving my accountant. He said charity work could get me some much needed tax credits."

"Har har…" Hale slid his hand from her shoulder to jab her in the side with his fingers.

Cass laughed as she used the blankets to shield herself from his attack.

"Seriously, what happened?"

"Alright, alright. But don't think you're off the hook." She tapped his chest, glaring up at him. "I've got a list for you after I get done with my story."

"Figured as much."

Cass sighed, "So I went to Sue's this morning…"

THE MORNING was cool. The sun had not been at work long enough to disburse the chill from the previous evening. Cass, one who enjoyed heat and despised the cold, bundled up in her bomber jacket to maintain her comfort. She lived in California to avoid the chill, but there was no way to defeat it in the early morning hours.

She stood on the porch, irritation gathering under her skin. Waiting always annoyed her. She felt like she should constantly be in motion. The 'Teddy Roosevelt ideology', she called it. She had seen a special on the History Channel about the former president. He believed it was important to keep oneself occupied and productive. Apparently, he constantly busied himself with personal projects when he did not have actual work to do. Cass enjoyed that philosophy, and attempted to act in kind with the former world leader.

Locks disengaged, the sound bringing Cass' attention back to the world at present. When the door swung open, Cass was met by a bleary-eyed Sue staring at her with an annoyed look on her face.

"Cass, what the hell?"

"Sorry, I know it's early," Cass said defensively.

"Early? It's 7:30 on a Saturday." Sue turned away from her to walk back into her apartment, leaving the door open for Cass to enter on her own. "Someone better have died."

"Again, sorry, I forget people aren't on the same schedule as me. I'm usually up early."

"Coffee…" Sue groaned as she shuffled into the kitchen.

Cass walked into the dining area, quietly seating herself in a chair. She remained silent as Sue clattered around the kitchen, fumbling through her morning routine. Cass was annoyed, as she had spoken to Sue last night and confirmed that she would be coming over in the morning. Sue's general distain in her greeting and whining about the time seemed contrary to their previous plans, and Cass was anxious to get this over with.

Sue shambled over to the table, clutching her steaming mug in both hands. She was bundled in an oversized sweatshirt for a college she did not attend, an inheritance from a previous relationship. The sleeves draped over her cupped hands, providing a soft barrier between the hot cup and her fingers. After flopping into a chair, she gave a pained sigh.

"Shiiiiit, did you want a cup?" She looked at Cass from under drooping lids as if begging her to refuse.

"It's okay. I'm fine." Cass waved away the offer. She folded her hands on the table, waiting for Sue to take a sip and gain some semblance of consciousness. After three sips, Sue continued to release belabored sighs and sit with closed eyes, letting the steam of her coffee waft over her face. Cass gathered that Sue would have to be forcefully drug into a conversation. "Sue, I wanted to talk to you about that thing with Phill and Hale."

"Oh, fuck, Cass, not this again."

Why the dog face? Always with the dog face. What could disgust you so horribly about this topic that it would cause you to make such a revolting expression?

"Sue, I'm sorry, but it's important."

"Should we start with Phill almost crying on me after you ditched him, or when you picked up some random guy right in front of him?"

"Sue, I feel the need to repeat that this is important." Cass held her tone, irritation with her drowsy companion making it increasingly difficult.

"Like you abandoning me isn't important?" Sue's attentiveness increased now that she had a reason to vent. It was the kind of self-centered reaction Cass had come to expect from her friend. "You know Phill actually asked me out last night?"

"Sue." Cass intertwined her fingers and brought them up to her lips. "I need you to drop that issue for a moment. I'll gladly entertain any questions or ridicule after the fact, but I really need to know some things."

"I'd like to know some things, too!" Sue set the mug down firmly, sending a few small drops flying, and placed her hands on the table as she gave Cass an incredulous look before proceeding with her lackluster interrogation. "Like, what do I do with Phill now? He's following me like a kicked puppy, and the rejection you put him through apparently pushed him to ask me out."

"Goddammit Sue!" Cass slammed her open palms on the table. The crack against the wood reverberated through the small dining area, snapping Sue to attention and causing coffee to erupt all over the table. "Stop being a selfish bitch and listen to me for one second!"

Sue, unfamiliar with this form of address from anyone, much less from the typically even keel Cassandra, sat frozen with wide eyes and a slack jaw. Coffee pooled around the base of her mug.

Cass took a deep breath, calming herself to prevent from lashing out again. She preferred a level headed approach to problems, and losing her cool would not make her feel that she had resolved the situation with the appropriate finesse. Despite her refocused calm, her palms remained flat on the table, and she glared at Sue from under furrowed eyebrows.

"I need answers to a few specific questions, and I need you to be candid. These are important, do you understand?"

Sue nodded her head. She took the moment of pause to shake back to herself. Her expression dropped the momentary shock and fell back into a more comfortable, cocky expression, albeit now on the defensive. "Y-yeah, of course. If it's so important, what is it?"

"Did you ever meet or speak with Hale?"

"The guy you met at the coffee shop when you were supposed to go on a date with Phill?" Sue cocked her eyebrow and threatened to make the dog face again, but then shrank back into a more complacent posture when Cass narrowed her eyes. "No, why would I know him?"

Having received what it is she needed, Cass ignored Sue's question. "You are sure Phill did not mention my name, or yours, when he talked to Hale?"

"Why is—"

"Sue, answer the question." Cass tensed, her tone conveyed her utter lack of desire to play games.

Sue shrugged and looked up, as if being accosted by an unjust accusation. She was desperately trying to regain the upper hand in the conversation by playing the victim. Cass was thoroughly unmoved. "How should I know, Cass, I wasn't there! Phill told me he didn't mention any names. He was very defensive about that, saying that he's paranoid about information security and strangers and identity theft and whatever else he was talking about. And Phill isn't one to lie."

Cass let the answers interact with the information she already had catalogued in her mind, attempting to gauge the sincerity of Sue's words as she did so. She let the moment hang for a few seconds, then spoke again, "Sue, if you are hiding anything else, I need to know now. I know you think this is all some big game, or just a series of events to screw with you, however there are bigger things at stake here."

Sue jumped at the presented opportunity. "Bigger things at stake?! You betrayed me, and now you want confirmation that this guy didn't know your name

before you got there, like I'm going to believe he wasn't planted there by you
anyway. And if I'm wrong, which I know I'm not, then maybe you have a fucking
stalker and should have just stuck with the date with Phill like you originally
agreed to."

Cass slid away from the table, slowing rising from her seat.

"What, you can't handle the truth being thrown back at you?"

"Sue, since you seem to be a fan of the truth being thrown, let me
reciprocate with some observations of my own." Cass leaned on the table, palms
pressed flat on its surface. Sue had pushed her too far and she was no longer
interested in the gentle approach. "You constantly complain about the lack of depth
in the relationships you pursue, whining that you want more, and that your
requirements are not too stringent. Yet, despite the evidence of a dozen past
heartbreaks, when presented with an individual who espouses what you claim to
desire, you reject them. Your reasoning varies, but typically it is something
shallow.

"You opt to instead chase after empty headed losers. While the
aforementioned losers generally possess good looks and passable personalities,
they are nowhere even remotely close to what you declare you are searching for.
The relationships are always doomed from the start, and you end up disappointed
and full of nothing but complaints.

"If you truly want to achieve the happiness you claim to crave, give Phill a
chance. Yes, there may be someone out there who is a better match. However, your
string of failures stretching back over the last few years beg the need for change in
your patterns of behavior, so perhaps he will be just what you need to broaden your
horizons.

"Alternatively, you can continue to lash out at everyone close to you, slowly
alienating those around you until you have thinned your social circle down to solely
spineless, sycophantic lackeys who don't know anything better than to take the
verbal abuse you seem eager to pummel them with."

Sue stood up with a look of indignation. She seemed unable to summon the

177

words to retaliate despite the dog face coming back in full force.

"Thanks for waking up to talk to me, Sue," Cass said flatly, then turned and left the dog face accosting an empty room.

———————

"I KINDA realized how much of a bitch I had been when I left," Cass winced, "But it was strangely liberating."

"Do you know if she's pissed at you?" Hale asked.

She shrugged. "She may be. Honestly, Sue and I have grown apart a lot over the past year. Something drastic needed to be done to catalyze either a reform of our relationship, or the formal break into our own directions. I feel good about it, regardless of how it ends."

Hale nodded along with her assessment. She overanalyzed and he wasn't surprised, but he did wonder if this time it was from defensiveness or guilt. "Fair enough, I guess. So what did you do for the rest of the day?"

"Hmm?"

"You said you met Sue around 7:30 in the morning, right?" Hale looked outside. "While we've spent a little time in here, it was already dark by the time you knocked on my door. What happened during the rest of the day?"

"Oh, well, yeah." Cass' cheeks flushed as she adopted an awkward grin. "I needed to think about everything that had happened. I typically think best when I pace around a room, drive aimlessly, or do some other arbitrary task that requires no real concentration."

"Tell me you ended up in Mexico," Hale smiled.

"Not quite, no. I managed to stay in So Cal, thankfully. I started driving north and ended up snapping out of a long mental debate somewhere around Santa Monica. I got off the highway, grabbed some food from this really great Greek restaurant on Santa Monica Pier–"

"Ew, Greek food," Hale grimaced.

"How can you not like Greek food?" Cass adopted the tone of a disappointed parent.

"Not my thing. Never have been fond of hummus."

"Well, it's not my fault you are mentally deficient. Greek food is amazing."

"Uh huh. Back to your embarrassing story."

"Ok, ok." Cass darted her eyes around as she shifted gears from the sarcastic repartee portion of her brain back to the anecdote section. "So anyway, full up on delicious, mouth watering hummus, and delectable beef–"

"Cass," Hale verbally prodded her.

"Right… so I got on the 405, heading back south." Cass' eyes wandered as her voice fell into an airy tone to reflect the mindset she had been in during the tale. "I just kept driving and driving, letting my mind argue facts back and forth for a while. I ended up exiting somewhere, cruising around side streets. Then, as the portion of my brain that was voicing support to come back over here and give you a proper chance to explain started gaining some ground, I realized I was in your neighborhood. Just a block or two away from your apartment, actually."

"Guess your subconscious was calling the shots while your active brain was distracted." Hale tried to call back terms he had learned in Psych 101 way back in the day. Whether he had used the correct ones or not, Cass seemed to get his message.

"Tell me about it." She rolled her eyes. "I had pretty much settled on the fact that you and Sue don't know each other. That meant either Phill spilled something, you're a psychic of some kind, or you have another-hopefully-non-creepy explanation for me."

"So was… this," Hale said, nodding down to their cuddling forms, "part of the plan?"

"Truth be told, no." Cass snuggled into his chest again, continuing the story as her eyes fluttered shut. "I grabbed some coffee from that place we met. Not bad stuff, really. I've had better mochas, but at least they don't burn their grounds. Anyway, I decided to enjoy my caffeinated beverage at your place while we talked.

But I had second thoughts when I parked out in front of your complex. I started a whole new internal debate, deciding that I would spend the time it took to finish my coffee to ensure I was making the right decision."

Hale did some mental math, "So you left Sue's around 8, I'm going to assume she's somewhere in Orange County, drove up to LA, had some lunch, then drove down here. That couldn't have taken you more than 5 hours, tops. What time did you park out front?"

Cass squinted her already closed eyes, pressing her face into his chest. Muffling her voice against his skin she answered, "Twelve."

"Twelve?!"

Cass rolled back onto her cheek and looked up at Hale. "I got the coffee around 12ish, then parked in your complex shortly after. I actually saw you get home about an hour later. You looked pissed, and obviously didn't see me."

"Yeah, long story." Hale rolled his eyes. "I'm surprised I didn't see you, though."

Cass shrugged. "I wasn't waving flags or anything. Anyway, my coffee cup timeline was a bad choice, as my mind knows how to mess with me to drag things out. My sips became smaller and smaller as time went on, til eventually I was sipping cold murk from the bottom of the cup. It's amazing how much I can justify. 'No Cass, you still have time to think. Sure it's been three hours, but there's still a little bit of coffee at the bottom that seems to have coalesced from the drops on the walls of the cup.'" She scoffed at herself.

"So you were sitting out in your car all afternoon?"

"When you say it like that I sound crazy."

"Is there a better way to say it?" Hale asked with a cocky grin.

"You could say I secluded myself to a quiet area to process data and corroborate stories." She offered.

"Right."

"Okay, so it was a bit crazy." She stuck her tongue out at him, which elicited him to return a smile and give a gentle pinch on her cheek. "The problem was that I like you. However, I have some very strict rules that cannot be ignored. Specific to this case, stay away from people who think their fantasies are real."

Hale opened his mouth to speak, but Cass held up a finger to shush him. He obliged her, remaining silent.

"The trouble is there are only a few ways you could have gleaned the information you did without the abilities you claim. Most of my suspicions aren't pleasant, but you don't fit the mold of a predator that would suit those circumstances. There were other theories, unlikely but possible, that I had to think about and dismiss. And finally, there is the possibility that you were simply telling the truth.

"Regardless, I have had a fantastic time with you during our brief time together. I couldn't justify pushing you away when all parties involved in this mess seemed so earnest and sure of the facts. So I finally decided to come up and talk to you, to give you a chance to explain it to me again."

"Um," Hale grinned. "Unless this was part of your interrogation tactic, you didn't grill me that hard."

"Har har…" She gave a mocking glare before continuing. "I was determined to stay outside until you had either satisfied my curiosity, or until I decided it was simply time to leave again. Then the door opened, and my logical reasoning broke down. Pathos arguments started assaulting me–"

"Pathos?" Hale asked, knowing he should recognize the term.

"Emotional. You know, Logos, Pathos and Ethos? Logic, emotional and ethical types of arguments."

"Right. Psych and speech classes are flooding back to me now."

"You should really know that term, you know, being a journalist and all."

"I admit failure on this one." Hale rolled his eyes and smirked. "Let's move on."

"Yeah, so my brain stopped wanting to hear all the Logos and started begging to listen to the Pathos. That doesn't happen to me often, but my gut feeling was that this was right. It didn't make logical sense, it was not supported by what I could properly deduce to be the correct decision, it just felt correct."

"Not regretting your choice, are we?"

"Nope," she said matter-of-factly.

"Making sure you can still look into the abyss and laugh, eh?"

"Nice reference," Cass said, eyeing him with a measure of respect. "I'm surprised you remember that and not Pathos."

"Yeah, well, Nietzsche had some entertaining ideas that stuck with me."

The two stopped, enjoying the moment. It stretched out over minutes, neither one of them willing to break the silence with the logical progression in the conversation. Instead Cass nuzzled into Hale's chest, playing the piano up his side again, while Hale brushed through her red hair and gazed down at her peaceful face. The moment had to end, and Cass' curiosity caused her to break.

"You know what we have to talk about next, right?" she asked, her eyes still closed.

"I have a good guess."

Cass lifted her lids to look up at Hale again. "You'll probably know a better place to start. I promise to interrupt you when I have questions."

Hale leaned back, eyes drifting to the ceiling. *Where to start?* He thought. *Do I give a general synopsis of how it works again, maybe talk about when it started, or even what I tried to use it for? How do I make this sound interesting, because past the supernatural nature of this ability, it's really nothing impressive.*

As if reading his mind, Cass offered, "You can start when you first realized what you could do, if you want. It's as good a place as any."

"Sounds good," Hale said. He suddenly wished he had a cigarette, which immediately segued into wishing he smoked. It was an odd wish, but it seemed appropriate for the moment. He could regale his tale like a hard boiled noir detective while motioning with a lit cigarette dangling from his fingertips, blowing perfect smoke rings through the air during each dramatic pause.

It took a few moments for him to realize he hadn't started speaking. Pulling himself away from the daydream, he conjured his disorganized thoughts into words, "I was really young. Maybe five or six. Memories are kind of hazy at that age, but this one stuck out. I was in a classroom, and I was playing with one of my friends. We were on a break or something, between exercises I guess. Either way, the teacher was occupied with his own things while the class took care of itself.

"I ran up to the phone. You know, the classroom phone that the teacher uses to call the office? Anyway, I grabbed it to make a fake call as part of a game I was playing with my friend. That's when I Wandered for the first time."

"Wandered?" Cass asked.

"It's what I call it." Hale moved his hands around as if arranging the story into order while he tried to think of how to explain himself without sounding utterly insane. "Divination, or whatever it is that I do. I refer to it as Wandering."

"Okay." Cass took a deep breath, trying to push aside her natural prejudice against this type of talk.

"Anyway, I dazed out when it happened, like I still do, and I saw some… things." Hale cleared his throat. "There was some racy conversation and some images of my teacher touching himself inappropriately."

"Your elementary school teacher was using his work phone to have phone sex while kids were away?" Cass made a disgusted face.

"I can only hope it was while kids were away." Hale rolled his eyes again. "Anyway, when I came back around, two of my friends were standing in front of me, waving their hands in front of my face and laughing. They saw me go all blank faced and empty, and thought it would be a good laugh to screw with me. They didn't know any better, they were just kids.

"Unfortunately, I was freaked out. It was like waking up in an unfamiliar place, it's still like that sometimes even now. It was like that initial terror of 'where the hell am I' that grips you for a moment when you wake up in a hotel, or from passing out. Unfortunately, that moment stretched on, and I just lost it. I started crying, which only made more kids crowd around. That didn't help my comfort level. Then Mr. Jennings came over to see what was wrong. That sent me into an even different type of terror. I ended up just curling up on the ground, crying my eyes out until I eventually was taken to the office where my parents picked me up."

Hale took in a deep breath, replaying the events in his head one more time before continuing with his verbal recount. "Apparently some of the kids reported what they saw, and the school nurse recommended I get checked out for epilepsy. The external responses I gave to Wandering apparently mimicked a Focal Seizure, followed by a hysterical fit, which they assumed was a panicked state due to the shock of the episode."

"Sounds like they were half right," Cass offered.

"You're not wrong. The freak out was pretty much all shock. Anyhoo, my parents weren't living in a life of luxury, but they also wanted to make sure I was alright. They took me to a doc and got me some basic tests. They drew my blood, gave me some behavioral tests involving motor skills and such, and even took an X Ray."

"What the hell is an X-Ray sup–"

"I know, I know." Hale cut her off. "This was like, early 90's, and it's not like my doctor was an expert in the field."

"Fair enough." Cass gave an irritated sigh. "Stupid doctors... continue."

"Anyway, I Wandered a couple more times in the Doctor's office. Once when the Doc went to give me a shot. Instead of experiencing my own needle, I Wandered into one of his other patients who had to be practically held down by his Dad. The second was while I was waiting in the room for the motor skills test. Apparently one of the previous kids had been so nervous he wet himself during a test."

"Did you tell anyone what you, uh, saw?"

"I did, actually. I was a pretty shy kid, so I waited until it was just my parents in the room, but I told them that the Doctor had to have a kid held down to give him a shot," Hale sighed. "They thought I was trying to be funny, I guess. They told me I had been very brave, and that they were proud of me for sticking through the process with such courage. At the time I thought they understood, but looking back I realize they just made assumptions to explain it to themselves.

"Eventually when we got home my mom took the time to talk to me more in depth. She asked me to recount what had happened in the classroom to try and find out why I had broken down so bad."

Cass listened attentively, curious about the following events.

"So I told her. I said that I saw Mr. Jennings saying weird things on the phone. It didn't occur to me to say *how* I saw it; I figured saying that I saw it was enough. I had to be prompted and cajoled into saying more. I was embarrassed. I felt like I had done something wrong. Anyway, my mom eventually got the gory details out of me, which prompted more crying until she repeatedly assured me I was not in trouble.

"I remember the details being muddied. I had told her I saw him on the phone, and that he was alone in the room, so I guess my mom had made the logical assumption that what I had seen had been before my little breakdown, and that something had just triggered the memory during class. She kept asking me leading questions, trying to logically deduce what happened, using my testimony to confirm her theories.

"In the end, she called the Principal and raised hell. Can't blame her. From what she knew, her son had walked in on a teacher having phone sex during recess. Well, technically I did, but not in the way everyone assumed. However there were no call recordings at the school, and due to the switchboard they used, the call log from the phone company didn't distinguish between the various classrooms, so they couldn't even verify if he had made outgoing calls."

"How'd you find out about all this?"

Hale chuckled. "My mom is a bit of a dramatic, and she'd rush to report her findings to my father. They'd make me go to my room, or somewhere else to play while they talked. I guess they didn't want me to be exposed to more of the scandal than I already had. Didn't matter. If I was anywhere in the house I could hear my mom shouting about the injustice of it all."

"She sounds like a peach," Cass grimaced.

"She's not bad, honestly. We don't get along great, truth be told, but she means well. I write off most of her idiosyncrasies because her heart's in the right place."

"That's admirable," Cass said.

"Thanks," Hale grinned. "Water?"

"You read my mind." Cass slid off of Hale's chest and stood at the side of the bed, dragging the sheet along to cover herself in a makeshift toga.

Hale pivoted sideways and rested his feet on the ground. He searched through the dark with his toes for a stack of discarded clothing before finally finding his jeans. Gripping them with his toes he pulled them up to his waiting hands. He fished his boxers from the tangled fabric and slid them on before getting up from the bed. He looked up to find Cass smiling at him.

"You ready, monkey man?"

"Don't discount dexterous toes." He lifted his foot up a bit, wiggling his toes. "I can practically write letters with these things."

"Uh huh." She arched an eyebrow and gave him a doubtful look, amusement shining through. "Come on now, you owe me water and the rest of this story."

Hale followed behind her, careful not to step on her train of sheets. After she took a seat on a barstool, Hale slipped past her, performing his practiced twist and bend to get past the bar and couch without damaging anything. The only light that guided him was the dim entryway bulb. He hadn't bothered to turn anything else on after stumbling out of bed to answer Cass' knocks earlier, and neither of them had been eager to turn on lights as they rushed to his bedroom shortly after.

He flipped on the kitchen light, bathing the apartment in a soft fluorescent glow. Cass groaned, leaning down to shield her eyes with her hand.

"Not a fan of fluorescent lighting?" Hale asked, pulling the refrigerator door open and retrieving a pair of waters.

"Not after my eyes were adjusted to moonlight." She gave an embarrassed grin.

Hale took a moment to look at her across the open counter space. The soft lighting provided unneeded aid by hiding imperfections of the body, making her seem that much more beautiful. Her skin was pale and flawless, with just enough curves to satisfy touch while still remaining pleasing to the eyes. He continued to take her in as he spoke in a soft tone. "Now that I can say this without risking a slap, you really have a phenomenal body."

"Hale." Cass continued to grin from under her hand-shield. "I'm a fan of flattery like anyone else, but if you don't give me that water and continue your story, I'm going to choke you."

"How'd you know I was into that?" His tone returned from low and complimentary to his normal sarcastic pitch. He placed her water in front of her, staying a full arm's length away as he did so.

"I'm going to hurt you." She stifled a laugh.

"I'll avoid the obvious follow-up joke and just continue." Hale unscrewed his water, smiling to himself as he took a few deep pulls off the bottle. He recapped the bottle, looking up to remember where he left off. "Hmmm, where was I?"

"Mom shouting about injustice."

"Ah, right." Hale leaned back on the kitchen counter, refocusing his attention on Cass. "So in the end, nothing could be proven, and I was put in an awkward position with my teacher. My mom wouldn't let that be, however, and demanded I at least be transferred into another class. The Principal obliged her, and I was moved under another teacher's care."

"So your parents didn't figure out how you actually gleaned the information?"

"Nope." Hale shook his head. "And if they suspected, they wrote it off. The doctor's diagnosis came back a negative. He said I was just a kid with an active imagination, and a tendency to daydream. What looked like potential seizures were just me letting my head float into the clouds. Between that and the lack of any concrete proof of my teacher's scandalous actions, they had no reason to think otherwise.

"Regardless, the entire situation scared the hell out of me. With one little Wander, I had turned my school year upside down, gotten moved out of the class with all my friends, been sent to a doctor, been put through painful tests, and finally gotten grilled by my parents on several occasions about what happened. The desire to come forward again when I started Wandering on a more consistent basis was slim. I made mention of a similar event a few years later after Wandering into the knowledge of my teacher potentially having an affair. That one had no witnesses to me freaking out, and no basis in reality since I was not at the teacher's home, which prompted my mom to sternly warn me against making up stories. That clamped down the last bit of desire to come forward with my insights."

"I can imagine." Cass sipped her water. "So did you figure out what caused it? Why you're able to 'see' things like this?"

Hale shook his head. "Nope, but I have an idea of what triggers it. Strong emotions, love, hate, sorrow, those are the most common things I Wander into, though occasionally I'll Wander into something completely benign and irrelevant. I borrowed Alex's phone once and saw some random wrong number he received."

"Speaking of –" Cass pulled her makeshift toga up around her shoulders. "He's not going to bust in again, is he?"

"I hope not. Just in case…" Hale chuckled as he crossed the few steps to his door and twisted the deadbolt into place. "There, now we're safe."

"I have to admit I was a bit mortified when he saw me." Her face flushed crimson at the memory. "I don't consider myself a prude, but I also don't go around showing my chest off to just anyone."

"I'll take that as a compliment." Hale straightened himself proudly.

"As you should." She narrowed her eyes and pursed her lips into a hidden grin.

"Alex's accidental voyeurism was a result of plans I made with him earlier today. I had no idea you were coming over, nor that you'd be in a compromising position on my couch, and he always comes in like he owns the place."

"And you don't lock your door?" She asked dubiously. "In this neighborhood?!"

"I mean, this isn't a five star complex but it's not like I'm in South Central or anything," Hale said defensively. "My neighbors are cool, and we rarely have any crime in the complex unless someone brought in the wrong guest."

"Okay," Cass shrugged. "But your open-door policy needs to change while I'm over. You can be all reckless when I'm gone, but I don't want Alex nor a lone gunman busting in here–" Cass cut herself off, blushing again as her eyes quickly averted.

"Whoa," Hale grinned. "Were you about to commit yourself to a repeat performance?"

"And look who gets all cocky after he gets lucky." She looked back up at him, cheeks still burning. "Now back to your story, hot shot."

"I'll just give myself a point of Karma for ignoring yet another obvious joke." Hale made a hash mark with his finger on an invisible chalkboard in the air. "Where did I leave off again?"

"You have the memory of a goldfish, you know that?"

"Hey look!" Hale's eyes shot open, and a broad, excited smile spread over his face. "A castle! … Hey look! A castle! … Hey look! A–"

"Okay weirdo, when was the last time you Wandered?" Cass asked, resting her chin in her hands. She kept the toga pressed to her chest with her forearms, letting the excess drape off her shoulders.

Hale dropped the goldfish impersonation, settling back into an amused grin. He thought for a moment, then got a little color in his cheeks as well. "Actually, last time I wandered was when we were, uh, on the couch."

"Really?"

"Yeah, I don't really know what I look like when I do it, or how long I'm out, but I can guess it's just a blank stare for a few seconds." He shrugged.

"What was it about?" Cass gave him a sideways glance, a bit of worry in her voice.

"Um…" Hale thought about the images he had gleaned, trying to sort through them to give Cass a complete answer. "One was you walking in a triangle and then calling me last night, the other was you and Sue. She was, uh, crying.

Crying on your shoulder, to be specific."

Cass froze.

"I didn't–" He paused, eyes darting while he thought of the ways he just screwed up. "I didn't touch on a sensitive subject, did I?"

"Hale, may I see your phone?" Cass asked politely.

"Probably, but before I commit to my answer... why?" His voice was tentative, nerves beginning to show in his posture. His cocky demeanor transitioned to tension as he lost control of the conversation.

"Honestly, I want to go through your call log and text messages." She looked down at the bar. "I'm sorry, I know it is a horrible breach of privacy, however I need confirmation that you and Sue have not shared information. There are only a few ways I can figure you knowing about this story, and I'd like to rule out the most likely to give more credence to your claims."

Hale continued to pause, trying to sort through his feelings on the matter. "I... honestly don't know what to say. Part of me wants to be offended for the lack of trust, but given the circumstance and your logical, very honest request, I'm having trouble thinking of a good reason to say no."

"Please?" Cass said without missing a beat.

"Uh, sure. It should still be on my nightstand." He motioned to his door.

The redhead wrapped in sheets quickly stood and shuffled back into the room. Hale followed her as far as the entryway, resting on the doorframe. He watched as she picked up his phone and sat on the bed. Still wrapped in sheets, she navigated through the menus with clicks and beeps. She slowed down after a bit, methodically clicking every few seconds and scanning the screen. After a few minutes, the phone was replaced on the nightstand, and Cass hung her head.

"I'm sorry, that was really paranoid of me."

"Again, given the circumstances, I'm lucky you're still here," Hale reassured. Feeling confident he would no longer taint her investigation with his presence, he inched over to the bed and sat next to her. "You have no idea how grateful I am that you came back. The fact you're willing to listen to my crazy claims and give a chance to prove I don't belong in a padded cell is something I've wished for my entire life!"

Cass kept her head low, but risked a look up at him through a screen of hanging red hair. "Wait, your parents never found out?"

Hale shook his head. "I got close a few times, but that initial scare kept me quiet for a long while. Over the years I'd get tempted, and occasionally something would slip. But what is a logical adult going to assume when a child comes up with a story regarding someone's intimate life? The one I mentioned about the teacher having the affair a few years after my first Wander had my mom warning me about mental institutions for people who can't discern between fantasy and reality."

"Point taken."

"Exactly," Hale shrugged. "I was either making something up, or I had found out through some rational method. Either way, the slip ups didn't happen often enough to warrant suspicion. The few times they did have to stretch to explain something were so few and far between, they were never suspicious enough to dig deeper."

"So no one else knows?" Cass sat back up, tossing the hair out of her face. Her jaw had dropped slightly to reflect her amazement, and a dip of sorrow in her eyelids showed him sympathy.

"No one else knows specifics." Hale had a moment of realization, rocking his head back and closing his eyes with a belabored sigh. "Except... oh shit... so yeah, I should probably tell you about Jeremiah and Imanu'el."

"Huh? Who?" She furrowed her brow.

"Yeah..." Hale grimaced. "Remember that guy in the gray sweatshirt?"

14

"So wait." Cass mentally reconstructed the series of events Hale had laid out for her. "The guy who attacked us outside of that bar is named Jeremiah, and you know this because he works for some evangelist guy who you saw on the TV named Imanu'el? And he just happened to bump into you on the street? This reeks of a scam, you know that, right?"

Hale nodded. "Trust me, I know. My biggest aversion to calling him in the first place was that very reason. I went out to the bar that night to clear my head and come to a decision. Now if I was some random Joe and they bumped into me and claimed I had some gift from God... well, I'd probably tell them to go fuck themselves." Hale shrugged. "However, I do have something different about me. And they had no idea I had even seen their broadcast, much less that I was even going to call them."

Cass winced. "Hmm... point. That would be pretty coincidental."

"So yeah, that's why I finally decided to call."

"And you arrive at a freak show that Imanu'el doesn't even bother to show his face to?"

Hale nodded. "Yup. I feel kinda bad now, truth be told. I really went off the deep end. I'm not usually like that."

"Well..." Cass pursed her lips. "You said it yourself; You were already on edge. The events of the previous night, which I can take a good portion of credit for–"

"It wasn't your fault."

"No, it wasn't," she agreed flatly. "It doesn't mean I didn't have a part in it. While I believe my reaction to have been, hmmm, logical, its negative impact on you was the same."

"Fair enough."

"So the previous night, the lack of sleep, and the lifetime of buildup only for what seems like a catastrophic let down seems like a good recipe for an unusual emotional response." She wiggled beside him, squirming closer to get into a more comfortable position. "And with Imanu'el as a no-show, that probably was the match to the powder keg."

Hale rolled his eyes. "Yeah, that definitely didn't help. Seriously, what could be more important than meeting with the new 'recruits' you just spent a bunch of time and money getting your message out to? Especially when these recruits are, I hope, rare and difficult to get your message to?"

"Yeah, the normal excuses about family emergencies and business trips just don't seem to fit."

"No kidding."

"Maybe his alien overlords requested a meeting, or the Government kidnapped him and are dissecting his brain right now!" Cass leaned forward, widening her eyes for effect.

"Ah, don't even joke about that." Hale cringed. "It's honestly one of my few phobias. I saw this movie when I was a kid about the government cutting up this alien while it was still alive. The alien looked human, of course, which didn't help with the parallels I drew in my head. Besides, this dude is a religious nut, so it'd have to have been a meeting with the Holy Trinity, cause aliens don't exist in his religion."

Cass giggled, sliding the rest of the way across the couch to lay across Hale's lap.

"Oh, speaking of…" Hale regarded her curiously. "Do you, uh, practice? Religion, that is?"

She arched an eyebrow. "No."

"With an emphatic answer like that, I imagine there's more to that answer than just 'no'."

She shrugged. "Not really. I believe most religions start with good intentions, but over the years their messages are muddled, the people who rise to power are not those with goodness in their hearts, and the overall execution of the faith ends up contradicting the initial intentions of the institution. Plus, I seat my beliefs in what can be proven. Saying there is a God because you cannot prove there is not is the same as saying there is actually a Flying Spaghetti Monster who actually created the universe until you can prove otherwise."

"I've heard of that 'religion'," Hale chuckled. "The followers are Pastafarians, right?"

"That's the one."

He laughed at the ridiculousness of the Pastafarian movement before continuing. "Well, I'm not far off from your beliefs. I'm firmly seated as an Agnostic."

Cass rolled her eyes. "Fence sitter."

"True, but saying something definitely does not exist in the absence of proof is just as fallible as making a definitive declaration that something does exist in the same scenario."

She eyed him for a long moment. "Touché."

Hale grinned.

"Anyway." She shifted tone to signify a shift in topics. "Now that our theological tangent is complete, we should get back to our original subject."

"That was pretty much it. You know as much as I do." Hale let his fingers drift over Cass' bare shoulder as he spoke. He relished the touch, reflecting on the luck and twist of fate that had brought her here. Not only was she physically attractive, they were well matched on a social and intellectual level.

Hale's only worry was that she was too smart for him. He'd rather have a challenge to improve himself than the other way around, but he also worried she might get bored.

He realized another benefit. In his reasonably short list of partners, he had been plagued with inconvenient Wanders during the moments of passionate union.

While Hale had no delusions that Cass hadn't been with others before, he seemed to have avoided that uncomfortable problem of Wandering into previous experiences in their first time together. Mostly...

"By the way, what was that whole thing with Sue crying on you? When did that happen? I'm guessing recently from the beeline to my phone, but it didn't really fit in your story from earlier today."

Cass bit her lip, a wry smile on her face. "You mean you're not going to let me distract you away from that little fact any longer?"

Hale arched his eyebrow. "You're sneaky."

"I can be," Cass grinned. "Okay, so remember I told you I just left Sue at the table..."

CASS CROSSED the room and was halfway out the front door when she heard the first sob. It wasn't expected, and it cut through the angry tension like a white hot razor. She stopped mid-step, turning to look back at her friend.

Sue was looking away, using her hair and the back of her hand to shield her face. The defensive demeanor was a clue on its own, and the sudden jolt of her frame as another sob escaped her lips confirmed Cass had heard correctly. She slowly stepped back into the room as Sue slumped back into the chair.

Cass didn't speak. She was naturally disposed to observing things that made her curious, though in this situation she found herself lacking the knowledge of what to do even if she had the inclination to actively interact.

The sobs increased in frequency as Cass closed the door behind her. Sue kept her face turned away, shifting in her chair to settle into the weeping rather than to shield herself. This confirmed Cass' inkling that Sue believed herself to be alone. The sobs continued into cupped hands, continuing until a sniffle signaled the presence of tears. Sue lowered her hands to wipe at her eyes and run her nose along the sleeve of her sweatshirt. It wasn't until she removed the shield from her eyes

195

that she caught a glimpse of a figure in her peripheral vision.

"Jesus!" Sue jolted, slamming her knee into the underside of the table. "Oh, fucking Christ..."

"Sorry!" Cass blurted, her demeanor remaining placid and inquisitive. The words came more as a consequence of surprise rather than a feeling of remorse.

Regardless of intent, Sue buried herself in her forearms, letting her puffy sleeves envelop her face. She remained there long enough to re-center herself, overcoming the embarrassment of being caught in what she had assumed was a private moment. The sobs did not return, and several deep breaths emanated from the fabric cave she had created for herself. Finally, she peered out from her cotton sanctuary, lifting puffy eyes up to gaze on the interloper in her home. "I thought you left," The blockage in her nose caused the words to come out as a muffled slur.

"Almost," Cass halfheartedly gestured to the door, keeping her curious eyes on her friend. "I... heard..." She trailed off, unsure of what else to say.

Sue allowed a few moments of silence to pass. Her eyes welled up again over the passing seconds. As tears slid down her cheeks, Sue stood and took quick steps to bridge the gap between the two of them. Her arms wrapped around Cass' neck and she resumed sobbing, the sound muffled into her shoulder.

"Whoa." Cass reeled back a few inches from the unexpected assault, but Sue held tight. She settled into the hug, vaguely aware that the arms wrapped around her had been used as tissue paper thirty seconds earlier. She tentatively patted Sue on the small of her back. "It's alright. Everything's okay."

"I've been such a total bitch," Sue choked out.

"No, no." Cass spoke the reactionary words, knowing immediately they were false. She bounced a few alternative responses through her head, and decided to continue with her usual honesty. "Well, yes. But honey, you're just confused."

Sue pulled away, bringing her sleeve covered hands up to her face again to wipe away tears. A small laugh crept through the sobs, causing a smile to spread across her lips. "Wow." She cleared her throat, wiping her face again before looking Cass in the eyes. "You really do suck at the whole empathy thing."

196

Cass couldn't help a grin. "Makes my Bachelors kind of a paperweight, huh?"

Sue gave a nod, the corners of her mouth sagging into a frown as the moment of levity passed. "I'm turning into my mom."

Cass returned to her somber observation. Sue might not have been the best friend lately, but she was still a friend. Cass knew what the comparison meant for the woman who had grown up with only her regularly-abused mother. It had been their single-parent households that had first brought the pair together as friends. But while Cass had inherited her strength by trying to be as strong as her father, Sue had come to her strength by trying to be anything but her mother.

"You'd think growing up with a woman who had bi-monthly ER visits thanks to her loving husband would have given me a clue." She sniffled, averting her eyes. "Looks like being shallow is genetic."

"Sue." Cass tried to draw her friend's attention back to her. "You're not like that. The guys you date can be assholes, but you're stronger than that. You wouldn't let yourself remain in a dangerous situation."

"Maybe not." She folded her arms, dropping her gaze to the floor. "It's not like I've made it far, though."

"You gravitate towards what is both comfortable and familiar." Cass winced. "Unfortunately, that isn't what really makes you happy. Fortunately, you're strong enough to stand up for yourself and socially dominate most people, which gives you an easy escape when you need it."

More sniffles, and another swipe across the sleeve. Cass hoped she would be washing that sweatshirt soon.

"I know what I want. I think." She gave an exasperated laugh. "But all I seem to do is the same stupid shit, and now I'm even pushing away my best friend. And what did you do to deserve it? Called me on my own bullshit!"

"This may be a blessing in disguise." Cass hated that phrase, but given the circumstances, she felt it was an appropriate application. She offered a supportive smile. "I think you just needed a wakeup call, and this may be it."

Sue looked up at Cass again, nodding and giving a sad smile. Fresh tears brimmed in her eyes. She moved forward, reaching out to pull Cass into another tight embrace. Her hands clutched under Cass' arms, desperate for the stability and comfort.

"Cass…" Tears streamed down her face and onto Cass' shoulder. "I am so sorry."

Cass returned the hug, both surprised and relieved that her earlier outburst yielded what seemed to be a breakthrough for her friend. "It's alright, Sue…" Cass consoled. "We're okay, and you're going to be fine."

"I'm lucky to have you as a friend." Tears ran down Sue's cheeks as she buried her face into Cass' shoulder.

"THAT'S THE part I Wandered into," Hale interrupted.

"So you know everything from there on out?" she asked.

"No," he admitted. "Truth be told, even parts of that last conversation were omitted. I just got bits and pieces. No idea where it went from there."

Cass clicked her tongue idly as she processed the information. "Interesting."

"So what else happened?"

"Nothing, really." Cass finished her water, placing the empty bottle on the table before continuing. "I apologized for going off on her. She thanked me for doing it. Sue's a good person at heart, she's just been on a bad streak lately. A little too much ego and a lack of consideration for others. Hopefully this will be a wakeup call."

"Here's to hoping." Hale finished off his water too, before taking both empty bottles back to the kitchen.

"What else did you guys talk about?"

"You." She blushed at the admission.

"Really?" He puffed up, his interest piqued. "What about?"

"You didn't see it when you Wandered?"

"Nope."

"Good," she smirked. "Because I'm not telling."

"Ouch. Walked into that one, didn't I?"

"Don't you mean 'Wandered' into that one?" Cass grinned.

"Punny!" He paused to grin before moving on. "While we're on the topic of me Wandering into your personal life, do you mind if I ask about the other one?"

"Hmm?" Cass asked. She kept her eyes forward to prevent Hale from seeing any of the sudden tension appearing on her face.

"The other thing I Wandered into, the one I brought up last night." Hale stumbled, trying to find a more politic way of describing it than 'when you were crying your eyes out'. "The one with you in the car, the guy saying Cassie on the phone."

"Oh, that one." Cass ensured her expression stayed even as Hale moved back around her and sat back on the couch. "Well, first it's your turn. What are you going to do about Imanu'el and his little cult?"

"What do you mean?"

"Well, Imanu'el will probably still want to meet with you when he gets back from whatever was keeping him away, right?"

"Maybe." Hale shrugged. "Doesn't really matter though. I never gave them my contact info, so they only get to talk to me if I want them to."

"Well, unless they're smart."

"What do you mean?" Hale eyed her.

"You called them, right?"

"Well, yeah."

"So if they check their phone records, or get real proactive and call the phone company, they can track down your number." Cass dotted plots on an invisible map with her finger. "Then they can call you, reverse lookup you from your phone number to get your personal info, get an address, etc. etc."

Hale grimaced and leaned his head back. "I actually tried to make a living as a P.I., and I can't figure out even the most basic stuff when it comes to tracking people down."

"Yeah, you mentioned that at the bar," Cass said absently.

"Yeah." He gave an embarrassed smile. "I had it in my mind that I could take an involuntary ability and turn it into a profitable career. I probably should have studied Criminal Justice or something instead of English Lit if I really wanted to commit to the idea."

"How long did your PI career last?"

"About six months. I ran out of money, got into debt, and realized I had very little aptitude for the job."

Cass substituted a giggle for a silent smirk, hiding it before Hale lifted his head back up.

"Pretty ridiculous, huh?" Hale asked.

"Not... too ridiculous."

"It's okay, you can laugh."

Cass did.

"Feel better?" Hale leaned his head on the back of the couch again, waiting for her giggling fit to subside.

"Yes, sorry." She rubbed her eyes, her laugh slowing as she returned to the conversation. "So, uh..." She wiped her eyes again, forcing a giggle back. "Question still stands. What about Imanu'el and his cult?"

"Assuming he has more skills as a P.I. than me?"

"Assuming he has more skills as a P.I. than you."

Hale gave a belabored sigh. His brain was rebelling against unpleasant thoughts, making it difficult to analyze the situation. "Well, I'm still curious about what he's trying to do, albeit significantly less so than a few days ago." Hale chewed on his lip. "Hmmm, I think the people who showed up were a little crazy, but I was harder on them than I should have been. I don't know, honestly. I'll probably listen to what he's got to say, but who knows. I'm kind of playing it by ear at this point."

Cass nodded, apparently satiated.

"So, your turn," Hale prodded.

Cass pursed her lips. "Could I... take a rain check on that one?"

Hale felt a knot tighten in his stomach. He knew he shouldn't be annoyed, as he was prying into an obviously sensitive area of her life. Still, he exposed the darkest secrets of his life, telling truths of things that no other living soul was aware of. He knew it was unfair to simply expect the same, but he was irritated nonetheless.

"I'm sorry." Cass cast her eyes down, clearly feeling a sense of shame at the small alteration in Hale's expression. "I know you've put a lot of trust in me, I'm just not ready to talk about that."

Hale nodded. "It's okay, I understand."

The two sat in silence, neither looking directly at the other. It was an awkward culmination to their conversation. The path they'd taken had precluded them from pursuing less important, jovial topics for the evening. Now they had hit a barrier that prevented them from exploring further. The tension enforced the continued silence, causing both to feel anxious.

In a sharp contrast to the somber moment, Cass let out a large yawn. Infected by its contagious nature, Hale returned the gesture.

"So, do you mind if I sleep here tonight?" Cass looked up at Hale with hope in her eyes. "I'm usually in bed way earlier than this, so I'd be a menace on the road."

"I see this as a great opportunity to improve my chances of getting more nookie, so yes," Hale grinned, trying to bring the mood back to a more jovial tone.

Cass returned the grin, grateful for the opportunity to slide the previous conversation under the rug. "Don't blame me, mister. I'm not the one whose body demands a sudden stop to our carnal activities. I'd be willing and able to stay up later if you could rise to the occasion."

Hale's eyebrows shot up. "That sounds an awful lot like a challenge."

Cass gave a mischievous grin and rose from the couch. She took graceful steps towards the room, allowing her makeshift toga to slowly slip from her shoulders, dip down her back, and finally float down to the floor. She cast a glance over her shoulder at Hale from the doorway to his bedroom, "What can I say, I like ambition."

As she turned back and stepped into the room, Hale scrambled from the couch to follow her.

15

Hale was awoken by a series of knocks on his door for the second time in 12 hours. He grumbled, unwilling to accept defeat in his effort to sleep in. His eyes fluttered open enough to realize light was streaming into the room before he fastened them shut again. The light pelted his eyelids, now annoyingly present in his semi-conscious state.

The knocks sounded again. Hale met them with a louder groan this time, prying his eyes open as if he could glare the intruder away. His eyes refocused to the crook of his arm. Commodore was curled there, looking up at his house servant with a lazy look.

Human, I am comfortable. If you believe you will be getting up and ruining this perfectly good sleeping area, I shall be disappointed.

Hale looked over his cat to the other side of the bed. To his surprise, disturbed sheets and an empty space were all he found. He pushed himself up, receiving a low growl from Commodore as a warning not to move further. He took a quick look around the room. Not being a morning person, it generally took him awhile after he woke up to regain his bearings, but he was sure something was out of place.

Cass was nowhere to be found.

The knocks sounded for a third time.

"I'm coming!" Hale shouted, pushing himself up to a sitting position.

Commodore sat up indignantly, staring up at Hale as if to chastise him for insubordination. He watched his house servant get up from the bed, yank on pants and pull a t-shirt over his head as he crossed the threshold into the main area of the apartment. The noble beast resigned to laying in the warm portion of the bed his servant had left.

Hale reached the entryway as he finished donning his wrinkled t-shirt, wiping his eyes with one hand as he opened the door with the other. "Yes?" he asked.

Light from the rising sun silhouetted a figure on his porch. Hale squinted, trying to block the bright rays emanating from the horizon and overcome the fuzziness in his half-asleep vision. As the figure came into focus, Hale picked out more details. He was a young man, no older than Hale. His sandy brown hair was neatly trimmed, and he had no facial hair decorating his features. His humble clothes were plain white, exuding an aura of purity.

"Good morning, Mr. Langston. I am Imanu'el. I know my presence is likely an unwanted intrusion, and I hope my early morning visit does not compound that agitation." He kept his hands folded at his stomach; a shallow bow of his head accompanied a smile as he greeted Hale.

Hale shook his head. Caught completely off guard and still trying to focus on the land of the living, he stumbled, "I, uh… what are you doing here? I mean, hi, uh, how did you find me?" He planted his face in his palm, rubbing his eyes and forehead again. With a belabored sigh, he looked up to try his opening again, but was beaten to the punch by Imanu'el.

"Again, I apologize for the intrusion, but I believe I owe you an explanation. My absence at our scheduled meeting yesterday was unforgivable. I wished to simply explain the situation and offer an apology. After which, should you decide I am not worthy your trust again, I will acquiesce your wishes to leave you be."

Hale paused, trying to gauge his opinion on the situation. He was still frustrated about Saturday, but the feeling wasn't nearly as fresh or as strong. His night with Cass had not only cleared up his fears that he'd lost her with his admission but had put him into an entirely new headspace. He felt almost rested and telling her his secret had relieved a burden he'd been carrying for so long, he almost hadn't noticed it anymore. Still squinting into the sun, Hale simply nodded

204

and took a step back. "Would you like to come in?"

Imanu'el nodded again, bending at the hips to give a short bow. "Thank you." He moved into Hale's apartment, crossing the threshold of the entryway and stopping near the back of the couch. He gestured. "Do you prefer to sit?"

Hale nodded as he pulled his wits back around him. He led his guest around the couch and sat. "Can I get you anything? Water, soda?"

"No thank you." Imanu'el averted his eyes to the floor in another half-bow. "I believe the hospitality you have extended me thus far is more than adequate."

Hale paused. He had always tried to give people the benefit of the doubt and thought being rude was simply unnecessary. This caused him to wrestle with a nice way to say 'What do you want' for a few moments. Fortunately, the silence spoke for him.

"You no doubt wish me to get straight to the point." Imanu'el returned his eyes to Hale's. They were calm and tranquil, though Hale could not miss a strong confidence behind them. As they locked gazes, Hale felt compelled to listen. "I will be more direct than I usually am with these topics. As you are aware, talking about certain gifts the Lord has bestowed upon us can garner awkward attention from anyone with a sensible outlook on the world. However, given the fact I believe we are both in the same Ark, if you pardon the metaphor, I will simply divulge what I know in hopes it will show you my trust."

Hale remained silent. Imanu'el was clearly intelligent and a competent speaker, which only made Hale exercise more caution. Cass would have been proud of him as he withheld his immediate questions and let the man offer more instead.

"I believe our Lord has reached down to this world to grant gifts to certain, special individuals. What purposes these individuals have are not yet known to me. Yet time reveals all, and I am certain it will be made clear if we are patient. What is important to me now is finding those who have been gifted by our Lord. I wish to gather those whom I call the Touched."

"What makes you think that's your purpose?" Hale asked.

"Good question." Imanu'el straightened. "I was truly without direction or purpose with my own gift. I was only made aware of its presence during my teenage years, and even then it was a miracle that my attention was drawn to it. It was not until recently that I was given a sign on how to proceed.

"Jeremiah, whom you've now had the pleasure of meeting twice, stumbled upon me. I would like to say I stumbled upon him, though it was truly he who extended the first hand. While I can imagine the Lord has gifted some of the Touched with truly extraordinary and fantastic abilities, it is Jeremiah whom I believe will lead us to the light."

Hale took a deep breath. The religious rhetoric was agitating and he'd heard it all before, in one form or another. While the 'Touched' certainly could provide more proof of a Divine existence than anything else ever presented to him, it could equally be proof of a scientific anomaly, mutation, or a host of other possibilities. For now, he remained silent. He was by nature a curious creature, and if listening to a zealot's preaching for a few minutes would get him answers, he would abide.

"Jeremiah has been Touched with a special type of hearing. I'd like to think it is attuned to heavenly frequencies, allowing him to better hear our Lord's presence here on Earth." He offered a hopeful smile, which Hale politely returned. "Regardless, I am certain it has given him the ability to hear others who are Touched. He describes it as a musical note emanating from the person's body. Sometimes it is more like a harmonic tone, or even a fluctuating wave.

"With his presence, my path became clear. I had been Touched with a divine gift, and now had the means to gather others with similar gifts to my side. It was a moment of clarity I had been seeking for years."

The front door opened, drawing both of their attention.

Cass pushed the door open with her shoulder, stepping across the threshold gingerly while cradling a cup of coffee in the crook of her left arm with another clasped in her hand. She began closing the door with her foot when she noticed the apartment was filled with more than just a sleeping Hale. The door clicked shut and she dropped her purse, allowing her to retrieve the cup from her arm with her free hand.

"Good morning," she offered.

Imanu'el stood, bowing his head in greeting. "Good morning. My apologies, I was unaware Mr. Langston had company." He turned to Hale. "Perhaps we should continue this at a later time."

"Um," Hale looked over at Cass. He saw a hint of recognition and suspicion in her eyes. "I think we're okay to continue. Cass is aware of my, uh, Touched-ness."

Imanu'el's eyebrows rose. "Oh? Very well then. It is a pleasure, Cass. I am Imanu'el. You must indeed be a trusted friend of Mr. Langston's to share such a valuable truth with him."

"Yes, we go way back." Cass stepped forward, extending one of the coffees to Hale. "Sorry, I didn't know we were expecting company, else I would have juggled a third."

"It is quite all right." Imanu'el held out a hand, palm forward to wave off any offense. "While I understand the benefits of the beverage, I choose not to partake myself."

"Weak stomach?" Cass queried, lifting her cup to her lips as she eyed the man in white.

"Quite the opposite. My body is strong, though I feel the caffeine negatively affects my ability to think clearly. I become a bit manic, I suppose. Regardless, it is probably for the better. A man in my position can hardly afford to be spending excess funds on such indulgences."

Cass nodded, swallowing a sip of her beverage. "Well, don't let me interrupt. I'll make myself sparse unt–"

"Actually," Hale cut her off, "you're free to stay, if you want. I'd like it, actually."

Imanu'el remained silent and stoic.

Cass did not hide her appreciation. "Even better." She grabbed a stool from under the bar and dragged it behind the couch by where Hale was sitting. She looked up at Imanu'el as she sat down. "If I'm not intruding, of course."

Imanu'el pulled his lips into a pursed smile. "No, of course not."

Cass smiled and sat on the stool, leaning onto the back of the couch to give her the best view of the conversation as she nursed her coffee.

"So you were saying," Hale guided them back on topic. "Jeremiah can hear music coming off of the Touched?"

Imanu'el lowered himself back onto the couch, resuming his collected posture before continuing. "In a sense, yes. It is no song, per se, rather just a distinct sound. One comparison he was able to give me was this: If you were to walk into a room where a television was on, but muted, you might hear the faint high pitched ring of the electronics on in the room despite the lack of volume."

"I think I follow." Hale nodded.

"Saturday was a learning experience for Jeremiah. He had never been in the presence of more than one of the Touched at once. Unfortunately, the experience was a cacophony of pain for him. Apparently the symphony of tones did not flow well together. Rather, they amplified and distorted, leaving him with a migraine that persisted to this morning."

"Which begs the follow-up question of why he was there alone," Cass asked.

"Quite right." Imanu'el nodded, bowing his head in shame. "Unfortunately, I was not able to attend the meeting due to an unforeseen and rather urgent opportunity. An elderly woman who lives here in Long Beach had seen my broadcast on television. She has a nephew in Utah whom she believed to be Touched. He had claimed wild things to her in the past, telling her vivid stories of his abilities and powers.

"The woman called me, acting as an intermediary between her nephew and I. It seemed he was reluctant to come forward. This did not seem strange to me, as all of the Touched that I have had the pleasure of meeting seem to follow a similar pattern of behavior. We tend to be withdrawn regarding our abilities, as the world is not yet ready to understand. Few, if any, will believe us. The rest will treat us with indifference at best, and cast us aside as outcasts or mad men, at worst."

Hale nodded slowly, his mother's warning about the 'men in the white jackets' replaying in his mind.

"A meeting was arranged," Imanu'el continued. "Though the man refused to come out to see us. What's more, he demanded to speak with me directly before he was willing to take any steps forward. We found a deal on a flight that left that very evening, and returned on Saturday afternoon. It was only one ticket, as we could not afford two, so I put it in my name."

After Imanu'el gave a long pause, Hale prodded, "I'm guessing Mr. Nephew didn't turn out to be everything he claimed?"

Imanu'el shook his head. "Not in the slightest. Mr. Nephew has been dragging his wealthy aunt along for quite some time now. She wishes to believe there is something special about the one male relative bearing her father's name, and he is more than willing to put on a show. Apparently heredity is important to her, and she believed that if Mr. Nephew was a success, their family name would thrive."

"So what 'power' did he show you?" Hale asked, suppressing a smirk.

"There were a few acts of prestidigitation, attempts to read my mind with cards, and even a strange trick where markings appeared on his arm." Imanu'el sighed. "While entertaining and creative, it was far from anything divine. I thanked him for his time, and excused myself. He seemed confused as to why I did not schedule a follow-up meeting."

Hale chuckled at the ridiculousness of Mr. Nephew. He found humor in the irony of the man going out of his way to seem special and different, something he wasn't, when Hale had done the very opposite.

"Imanu'el," Cass interjected. Hale noticed her pursed lips and narrowed eyes, the face she made when her curiosity was in full effect. He'd seen it directed his way more than once and suspected he would become all too familiar with the expression. "Hale told me of the sermon you broadcast out on public access."

"Yes," Imanu'el confirmed. "I decided to throw caution to the wind in hopes of finding others who were Touched. Fortunately, the negative backlash has been minor, and the yielded results have been great."

"Yes, of course." Cass quickly acknowledged his comment to afford the bare minimum of social etiquette, and then transitioned back to her question. "Your broadcast mentioned you were 'Touched' as well, and that a demonstration would be given once you met in person. Is that offer still on the table?"

Imanu'el hesitated. His brow furrowed and his lips pursed. An emotion akin to fear crossed his eyes for a moment before he cast them down and responded. "If you wish, yes. I do not extend it often, and was actually hoping to gather the Touched together again for a mass demonstration. While not ideal, due to the circumstances, I believe I can afford to display it privately for you. Is that your wish?"

Hale cocked his head. "You make it sound quite... ominous."

"It is not my intention to worry you, and I apologize for seeming dramatic. However, my gift will require one of your participation, and it will require a small amount of pain."

"Excuse me?" Cass asked, her eyebrow arching.

Imanu'el extended his hands out, palms forward. "Again, I apologize. Perhaps you now see the cause for my hesitation. It is not a gift that displays itself with flashes of light or any prestige, it simply is... a gift." Imanu'el struggled with the last words, then looked back up to his audience. "Shall we proceed?"

Cass continued to eye the man as if he needed a straitjacket. Before she could voice any more questions or protest, Hale responded for both of them.

"Yes, I will do it." As Cass turned to him, an objection already forming in her mouth, he spoke again. "Please, I need to see if this is for real."

She remained silent, though he could see it in her face. Every logical piece of her body screamed to eject this intruder from the apartment and to go about their lives without him. However, she was inflicted with the burning need to know answers almost more than Hale, so she complied.

"What do you need me to do?" Hale asked.

"Do you have a sharp knife, or perhaps a straight razor?"

"I'm assuming a steak knife won't work."

"I'd... prefer not." Imanu'el paled a bit.

He took a swig of his coffee and placed it on the table. "One sec, lemme look." Hale pushed himself up, shimmied past his guest and ventured towards his room.

He almost tripped over Commodore as he passed through the doorway and turned into his bathroom. The regal feline had assumed a crouched position at the corner between the bedroom and bathroom doors. This allowed him to have a clear line of sight into the living room from a position of stealth.

The cat did not move. Rather, he let out a low, guttural growl and continued staring around the corner. He only allowed one eye to peer out around the wall, ears pulled back and head lowered to keep himself as hidden as possible, and kept his gaze fixed on the intruder dressed in white.

"What's wrong with you, cat?" Hale looked down at the vigilant predator.

Commodore ignored him, his focus unchanging.

"Whatever," Hale sighed, searching through his drawers.

Everything is fine, he told himself. *This is a necessary step to prove I'm not alone in the world. He can show me, with no special effects or chicanery, that he is Touched too.*

Then why are your hands shaking? The Poet asked.

Hale steadied himself, realizing that his hands were vibrating relentlessly as he pushed through the junk in his drawer.

I think it is a little natural to be nervous.

It is, The Poet confirmed. *Just don't let your desires get the best of you.*

And remember! The General jumped in. *The best defense is a STRONG DEFENSE!*

Thanks for that.

Anytime, sir!

Hale pulled out one of his old safety razors. He walked back out into his bedroom, maneuvered around his watchful pet, and stepped back into the living room. Doing his practiced bend he slipped between the couch and bar before curving his path around into the kitchen. As he fished through kitchen drawers, Cass called out for him,

"What are you looking for?"

"Screwdriver," Hale muttered. "I have a safety razor, I just need to pry off the plastic."

"Look for a lighter, please," Imanu'el said. "Or matches. They will work as well."

Hale found both, then went to work on the kitchen counter. With a few deft moves and a small application of strength, the plastic prison in which the triple razor set was kept popped open. Hale pried them apart further with his fingers, excising the three small razors inside. He brought them back around the counter and deposited both the razors and the lighter into Imanu'el's waiting palm.

Imanu'el took a deep breath, held it for a few moments with his eyes closed, and then let it out slowly. His eyes opened and refocused on Hale. "Let us begin."

212

16

Imanu'el ran the bare razor through the flame. His movements were methodical, clearly practiced. The metal blackened quickly, and after a few slow pulls over the lighter, he released the trigger. Curving his lips into a tight circle, he blew a stream of air over the thin sheet of metal to cool it.

"Are you left or right handed?" he queried.

"Right," Hale answered.

"Please give me your left hand." Imanu'el extended his own left hand, palm up.

Hale willed his body to relax, and calmly extended his hand.

Imanu'el took Hale's hand in his own, turning it palm up. He lowered his right hand, razor pinched between his index and thumb. The razor hovered over Hale's flesh as Imanu'el rested his right hand on Hale's outstretched fingers.

. . . "None for me, thanks."

. . . . . . "It's on me. Make that two,

please." The man behind the

counter in the orange apron

pressing buttons on the register.

. . . . A man in a navy suit with an expensive-

looking tie smiled like a predator.

. . . . The man shook Imanu'el's

hand. The Washington monument stuck

out over his shoulder.

"Oh my God!" Cass exclaimed. "Hale, are you okay?"

Hale shook from his Wander and looked around. Cass was gripping his shoulder tightly, her eyes fixated on his hand. He followed her gaze and saw the source of her alarm. In the time he had been Wandering into Imanu'el's past, a small gash had been opened up on the palm of his left hand.

Pain welled along with blood as realized he'd been hurt.

Hale bit back the urge to yelp in surprise, managing simply to shift uncomfortably as he concentrated on pushing back the pain. Blood gathered into a small pool, alerting Hale that the depth of the wound was more than a superficial scratch.

Mental note, I don't feel pain while Wandering.

"Please remain calm," Imanu'el coached. He rolled his sleeve up over his own elbow, exposing the entirety of his forearm. His skin was pale and smooth, though what drew both Cass and Hale's collective attention were the two thin strips of gauze taped to his arm. One bandage was clean, the other exhibited a small stain of red blood as if to advertise the freshness of the wound.

The razor lowered to a new section of bare skin just below the bloody bandage. His flesh depressed at the application of the razor, but did not break. The skin seemed unwilling to relent to the sharp instrument.

Cass averted her eyes, pressing her cheek against Hale's shoulder as she looked away.

Hale remained transfixed. There was something odd happening. He had not borne witness to the infliction of his own wound, but he could imagine the ease with which the razor penetrated his skin. What he watched now was not what he surmised had occurred.

With a slow inhale, Imanu'el redoubled his efforts and pressed harder. The skin finally snapped around the tip of the razor and folded slowly around the blade. The instrument steadily split through his forearm, though not without concentrated effort. Imanu'el had to saw several times to get the razor to catch and sever the next portion of flesh.

Hale imagined the effort it would take to inflict a wound on one's self would be great, however there seemed to be an additional exertion of strength on top of the application of will. This wasn't easy for Imanu'el, physically or any other way, if his apparent struggles were to be believed.

Imanu'el's breath released in a rush as he finished the incision. He tossed the bloody razor onto the coffee table before cradling his injured arm. With a sense of urgency in his voice, he said, "Hold out your hand."

"Huh?" Hale balked. He wasn't sure what he was expecting, and now was overcome with a sudden wave of reluctance.

"Quickly." Imanu'el slid towards him on the couch. Blood pooled above his own wound. He pressed the skin on his arm to keep the blood from running.

"I'm going to be sick…" Cass stood and quickly maneuvered around the couch. Untrained in the art of the couch/bar bend to which Hale was so well practiced, Cass clipped her side on the jutting out wood as she hurried past. The thud drew Hale's attention up in time to see Cass stumble over the corner of the couch and fall to the floor in front of his bedroom door.

"Cass?!"

"Mr. Langston!"

Hale's attention darted back towards Imanu'el. The man's eyes pleaded for him to comply. The sweat beading on his brow and the tears brimming in his eyes reminded Hale of the lengths the man was going through to prove himself.

Hale pushed his hand forward.

With consent reaffirmed, Imanu'el maneuvered his arm over Hale's hand. He twisted at the shoulder, positioning his cut directly onto Hale's.

Their flesh touched. Their blood mingled.

. . . "No shit…" The predator in the suit gazed
   at his hand, an impressed smirk on his
   face.

                . . . . . . "–right about you."

215

. . . . a searing pain shot through
Imanu'el's ribs as laughter echoed in his
ears.

. . . . "Hot damn! He does bleed!" a voice shouted
as blood spurted from Imanu'el nose.

. . . . "–the fuc–" The latino man
yelled as Imanu'el pulled him to
his feet. Blood ran off both their
hands.

. . . . . . "Just a taste. I'm real thirsty…" Imanu'el's
skin was pulled taut over his bones. "Tio, come
on-"

. . . "–ckin broke, and you go through
this shit faster than anyone I–"

"Mr. Langston? Mr. Langston!"

Hale's eyes lazily rolled down to observe the source of the voice in front of
him. The world was distant, less real than the flurry of visions that had just
assaulted him. He wanted the voice to go away. It was a distraction. An annoyance.
A–

"Mr. Langston!" Imanu'el shouted.

"Wha–?" There was a fuzzy image of the man in white in front of him. Was
that concern on his face? Yes. Concern. Maybe panic. What could possibly be so
important? There were things to be sorted out. They didn't make sense yet. The
puzzle was laid out in pieces before him, and it was unsettling to leave them in such
disarray. If the voice would just shut up for a moment, surely he could properly
assemble them.

"Hale!" The shout was accompanied by a sharp slap across his jaw.

Hale reeled, the dreamlike world he had fallen into was pulled away
abruptly. The room came back into focus. Imanu'el was staring, a turbulent mix of

horror and wonder exuding from him. The man had ruined his outfit, as blood had trickled off his arm and onto his pristine white pants. Likewise his right cuff had been marred with splotches of red as the fabric touched his bloody hand.

"Yes, what?" Hale stuttered as he struggled to regain his conscious thoughts. "What's wrong?"

"You... I don't know." The panicked man breathed a hard exhale of relief. "You looked like you were having a seizure."

"Hale?" A wavering voice called out from the floor.

"Cass!" He shot up from his sitting position. The quick achievement of altitude was met with an equally fast descent back onto the couch. His legs apparently worked on a slower recovery time than his sight and hearing, and they were in no mood to humor his desire to remain standing. After realizing he was in no position to rush to her aid, he called out again. "Are you okay?"

"Yeah, fine," she groaned. "Pain seems to be a phenomenal counter to nausea. I'm going to have a hell of a bruise on my hip. What's happening up there?"

"I, uh..." He looked back to Imanu'el. The man in white seemed equally eager to hear an explanation. "Imanu'el put his arm on my han–" Hale looked at his hand as he spoke. The broad smear of drying blood was shocking enough, but what drew his true amazement was his wound. The fresh cut had not only clotted, but seemed to already have formed a thick scab.

"Mr. Langston?" Imanu'el prodded.

"Hand," Hale finished. "He put his cut on mine, and it... is it healing?" Hale looked back up to the man on his couch for confirmation.

Intrigue mirrored in their faces.

"Mr. Langston," said Imanu'el, clutching his arm tightly. "Might I trouble you for a towel?"

"Uh, shit, yeah. One sec." Hale gingerly rose to his feet. He leaned to and fro, testing his balance for a moment to ensure he did not end up on the floor. Satisfied that his legs had solidified past their jellified state, he hopped over the back of the couch and grabbed a roll of paper towels from the kitchen. Spinning the roll on his fingers he let loose a half a dozen sheets, tearing them off and tossing them into Imanu'el's lap.

He put the roll of towels on the bar. As Imanu'el cleaned himself, Hale took the opportunity to check on Cass. He slid through the gap and knelt down next to her prone form. "Hey, you okay?"

She lay curled into the fetal position. One hand pressed to her hip as if force would prevent the broken blood vessels from purpling her skin. The other arm curved up over her head, hiding her face. "I feel ridiculous."

Hale chuckled in spite of the situation. "Well, if it makes you feel any better, you are the lowest ranked contestant on the comedy of errors show for today."

"So what happened?" She kept her face covered as she spoke.

"Um," Hale looked at his hand again to confirm he hadn't been hallucinating. "Well..."

"I healed him." Imanu'el spoke from the couch. Hale returned his gaze to the preacher.

Imanu'el finished dabbing away the last of the wet blood on his hands and arm, pressing the remainder of the towels to his seeping wound. He turned to the two on the floor, careful not to lean on the armrest of the couch in fear of staining it. "As simply as I can describe it, the Lord has gifted me with the power to purify the flesh and blood of his children." He stood and walked around the couch, heading towards the kitchen as he spoke. "Your wound is already scabbed over. By tonight, it will be thick and rough scar. You will retain a small patch of rough skin over that spot for some time, though eventually it will go back to being as it was before today."

Hale stared in disbelief. It was a rare occasion when he was amazed. There was a magician who had accomplished the feat at his seventh birthday. He had performed a trick involving a signed card wildly jumping through the deck. The finale involved bending the card, placing it in the center of the deck, only for it to suddenly snap to the top right in front of his eyes, still bent. Hale had known even then there was a trick to it, but he had wanted to believe it was something more.

This was real.

Hale did not have to stretch his imagination. He did not have to suspend his disbelief. He had witnessed something truly spectacular. Whether it was magic, miracle, or mystery of science, he had watched a wondrous ability performed, and could not deny its grandeur.

Questions were already forming in his mind. Hale stared up at Imanu'el through the bar as the man in white scrubbed the blood from his hands and attempted to blot out the fresh stains on his clothing. He needed to know more about this man. More about what he could do. Maybe he had answers.

"Is it gone?" Cass' voice was low and flat, clearly embarrassed.

"Huh?" Hale broke away from his train of thought. "Is what gone?"

"The blood," she sighed, arm still covering her face. "I have a problem with blood. I kinda lose it. I figured I'd be okay in this situation because it was important. I was wrong."

Hale looked down at his bloody palm. "Um, no, one sec." He pushed himself up and sped into the bathroom. His mind raced over the past few minutes as he ran water and rubbed his hands under the faucet.

Okay, he cut my hand. Cass saw it even if I didn't. I felt no pain until after I Wandered, but the pain was definitely there when I snapped out of it. Dry it off, see if it is still bleeding. No. No it is not. It looks like the scab is days old already, and I don't feel a damn thing.

The skin is rougher, The Poet added. *Almost rubbery, just as he said.*

I believe we are overlooking something important here. The General chimed in.

I am missing something, but what is it? Something is off.

More than one thing. The General grumbled.

Perhaps his injury? The Poet offered. *There were several items demanding his attention at the creation of the wound and directly after.*

He was still bleeding even after I stopped. Hale felt his blood go cold. *No.*

No that doesn't make sense. How could his blood have healing properties when he was still bleeding after I was?!

Do not forget his bandages. The Poet added.

Why would he need them?!

I still think you're missing the important part here. The General chastised.

I need to see it to be sure.

Hale finished drying his hands, ensuring the blood was completely gone before he moved back into the living room. Cass lay still on the floor. Commodore watched her intently from his makeshift foxhole, his primary target still out of his sight in the kitchen.

"Okay, all gone." Hale knelt down next to her, lightly touching her arm.

Cass peered out from the crook of her arm as if to verify it was safe to venture out once more. She tentatively removed her arm from her face, allowing Hale to help her to her feet. Her fingers found her temples as she leaned against him for support. "Please don't make fun of me." She rubbed in a circular motion with her fingertips as she spoke into Hale's chest. Her voice still sounded defeated.

"Don't worry about it," he spoke calmly. "I think we both freaked out a bit. Consider me thankful that you tried to stick it out despite your phobia."

Cass just groaned in response, releasing her temples and wrapping her arms around his waist.

Hale kissed her on the side of her head, and then glanced over her shoulder into the kitchen.

Imanu'el stood there calmly, watching the two with a placid expression as he pressed fresh paper towels to his forearm. Aside from the minor red splotches on his pants and right cuff, he seemed just as serene as when he had arrived at the apartment.

"Mr. Langston," the man in white spoke softly. "Are you ready to continue?"

"I have questions," Hale stated.

"As do I."

17

The trio settled back in the living room with Hale on one end of the couch and Cass sitting on the armrest next to him. Imanu'el, still pressing a folded stack of paper towels to his forearm, sat quietly at the other end. Cass rested her arm on the back of the couch, hovering over Hale as she eyeballed their guest.

"May I begin?" Imanu'el asked.

"Actually, there's a couple things I need to know first," Hale said.

"Very well." Imanu'el focused his eyes on the floor, letting them gently close as he continued to place pressure on his arm. He was in a relaxed, almost meditative state, though he remained alert enough to answer Hale's questions when he asked.

"When did you learn you could do that?" Hale started, eyes drifting down to Imanu'el's arm.

"While an interesting story," Imanu'el responded softly. "It is hardly relevant in comparison to other questions both of us have. Perhaps we should delay the tale for a later time?"

Hale stopped for a second. "Fair enough."

"Why is your arm still injured?" Cass interjected.

Half comatose on the floor, and she still manages to notice the little details, Hale thought.

"Because I was cut," Imanu'el said flatly.

"That's very astute of you..." Annoyance dripped off her words. "But so was Hale. His cut is fine now, why isn't yours?"

"Good observation." Imanu'el nodded. He inhaled deeply through his nose, the serene expression and tone rejuvenating as he did so. "The Lord has gifted me with the power to heal his children. He has bestowed upon me the divine ability to knit flesh back together, mend wounds, and cleanse sickness from the body. This is not, however, a gift I may bestow without personal sacrifice.

"To exercise His divine right over life, I must sacrifice some of my own. I may assist in the nurturing and chirurgic treatment of my fellow man, though in doing so I will impose wounds upon myself that will not heal so easily. In fact, I would gauge that my own rate of healing is slower than that of a normal human being.

"It is my gift," Imanu'el said softly. "And the price is insignificant in the shadow of His favor."

"You can heal any injury?" Hale asked.

Imanu'el nodded. "I have performed this miracle a number of times on various types of wounds, all of which were cured in a short period of time." He took another steady breath and flexed the clamped fingers on his arm. "Might I venture a query?"

Hale knew what was coming. The chill that rushed through his body and landed in the pit of his stomach accompanied the realization. Reluctance brewed hesitation, though he managed a confident answer, "Yes."

Imanu'el nodded, eyes still downcast with their lids gently pulled over them. He took another slow, methodical breath before continuing. "How have you been Touched?"

"Funny enough," Hale chuckled. "I really don't have a good way to explain it yet."

"Please try," Imanu'el encouraged.

"Will do." Hale pursed his lips, preparing to speak when a tap from Cass pulled his attention.

She gave him a worried look, furrowing her brow and glancing at Imanu'el.

He shrugged, holding out his palm with the cut exposed as a retort to her non-verbal protest.

She pursed her lips, but made no other move to stop him from proceeding.

"Well…" Hale cleared his throat. "I, uh, see things."

"Go on." Imanu'el said, patiently.

Hale proceeded. The words, choppy at first, picked up momentum after he stumbled through the first few sentences. He found himself repeating many of the same stories he had shared with Cass the night before, finding additional comfort in the familiarity of the tales. It was easier than he had imagined. A week before he could not dream of sharing his darkest secret with another living soul, yet here he was, speaking freely and easily as if he was repeating a common anecdote.

Imanu'el remained silent and stoic as Hale regaled him with his past. Aside from the occasional furrow of his brow and the flex of his fingers, he remained motionless. Finally, when Hale finished, his eyes fluttered open and he faced his conversational partner once again.

"You have given me several examples of your 'Wandering'." Imanu'el spoke softly. "When was the last time you Wandered?"

He has shown you trust, The Poet whispered. *It is only right you return it in ki–*

STRONG DEFENSE! The General shouted over the Poet.

"When you showed me your gift," Hale replied.

The muscles in Imanu'el's face tightened, and his eyes flared for a brief moment before returning to his previous demeanor. "Really?"

"Yes. Once when you touched my hand to cut me." He stopped to relive the moment before attempting to describe it. "And the second time when your blood touched mine. It was… different. The images were much stronger than usual. I think I would have seen a lot more had I not been physically shaken out of it."

"What did you see?"

"The first time I saw you speaking with someone. I didn't recognize them." Hale closed his eyes, conjuring the images back up. "Navy suit, confident smile. You guys were getting drinks, I think. The second time, it was different, there–"

"Hale." Cass leaned forward, gripping Hale's shoulder for support. "I'm really not doing well…"

"Huh?" Hale spun to look at her.

Cass had her free hand pressed to her forehead. She was pale, and was leaning most of her weight on him just to keep upright.

"I'm sorry," she moaned. "Imanu'el, I hate to ask this, but could we postpone the rest of this conversation for later? I am really not feeling well."

"I…" Imanu'el balked, clearly flustered. His face flushed, shattering the serene image he had been maintaining. With concerted effort, he forced his objections back, settling on a more polite response. "Of course. If I could simply ask for the means by which to contact you in the future, Hale, I will excuse myself and allow you to tend to your lovely companion."

Hale pulled out his cell phone. "Do you have email, or a cell phone?"

Imanu'el gave him his email address.

"Alright, I've got you in here. I'll email you my phone number later tonight." Hale stuffed his phone back in his pocket. He stood and put his arm around Cass to support her. "Feel free to call me this week. We'll set up a time to meet."

"Of course." Imanu'el reluctantly stood. "It has been a pleasure meeting you both. I can show myself out." He maneuvered around the couch, crossed the entryway and quietly exited the apartment.

After the door clicked shut, Hale didn't even have time to open his mouth before Cass lifted her head and spoke. All pretensions of illness immediately drained away. "We need to talk."

Hale's eyes widened as Cass lithely stood from her perch on the couch and crossed the entryway to lock the door. She looked through the peephole to ensure Imanu'el had indeed left, then returned to find Hale as speechless as the couch he sat on.

"That guy is dirty," Cass said flatly.

"Wait…" Hale shook his head as if it would reboot his perspective. "You were faking being sick that whole time?"

"No, not at all." Cass slid down onto the opposite side of the couch where Imanu'el had just sat. "I am extremely hemophobic. The sight of blood makes me freak out, get sick, sometimes even lose consciousness. That whole lying on the floor thing was very real. Now, I may have dragged it out longer than it actually lasted to benefit our situation, but I was legitimately about to vomit all over your living room when I saw... eh, just pictured it again." Her face sunk into her hands.

Hale looked at the door, wondering if it was too late to run after Imanu'el.

"What did you see?" Cass asked, her voice muffled by her hands.

"I think I should go get him," Hale ventured.

"Wait." Cass' tone was one of warning. "If you tell him everything now, you can't take it back. If you wait 24 hours, you can still tell him everything, but at least we'll have some time to talk this through. We're both emotional right now. That was the strangest thing either of us has ever witnessed... I hope. All I'm saying is it would be beneficial to take a step back and look at this objectively before you commit to anything with the messiah."

Hale settled back into the couch, teeth clenched in frustration as he mentally wrestled his options. "I don't want you to be right, but I can't deny your reasoning." He grudgingly sat back, getting comfortable. "So what now?"

Cass straightened herself. She took a few breaths to regain her composure, allowing the blood to flow and bring some color back to her already pale skin. "First, tell me what you saw."

"The first or second time?"

"The first one," Cass said adamantly.

"Do you know something I don't?" Hale eyed her.

"Yes, and I'll be more than happy to share it with you," she promised. "Just trust me on this, you won't want to hear it until after you've recounted what you Wandered into."

Hale's curiosity was piqued. Placing his trust in her as she asked, he delved back into his memories to bring back as many details as possible. "Two guys... one of them in a navy suit with a sleazy car salesman smile. The second one was

Imanu'el, I think. Guy behind a counter serving drinks… orange apron, messed up hair… Then they were outside shaking hands." Hale's eyes opened as he remembered an interesting detail. "The Washington monument was right behind the guy in the suit. They must have been in D.C.!"

"D.C.? Interesting." Cass' eyebrows shot up. Thoughts raced behind her eyes for a few moments before she visibly forced herself to return to the topic at hand. "We'll come back to that. When you've Wandered in the past, what's the longest period of time between the event you witnessed and the time you Wandered into it?" Cass asked inquisitively.

"Um…" Hale furrowed his brow while he thought. "I can't be sure. I don't know all of the people or events that I Wander into, so I don't have a good frame of reference."

"Let's go through some of the ones you do know about," Cass suggested. "You Wandered into several conversations between Sue, Phill, and me, right?"

"Right," Hale confirmed.

"Go through them for me."

"Let's see." Hale counted off on his fingers. "There was Sue and Phill talking about the date, including her begging you to do it. Sue and you talking as you got ready… I like vanilla perfume better too, by the way."

Cass blushed over a hidden smile.

"There was the time Sue ended up crying on your shoulder, and…" Hale hesitated, remembering the last one regarding Cass. "The time you were in your car, the phone call."

Cass nodded in affirmation, unable to hide the lines of tension in reaction to his words. She forced out words, attempting to move away from the awkward subject into something more familiar: analytics. "Okay, I know you Wandered into all of those except the crying one… Sue crying," she quickly corrected, her cheeks flushed. Even an accidental allusion to his vision of her in her car was enough to make her uncomfortable. She took a breath, centering herself.

"Do you want to talk about anything?"

"No," she said quickly, returning to the previous subject. "So I know you Wandered into all three of those on the day we met. Sue had set up the date the night before, the pre-date meeting was obviously the same day, and the, um, phone call you witnessed was a few days before. That suggests you only Wander into information that is recent, maybe within 72 hours from the event."

"Sometimes," Hale nodded. "I've also Wandered into other things that seem a lot older. Like my boss at his son's funeral, and this author I met talking to her husband before the book even came out. Those could have been weeks, months, even years old."

"I... huh." Cass put on her intuitive face, pursing her lips and furrowing her brow. She remained silent and stoic for a few moments, and then began brainstorming out loud. "You told me you Wandered due to various stimuli, correct?"

"Right," Hale confirmed. "Sometimes it's touching something, catching a smell, hearing a voice."

"What if different stimuli have different, um, timelines? Is that the right word?"

"I don't think they have a word for this."

"You realize this is not scientifically possible." Cass stubbornly crossed her arms, attempting to deny the variation to reality she had just presented.

"I don't make the rules." Hale shrugged.

"Let's continue disregarding the basic laws of biochemistry for a moment." She donned her intuitive face once again. "Tell me the last thing you remember doing when you Wandered into the information with the date stuff and the phone call."

"You realize my memory is not that great, right?" Hale protested.

"Hale, we're not having sex again until my curiosity on this is satisfied." She arched an eyebrow.

"See, that's all I need." Hale held out his hands, palms forward. "A little motivation, nothing to get overly excited about."

She gave a wry grin.

"Fuck, let me think." Hale pinched the bridge of his nose, sifting through his memories to zero in on the information Cass requested. "The first one was off a dollar Phill handed me, that showed me him and Sue. The second one, you and Sue before the date, was off the smell of your perfume. The phone call was when we were in the car. I leaned my face against the headrest right before it happened."

Cass nodded. "And when Sue cried on my shoulder?"

"We were, uh…" Hale grinned at the thought. "Getting touchy feely on the couch."

Cass seemed to disregard Hale's giddiness. "All four of those triggered from some sort of tactile or olfactory sense. Yet you're saying the ones set off by hearing something seemed to be older?"

"It's a guess, but yeah." Hale didn't want to make a committal response. *How am I supposed to know how long ago Ockie's son died, or when a conversation happened between a husband and wife regarding a book's ending?*

"That at least gives us something to go off of." She looked him in the eyes. "Anything else?"

Hale remembered the clarity of his most recent visions. "The blood!"

"That's right, you were starting to mention that when I interrupted. What happened?"

"It was unreal." Hale's eyes widened as he spoke, in awe over the memory. "I can normally tell my Wanders are around the same timeframe. I usually get multiple flashes of events, but it's obvious they are part of one conversation, or part of a series of consecutive events.

"This was different. Real different." Hale stressed the words. "These all seemed to be from very different times, different places, involving different people. And it was clear. Like IMAX HD vivid, it was insane."

"What did you see?"

"I saw the same guy in the navy suit. He was looking at his hand all impressed about something." Hale glanced at his own palm. "I can only guess he was given a similar performance."

"You also saw him when Imanu'el touched you, and he had fresh wounds still bandaged up on his arm." Cass verbally put the pieces together. "So that corroborates our assessment of your time windows since this must have happened recently."

"He mentioned something about 'being right about him'. I only caught the end of the memory before it flashed to something else, so it's out of context."

"Let's move onto the next one," Cass urged.

"The next one was a little… violent," Hale warned. He ran over the memory once more before continuing on. "Imanu'el was on the ground, curled up on his side. There were people laughing around him, and he was clutching his ribs. It felt like he was in pain, like his ribs were cracked. Then it switched to him bleeding from his nose while someone shouted that 'he does bleed', like they were all surprised. Then it flashed to him lifting someone else up off the ground. They were all wearing jumpsuits… maybe maintenance or janitorial gear? Anyway, the guy on the ground looked like he was in pain, and blood was running off both of their hands."

Cass looked a little green.

"Something else." Hale leaned forward. "Did you see him cut my hand?"

"Yes." Cass shifted uncomfortably.

"See, I didn't. Apparently when I Wander I'm completely oblivious to the real world. I didn't even feel the pain until I came back. Did he have a lot of problems cutting me?"

"No," she responded shortly. Her fingers lifted to rest on her lips for a moment as she cleared her throat. "It took maybe a couple seconds and it was done."

"I figured." Hale looked down, scrutinizing the events he witnessed. "When he cut his hand, it seemed like it was a lot of effort. I mean, sure he was cutting his own flesh, which has got to be difficult, but it was like cutting through rubber–"

Cass jumped up from her chair and stumbled into Hale's room, taking a sharp right after clearing the doorway to head into the bathroom. Commodore shrieked as she passed, cluing Hale in that Cass had not been too careful where she was stepping.

"Cass?" Hale asked tentatively from the couch, staring after her through the empty doorframe.

The sounds of vomiting emanated from his bathroom.

"Right," Hale said quietly. "Probably should have cut back on the vivid imagery for that one." He stood from the couch and timidly walked into his room, looking through the second doorway at the redhead kneeling in front of his toilet.

She breathed heavily, elbows resting on the toilet seat so both hands could support her head and keep her hair pulled away from her face. Her skin had paled a shade, giving her an almost corpselike pallor.

"I'm really sorry," Hale ventured.

"Keep going." Her voice was uneven, and her breathing still heavy, though the conviction in her voice was undeniable.

"Maybe we should take a break–"

"This isn't going to make sense to you yet, but I need to know. Give me details." Cass leaned her head back, hair tumbling back over her shoulders. She balled up a wad of toilet paper, wiping it across her mouth before unceremoniously tossing it into the bowl. "Please, just keep going. Just turn your back if I get sick again."

"I'm going to trust that you aren't just being a masochist, and rather there's something I'm just not getting here."

"Please." Cass rested her head on her hands again, peering up at him through a few rogue strands of hair that veiled her face.

"Alright." He took a deep breath. "All I was saying was that his skin seemed really... eh, solid? Is that a good word?"

"Resilient?"

"Better word."

"Thank you." The toilet bowl created an odd resonance to her voice.

"The last one was him talking to someone. He looked… sick. Real sick." Hale furrowed his brow. "He said something about getting a taste and being thirsty."

"He looked strung out?" Cass asked.

"Yeah, all thin and–"

"Like 'druggie' strung out?"

"Yeah," Hale said slowly. "Just like that. I saw a movie once where they referred to heroine junkies as being 'thirsty'. You think it could be that?"

"Probably," Cass rolled back off her heels and sat on the tile floor wiping her mouth with her hand before leaning back against the wall. She tilted her head back and closed her eyes again.

"There was a fragment of a response. It sounded angry, screaming about him being broke or something."

"Couldn't pay for a fix?"

"Sounds like it." Hale nodded. "Also something about him going through heroin, or whatever it was, faster than anyone else."

Cass breathed calmly through her nose, color slowly returning to her cheeks. "What else?"

"That was the last of it." Hale slid down the bathroom doorway to sit near her. "Can I bring you anything? Water, soda, bread?"

"Laptop."

"Listen, you're awesome and all, but you're not eating my laptop." Hale grinned in attempt to make light of the situation.

"Don't worry, they'll have food on the plane."

"The wha–?"

"The plane." Cass repeated. She lowered her head to look Hale straight in the eyes. "We're going to D.C."

18

Hale looked at Cass incredulously. An uncomfortable chuckle attempted to signal the joke was up, returning to a disbelieving smile when she did nothing but stare back up at him. She remained motionless as he went through his bevy of visible reactions, as if waiting for the sincerity of her declaration to sink in.

"You're serious." He broke the silence by converting a question into a statement.

"As a death sentence," she confirmed, a grim smirk creeping to her lips.

"Wh—" He cut off his own flurry of questions in an effort to provide his own answers. After a few moments spent wracking his brain, he realized he had failed at following her logic, and instead only succeeded at remaining frozen with his lips curved into a 'Wh–' sound. Fortunately for his lips, they did not have to move to continue where he left off. "Why is this so important? I mean, that's a big trip to make on a whim!"

"Yes and no. However, if you bring me your laptop, I will nonetheless reserve two tickets so we can go."

"Cass." Hale held his hands out, keeping a supportive smile as he changed his tone. "We can't just fly to D.C. It's Sunday. I have work tomorrow."

"You're a journalist who doesn't work weekends. They can miss you for a few days."

"That–" Hale stopped himself mid-sentence to take a breath and collect himself. She was right. "Seriously, that's more by choice. It's a cut in pay, but I like my job much better."

Cass smiled at him, her head lazily leaning against the wall. "I wasn't attempting to belittle your competency, merely stating a fact. If you're not working

232

weekends, chances are a local newspaper can afford to miss you for a few days, am I right?"

Hale pursed his lips.

"Alright, so you take a couple vacation days and fly out to our nation's capital on my flyer miles." She gave a weak smile, the bathroom antics clearly having taken their toll. "And as a stipulation to our trip, I promise to answer those questions that have gone unanswered. It will also help explain why I am so adamant about not only going, but bringing you with."

Hale continued to look over her as he thought the matter through. She looked physically weak from exertion, yet the words that came from her were laden with confidence and conviction. She was sure that this was the right thing to do.

And you do have over two weeks of vacation time, The Poet reminded him.

Let's not forget R&R in the hotel room with a new lady friend, The General sounded off.

You two are not helping, Hale admonished his own internal voices.

Yes we are, They said in unison.

Aren't you supposed to be giving me perspective from multiple sides?

I say we drop this 'sides' nonsense for once and sue for peace, The General chuckled.

Pacifist pussy, The Poet murmured.

That's my line!

With a defeated sigh, Hale said, "I better get some good answers." He leaned forward to kiss her on the forehead, then stood and went to retrieve his laptop.

———

"No no, Ockie. Everything is fine," Hale assured him over the phone. "I just need to cash in on a couple vacation days. I'll be back by Thursday, and I'll put in some hours this coming weekend to help out with the Sunday edition." Hale gave a comical glare at Cass before returning back to the call. "Definitely. Thanks again for the understanding."

Cass laid sideways in her seat, watching Hale as he tossed his phone on the dashboard.

"Your boss seems nice," she commented.

"You have no idea," Hale grinned. "He's an awesome guy, great with people, and fun as hell to work for." His wide grin faded a bit as he remembered Wandering into Ockie's son's funeral. The source of Mr. Ockerman's leniency towards Hale tumbled back to him.

"My boss is highly effective, not so much with the nice."

"How so?"

"You ever see that show Hell's Kitchen?" she asked.

Hale chuckled. "Gordon Ramsey kicking trash cans and screaming into people's faces? I love that show."

"I smell a streaming marathon," she smiled. "Anyway, he's like Ramsey. Not yelling all the time, mind you, but he doesn't shy away from confrontation, and he is not afraid to tell you if you're screwing up. On a good note, just like our favorite chef with anger management issues, he will give you glowing feedback when you've done well."

"Well, at least when he gives you a compliment you know you really earned it," Hale offered. "He's not just trying to make you feel better."

"That's true. Still, there are days where my head is just not in the game, and I really could do without the berating."

"Being berated on normal days is fine?" Hale grinned.

"Well, duh!" Cass stuck her tongue out at him. "Brat."

"Yeah," he smiled. With a brief glance around to get his bearings, he continued. "Are we getting near your place? I'm not too familiar with Irvine."

"One more street, then make a right," she directed.

They navigated through the streets until they pulled up to the gate of the Playa Norte apartments. Hale didn't hide his gawking as Cass waved to the guard and flashed her resident ID card. The apartments featured two towers, each at least fifteen stories high. Floor to ceiling glass windows were present on almost every story, and an Olympic size pool with a neighboring tennis court sat neatly between the two buildings. The gates slid open, forcing Hale to stop from staring out the windshield so he could drive.

"This is ridiculous!" he exclaimed comically.

"Jealous?" Cass arched an eyebrow.

"Yes!" He maneuvered down the small street towards the underground parking garage. "How much do you fricken make to be able to afford this?"

"Enough. They're not as expensive as you may think."

"I'm thinking over two grand a month for a one bedroom, at least."

"Well," Cass shrugged, suddenly a little bashful. "Yes."

"I'm not even close, am I?"

"Right over there, that's my guest spot." She pointed, sidestepping his question.

"This is ridiculous," Hale repeated softly.

He pulled into the spot as directed, throwing his car into park. He donned a playful smile as they exited the vehicle. Cass, giving a modest blush, noted the look.

"What?" she asked.

"Oh, nothin'." He sidled up next to her, putting his arm around her waist as they walked. "So, do you usually drive to work, or do you use the helipad?"

"Shut up." She hid a grin as she jabbed him in the ribs, the redness in her cheeks spreading up to her ears. "I'm not going to let you make me feel guilty for doing well for myself."

"No, not at all." He gave a satisfied sigh. "I am just glad to know that I can retire early if we start to get serious."

"I will hurt you," she warned.

"That's the second time in 24 hours you've threatened bodily harm on me."

"I'm small, but that just means the aggression is condensed down into a more pure, volatile form." She prodded him again. "Don't test me."

"Yes ma'am."

The two shared a laugh, linked at the waist as they walked towards the elevator. After a short trip down to the ground floor in the glass walled transport, they exited the parking garage and made their way to the Western Tower. Cass waved her badge across the security panel, receiving a pleasant beep and a flash of green light, followed by the click of the front door admitting the pair entrance. Hale opened the door for her, bowing like a humble servant as she passed by. She returned the gesture with a wry grin and another poke to his ribs. Laughing, he scooped her up from behind and carried her across the threshold.

"You're fun." She said with a smile, wrapping her arms around his neck for support.

"I try." He returned her smile, and then leaned in for a kiss.

They stood there enjoying the moment. Suspended in his arms, enveloped in their kiss, the rest of the world seemed to fade into the background. No more luxurious towers. No more bleeding prophets. No more spontaneous vacations. No more intrusive friends.

"No more!" a voice scolded.

The two pulled away from each other, the outburst jolting them out of their oasis.

"No more!" the voice repeated.

Looking over, Hale and Cass saw an elderly woman trodding down the hallway towards them.

"You no do that here!" She continued to reprimand them, swatting at the air near them as if to shoo them away. "You have privacy room! You use privacy!"

Hale released Cass' legs, letting her slide back down into a standing position. She grinned back up at him, "I give you credit for trying to have a sweet moment."

"I appreciat–"

"Go now!" The woman barked.

"Jesus Christ." Hale walked through the lobby with Cass to get away from the old harpy, migrating them towards the elevators. "Fucking PDA Nazis must have a headquarters here."

"They've actually changed PDA from Public Displays of Affection to Parental Disobedience in Action. It's very sad."

The old woman followed their movements with a scowl even as they gained distance. Hale returned her stare with a glare of his own, narrowing his eyes to reflect her animosity in a mocking, comical fashion.

The elevator sounded its arrival. Cass ushered Hale through the open doors, breaking his staring contest with the old woman, who was now wagging her finger to accentuate her angry glare.

"You were antagonizing her." Cass mocked her disapproving grin.

"She had it coming." He pointed at the closing doors to reference the woman out in the hall. "Did you see the way she was dressed?"

Cass punched him in the shoulder. "If you would have said 'she only had herself to blame' you would have gotten a kiss instead of a punch."

He pulled her in for another kiss. When she was in his arms and he could feel the warmth of her skin under his hands, and feel the softness of her mouth, he lost time.

When they pulled away she looked up at him with a content smile. "I'm not usually this affectionate. What did you do to me?"

"I'm a hopeless romantic," Hale admitted, returning the smile. "Maybe it's just rubbing off on you."

They continued to beam at each other for another few moments before the elevator signaled their arrival. The doors slid open, and the pair walked arm in arm into the hallway.

"So this entire floor is yours, right?" Hale ventured.

An elbow jutted into his side and he released her arm to get some distance between the two of them, still donning a mischievous smirk. "Ah! Sorry! Just kidding." A few seconds of silence bridged the gap between his next comment. "So this floor and the few above it, then?"

Had there been an old woman to scold them, she would have been given plenty of ammo. The pair arrived at Cass' door giggling. Hale relented from his mockery of her income after Cass found a ticklish spot. Realizing he had lost any advantage from physical size, he admitted defeat and resumed a peaceful escort to her door.

The door opened to her apartment. Like Hale's, a kitchen was immediately to the right. Unlike Hale's, the living room was spacious, including a dining area to the immediate left past the entryway. Hale took steps inside with a look of awe on his face.

"Holy shit." He moved past the leather sofa and glass coffee table, stopping just before the windows.

"That's where I can gaze down at the masses of plebs begging for bread." Cass moved through the dining room to her bedroom.

"Hey!" Hale looked back at her. "How come I–"

"I can make fun of myself. I'm allowed."

"Something isn't fair about this," he protested.

"Oh, don't worry, you'll get over the whole 'equality' thing soon enough."

Hale chuckled, staring out over the city of Irvine. He heard Cass packing up a suitcase in her room as he watched traffic speed by the main road. "You do have a really nice place," he called out over his shoulder.

"Thanks," she responded. "And all jokes aside, I really do work my ass off to afford this place."

"I'm sure you do," he said sincerely. "I just like giving you shit."

Minutes passed. Hale watched the sun dip down over the horizon. He couldn't see the ocean from this elevation, in place of its beauty the sky lit up with a pleasant hue of pink, illuminating the few clouds in the sky with a dark tint. The landscape of Irvine was amusing. There were trees, bushes, and flowers, though all were carefully engineered to fit in with the surrounding structures. There were no open fields in sight. No empty lots. Everything was developed, groomed, and beautifully maintained to fit in with the image of perfection the city enjoyed projecting.

    . . . Cass walked past the window, deep in

      thought.

        . . . . . . "–evening was derailed on

        Monday, and my week–"

"Hey," Cass called out.

Gauging from her tone, it was not the first time she had called out. He turned around, "Yeah?"

"Wandering?" She asked.

"Sorry," he said, feeling sheepish. Wandering while in her home seemed like an invasion of privacy, like he had been rifling through her drawers while she was away. "If it makes you feel any better, I think it was just about you calling me the other night. So nothing I didn't already know. Uh, I'm not trying to snoop, I mean."

She eyed him for a moment, looking more intrigued than offended. Finally, she broke the stillness in the room. "Our flight is in three hours. We should go."

———

"I'D LIKE to point out that liquids do not show up on metal detectors, either," Cass fumed.

"Huh?" Hale walked through the terminal alongside Cass as she ranted.

"They confiscate a thirty two dollar bottle of makeup because it was over three ounces of liquid."

"Right, cause the whole terrorists trying to smuggle liquid explosives onto planes thing."

"Except for the fact that metal detectors do not pick up liquids, explosive or no."

"Can you, uh, keep your voice down?" Hale looked around nervously.

Cass continued on as if uninterrupted. "Which means I could put many ounces of whatever liquid I choose on my person." She counted off on fingers with her free hand. "Pockets, jacket, taped to my body, etc."

"Seriously, maybe just a few notches," Hale whispered to her, putting his hand on the small of her back. He kept his eyes on a mother covering her child's ears. The woman fixated her stare on the pair walking by.

"You know," Cass continued in a huff, "Benjamin Franklin once said that 'He who would sacrifice liberty for security will receive neither'."

"Yeah, and while I agree with the sentiment, Mr. Franklin didn't live in an era with nuc–" He paused, doing a quick look around before lowering his voice back to a whisper. "Nuclear weapons, either."

"You're not wrong," she conceded before launching into a new point. "And I don't necessarily disagree with the enhanced security precautions; I just disagree with the shoddy implementation. If they're going to make rules that inconvenience people, at least make them effective."

"If you like, I'll help you write an angry yet well-composed letter to your congressman about it."

"I just want my MAC back," Cass pouted.

Hale grinned and kissed her on the temple. "Make you a deal. If you cut all the terrorist talk, I'll buy you a new bottle of whatever that stuff was."

"Face and Body Foundation," she grumbled. "But I'd like to say I'm still frustrated due to the principle."

"Duly noted."

She nuzzled into him as they walked, letting go of the rant.

Hale held her close as they walked, smiling at the situation. "You're kinda funny, you know that?"

"Because of my ineffectual outrage at inadequate security systems?"

"Partially. It's just that 90% of the time you are this confident, cutthroat, and decisive woman, and then you go into these cute little phases where you are all soft and adorable."

"I'm going to take that as a compliment so I don't have to disembowel you in front of airport security," she said with a smile, still nuzzled into his shoulder.

"Thank God for TSA."

The pair continued to move through the airport, navigating past the various terminals and airport shops. Hale chuckled at the $14 'value meals' featured in various fast food restaurants as they passed. Cass grumbled about whether they limited customers to 3 oz drinks.

They arrived at their gate. Joining the other passengers in the waiting area of the terminal, they took a seat and waited for the boarding announcement to sound.

. . . "–going to miss you."

. . . . . . the couple embraced tightly,

tears running down their cheeks.

"Hey spaceman." Cass poked him.

Jerking out of the Wander, his eyes darted over to her. "Sorry," he said instinctively.

"Nothing to be sorry about." She looked at him with curious eyes. "What did you see?"

"A couple crying into each others' shoulders. Looked like a tearful goodbye."

"Odd... unless maybe they were getting on different planes," Cass hypothesized. At Hale's questioning look, Cass clarified. "There's no way anyone but a ticketed passenger would get back this far. And for someone to be having a tearful goodbye, it suggests they are not getting on the same plane."

"True," Hale nodded. "That's part of my gift, I guess. Limited information, limitless questions. I'm fairly curious by nature, too, so it drives me crazy sometimes."

"You'd think that would be driven out of you by now." Cass dug through her purse for some gum. "After having to let matters drop for so long, you'd just learn to stop questioning things."

"Nah, I'm no quitter."

Cass grinned, offering him a stick before taking one for herself.

The floor to ceiling windows of the Los Angeles International terminal provided an open view of the runway and taxi lanes. The pair stared out, watching planes maneuver past each other, jockeying for position until they were on the final strip. When in position, the planes would pause to radio into the control tower and do their final checks, after which the giant aluminum avians would jet forward, lift their noses and coast into the sky.

Hale fidgeted.

Cass noticed the twitch. "You've flown before, right?"

"Yeah," Hale nodded confidently. He pulled his lips together, shattering the confident image. "Once, actually. I was seven. My grandmother died. We flew out to make her funeral. I don't have any abject fear of it or anything, but I'm not a huge fan of it."

She nodded, looking down.

Hale noted the evasive gesture. "And you…?"

Her smile faced the floor. "A bunch of times, actually." She lifted her gaze to meet his. "I flew a lot when I was a kid, and a bunch of times on business with my company. So I'm used to it, I suppose. I just get a little freaked out during takeoff and landing."

"Define freaked out," Hale said with a smirk.

"Usually just some tension," she said with an unconvincing nod. "Well… no, lots of tension. I usually have a few drinks and a pill before I board. Sometimes I hyperventilate, but I've only cried once." She flushed at the sudden admission. "Why did I tell you that? It was a really odd occurrence. So… yeah."

In an attempt to relieve Cass of her embarrassment, Hale shifted topics. "So you promised some answers on this trip. Do you want to just start somewhere, or should I begin peppering you with questions?"

The intercom crackled. "*Attention all passengers for Flight 1271, nonstop to*

Washington D.C., we are now boarding Group 4 . Now boarding Group 4 for Flight 1271 to DC. Thank you."

Cass looked up at the speaker on the ceiling, then across to Hale with masked relief on her face. "Looks like we're up."

19

The crowd filed through the jetway, inching forward as the passengers at the head of the line stowed their baggage and wedged themselves into their designated seat. Hale watched faces, expressions, and body language. He was amused at the non-verbal behavior people communicated when forced into close proximity with other human beings. It was reminiscent of a course he took back in college.

Next time you get into an elevator, his teacher had lectured, *take a look at everyone around you. Unless you're in a bigger city where these situations are now commonplace, the occupants will have their hands in their pockets, clasped at their waist, and might even be physically leaning away from the nearest person. Eyes are generally downcast, fixated on the ceiling, or watching the numbers as they count towards their destination. This is because people's personal space is being threatened. The forced close proximity of others is socially awkward to them, causing them to act unnatural until their comfort level has been restored.*

Hale's eyes canvassed over his fellow passengers, stopping when he reached Cass. She was the picture of discomfort with her carryon bag clutched with both hands, her gaze cast down to the floor. Her mind may have been wandering, with cheeks still pink from their previous conversation, but her eyes were wide and alert. He cocked an eyebrow at his observation, but said nothing.

Shuffling along the raised walkway with the rest of the line, Cass remained silent. The few times she looked at Hale she found him looking down at her with a comforting smile. She only gave a half-hearted grin and quickly looked away. The evasion was obvious, however Hale wasn't going to let her drag him across the country without holding up her end of the deal.

The pair crossed over the end of the jetway and into the plane where Hale had to walk sideways to avoid slamming the shins of the gentleman in 1B with his laptop. Shimmying past row after row of seats, Hale and Cass made their way to their section. Leading the way, Cass was the first to stop when they arrived.

Hale looked at the row. "The emergency row?"

Cass gave him a sideways glance as she threw her bag into the overhead cabin. "Yeah?"

"I don't know, seems kind of weird to sit there, doesn't it?"

"I paid extra to get a seat here." She slid into the window seat, stretching out her legs. "See? More legroom."

Hale stopped for a moment, pulling his lips down as he gave an impressed nod. "Fair enough." He joined her, plopping down in the middle seat. With a practiced motion he swung his laptop bag atop his knees and began to free the computer.

"Uh uh, not yet." She put her hand on the laptop pocket to halt his progress. "Not until after takeoff. You'll get scolded by the nice woman in uniform."

"Aww," Hale protested, looking for a place to shove the bag under the seat in front of him.

"Nope." Cass leaned on her hand, grinning. "No storage in this row. Gotta go up top."

Hale turned to her, clutching the bag to his chest. With a comical look of horror he said, "If anything happens to my baby, I'll never forgive you."

Still grinning, she replied, "Well, I'll pray the fates aren't against me."

Hale stood, noticing there was a solid wall of people blocking the aisle. He moved out a foot, trying to get to the overhead bin from underneath.

"Watch it!" A man in the aisle warned as he leaned back sharply to avoid collision.

"Sorry." Hale pulled the bag back to his waist, realizing another attempt with a less perceptive passenger in the aisle may have resulted in a concussion.

The man inched past, giving a wary look to Hale as he did.

"Excuse me," Hale smiled at the next person in line, pushing himself out into the fray. He received a bitter grumble, to which he responded. "Trust me, the line is going slow enough you won't even realize I'm here."

Upon closer examination, the overhead bin was near full, and he didn't have the desire to shove his breakable computer between two travel-hardened suitcases. Giving a longing look to the front where he had seen a coat closet, he realized the multitude of growls and grimaces he would receive by making people move out of his way. Admitting defeat, he slid back into his seat, placing the bag between his legs.

"You're gonna get yelled at," Cass warned in a childlike pitch.

"Actually," Hale raised a finger triumphantly, then pulled the blanket out from behind him. With a few quick shakes, the fabric unfurled around his legs, covering his bag from view. "Voila!"

Soft applause came from the window seat.

He smiled, leaning back and resting his hands on the armrests.

. . . the man gripped the armrests,

knuckles turning white.

. . . . . . sweat beaded on his forehead.

His hands shook as they held a

white bag.

. . . . moans of disgust and protest erupted

as the man vomited repeatedly.

Hale came back to himself, wide eyed and transfixed on the seat in front of him. He exhaled a held breath, blinking a few times to begin the process of collecting himself.

"You look… green," Cass said hesitantly.

"Sorry." Hale took a deep breath. "No offense, but I think this is going to be the last trip I take on a plane for awhile."

"Makes sense," Cass said quietly. "Emotions run high here. What was it this time?"

"Someone who looked greener than me, let's leave it at that."

"Fair enough."

"Speaking of, what do I look like when I Wander?"

"I wondered when you were going to ask that," she grinned. "I've been watching whenever I think you're doing it, which is why I've checked after each one to make sure it was what I was seeing."

"Makes sense."

"It honestly changes each time." She kept her voice low as she described it, realizing Hale was getting increasingly anxious as the conversation went on. To keep their words private, she leaned in closer to speak. "At my apartment, you had a relaxed expression on your face when you looked out the window, except towards the end when you bit at your lower lip. I did that when we talked, by the way."

Hale blushed, suddenly embarrassed for a reason he could not place.

"Out in the terminal you got this sad look on your face. Your lip pouted out a little, but other than that it was completely unnoticeable. Had you not briefed me, I would have assumed I just misread your expression."

"And this last one?"

"You looked kinda horrified."

Hale chuckled. "Yeah, that fits."

The two sat quietly for a bit. Hale people watched, noting the expressions on faces as they moved by. An elderly man with a scowl permanently affixed to his face. A woman with a small child, no older than four. The child seemed just as interested in Hale as he was in them, as she gave a toothy grin and waved. Amused, Hale smiled and waved back. The next in line was a grumbling man in a sharp suit. He fumbled with his bag, shoving it between two larger suitcases in the overhead bin across from Hale, then sat down in the seat directly opposite from them. He proceeded pushing buttons on his Blackberry, ignoring the world around him.

Eventually everyone was seated and the flight attendants went to work. Two of them stood at different intervals in the plane, giving a safety demonstration to their attentive audience, while the rest made their routine checks. They moved quickly up the aisles, smiling and correcting problems as they saw them. They reached the emergency exit rows that Hale and Cass occupied, finding the businessman still at work on his phone.

"Sir, you'll have to turn that off until we are in the air," the attendant said. Her blonde hair was neatly pressed straight, pulled back over her shoulders. The smile she wore was professional and courteous, however gave no implication of being truly friendly. Her tone conveyed authority, and the expression above her row of pearly whites stated clearly that this was not something to be argued.

The man looked up from his phone with an annoyed expression, ready to challenge the order to relinquish his device. His determination quickly faded at the glint of challenge in her eye, to which he gave a mumbled apology and stuffed his phone in his jacket.

"Ya know," Hale said, leaning into Cass. "I'd have paid good money to see him throw a fit, only to have her Indiana Jones him right out of the plane."

"I think that's why they take so long loading luggage," Cass offered. "Just in case a passenger gets uppity."

They grinned at each other.

"Ladies and gentlemen, thank you for flying with us. We're going to begin our taxi out to the runway, after which we will begin our nonstop flight to Ronald Reagan airport. Flight attendants, prepare for takeoff."

The plane jerked as it backed away from the jetway. Cass immediately tensed, hands sliding around the end of the armrests to both sides, gripping them as if to hold herself in her seat.

Hale made a mental note of the similarity of her actions to his last Wander. Watching over her for the following minutes did little to differentiate her mannerisms from the memory he had stumbled upon. Unwilling to let Cass succumb too deeply to her fear, he decided to distract her. "So, where are we staying when we get to DC?"

"Uh, hotel," she answered absently, eyes focused out the window.

"Figured as much, unless you have a summer home you haven't been telling me about." Hale leaned in, trying to pull her attention away. "Which hotel?"

"The airport," she muttered.

"I don't think they have rooms at the airport."

Cass remained fixated on the runway as the plane curved out onto its starting point.

"Figures," Hale scoffed. "I knew this trip was a stupid idea."

"Wha–?" Cass pulled away from the window to risk a glance at Hale.

"Here I am, ready to fly across country with a girl I barely know." He flopped his hands down in defeat. "And for what? Some answers to questions that will either be completely evaded, or answered half-heartedly?"

"What the hell is that supposed to mean?" Cass pulled her eyebrows in, jaw jutting forward as his words cut into her.

"I think you know damn well what it means," Hale snapped, raising his voice slightly as the whine of the engines rose up to a crescendo, but not loud enough to draw the stewardess' attention. "You dragged me out here under false pretenses."

"Excuse me?!" Cass straightened in her seat.

"All this crap about giving me answers about your family, and assuring me I would know exactly why it was imperative to rush across the country on a whim." Hale shook his head, curling his lips in disgust. "I haven't figured out your ulterior motive yet, but it's clear by now that you have one!"

"You self-centered prick!" She exclaimed. Several heads turned to watch the drama unfold. Engines roared in the background, pushing the plane forward with a steady acceleration. "You know damn well my family is a difficult subject for me. Either that or you are completely dense. Don't you think I might just have trouble talking about it, especially in this environment?"

"That's a good excuse for now," Hale shrugged with a mocking smirk. "Then you'll be tired, or you won't feel comfortable, or the stars won't be aligned.

Here I am, an open book to all your questions, and you are still playing cloak and dagger like your secrets are all that important."

She jerked herself around as if she was going to slap him. Reined in by her seatbelt, the sudden jolt stopped whatever momentum she had, causing her to clumsily shift to face Hale instead. Face flushed with anger, she continued on through gritted teeth. "Just because your secrets were different doesn't make them any more important. You have no idea what I have been going through over the past few weeks, and you have no right to assume your problems are so much easier than mine."

Hale leaned back in his seat as the plane tilted its nose towards the sky. "Well, I'd like to say let's compare. However, that would require you to actually be forthright."

"You fucking bastard," Cass hissed. "How dare you downplay my problems. You have no idea what you are talking about, nor how offensive you are being. I have a literal life and death situation on my hands. It was my hope that we could help each other given our recent experiences, though it seems you've decided to instead follow the road of the asshole. Don't worry, once we touch down in DC I can make arrangements for you to have a free flight back so you don't have to deal with my petty little issues anymore."

Hale turned to Cass and gently put his hands on top of hers. Her face shifted from furious to contemptuous, then confused as he leaned forward, placing a soft kiss on her pursed lips.

"What the hell are you doing?!" She pulled back.

"I'm sorry. I didn't mean any of that," he said calmly.

"Bullshit," she spat. "You can't just blow up on me and expect me to brush it off."

"No, seriously," He smiled warmly. "Look out the window."

She shot him an irritated glare before complying with his request. Outside the window, the city of Los Angeles was quickly receding as the plane gained altitude. Her eyes lingered for a few more moments before she turned back to Hale.

Though the bulk of her anger had been pulled out the window with her realization, remnants caused her jaw to set and her lips to remain pursed.

"I'm sorry," he repeated. "You were on the verge of freaking out, and being nice didn't seem to be getting through. You have a little bit of a temper, so I figured being pissed for a minute would be better than crying from fear."

The lingering anger gnawed at her to tear into him. Fortunately, it was losing ground against logic and an even temper. Despite its rapid decline in tenacity, it was able to prompt one last question in its death throes, "You didn't mean *any* of that?"

Hale's eyes shifted to his left, thinking his answer over carefully. "Most of it, no," he admitted quietly, depriving their audience of the finale. "Granted, I am very curious, and a little annoyed that I haven't got my answers yet. But like you said, this is a busy place, and not the best locale for a private conversation."

Her teeth unclenched and her jaw muscles relaxed. The vestiges of anger slipped from its conquered hill, being forced back into submission by his words. "I can't say I wholeheartedly appreciate that, as you were mean, but I understand the intent. So... thank you. But don't do that again."

He placed another soft kiss on her lips. This one she returned.

"Tell ya what." He reached down under his blanket with a smile. "I've got something to get our minds off the flight."

"I think you can be arrested for that," she said wryly, releasing the last of her anger.

"Funny." He pulled his laptop bag up from between his legs. "But not quite what I meant. So are you a Chess player, or do you prefer Family Feud?"

"Which will be less painful to your ego when I leave you defeated on the field of battle?" She arched her eyebrow confidently.

"Since you put it that way, I think I'll school you in Chess *first*, then we'll move on to the Feud."

———

A LINE of people steadily funneled out from the terminal gate, fanning out onto the main walkway towards the baggage claim. Phones were clicked on, and the chatter of conversation filled the air. From the mouth of the gate, a shrill laugh sounded, cutting through the indistinct banter.

"You're just upset!" Cass said jovially as the pair exited the jetway.

"The game was rigged, you can't deny it." Hale matched her grin and shrugged.

"'Things you find at an airport'…"

"Hey, my answer should have at least been number three," he said defensively. "There's no question about it."

"Al Qaeda?" She lowered her voice to a hushed whisper, still stifling laughter.

"You think the more generalized term of 'terrorist' would have been better?"

"I think you've lost it." Her voice returned to its normal volume.

"Meh," Hale shrugged. "At least I have not one, but two of your Kings in captivity."

"I still want a rematch." She prodded him. "Best three out of five."

"Well, that only puts you three wins away from victory," he smirked. Adopting a contemplative look, he put his index finger to his chin. "Hmmm, let's see. For the first King, a lifetime of imprisonment and torture. For the second… yes, enslavement in the castle. He shall serve my every whim lest he be flogged for his insolence."

"Ugh." She stuck her tongue out. "Give me the first punishment any day over the second."

Arching his eyebrow, he lunged to the side and grabbed her around the waist, squeezing her sides.

"AH!" She jolted, laughing uncontrollably. "Ok! I give up, eternal servitude it is… please stop tickling me!"

After another sharp yelp that drew the attention of several travelers towards them, Hale released her and smiled triumphantly. "I see I'm not the only one who's ticklish."

"Touché." She brushed the newly-made wrinkles out of her shirt, regaining her composure. Hale slid up next to her again, snaking his arm around her waist to pull her close rather than tickling. He placed a kiss on the top of her head, then walked with her snuggled comfortably next to him.

The pair proceeded through the airport in silence. Hale found his attention drifting to the various decorations and informational displays erected around the airport. Having never been this far away from home, he took the opportunity to gawk at the new sights and smells being presented.

"You look like a tourist," Cass said, eyes lifted up to his face.

"Feel like one, too." His head whipped around to another statue to his left. "Never been to DC before. Wish I had a camera."

"Don't you have a phone?"

"Yeah," Hale stopped as he caught her meaning. "Ah, good point."

"Oh, wow." Cass pulled away, face flushing again. "Please don't."

"Ah, who's gonna care?" He pulled out his phone, switching the camera on so he could snap shots as he went by various points of interest.

"You are such a geek."

"Yep," he grinned. "This place is damn near empty anyway."

"It is Sunday night," Cass explained. "And most people use Dulles airport… at least they used to. Not sure anymore."

"Well, aren't you a fountain of trivial information."

She stuck her tongue out at him.

Hale continued to snap shots of the golden vaulted ceilings, commenting on the architecture as Cass shook her head and walked quicker. He kept pace, making brief pauses to capture images of interest along the way. Eventually Hale's options were limited to the baggage claim, and his phone was stored away.

"Watch for the bags, I'm going to grab our keys." Cass walked off.

"Keys?"

"For our car," she answered over her shoulder. "Unless you like walking."

"Not particularly."

She continued on to the rental kiosks, where she was greeted by a smiling man in a red vest. Hale turned back to the slanted conveyer belt just as a loud buzzer sounded. The buzzer repeated every few seconds. The cycle of repetitions were long enough for everyone's attention to be drawn, but far too long for anyone without some patience to spare. After the buzzer finally stopped, the nylon conveyer belt lurched into motion and bags poured out onto the now moving turnstile.

He let his mind meander over the events of the weekend. He found it hard to comprehend that Mrs. Dowling had murdered her husband just two nights ago, that he had trashed Imanu'el's studio and gotten a ticket just yesterday morning, and that Imanu'el had been in his apartment the afternoon after Cass and he spent the night discussing secrets he had never shared with anyone.

It had been an interesting weekend.

Cass' bright green bag caught his eye. He leaned forward, fishing it out of the river of bags flowing past. He set it next to him, returning to the search for his bag. With his mind falling dormant, he found a curiosity tugging at the back of his brain.

The car may be a good place to broach the subject. The Poet suggested. *After all, you've travelled three thousand miles. It will be a private place you can discuss the circumstances that brought you out here.*

I would like to state for the record that this is a foolhardy endeavor, sir, The General chimed in. *You appear to be thinking with your pecker, and not tactically approaching your situation.*

She is smart, and seems trustworthy, The Poet cooed.

She's crafty and good looking, The General scoffed.

A potential confidant.

A likely spy.

"That was quick." Cass slid up next to him.

"I could say the same." Hale looked down at her. "Got the car already?"

"Yep," she smiled. "We just pick any car out of Section 1A. They'll scan it when we leave the lot."

Hale's eyebrows shot up. "Well that's incredibly convenient."

"Isn't it though?" She cocked her head. "Reward Points well spent."

"Fair enough." Hale turned back to the turnstile just in time to see his bag moving past. He jumped forward, nearly bowling over the businessman who sat across from them on the plane as he chatted away on his Blackberry. "Sorry!" Hale grasped his bag, leaning one hand on the man to keep his balance and stop from pushing into him further.

> . . . The office was quiet. Perspiration
> beaded just under his collar as he
> waited.
> . . . . . . "–and close it. You're on
> the afternoon flight to–"
> . . . . a shrill woman's voice
> accentuated a hearty slap to his
> face.

"Sorry, thank you," Cass said, standing in between the man and Hale. "Bad back, seizes up on him sometimes. Thank you so much."

Hale took a quick accounting of his situation. His bag was in front of him. He was still stooped over. Cass was speaking to the man in the suit, who for the first time seemed pleased with his situation. He gave a forgiving smile to the attractive young woman offering apologies, allowing her to give her explanation and move away.

Hale picked up his bag as she moved into him, ushering him away.

"That was awkward," she whispered as they moved towards the doors.

"You're telling me." His eyes darted about. "What'd I miss?"

"You just kinda stood there." A small grin spread across her lips. "Bag halfway off the turnstile, one hand on the man's shoulder. You were getting some weird looks, so I decided to intervene."

"Quick thinking. Thanks," he sighed.

"What did you see?" Curiosity crept into her voice.

"A fragment. Another story that'll remain a mystery." He grimaced. "Annoying, isn't it?"

Cass mirrored his expression and nodded. "I think I'd end up institutionalized. I'm too curious for my own good. I'd be going up to people trying to ask leading questions like a crazy person."

"Yeah, let's not joke about that," Hale said uncomfortably. "I saw One Flew Over The Cookoo's Nest and Marathon Man when I was a kid, both of which gave me some pretty hefty nightmares about what could happen if I wasn't careful."

"Sorry," she winced, walking the rest of the way across the street in silence. Finally, she broke the stillness, "Wasn't Nicholson was great in Cookoo's Nest?!"

Hale chuckled.

The two walked onto the rental car lot, perusing up the first aisle for a car that fit their tastes. There were twelve choices in all, all reasonably similar in quality. There was a miniature SUV, giving the fence sitters their option to have more room than the standard car without having gas efficiency in the single digits. After that, the economy car for the environmentally friendly consumer. Finally, there were several sedans for those who wanted a more standard vehicle and weren't conscientious about their image.

"Eh?" Hale pointed at a black Ford Taurus.

"Inconspicuous." Cass nodded her head. "And enough trunk space for at least two bodies. Works for me."

"Not that funny when I still don't know why we're out here," Hale grinned nervously, moving towards the driver's side.

"No, we're not here to murder anyone." She reassured.

"Or move previously murdered bodies?" His eyebrow arched.

"Or move previously murdered bodies." She confirmed.

"Alright, you seem trustworthy." Eyes narrowed with mock suspicion. "But I'm watching you…"

"Right…" She grinned, tugging on her door. "Now can you unlock my door, Sherlock? I put you on the rental as a driver so you could be my chauffer."

Hale opened the driver side door, sliding into the seat and closing the door behind him. The key was conveniently left in the center console, a tag with the car's information attached to the ring. Hale picked up the key and slid it into the ignition. With a twist and a satisfying roar, the engine came to life. His next stop was the heater, which he cranked up to 80 to bring the car to a more comfortable temperature.

Several raps on the window drew his attention.

"It's cold." She gave a pouty face.

"What?" He mouthed the words quietly, putting a hand to his ear. "I can't hear you over this wonderful heater!"

"I think it's starting to rain…"

"Wow," Hale continued. "This interior of this car is so spacious… and dry!"

"I feel the need to remind you of three important things," Cass said into the closed window. "One; I have your plane ticket home. Two; I have answers that you want. Three; I can, and very likely will, hurt you if I feel another drop of rain on my head."

Hale grinned and hit the unlock button with a slow, dramatic descent of his finger.

Cass quickly opened the door and slid into her seat. She released a sigh, followed by her hands clapping together and rubbing in front of the warm air flowing out of the vents. "Ohhhhh… that feels good." She let several seconds pass to warm up her joints, flexing her fingers as they returned to a comfortable temperature. Bringing them up to her mouth, she blew warm air into her palms, letting the breath travel up her skin and over her fingers. Confident her hands were back in good working order, she quickly turned and jabbed Hale in the ribs.

"Aah!" he laughed as he jerked away from her and pressed into the door.

"You can be a jerk sometimes," she grinned, jabbing at him again.

"It's just my passive-aggressive way of combatting your superior intellect and upper middle class paycheck." He deflected another incoming jab. "You know, sticking it to the Man."

"Ugh!" She sat back, crossing her arms while hiding a smile. "You are an insufferable pleb, you know that?!"

"Apologies, m'lady." He ducked his head subserviently. "Does mistress wish me to divert the carriage?"

She pressed a few buttons on her phone. "Head towards the exit, GPS will be your Cleopatra and tell you where to go."

"Yes, your highness."

Hale pulled the car out of the spot. The sun had set, leaving what was a muggy, overcast day as a dreary and drizzling night. The parking lot offered orange florescent lighting to offset the dismal atmosphere, and it only succeeded in providing minimal illumination to their destination.

The man in the exit booth greeted them with a tone that matched the weather. He had them shut off the vehicle, hand over the key with attached card, along with Cass and Hale's driver's licenses. Once all the pertinent data had been scanned and entered into the system, he handed them back with a half-hearted goodbye before closing his booth up and raising the gate for them.

"So where are we headed, navigator?" Hale asked as he pulled out onto the main road.

"Not far. Hyatt Regency, right down the road here."

"You been here before?" Hale asked.

"No," she responded. "Not since I was a little girl, at least. I picked a hotel close to the airport, though, so I know we're not going far. Turn here."

Hale turned as directed, remaining silent as he drove.

"And to answer your unspoken question: when we get to the hotel."

"Thanks," he smiled.

20

The room at the Hyatt was a reasonable size. With a king sized bed, bathroom, a dresser, 36" TV and a small sitting area with a standing table, the room was close to rivaling Hale's apartment in size, and clearly beating it in cleanliness. A honk sounded outside. Muffled by the windows, it was far from obtrusive, leaving the room's stillness intact.

"Okay," Hale said with a content sigh. "You've stalled enough. Let's hear it."

"I claim no responsibility for the most recent 'stall tactic,'" Cass grinned, playing her fingers across Hale's chest.

"Well…" Hale stumbled comically, looking down at the disheveled sheets. He wondered where the comforter had ended up after he'd tossed it off the bed. "I may have delayed us a little upon arrival, but you can't pretend you didn't provoke me."

"Provoke you?" Cass leaned up on her elbows, looking at Hale with her mouth open aghast. "I just looked at you when we were coming in the room!"

"You bit your lower lip," Hale said smugly.

"I bi–" She cocked an eyebrow. "How is that provoking you?"

"I'm a guy. It doesn't take much." At her unchanged expression, Hale smiled. He wrapped his free arm around her waist to give an affectionate hug. "You said more with that look than you could have with words. You might as well have shouted 'Hale! We've just survived a 3000 mile trip across the U.S. Help me christen this room to celebrate!'"

Cass dipped her head down, peering up at Hale from behind his chest.

"See?" A victorious smile spread across his face as he leaned back, closing his eyes. He released her with one arm, keeping her cuddled close. "Seriously, I know you beat me on the curiosity front, but I am still a curious person. I'm going to have an aneurism sooner or later if I don't find out why we're here."

"Can I start with the more altruistic reason before I move onto the selfish one?"

"Sure," he grinned.

"Thanks." She rested her head on his chest, gathering words. After several moments of silence passed, she took a deep breath and spoke. "Something is up with Imanu'el. I watched him as you two talked... well, when I wasn't immobile on the floor. He's confident and he knows what he's talking about. Had we met the guy in a church, I'd say he was a priest intoxicated by his faith. However, due to the circumstances, I had my guard up.

"At first I could write off most of my observations to bias and paranoia. I wanted him to be dirty. I needed him to be lying to prove my instinct right. But I didn't want to confuse an already jumbled situation, nor corrupt something that may very well be a good thing for you. So I kept my mouth shut and watched."

"He's a weird guy, Cass, but–"

"Wait," She cut him off gently. "Just hear me out."

"Alright." He resumed his silence.

"You talked for a while about your past." Her eyes shifted, regaining her footing in her story. "He maintained his tranquil demeanor for most of it. However towards the end, he showed true emotion for the second time in the entire conversation. See, he was masking his emotions more than normal people do. I explained it away as an attempt to put up the proper image. As a pious man and zealot of peace and healing, the quiet messiah is a good persona to project. That part didn't bother me. Fixers will do that, many professionals do too."

"Fixers?"

"Sorry, middle men, confidence artists, generally on the other side of the law," Cass clarified.

"Ah, continue."

"Anyway, the problem with masking your emotions is simple. Most things will get covered, leaving you with a blank slate for a face. However when something does get to you, and I mean really get to you, you show it. This gives anyone watching a clear indicator when something strikes a nerve. Imanu'el only broke his mask twice in the entire conversation. The first time was during the–" She gulped a little. "Sorry... ugh... cutting. Can't even think about that without feeling sick."

Hale gave a squeeze to comfort her.

"Anyway, he paled when I mentioned the steak knife, and was obviously emotionally exposed during the... process." She took a deep breath to steady herself. "The second time was at the end of the conversation. When you were recounting what you Wandered into, specifically about the man in the navy suit and D.C. The look on his face was very telling. His eyes widened. His lips tightened. He was terrified of something. I think he was worried you uncovered information that he didn't want you to know."

"That's what caused you to fake being sick to get him away?"

"Yes," she answered.

"Why not just ask him about it?"

"If I'm right about him, he could have spun a tale that sounded pretty and made a lot of sense, and it would have only given us more reason to trust him. If I was wrong, then I just delayed your conversation. At the time, I didn't realize we'd be leaving the state within the next few hours."

"Okay, so you saw him react poorly to information, giving more support to your theory that he's dirty," Hale collected. "What made you jump to the decision to pay for a flight, car, and hotel room?"

"It's not that big of a deal." She nestled into him sweetly. "I used your credit card."

"Ha! Like my credit limit would support such a lie." He fingered her ribs, causing her to squirm and giggle. "Back to serious mode. The suspense is killing me. I need to know what I'm doing in D.C., aside from spending time with a gorgeous woman."

"Nice addition."

"Thanks." He squeezed her again. "Now out with it."

"The altruistic part of the decision was conceived when you talked about the time frame on your Wanders." Her leg wrapped around Hale's, her gaze staying perpendicular to his. She felt more at ease speaking without eye contact at the moment. "I realized that if we were going to get to the bottom of your issue with Imanu'el, we would have to get out here immediately to do some investigation. That way we could get some conclusive evidence, and figure out whether or not you were getting involved with someone who was on the level... hopefully."

"Okay..." Hale trailed the word off as he let her explanation sink in. "Now for the non-altruistic part. I think the picture might get a little clearer then."

"I need you to understand something."

"Okay."

"There are few people in this world I've had this conversation with. Now I know you understand the importance of personal secrets, so I won't overstate the obvious." She met his eyes to finish the sentence. "But I need you to treat this like you treat your own secret, okay?"

Hale paused briefly to let the gravity of the statement sink in. "Understood." Hale nodded solemnly.

Cass resumed her averted gaze, head resting on Hale's chest. "My dad is a wonderful person. He is intelligent, caring, and very loving. He raised me by himself. My mother passed away at an early age. I don't even remember her. But my dad never let being a single parent slow him down. He spent as much time with me as he could, and provided me with a great start to life."

Hale's mind immediately started searching for where this went wrong. Horrible images of debauchery and misfortune crept behind his eyes, though he focused on remaining silent and stoic to avoid betraying his thoughts in case Cass looked up again.

"My dad was always honest with me. Despite anything that would happen, I knew I could rely on him to give me the truth. It was important. More important than normal father-daughter relationships, I guess." She bit her lip, wrestling over her choice of words. "It was more important because of what he did for a living."

Hale let his silence ask the question rather than interrupt her momentum.

"My father is what you call a Fixer. There are other names for it: grifter, con, face, hustler, and dozens more that get less kind as you go. Call me bias, but I don't like those. They sound sinister. They add unnecessary menace to what is a relatively harmless profession." She emphasized the last words, as if the practiced phrase had been given to convince more than her audience. "It's not like he is out selling snake oil to old ladies, nothing like that. He acts as a negotiator between rival factions, he'll broker deals between less than reputable businesses, he'll solve problems with creativity rather than muscle and manpower. He uses his mind to achieve his goals, exercising will instead of strength. He always said it was important to study a problem and really get to know it, as there was probably an easier solution than what most people would use. There are many people in this world who operate on the edge of, or just outside, the law. Those people find my father's talents very valuable."

Hale gently stroked his fingers across the bare skin of Cass' back. He meant it to be comforting, to let her know he was still with her. Still, he feared his jerky movement only projected nerves and distance.

"The important thing is my dad didn't hurt people. He has a sense of right and wrong, and he made sure I did, too." She met Hale's eyes again, anxiety creeping into her voice as if she needed him to believe as much as she did. "Remember what I have my degree in? Psych with a minor in Criminal Justice? I was going to be a lawyer. I remember deciding it when I was nine. My dad had gotten into a little trouble, nothing he couldn't handle, but it was enough to shake up our daily routine for a while. Things got tense, and I noticed his biggest problems were with his lawyer. I thought, what if I did that? What if when I got older, I could protect my dad for once? You know, reverse the roles."

She slumped down, resting her chin on Hale's chest. Her eyes lifted up over his head, staring off as she continued. "It was a childish dream, but not a bad one. It wasn't until my Junior year in college that I had a conversation with my dad about it. I mentioned my desire to go into law after I got my Bachelors, and that I'd gladly work for him for free if it ever became necessary. 'Think of it as a bonus,' I said. 'You helped put me through college, so now you get a return on your investment.'

"I always imagined him being happy. I pictured his eyes welling up before he pulled me close and told me how proud he was of me." Cass continued as if unfazed despite the tears brimming. "No. He loved me too much for that."

"He turned you down." Hale made the question a statement of fact.

Cass nodded. The corners of her lips dipped into a frown for a moment as a tear freed itself and rolled down her cheek. She quickly recovered and continued. "He painted the picture for me. Me, standing in the courtroom. Him, being dragged off by the Bailiff in handcuffs. An angry judge pounding a gavel while shouting 'GUILTY'!" She stopped, a frown tugging at her mouth again. "He put it in a much nicer way, and made sure I knew he thought I was brilliant and would be a fantastic lawyer. But the message was clear: if I ever defended my father and failed, no matter how hard I tried, nor how skilled I was, I'd never forgive myself."

She turned her head away to lay her cheek on his chest again. Hale felt warm drops fall from her eyes onto his skin.

"Cass," Hale said hesitantly.

"My father doesn't hurt people, Hale," Cass repeated, voice cracking. "He may be a criminal in some people's eyes, but he doesn't hurt people."

"Cass." Hale's voice gained force, nerves and suspicions pressing his need to know. "Why are we here?"

"He has always been honest with me. We have no secrets!" She was crying freely now. Words escaped through sobs, and tears flowed from Cass' cheeks down Hale's chest. "He solved problems. He found solutions. He didn't hurt people."

"Cass." Hale's mind raced. It was clear now; he just needed to hear it.

"My father is in jail!" she exclaimed, burying her face in his chest in shame.

"He was arrested for murder two weeks ago."

21

Cass' sobs filled the room. Hale remained silent. He couldn't decide from the myriad of obvious reasons why he maintained his taciturn demeanor. Was it due to shock? Perhaps it was the realization that Cass would not be in the mindset to answer the plethora of questions he had. Alternatively, it may have been the knowledge that she was not yet finished, and answers would come in time. Finally, he realized nothing he could offer would be any more comforting than simply holding her and showing support.

This is a complex situation, The Poet murmured.

Complex my ass, The General countered. *This is a goddamn clusterfuck.*

You know what is coming next, The Poet continued.

More pain in the ass? The General answered.

I'm aware. Hale cut both voices off, refusing to deny the merit of either point. *Regardless, I think I'm okay with helping her. I really like Cass, and if she asks what I assume she will ask, maybe I can finally do something useful with my gift.*

Minutes ticked by. Cass regained her composure, wiping her face with the sheet to clear away tears and smeared makeup. She averted her eyes, staring down at the corner of the bed with her cheek resting on Hale's chest. She rose and fell slowly with his breaths, an arm draped around his stomach as if she was preventing him from sliding away.

Silence persisted. The sounds of their breathing were soft accents to the low hum of the room's heater. The stillness was disturbed further as Hale slid his hand from Cass' shoulder, rustling the sheets in its ascent. Fingers descended softly into her twisted hair raking back slowly to pull it away from her face and into organized rows. A soft sigh escaped her lips in response.

"I need you to believe me." She finally said, the words fighting through her tightened throat.

"I know," Hale responded, stroking her hair. "And I do. Given the circumstances, I can't see why you would lie to me."

"Okay," she sniffled, taking another breath to steady her voice for her next question. "Then you'll understand–"

"Of course I will," he cut her off.

"What?" Her head popped up, spinning to look at him directly. Streaks of stray mascara darted from the corners of her eyes, giving her a desperate and disheveled look.

"If I haven't mistaken your intentions…" He gave a supportive smile. "You want me to see if I can help. Use my gift to help clear your dad's name, right?"

Her lips tightened into a smile, forcing back more tears as she did. "Yes, please. Hale, I'm so sorry." She shifted, dragging the sheets around her into a makeshift toga so she could sit up while she spoke. She hovered over Hale, looking him in the eyes as she continued. "I know it is extremely selfish of me, but as soon as you said D.C., the idea just kind of came to me."

Hale came to a silent realization. Cass' revelation on the coinciding location of D.C. came before the altruistic plan for the trip to help him. He tactfully kept this realization silent.

"It was just such a coincidence, you know?" She continued on. "My dad is locked up, right here in the same city that you were Wandering into. I hoped you could help, otherwise my dad is facing a Murder Two charge that he doesn't deserve. But this isn't just about that!" She quickly added, frantically patting his chest quickly with her free hand as if to pull his attention back to his own goals. "I can help you, too! We'll track down whoever Imanu'el was talking to, and we'll solve both of our problems."

Hale took Cass' hand in his own, looking up at her. "Cass, it's okay," he assured. "Yeah, hijacking me all the way out here wasn't the best thing to do, but I understand why you did it. You want to protect your dad, and I am in a unique position to help."

"I want to be clear I know this was manipulative." She frowned, her eyes threatening to let loose more salty water. "Waiting to tell you out here was both cowardly, and a shitty tactic to make it less likely that you'd turn me down."

"The fact you just swore for the first time that I can remember shows me how emphatic you are about your apology." He gave another supportive grin. "I mean, other than on the plane."

"That doesn't count." She pursed her lips. "You provoked me."

"That is true." He agreed. "Look, it's okay. I see exactly what you did, and while I'm not wholly happy with the way things happened, I understand, and I'm not mad."

Her lip pouted out, clearly wanting to say more, though fighting back tears of shame took precedent. She finally just leaned forward, wrapping her arms around Hale's neck and hugging him. "Thank you. Thank you so much."

"Don't thank me yet," he replied, returning the hug. "I don't know for sure I'll be any good to you."

"No, you will," she said assuredly. Her body rose back up into a sitting position. She wiped her cheeks, sniffling again to clear her voice, and then looked back down into Hale's eyes. "I have a plan."

"WE REALLY don't have to do this first," Hale repeated. "Your investigation is much more important." Just using the word 'investigation' sent a strange chill of joy up his spine. He could imagine Peter Faulkner walking beside him in a brown trench coat and fedora, giving him a smile and a wink as they approached a crime scene.

"We really do," Cass insisted. "Given what we know, the trail on Imanu'el's activities may go cold in the next day or two. The crime my dad is being accused of happened weeks ago, so another couple of days shouldn't make any difference. It's either still there, or it's gone."

"I'm only conceding because you dragged me out of bed at this god awful hour, and I can't yet think straight."

She planted a kiss on his cheek without breaking stride. "I'll accept your surrender without gloating."

The two walked arm in arm down the street in the cool morning air. The link at their elbows allowed them to keep their hands in their pockets as they moved, shielding their extremities from the chill. Cass bundled up in a puffy jacket with faux fur lining around the neckline. Hale had both hands shoved in the front pouch of only his white hoodie. His wardrobe was clearly not ready for colder weather.

Despite the early morning hour, the citizens of D.C. were up and bustling. Cars moved steadily through the building traffic of Independence Avenue, and pedestrians choked up the sidewalks as they moved through various stores and across intersections.

"I don't understand people who are this alert and busy at 7:00 AM," Hale groaned. A sharp gust of wind stung his cheeks and brought him to a state of alertness. "You realize it's 4:00 AM our time, right?"

"I don't mind," Cass said cheerily. "I'm a morning person. I used to get up at 4:00 all the time in college. Now I spoil myself and sleep in 'til 5:00."

"You're a mutant," Hale grumbled.

"I suppose I'll play the role of the Kettle in this conversation."

Hale grumbled again in response. A nervous part of his brain itched at him to tell her he was trying to be funny, and wasn't really as grumpy as he was acting. Realization came shortly after.

Remember who Cass is, genius. She's more observant than you.

"Here we are, Grumblecakes." Cass stopped in front of a shop, opening the door with a cheery smile. "This should help your mood."

"Huh?" Hale looked up. The sign read <u>Monument Mochas</u>. "This looks familiar." His brow furrowed, trying to rustle his memory.

"Good," she said contently. "Look behind you."

He did. Over the rooftops of buildings he saw the steeple of the Washington monument pointing straight towards the sky. It was the first time he had seen the obelisk with his own eyes. He was surprised how much more impact the real tribute to their first president had. Seeing pictures just didn't do it justice.

Realization visited him for the second time in their conversation.

"This is the place!" he said, turning back to her.

"It very well might be," she nodded. "Now get inside, you're letting all the heat out."

At the promise of heat, Hale shuffled after her. Greeted by warm air, he let out a content sigh and removed his hands from his pouch. With brisk strokes, he rubbed them together and forced feeling back into his cold extremities. It took a moment, but a certain familiarity set in.

"This is the place," he said confidently.

"I hoped you'd say that." Cass sidled up to him. "It's the only coffee house listed near the Washington Monument that has orange-uniformed baristas."

Hale looked at her incredulously.

"I did a quick search for coffee houses on the white pages, built a list, vetted everything that was a recognizable national chain, and finally scanned through websites, Twitter feeds and Facebook pages for pictures of uniforms. This one was the only one I could find with orange aprons." A look of worry crossed her face. "You did say orange, right?"

"Yes, just… wow." He felt a pang of jealousy. "You're good at this."

"Thank you." A genuine smile met his compliment. "Now, treat me to a caramel latte with no whipped cream, skim milk, and an extra cup. I'll tell you what we're doing next after that."

"Yes ma'am."

They stood in the shrinking line, waiting their turn until they could be served. The barista who greeted them had either suffered a horrible shrapnel injury, or thoroughly enjoyed the art of body modifications. Hale judged by the symmetrical arrangement of metal protruding from the individual's face, and the unlikely event that shards from an explosive would launch out and attach as perfect cones and 6 gauge barbells, it was likely the latter.

"A café mocha and a caramel latte with skim milk and an extra cup."

"You want whipped cream, bro?" The barista asked. A new, thick barbell protruding through his tongue caused 'cream' to come out 'cweam', and 'bro' to sound more like 'bwo.'

Hale couldn't help a grin. "Yes."

Cass jabbed him.

"On the mocha, not the latte," he corrected.

"No pwobwem, bwo." He punched some keys on the register and gave Hale his total. With a swipe of plastic and the handoff of a noisily printed receipt, the transaction was completed.

"Oh, before we go," Cass interjected, stepping forward to address the barista directly. "Were you working here on Saturday?"

"Nah, got this done on Satowday." He pointed at his mouth, showing off a thick gauged set of twin barbells sticking through the center of his tongue. "Will was though." He motioned to the other man behind the counter.

"Can we talk to him for a quick second?" she asked, giving a flirtatious grin.

That's not fair. Hale thought. *If I moved my shoulders and smiled like that I'd probably get punched.*

"Uh." He looked past them to the building line. "Suwe, but make it quick. Will!"

"Sup?" The man behind the espresso machine finished moving various cups and shots around with lighting speed and looked up.

"They wanna tawk to you. Nesst!" he called over Hale and Cass, hinting for them to move over so the next customers could take their place.

"How can I help?" The man moved over to an open spot in the counter where the three could speak. The anxious look on his face let them know he was busy, and any conversation would have to be kept brief.

"Will, right?" Cass asked. "You worked her on Saturday?"

"Bill, actually. Pincushion just can't speak straight." He gave a look over at his co-worker.

"You'we jus' jewous." The barista said, punching away at the register. He looked nothing like Alex, and Hale was sure he didn't party like Alex either, but the cavalier attitude reminded him of his friend. Alex, who was certainly wondering where he was and how he'd managed to end up with Cass in his apartment again. Hale ignored the sudden surge of guilt that he'd left without explanation or warning, but it was quickly overtaken by curiosity as Cass worked her magic.

"Did you work in the morning, afternoon…?"

"Pulled a 12 hour shift that day," he smirked. "I was here til almost closing. What's up?"

"To be brief, we're running a study on memory and retention for UDC. If you can spare 10 minutes when you're not so busy, we'd love to talk to you."

"Eh…" He scratched the back of his neck, clearly trying to find a polite way to brush them off.

"We'd pay you for your time, obviously," Cass smiled. "$20 for a 10 minute conversation isn't that bad, is it?"

His face changed almost immediately. "Uh, yeah, sure. Why not?" He looked at the line. "Give me about 30 minutes, then I should be able to spare some time."

"Sure thing, thanks!" She gave a bright smile and an excited bounce before turning to go grab a seat.

When they were out of earshot and Bill was focused back on his work, Hale leaned in. "You are shameless, you know that?"

"It worked, didn't it?" She flashed a smile and slid into a booth. "It's amazing how much cooperation you can get from a little lean and a smile."

"You're a regular Al Capone." He adopted a cheesy gangster slur, sliding into the seat across from her. "You can get more with a kind word and a gun than you can with a kind word alone."

"DeNiro delivered it best in Untouchables," she agreed.

"God awful movie, though." Hale curled his lip.

"Not god awful," she said defensively. "Just the parts with Costner. Sean Connery and Robert DeNiro were fantastic."

"Okay, I'll give you that." Breaking away from the movie interlude, Hale realized he was still in the dark about a lot of what just happened. "By the way, what is UDC?"

"University of District Columbia," she answered. "I figured it was a good cover."

He shook his head and chuckled. "So, care to fill me in on your plan?"

"Absolutely." She leaned in with a crafty grin, eager to share. "So you told me it was daytime in your Wander, right?"

"Yeah." Hale thought for a moment to confirm. "Yeah, looked like early to midday."

"And he missed the uber important meeting on Saturday afternoon, right?"

"I think I see where you are going with this."

"And he was obviously back by Sunday," she continued on. "So if the Saturday meeting was so important, he wouldn't have met on Friday afternoon and just hung out for another day, right? Well... I hope not, cause that's going to make this more difficult. Either way, we have a starting point. I just hope double-shift-boy isn't too brain fried to remember anything, else I'm out 20 bucks."

"You're shelling out a lot of cash for me." He arched his eyebrow. "Tickets, car, hotel. I mean, sure, I bought coffee, but I don't think that makes us even."

"Do I need to remind you what you're doing for me?" She said evenly.

"Point, but still..." He shifted uncomfortably.

"Plus, the tickets and hotel were acquired with reward points from my credit card, meaning I paid next to nothing. So stop fretting."

"I guess I mean to say 'thanks'." He grinned.

"Thank you, Hale." The downward shift in her tone from jovial and light to low and somber accentuated the words. Hale knew the second part of this trip was important to her, and that simple statement served as a great reminder.

He nodded, pursing his lips into a somber smile. "You're welcome."

They passed the next few minutes in silence. Cass retrieved their drinks when Bill finished them, giving him a flirtatious 'thank you' before returning back to the table. Hale suppressed jealousy, reminding himself it was an act to further their agenda. Still, something gnawed at him to jump over the counter and establish dominance over the espresso peddler.

The queue of customers dwindled away as each cup was successfully ground, strained and mixed. A few customers stayed to enjoy their drink at a table, while others whisked off to their early morning destinations. As the last of the morning rush received the caffeinated start to their day, Bill moved around the counter, a cup of iced tea in hand.

"Taking a break, Marty." He strolled over to the waiting pair at their booth, dragging a chair behind him to sit at the end of their table. "Okay, I've got ten minutes. How can I help you?"

Cass fished out a pocket notebook from her jacket, clicking a pen as she shook the cover open. "To bring you up to speed, this is a psychological study for UDC as part of a group project. Our group is studying workplace behavior and memory retention. Part of our group went to various sites around DC, visiting establishments and attempting to stand apart from the normal crowd. My part of the group…" Cass smiled and placed her palm on her chest, drawing Bill's eyes there and further numbing any resistance he might have had against playing along. Hale marveled at her subtle tactics. "Is in charge of data collection. We are going to the places our group visited, interviewing employees of said establishments to gauge their retention of our group's presence. Ready?" Cass held up the pen and grinned.

"Sure." Bill cocked an eyebrow and stuck the straw to his iced tea between his lips. Hale surmised their interviewee's mannerisms suggested he might be suspicious of Cass' bogus tale, or that he was simply trying to put on a guise of mystery to look good for the cute college girl.

Hale's primal urge to throttle his competition was quashed again by his logical mind.

"Great!" She squeaked, playing the boppy student down to the letter. "Now, there were two individuals that came in during the day on Saturday. Both were male. One was wearing a navy suit–"

"I hope the other one wasn't in a suit, too." He smirked and sucked on his straw. "This is DC, after all. Everyone is in patriotic colors and business wear."

"No," she smiled patiently. "That's part of the control, actually. The man he was with was dressed in all white."

Bill paused for a moment, biting the end of the straw into a mangled mess as he thought. His eyes shot up as a memory hit. "The Hari Kari guy?"

"Do you mean Hari Krishna?" Hale asked, unable to suppress some type of reaction to the man's stupidity.

"Yeah, those guys. Wait." He furrowed his brow. "What's the other thing I said?"

"Ritual suicide," Cass answered pleasantly. "Moving on, I think we've passed stage one, but just to be sure, describe the two gentlemen to ensure we are talking about the same people."

"Uh, let's see." He chewed vigorously on the plastic between his teeth. Hale wondered if he would ever get a sip of his drink through there again. "The guy in the suit was, well, a guy in a suit. Looked like a generic lobbyist. Tidy hair, white guy, decent looking… not that, you know, I'm into guys or anything. I'm straight, and recently single!" He looked at Cass as he pleaded his case.

"I hoped so…" She averted her eyes and blushed timidly. "Um, you were saying?"

Hale reclined back on his side of the booth. *This is better than going to the movies,* He thought, forcing himself to look stoic. He couldn't play a part as well as Cass but he could at least try.

"Um," Bill grinned, trying to get himself back on topic. "Anyway, standard lobbyist dude. You've seen one you've seen them all."

"Any specifics you can remember about him?" Cass prodded.

Bill wracked his brain for a bit, unconsciously going back to gnawing on his drinking implement as he tried to fish for details to impress the beauty before him. "No, honestly. I probably wouldn't have even remembered him at all if it wasn't for the Hari Krishna guy. That kinda stuck out."

"Okay." Cass scribbled on the notepad. "And what do you remember about the other man?"

"Let's see." Chew chew chew. "Clean cut, short guy, no facial hair. Oh, same with the other guy. No facial hair I mean, the guy in the suit was tall. Uh, white clothing. No beads or bibles or anything. Um…"

"We're definitely talking about the same people," Cass smiled. "So you noticed them due to the white outfit, but you don't think you would have remembered if they were both wearing suits?"

"No," Bill said flatly. "We get a ton of people in here like that. They would have just blended in. Unless, you know, they did something out of the ordinary to catch our attention."

"Fair enough." Cass pursed her lips and pretended to act interested as she jotted down notes. Hale realized she may very well be interested, as there was subtext that Bill wasn't party to. "Speaking of out of the ordinary, let's move on to behavior. Did you notice what the two did after you initially saw them?"

Bill rolled his eyes as if the task was monumental. Letting out a deep sigh, he visibly wracked his brain. His poor straw suffered the worst of it. "Shit, um… I think they sat over there." He turned and pointed to a booth in the corner. "It was early afternoon, so it was slow. I remember hanging out and talking with Regina most of the day. She's my co-worker, not, you know, my girlfriend or anything," Bill quickly corrected himself.

Cass smiled, playing into his awkward advances. "I've actually found it easier to recollect memories if you reconstruct the scene," she suggested. "Replaying it in your mind, maybe even standing where you were when you watched them."

"Well, I didn't really watch them." He shrugged. "Truth be told, I glanced over a couple times, but otherwise kinda ignored em.”

"Humor me,” she grinned. "Let's walk you back over there, see if there's anything else that springs to mind.”

"Uh, sure.” Bill checked his watch before standing up. "I got a few more minutes.”

Cass walked with him to the edge of the counter where he parted from the trio. He leaned against the back counter, resting both palms on the ledge as he looked out over the coffee shop. He looked over at the booth again, biting his lip as he conjured up the memories. "Uh, the guy in white sat on that side.” He pointed. "So I could see his face. The other guy had his back to me.”

Cass scribbled away. "If they did their job, you couldn't hear what they were saying… but do you remember facial expressions?” She looked up at him, pen at the ready.

Hale watched the man struggle with memories, amused at the process Cass was using to pull information. He wondered how much of it was legitimate science, and how much she was making up on the spot just to dredge up as much info as she could. With a glance around, Hale noticed he wasn't the only one that was entertained. A curly haired man in a tweed jacket with thick rimmed glasses and a pudgy face sat in a nearby booth. He watched the interview progress with a mild look of interest. Hale gave the man a smile and a nod, which was returned in kind, and then looked back to Bill behind the counter.

"Fuck, uh, no.” He rubbed his head. "The guy in white was really quiet… uh… It was a couple days ago, I really don't know.”

"Okay, no problem. Remember, there's no wrong answers here,” she spoke calmly, jotting down a few more notes. "This is the last phase of questions. We've gone through the superficial and first tier stages of memory. Our last test is to see if replication can assist in the retrieval of memory. Ronny,” She turned to Hale. "Can you please sit where our quiet Man in White sat?”

A flash of understanding crossed his features, leaving a wry grin in its wake. *She played this well*, he thought.

He moved past her, slowly sliding into the booth and placing his hands flat on the table.

     . . . "Power," The Suited Man said from across the table. "What is the most desirable–"

      . . . . . . The Suited Man shot a look of disdain at Imanu'el.

        . . . . "–determination, or as I like to call it, will." The Suited Man flashed his signature predatory smile.

"–eah! Just like that!" Bill exclaimed.

Hale looked over, trying to look natural.

"He seemed, you know, freaked out. I had to see him mimic it to remember, but yeah, you're right. Wow, that really did help!" Bill curbed his excitement with a cough. "So, yeah, you really know your stuff."

"Thanks. Well," she smiled, crossing her fingers. "I'm learning. Here's to hoping I can actually use it sometime in my life."

"Oh, definitely," he said encouragingly. He licked his lips and held his breath, drawing his confidence. "So, uh, are you doing anything later? I'm off at 3. Do you wanna grab a late lunch or something?"

The dipshit behind the counter has no chance. Hale repeated the mantra in his head.

Cass pulled the notebook to her chest as if she were shy and almost at a loss in the face of his flirting. "Um, I'm going to be elbow deep in this project for at least another week. But, maybe I could drop by next Saturday after we're done?"

"Sure, yeah, that'd be great," he said with a smile.

"Great!" she agreed, giving another little bounce. "I'm Sara, by the way."

"Bill," he said, giving a small wave of introduction.

Hale had to fight not to roll his eyes. He almost felt bad for the guy, but not bad enough to offer any kind of assistance.

"Okay, Bill," she grinned flirtatiously, cheeks flushed red. "We gotta get going to the next location, but it was really great talking to you."

"Yeah, thanks. That was really, uh, informative." He smiled again and nodded.

Must not punch the idiot. The mantra evolved.

"Alright Sara," Hale said, sliding out of the booth. "We gotta get rolling. It was nice meeting you, Bill."

"You too." Bill gave a polite nod and wave.

The two faux students turned and made their way for the door, Cass still blushing and holding the notebook close to keep up the charade. Hale played his part, moving casually next to her like a disinterested classmate.

"Oh, hey!" Bill called out.

The two spun around.

"Yes?" Cass responded. "Did you remember something else?"

"Yeah, uh," he continued nervously. "Could I get that $20?"

22

"**U**gh! The nerve!" Cass griped, teeth gnashing as she walked. "Seriously!" Hale couldn't help smiling. "How dare he?"

"Don't even!" Cass warned.

"What? It's kind of poetic justice, don't you think?" he said defensively. "I mean, you had no intention of following up on your little date, so it was almost karma's way of paying you back."

"I don't care about the money," Cass growled. "I just can't believe someone would have the nerve to ask me out, followed immediately by asking me for money. That's just... bad etiquette."

"Fair enough." He continued to smile, letting the moment linger. "From an outside perspective, you have to admit that was a little funny, though."

"No wonder he's single." She scowled.

"Excuse me?" A voice called out from behind.

The pair turned to meet the voice. Hale recognized him from the shop. It was the man in the tweed jacket who had watched their interview of Bill. He pressed his thick square glasses up his nose and smiled. The skin of his jaw drew up when he moved his lips, accentuating his pudgy cheeks and adding to the bland fleshiness of his face. His receding hairline completed the look, and Hale gauged he was definitely not a good looking man. In fact, he was a bit comical with his odd combination of features.

"Yes?" Hale responded.

"Sorry to interrupt." He stopped a few feet away, clasping his hands timidly at his waist. "I don't mean to intrude, but I couldn't help but overhear your case study in there."

"Oh, yes, um–" Clearly caught off guard, Cass attempted to regain her footing.

"My apologies, I'm Dr. Lyman." He extended a hand. "You might have seen my name on the rosters at UDC. I teach upper division Pysch. I come here so often, I'm surprised we haven't run into each other before!"

"Oh, yes, of course," Hale lied, taking the man's hand and giving it a firm shake. "Great to finally meet you in the flesh, Dr. Lyman."

"A pleasure to meet you," Cass smiled politely, shaking the professor's hand in turn.

"Again, sorry to interrupt, I was just curious what curriculum this case study came from. I'm very interested in following up with you to hear your results," he smiled eagerly. "What are you hoping to find?"

"Oh, well–" Cass stumbled.

"This is actually a side project," Hale interjected. "We're not doing this for any particular class, but rather as an independent study we hope to write a journal on."

"Oh." A frown revealed his disappointment. "I see. Well, I hope the University can at least benefit from your findings. Ah, would you mind terribly if I took your contact information? I would love to follow up with you on this, maybe even share some notes."

The two stumbled for a moment, giving the professor a chance to speak up again.

"Here." He held his hand out. "Let me at least put my number in one of your phones. That way you can look me up at the University and check out my credentials before giving away any personal information. Fair?"

Cass nodded, slipping back into the role of the student. "Of course. Sorry, you know how careful you have to be these days." She pulled out her phone and handed it over.

He smiled, punching in keys as he continued talking. "It's so rare these days to find good talent, you know?" He pressed a few more keys before pausing.

"Would you mind if I put this under my first and last, Nicholas Lyman? Some students prefer Professor Lyman, but I think that is rather formal in cases like this."

"Nicholas is fine," she said.

"Good. Right." He raised the phone in salute and smiled back, then returned to pushing buttons. "As I was saying, good talent. Your study seems very interesting, and I'd be interested to see what other data you collect. Just give me a call anytime during my office hours, 11 to 3 Tuesday through Saturday, and we'll set up a formal time to meet." He pushed the last button and handed the phone back. "There we are, Nicholas Lyman."

"Perfect," She pocketed the phone. "And sorry again for the phone thing. Young girl, gotta be careful, you know."

He pursed his lips and held his hands out, palms forward. "Not a bit of offense taken. That said, I am surely taking up valuable research time. I'll leave both of you to your studies. Thank you again." He smiled and nodded, backing away a step before turning and retreating to the coffee shop.

Cass and Hale turned, continuing down the pathway.

"That was close," Cass breathed.

"Not to steal your role as the collected one with a plan, but what could he have done?" Hale posed. He adopted a stern voice. "You durn kids and your fake University studies! I bet you're smokin' that reefer and listening to that rap music!"

Cass gave a nervous chuckle. "I don't know, I just locked up. I guess it's the old student in me, I felt the need to avoid reprimand by a professor."

"This probably isn't a good time to discuss that one fetish I have, is it?"

She jabbed him, causing him to jump and nearly lose his balance off the sidewalk.

"Ah, good one." He rubbed his side. "Seriously though, that was kinda weird, right?"

"He's odd, but a lot of the Psych professors I had were, so I guess that's what I expect."

"Fair enough. So what's next?" Hale jabbed his hands in his pockets.

"First item on the agenda: what did you see?" She opened up her notebook as if to write notes again. Hale saw the first page was filled with doodles of flowers and stick figures in various Neanderthal poses.

"Let me guess…"

"Pictures of our interviewee," she confirmed.

"You didn't let me guess." He gave her a stern look.

"Deal with it." She flashed a smile. "Now what did you see?"

He told her, confirming The Suited Man with the predatory smile did sit with Imanu'el at that table.

"Okay, so the Salt Lake nephew story was 100% bogus." Cass paused to mentally gather the data. "Why would he lie? What was so bad about coming out here?"

"His cover story involved meeting with a 'diamond in the rough', but all he needed was a plausible excuse on why he'd miss out on his first meeting with the Touched, so it must have been important," Hale grimaced. "I really don't like that name, by the way."

"What do you want to call it?"

Hale thought for a moment, his mind offering nothing better. "Touched it is. I'll come up with something better later. Anyway, what's next?"

Cass walked in silence for another half a block, pondering. "Well, unless we somehow get security footage or credit card records from that place, I think that's as far as we're going to get out here."

"Unless we stake it out and wait for him to come back."

"That is assuming he frequents the establishment," she pointed out. "For all we know it was a one-time venture. After all, if this was supposed to be secretive, you wouldn't meet in a place you could be found at later."

"And truth be told, I'm not patient enough to sit in a car for a week watching for a person I might not even recognize," Hale admitted.

"At this point…" Cass pulled her lips back into a frown. "Confronting Imanu'el may be the best course of action. He's got less wiggle room now, so you're more likely to get a true story out of him. I don't like it, but I'm running out of ideas."

"Well…" Hale sidled up next to her, pulling her close with an arm around the waist. "I honestly don't expect you to scour the streets for more answers, and you've done more than enough already. I say we call the Imanu'el investigation quits here and move onto more important things."

"Are you sure?" She nuzzled into his shoulder. "I don't want you to feel cheated, and I did drag you all the way out here for my own selfish expedition."

"It's less selfish when you're doing it for the benefit of another person. And I'm sure your dad will appreciate it."

He couldn't see her eyes tear up.

"So what's the plan? Where do we start with this new investigation?"

"The DC Central Detention Facility." She said calmly. "We need to talk to my dad."

———————

THE PAIR walked through the second security checkpoint of the jail, holding their arms out as a baton waved over their bodies. The redundant checks had seemed like overkill to Hale until Cass explained the need for additional security. While primarily a place to house convicts of misdemeanor crimes, there were also plenty of criminals awaiting adjudication of major criminal trials, or on the list to transfer after being convicted of a felony. Therefore smuggling in weapons and contraband was both more likely and threatening to those inside.

The guard waved them through one last metal door, opening up to a square room of chairs and Plexiglas windows. With cautious steps, the pair moved down the rows to their designated booth. On the way they passed several interesting conversations. One woman spoke quietly into the phone to a man on the other side of the glass, tears pouring down her cheeks as her body wracked with sobs. Another booth featured a woman who had abandoned her phone, opting instead to open up her blouse and lean forward, giving the man on the other side a not-so-private show. The last booth they passed featured men on both sides of the glass. They each had their hands pressed up to the transparent divider, heads down, eyes closed. They spoke softly and in unison.

Cass and Hale reached their designated aisle, taking their seats across from the empty chair on the other side of the window. The plastic frames of the furniture clattered noisily as they slid into a comfortable position, though the racket was lost in the mix of conversations taking place around the room.

Hale shifted uncomfortably, leaning in to talk to Cass. "You sure you want me here?"

"Yes." Her voice wavered as she continued. "If there's anything you can Wander into that may help narrow down what we're looking for, I want to be sure you can see it. Maybe you will see a face of someone who can give him an alibi, or recognize some type of emotion on someone else that gives us a suspect."

Hale knew she was reaching, but said nothing to counter her. She confirmed everything he could have said with her tone. He suspected the primary reason he was here was for emotional support, which he was happy to give. He leaned forward onto the small table in front of them.

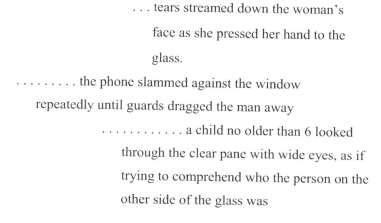

. . . tears streamed down the woman's face as she pressed her hand to the glass.

. . . . the phone slammed against the window repeatedly until guards dragged the man away

. . . . a child no older than 6 looked through the clear pane with wide eyes, as if trying to comprehend who the person on the other side of the glass was

He sat back quickly, rocking his chair with his momentum.

"Everything alright?" Cass looked over at him, brow furrowed with concern.

"Yeah… yeah." He took a breath. "Sorry. I… sorry. Just an intense Wander."

"Do I want to know?" she asked.

"A bunch of different things, different people," Hale's eyes dropped as he recalled the images. "Sadness, anger, pretty standard stuff, even if it was a little shocking to watch. But the worst was seeing a kid's face and feeling his confusion as he tries to figure out if that really is his dad on the other side of the glass."

He paused, trying to shake the feeling. He started to gather his words when he noticed Cass move out of his peripheral vision. She looked down, running her finger along the bottom lids of her eyes.

"I am a tremendous dick, I'm sorry," Hale sputtered, realizing his callous mistake. He placed a hand on her back, "Are you okay?"

"I'll be fine." She lifted her head and forced a smile, eyes still glistening with the threat of tears. Her voice shook, threatening to break. "Let's just… not talk for a bit, okay?"

Hale nodded, leaning back in his chair to gift Cass with some more space.

The minutes passed, each long and excruciatingly slow. Hale spent the time monitoring Cass to ensure she was holding up as well as she could be. He also took an accounting of the 'dangerous' places for him to be in the room. He didn't want to Wander again. Not in this place.

The door to the inmates' section opened and a man in an orange jumpsuit was escorted out. A guard led him towards the booth where Cass and Hale waited. His smile reached his eyes as he looked through the glass. Brown hair with streaks of gray hung towards his collar and continued in a similar color scheme through the short stubble adorning his face. Hale took note that Cass had received her soft hazel eye color from her father as well. Despite the somewhat weathered look the man had taken on during his stint in prison, Hale could easily imagine him in a suit with a briefcase walking towards Capitol Hill.

He picked up the phone on the other side, attention completely focused on

Cass.

Cass reciprocated, attempting to lift her phone as calmly as she could so as not to give away her nerves.

He spoke with a smile, resting his fingertips on the transparent barrier between them. While Hale could not hear his voice, he could clearly see the convict mouth the word 'Cassie.'

"Hi Dad." The strain could be heard in her voice. She rested her fingertips near his.

He responded with a calm face, love reflecting in his eyes. He seemed to be speaking softly. Hale could imagine from his expression he was attempting to keep Cass' fears assuaged.

"I know." She sniffled, running her fingers across her nose in a quick motion as if trying to hide any sign of emotional weakness. "But I had to see you. I don't like the thought of you in here."

He smiled warmly and spoke, fingers moving idly against the glass.

"Do you need anything?" she asked weakly. "I know I can send money. Do they allow other items? Or do you need me to call anyone?"

His warm smile persisted as he shook his head softly. He spoke again, eyes lighting up as he did. He pressed his full hand against the glass.

Cass bit her lip in an attempt to hold back a wave of emotion. The effort was in vain. Tears poured from her eyes and slid down her cheeks. Within seconds, she looked away and shielded her face with her free hand to conceal her sobs as best she could.

Hale made a move to console her, though a quick motion from behind the glass caught his notice. The gesture was subtle, but it immediately drew his full attention. Cass' father turned his head sharply to look at Hale, his eyes immediately widening into a fierce glare. His lips pulled in and his jaw set, fixating his eyes on what clearly was an intruder into his conversation. A chill ran up Hale's spine, and he withdrew back into his seat.

After lingering for another moment on the interloper, the prisoner's gaze returned to his daughter and his features softened again. He spoke in soft words, trying to coax her back out of her shell.

Slowly, Cass regained her composure. She wiped her eyes with her fingers, trying to minimize the smear of makeup as she did. After a few final sniffles, she returned to the conversation fully.

"I know, I know. I'm sorry." She took a ragged breath. "I am glad to see you. I just wish–" her voice cracked, and she took a moment to steady herself. "I just wish I could give you a hug."

He nodded and gave a comforting smile, speaking a few words to accompany the gesture.

Cass took a deep breath, and Hale recognized the look of determination beginning to smooth over her features. This was common right before one of her inquisitive moments.

"Dad, can you tell me what they are accusing you of?" She kept her voice steady. The familiar mindset of analysis gave her a renewed sense of calm. "I need the specifics. Where were you? Who was involved? All of it."

He cocked his head and furrowed his brow, clearly asking a question.

"Call it curiosity," she responded. "I would rather not have to hear it in the courtroom for the first time."

He shrugged and nodded. A few moments passed as he gathered words, then he spoke again. His face remained even, and though his expression remained soft, the look of tenderness and love faded for the telling of grim details.

Cass remained as stoic as she could, nodding and giving feedback where appropriate. Finally, she interjected. "Where?" She paused for his retort, responding in turn with a firm voice. "Because it helps me to know the details, you know that Dad."

He paused on the other side of the glass. Calmly, he spoke a few words and looked at her with an arched eyebrow. Hale could picture the same expression on his face had he been asking his own child if she had stolen a cookie without permission.

"I'm not dumb, Dad." She pulled her lips back into a thin line and lolled her head forward, as if accentuating the stupidity of the question.

He watched her for a few moments, studying her features. Finally, he released his expression and nodded, speaking into the phone again.

Cass listened carefully, nodding as he spoke. When he finished, she gave a final query. "Is there anything else?"

He shook his head, tapping the glass with his fingers. The warm, fatherly look returned as he spoke again.

"I miss you too, Dad." She pressed her hand against his.

A guard came up behind the prisoner, speaking a few quick words.

The jumpsuit wearing man turned around, speaking with the phone covered and flashing a beaming smile. Excitement and pride radiated from his face as he held one finger up.

The guard stopped, pursing his lips for a moment before returning a smile of his own and nodding. He gave a 'go ahead' gesture, and walked a few paces away.

Cass' father turned back to the phone, speaking some quick words and glancing at Hale. "Hale?" She asked with a confused face. "No, we're... Dad, did you tell that guard I was engaged just to get an extra minute?"

Her father's face lit up, as if they were still talking about great news. An emphatic 'Yes' could be seen from the other side.

She smiled, playing along. "I love you, you know that?"

He grinned back at her, returning the sentiment. He glanced at Hale again as he continued to speak.

She paused, eying him suspiciously. "Okay, but be nice." Tentatively, she turned and offered the phone to Hale. "He wants to talk with you."

Hale took the phone, looking through the glass at the man waiting with a pleasant smile. Memories of the fierce look that stabbed him through the solid barrier still reverberated in his head as he sheepishly put the receiver to his ear and spoke, "Hi..."

"Afternoon," the man said. His voice was rich as chocolate. Even with the minor mechanical distortions due to the old phone lines transporting his words, Hale knew this man's voice was an asset in compelling people's attention. "My name is Wilmer Voss, but you can call me Will. And you?"

"Hale." He cleared his throat. "Hale Langston."

"Well Mr. Langston," Will continued in his genial tone, "since I can't make introductions properly, I'll have to substitute a smile and a nod for a handshake." He did so.

Hale returned the gesture.

"Now on to brass tacks." The receiver tilted up to his mouth, the angle of the phone's arc covering his lips from Cass' view. While his facial features remained ingratiating and friendly, his voice dropped a pitch. Hale could imagine this tone was what would have accompanied the menacing glare he had received earlier. "You don't need to give any feedback from here on out, just look happy and nod to show you understand."

Hale mustered a friendly smile and nodded.

"Good. Now I need you to understand the woman you are sitting next to is the most important person in the world to me. Do you understand?"

Hale nodded again.

"I also need you to understand the fact that these walls do not prevent me from remaining in contact with the many friends I have made in this world, and that I would expend a lifetime worth of gathered associations and favors to make miserable the man who treated my daughter poorly. Do you understand?"

Hale's eyes were drawn to the orange jumpsuit. He returned his gaze to Will's eyes and nodded.

"Good, now that you understand my baby girl is not a conquest to notch in your bedpost, I give you my blessing to make her as happy as you possibly can. Just don't let me hear any stories to the contrary. Now say you were glad to meet me, and promise you'll treat her well." The receiver dropped away from his mouth by an inch as he shifted posture, allowing Cass to see a dazzling smile aimed at Hale.

"It's been a pleasure meeting you, sir," Hale repeated as instructed. "And don't worry, Cass is one of a kind, I'll treat her like the treasure she is."

"Very touching," Will said flatly, smile still gleaming. "Please hand the phone back to my daughter."

"Here you go." Hale turned and handed the phone to Cass, who was boring a hole into him with inquisitive eyes. "Uh, he wants to talk to you."

She took the phone, returning her gaze back to her father. "Dad... what did you say?"

He became animated, smiling and speaking with his hands.

"Uh huh," she said, eying him suspiciously. "And that was done in the nicest way possible, not in an attempt to scare him at all, was it?"

He grinned and said some words to reassure her.

"Yes, I'm sure he is," she said, her voice and expression still skeptical, but more amused now.

The guard made a motion and spoke behind Will.

Will nodded to him, then turned back to the glass. Hale saw the words "I love you, Cassie" clearly through the glass, after which he placed his hand on the clear barrier.

"I love you too, Dad." Tears brimmed again as she placed her hand over his.

He gave a reassuring smile, hung the phone up, and then slowly stood and pulled his hand away. Minutes later, long after Wilmer Voss had been escorted out, Cass finally pulled her hand away from the window.

23

Cass navigated through the roundabout, shooting an eye roll Hale's way when she was at a comfortable distance from other cars. "That's a load of crap."

"No, really," he said. "While a little more creative than anything I've heard, he was legitimately just looking out for you. He wanted to make sure I was treating you right."

"I don't disbelieve that." She righted their path, continuing down the street. "I still think he threatened you."

"Those phones are probably recorded," Hale ventured. "I don't think anyone would make that bad of a threat while being recorded in prison."

"'That bad' of a threat?" She shot him a knowing look. "So he did threaten you."

"Well… yeah." Hale blushed. "A little."

Cass smiled, returning her gaze to the road.

"So, what's next?"

"I convinced my dad to tell me where the crime scene was." She continued driving, as if the statement encapsulated the answer he sought.

Hale took a deep breath and exhaled. He knew this was a step in the process of finding the truth, though its proximity to a crime made his nerves begin to jump. The last thing he needed was to join the Voss family in prison for tampering with a crime scene.

His gaze shifted over to Cass. She was absolutely stunning. Her red hair shone in the afternoon light, and the slight upturn of her lips denoted happiness in spite of the turbulent times she weathered. Devastation had wrought her face not ten minutes earlier as they left the Central Detention Center, and Hale knew that her spark of happiness was due to hope. Hope that he was the key to.

He had to go through with this.

"So he wasn't too happy about you asking for details?" Hale ventured.

"He probably suspected I was going to do something foolish," she said, turning as the GPS offered instructions. "I feel bad for fibbing, but I know he wouldn't have told me otherwise, and that would have created extra research work to find it on my own."

Hale chuckled. "So had he forbade you from looking into it, it wouldn't have dissuaded you at all?"

"The same way telling him to be nice to you didn't dissuade him at all." She grinned, keeping her eyes on the road.

"Fair enough."

The streets took a turn for the worse. Potholes and cracks become more consistent, cars parked along the streets diminished in quality, and buildings started to show their decrepitude. Hale examined the various complexes as they drifted past, drawing comparisons to his own neighborhood. Rotting wood in cosmetic areas, old colors mixed with patchwork jobs of new paint and drywall, and an increasing presence of cheap motels and barred up convenience stores signaled this was no longer the tourist section of D.C.

"Starting to remind me of home," Hale mumbled as he looked out the window.

"I'm starting to feel like a minority." She commented.

"In this neighborhood, you might be." He said, looking around.

"I promise, in and out," she reassured. "We won't stay longer than we have to."

"I'm not worried," Hale responded. "I live in a bad neighborhood, so I'm kind of used to it. And our newly found minority status will probably get us some looks for being out of place, but I highly doubt it will come to anything if we're not antagonistic."

"How politically correct of you."

"Seriously," he said. "It's a pet peeve of mine. The way the news pitches areas like this, it's like they expect you to be beaten, robbed, raped, murdered, or a grisly combination of the quartet just by walking through the streets. Truth is, while it may not be the safest place, chances are if you don't go looking for trouble, you won't find it."

"I know, I know," she sighed. "While it may be a statistically low chance that I will be mugged and raped in a bad neighborhood, doesn't mean I want to test the odds."

"I don't know if this is the best time to bring it up, but you know my neighborhood isn't much better than this, right?" Hale looked over at her. "And you're definitely not a minority there."

"Look who's getting a guest pass to my complex!" She announced excitedly. He chuckled, looking back out his window.

The GPS directed them around the last few streets before it finally announced their arrival. Cass parked on the curb down the street from an old apartment complex. The walls were a faded blue with white trim around the awnings. Old brown doors added a strange contrast to the exterior colors, and the metal gate surrounding the complex did not provide an inviting atmosphere.

Hale looked back at Cass after taking the sight in. "In and out, you say?"

She nodded and the pair exited the vehicle. They stepped over the buffer of dead grass between the sidewalk and the street, up the path and to the waiting gate. An intercom system sat next to the locked entrance to the complex, featuring a list of names with 'Leasing Office' at the bottom. Cass hesitated, looking over the buttons.

After a pause long enough for Cass to examine the panel, Hale voiced an inquiry. "Did he tell you what apartment?"

"Ahh… no." She said, looking up at him. "Just that it was at Liberty Apartments downtown. I figured asking more was tipping my hand."

"There's a couple ways we can do this, then," Hale suggested. "We can snoop around the apartments and look for anything out of place, check on the internet for anything in the news about the crime, or just ask the leasing office and see if we can convince them to let us take a look."

"I doubt they'll let us go poke around a murder scene like a couple of freaks."

"We could say we're here with the police."

"You don't look like a cop." She smiled and arched her eyebrow.

"Hey," he said defensively. "I was a P.I. for a while."

"Yeah, a bad one." She stuck her tongue out playfully.

"Point," he smirked. "Okay, what about contractors to clean up and turn over the room for the new tenets."

"They might have already done that."

"If they have, we know the likelihood of finding something is slim," he shrugged. "But if they haven't, we might get a guided tour of the place."

"Risky, but it may be worth it," she conceded. "I'm just worried that we'll get made and our hands will be tipped. I need to make sure we get in there."

"Well if we get caught snooping around, you can bet we're not going to get another chance. We should leave sneaking in as a last resort."

Cass nodded, weighing their options.

"So, should we go get some suits and fake business cards?" Hale broke the silence after Cass pondered for a while. He could see she was deliberating on this problem more than she usually would, likely because of the personal investment she had in its outcome.

"I'm thinking we can just try the contractor angle as is. Say we're here to make an estimate or something, no need for cards. We'll just use the laptop." Her voice suggested she was not sure of herself.

Hale believe it was their best option, mentally agreeing that finding a suitable business card or fake ID would be time consuming, costly, and difficult. "I think it will work, and worse comes to worse we'll just say we're out of cards." Hale reassured her. He held his finger over the 'Leasing Office' button. "Shall we?"

She pursed her lips and nodded.

Hale depressed the button. A crackle sounded, immediately cutting off as he released pressure. He studied it for a moment before turning to Cass. "Is that an intercom button?"

As if to respond, a voice sounded out from the panel. It was female, and there was no attempt at civility in her tone. "We're closed."

Hale pressed the button again, holding it down. The panel clicked. He leaned forward. "Uh, sorry, we're late. We're supposed to take a look at a room to give an estimate."

"Who?" The voice asked, annoyed.

"I'm sorry?"

"Who are you here to see?"

"There wasn't a name given," Hale continued. "We were just told to speak with the complex manager and give an estimate for a room that had been damaged."

"We're closed." The voice repeated, annoyed.

Hale pressed the button again. "I apologize, but we need to fill this order. If you can just point us to the right place, we'll let ourselves out when we're done."

Silence.

They waited for a few minutes. Hale tried the intercom again with no luck. During their silent contemplation on how to adapt to the situation, a set of foot falls approached.

A heavyset woman walked down the path towards them. A light green blouse contrasted well with her black slacks and dark, chocolate colored skin. A pair of oval glasses rested on her nose, and she gauged the two individuals with suspicious eyes as she closed the distance. Head held high, and lips pouted out to accentuate her distrust, she called out, "I done told y'all, we're closed. Come back another time."

"My apologies, ma'am," Hale pleaded. "I know we're late, but we really need to get this claim written up today. Is there anything we can work out?"

"Your company puts me off for a week, and now you want me to accommodate your schedule?" She tilted her head down, eyeing Hale over her glasses. "I don't think so. I done worked my day an' I'm goin' home."

Hale noticed she had a street slanted drawl to her voice, and there was a prevalence of slang in her lexicon. However, her words were enunciated clearly and well chosen, leading him to believe she was playing a role of ignorance to try to get rid of her unwanted guests.

"I apologize for the inconvenience, and I'm sure I can talk to my boss about getting our fees cut back for the poor work ethics," Hale continued. "I'm sure something can be worked out."

"I don' care about fees," She exclaimed as she reached the gate. "It aint comin' out of my paycheck. Now back up, git git git." She shooed them back, putting her key in the gate on the other side. With a twist, the lock came undone and she pushed it open, sliding through and slamming it shut tight. She held it there for a moment, as if they would rush past her if she let it go. "Go on now, I'll be here tomorrow. You can come by then."

"Ma'am–" Hale protested.

"Go on!" she said adamantly.

The two looked at each other, trying to come up with a last minute plan.

"These two botherin' you, Gerda?" A voice called out from behind them.

The pair turned around. Walking up the path was a tall man with an air of authority. His hair was clean cut and short, his goatee neatly trimmed, his skin a shade darker than Gerda's, and his clothes clean and new. The dark green, un-tucked dress shirt gave an odd contrast to the deep blue and grey jeans he wore. He walked forward confidently, a swagger to his step as he eyed the two interlopers on his street with gravitas.

"Slowin' down my trip home, but that's all." Gerda lifted her chin to Hale and Cass. "Good night to both of you." With that, she turned and walked down the sidewalk. Hale glanced at Cass, who nodded in silent agreement that it was time to leave.

"Now hol' on." The tall man side stepped, holding his hand out to halt their progress. A wry grin spread across his lips as he looked over them. He stood casually, bringing his hand in front of him to rest with one fist loosely in the opposite palm. The glint of a gold watch disappeared under the cuff of his sleeve, leaving several thick rings as the only visible jewelry on the man.

Somewhere in the back of Hale's mind he remembered a martial artist in a kung fu movie doing the same hand gesture during a bow. Somehow he didn't think this man's intention was to show respect.

"Now what brings y'all fine, upstanding citizens to this part of D.C.?" He smiled, revealing a row of pearly white teeth with two golden rimmed caps.

"Just here to do an estimate on an apartment that got damaged," Hale lied, looking away nervously. "Guess we'll be on our way."

"I said hol' on." His voice dropped an octave, head tiling back to look down his nose at the pair. "Who you work fo'?"

"I'm a contractor."

"I must look like an ignant nigga to you." His voice returned to a soft, calm tone for the declaration. Somehow, the peace in his voice mixed poorly with the harsh words, making them that much more sinister. "You really going to lie to me on my own stoop? You can' bother to come up with a good one? Try again."

"Listen, we don't want any trouble," Cass started.

"And you aint found none, yet." The man's head snapped to look her in the eyes, the intensity within them sending their own message. He released her gaze after a few moments, returning back to Hale. "Now back to your bullshit. Lie to me, boy, and make it good."

Hale's heart was pounding. The man was not much bigger than Hale physically, but he was clearly stronger, and stood like knew how to handle himself. He didn't look like the common street thugs he was used to seeing near his neighborhood, which in a way scared him more. He wouldn't be surprised if this man was an entrepreneur of sorts, though his business was likely not one he paid taxes and fair wages for.

"We're here to see an apartment." Hale summoned his courage, knowing that showing weakness in situations like this was more damning than the wrong words. "That's all."

"I don' think you tryin' to put cream in the coffee, so this just a visit?"

"Yeah, coming and going," Cass said nervously.

"You here for party favors then?"

Hale hesitated, taking a breath. "No."

"White boy," The man pointed a finger at Hale's face, raising his tone slightly to show his aggravation. "Your type don' come around here but for two things, pussy and plants. Now I am tolerating your bullshit cause I expect to see some ducats for my troubles. I'm a businessman, so stop wastin' my time and tell me what the fuck you want."

Hale looked at Cass for a second, then quickly back up to the man.

"Deal," Hale said confidently.

"Speak, homie, I ain't got all day."

"How much for a tour?"

"A what?" The man dropped his hands, taking a bold step forward into Hale's space. "What the fuck you got me confused with, a goddamn limo driver?"

"No, I mean–" Hale instinctively backed up.

The man pushed forward, throwing Hale off balance and down to the curb.

Cass jumped backward, clutching her purse and standing flush against the community gate.

. . . "-treated with respect, not a damn punching bag"

. . . . . . "–gonna be aight. I gotchu"

. . . . Obie took a handful of money

from another man. "Good work. Now

follow me, gotta take care of someone."

"I said what the fuck you doin' on my street?" The man towered over Hale, leaning in to get within swinging distance if he didn't like the answer.

"We'll pay!" Hale said, shaking out of his sudden Wander while holding his hands out. "Cash! We just want to see one fucking apartment. Swear to fucking god."

"Why?!" He lurched forward to feign a swing, causing Hale to push himself back along the ground to stay out of the man's reach.

"Someone was killed there." Hale realized honesty was the best option at this point. "We just want to see the crime scene."

The man paused, looking down at Hale with curious eyes. After the long silence he spoke again. "Five-oh already been up and through that joint, they got everything locked away. You's a little late for a cover up."

"We're not trying to cover anything," Hale promised.

The man eyed Hale, "You two some sort of freaks that get off on this shit?"

"No man," Hale said, hands still out as he kept his eyes locked with the man towering over him. "Just... it's kind of a long story. We just want to see it, alright?"

A few more seconds passed before a hand was extended down. "See, why didn' you just open with that?" he asked, his voice returning to a much friendlier temperament.

Hale tentatively took the offered hand, allowing the muscular man to pull him to his feet.

"Name's Obie." The man shook Hale's hand before releasing it.

"Hale." He nodded, forcing himself not to take a step back. "So, uh, how much do you want to let us in to take a look?"

Obie looked back at the gate, chewing on his lip as he thought. "Well, I gotta get you through that gate, an' I'm guessing y'all will want to get into the apartment, too, right? Make it a clean C-Note and we happy."

By the time Hale looked over at Cass she was already digging through her purse.

"I don't suppose you take checks."

"Nah, and my Square is broke," Obie played along.

She pulled out a few bills, counting them out. "Here, that's $87. It's all the cash I have on me."

"Hold on, I hate cash, but…" Hale dug out his wallet, pulling out a $20. "I always carry one on me, just in case. Call it a bonus."

"Ain't you two generous." Obie took the money and thumbed through it. After shoving it in his pocket, he turned towards the gate. "For that I'll make sure yo' ride don' get jacked."

He pressed on the mesh of the gate, causing it to swing inward with little effort. He shot a grin over his shoulder as he walked through.

"But she–" Cass protested, looking down the path after Gerda.

"–don' want y'all knowin' the gate's busted," Obie finished for her. "My cousin Keenan works here, fixes shit up, turns over apartments, you know." Another grin. "T'sow Gerda knew you was bullshittin', too. She knows who works here."

Cass put a hand on Hale's arm, giving him a look that showed she still thought their gambit had been a good attempt.

Obie moved through the gate and walked past the first row of doors, looking up a staircase at a youth playing on the steps. The large man called up to him, "Hey little man, go on an' watch these two tourists' car. Make sure no one fucks wit it, aight?"

There was no hesitation or question. The kid simply nodded and ran down the stairs, shoes blinking with little LED lights with each step. He barreled past them and down the sidewalk towards the street.

"How will he know which one is ours?" Cass asked.

Obie chuckled, turning down another corridor of apartments. "It's gonna be the only one he don' know. Shit, y'all are lucky I ain't an evil man. Y'all would be out money, a car, and have no story about a crib with blood on the floors to tell your friends. My advice, stay out tha hood. Y'all got no idea what the fuck you doin' out here."

"Thank you," Cass said meekly.

"Don' thank me yet, shortie," Obie said over his shoulder. "I ain't come through on nothin'. Fo' all you know I'm taking you to my homie's crib where your world will get all kinds of fucked up."

Cass remained silent, unconsciously clinging to Hale's arm as they walked.

The path they took led them to the back of the complex. Obie led them on, shouting greetings and throwing various signs of respect to men and women he passed. One man received a nod and a shout, another a half bodied hug and a few sentences of conversation before seeing the other off. A woman was stopped and handed the pocket full of money he had just obtained from Cass and Hale. She looked to be in her thirties, though her face was weathered and the bags under her eyes could almost be called luggage. She took the money with a surprised and gracious smile, wrapping her arms around Obie's neck and thanking him heartily. He unraveled her arms after a few seconds, nodded dutifully and moved on.

Hale watched the interactions with interest, examining facial expressions, body language, and voice inflections. Each one regarded Obie with a measure of deference, and while they all gave the Caucasian pair an inquisitive eye or look of contempt, none questioned their presence. Hale looked to Cass to see if she noticed this too. Cass had instead fixated on the ground in front of her, both hands still attached to his right arm. It looked like a well-learned response; don't look for trouble and you don't find it. For the first time, he saw he fear win out over her curiosity. He looked back up at Obie as the guide swaggered on down the sidewalk.

"Do you live here, Obie?"

"Nah, my crib up tha street." He gestured back with his thumb.

"You have a lot of friends here," Hale observed.

"And what makes you think any of these niggas are my friends?"

"They have a lot of respect for you," Hale continued. "Maybe a little fear, too."

"Yo Ted Koppel," he barked. "You done writin' my biography?"

"Just curious what you do here."

"I'm a businessman, and a supporter of the community. Thas' all you need to know," Obie pointed. "Right up ahead, that be the place."

Hale and Cass looked forward. There were two floors of apartments, each looked the same as the next. The pair came to a simultaneous realization, the small labyrinth they had been led through would have been nigh impossible to navigate without their guide, especially with the interference they would have encountered by the residents. Sneaking in would have been a dismal failure.

Obie led them up a wooden stairwell. The wood creaked and bent, made brittle from age and weather. The structure withstood their presence, exhibiting much more resilience than an outside observer may have guessed.

They reached the top, hooking around the iron banister and moving down two doors to the right. Obie rapped his knuckle on the door twice as he passed it, then turned back to his fare and leaned against the wall. "This it."

"Let me guess," Hale spoke up. "It's unlocked, too?"

"Hell naw, man." Obie cocked his head and squinted his eyes as if he was trying to find the source of the inane comment. He reached into his pocket, pulling out a metal object. With a flick of his wrist, a three inch blade flew out, clicking into place.

Cass inhaled sharply, taking a quick step back.

Obie chuckled, shaking his head as he turned towards the door. He fished a key out of his other pocket, sliding it into the deadbolt. With two quick motions he slammed the butt of the knife onto the back of the key, then slid the blade into the doorjamb next to the handle. He twisted the key with his free hand, clicking the lock out of place, then levered the knife to depress the catch in the door. Within seconds, the door swung open. Like a butler greeting servants, Obie smiled and extended his arm out, inviting them in.

Hale gave a nod to Obie before tentatively stepping past him and into the apartment.

While the apartment didn't look like the scene of a grisly murder, it certainly lacked an inviting atmosphere. Aside from relatively new carpet, the rest of the living space was in less than great condition. Countertops featured chips in the surface, paint on the walls was old and yellowing, and the baseboards featured several areas of wood rot and physical damage.

Hale and Cass moved through the entryway, taking a gander around the room.

"There it is," Obie said, clicking his knife closed and slipping it back in his pocket. "Now you can tell your trust fund club you've been down in the shit."

"Where did it happen?" Hale asked, eyes scanning the floor.

"Heard the dude got done right there." Obie pointed to the floor where they stood. "Way I hear it, cat got blasted a few feet from the door."

"There's no blood." Cass sounded a little panicked, looking around the floor.

"Bad enough someone got done here." Obie crossed his arms, leaning on the doorframe. "You think a nigga wanna rent out a crib with bloodstains on the floor? Hell naw. Gerda had that shit fixed up soon as tha police took down tha tape."

"Shit…" she cursed, bringing her fist up to her lips. She paced.

"I tol' y'all a coverup was a bit late." Obie cocked an eyebrow.

"No." Hale held up a hand defensively. "Nothing like that. We were just hoping to get an idea of what happened. Can we, uh, just take a look around?"

"Ain't nothin' to steal, an if you jus' tryin' ta fuck in a murder scene, be quick and clean up after." Obie straightened, digging a green pack of cigarettes out of his pocket. "Ima have a smoke out here. I'll grab ya after and take you back to ya car."

"Thanks Obie." Hale nodded. "I appreciate it."

Obie turned and moved down the walkway to the staircase, taking a seat to enjoy his cigarette in peace.

"What do we do?!" Cass whispered, eyes wide with anxiety.

"Everything we can," Hale answered confidently, putting his hands on her shoulders to calm her. "I'll try to trigger a Wander off of everything in this room. Hopefully they haven't wiped the trail completely clean."

She nodded, clearly unconvinced. "What should I do?"

"Hang out here." He pointed to the small linoleum entryway near the door.

"Let me know if he's coming back."

Her eyes watered, clearly frustrated and upset with the situation. While she had not expected a gift wrapped package with the evidence to clear her father's name waiting inside, she had hoped for a slightly more tenable situation. Understanding there was little she could do from this point, she assumed her post in the entryway and watched Hale as he moved.

Unsure how long they had, Hale got on his hands and knees and started feeling around the floor. He probed with his fingers, smelled the carpet, ensuring his skin touched as much surface area as possible. He felt ridiculous. Like a dog sniffing for a treat with their owner watching for their own bemused entertainment. He knew... well, he hoped Cass didn't have anything except for wishful thoughts that he'd find something. A nagging theory prodded him from the back of his mind that she would be mocking him mercilessly for this later.

Focus, Hale. He mentally kicked himself. His fingers ran along the line of carpet bordering the linoleum entryway.

> . . . a crack of a staple gun was followed
> by a sharp cry of pain.
> . . . . . . "Fuck this shit!" the man
> exclaimed, standing from his work.

"What did you find?!" Cass' voice found Hale's ears as he exited his Wander.

He shook his head ruefully. "Just a worker, probably Obie's cousin. Hurt his hand when he was putting in the new carpet."

She wrung her hands nervously, eyes focused on him as if the true revelation was near.

He stood, moving over to the kitchen. His hands moved across the countertops. The divots and chips in the wood surface acted as small hills and valleys for his fingertips, however nothing sparked any insight. He inhaled deeply, smelling the faint lemon scent of the disinfectants used to clean the room during its turnover. Aside from the faint odor of citrus, Hale received no hints to the history of the apartment.

He walked through the bedroom. He explored the bathroom. He did a quick once over on the living room and entryway again. Each room was examined as quickly and thoroughly as possible, doing his best to focus on the well trafficked areas. Each room met with the same silence, as if the secret was determined to stay buried.

Hale paced in the living room, unwilling to look up and see the disappointment riddled across Cass' face. He needed to do this. He needed to help her. He refused to be thwarted by a fast approaching deadline and the small threat of danger. She brought him here to help her family, her flesh and blood, and he would not let her down.

"Blood…" he said quietly.

"What?" she asked, taking a quick look outside.

Obie's voice could be faintly heard speaking into a cell phone. Perhaps they had enough time after all.

"Blood," he repeated in a hushed voice. "The blood from the wound had to have seeped through the carpet. It's probably right under here somewhere. When I Wandered from Imanu'el's blood, it was the most powerful imagery I had every received. I don't know what the, uhm, shelf life will be. But at this point, we're running out of options."

Cass stepped forward. "How do we get to it?"

"Unless Obie wants to lend me his knife to cut out strips, we're just going to have to pry it up." Hale knelt next to the dividing line of carpet and linoleum again. The carpet had been roughly stuffed under a metal divider to clamp it down to the floor.

Hale wished Alex was here with them. He would have been able to deal with Obie much better, and his knowledge of construction would have been useful. However, knowing his friend's assistance was 4000 miles away, he returned to the task of figuring out how to achieve his goal.

Pinching a tuft of carpet between thumb and forefinger, Hale tugged at the edge. A small portion pulled loose. The progress halted suddenly, fastenings taking purchase and holding the carpet tight. From the looks of it, Keenan had only bothered to attach the carpet at large intervals, counting on the metal divider to act as a cover and supplement to his work. Hale remembered a conversation over beers with Alex about this.

"*Alex!*" Alex imitated his foreman. "*Every three inches. I want a purchase on that carpet to the floor every three inches. Use your dick as a measuring tool if you have to!*" He dropped the impression. "*I wanted to ask him why his wife thought my three inches was bigger than his, but I figured a paycheck was better than one-upping that jackass.*"

Hale smiled at the memory, then curled his fingers under the small lip of carpet he had exposed. With a sharp rip, the fastenings to the left and right of the opening snapped loose. Another sharp tug pulled up enough of the flooring to see a couple feet underneath. Hale slid out onto the linoleum, looking into the makeshift cave he had created.

There it was, plain as day.

It was a dark stain of crimson in a sea of lumber. While faded from obvious attempts to clean and scrub it out, the stain was permanent, and had soaked into the wood beneath the padded flooring. Hale looked back at Cass, who could not see the residue from her angle. His eyes said everything, and he turned before questions could be asked.

He reached out a hesitant hand, hovering centimeters over the dark splotch. The memories of the Wander from Imanu'el's blood flashed back to him momentarily, reminding him how vivid this experience could be. He didn't want it. He wanted to pull away, just say he found nothing. He wanted to just leave with Cass and comfort her like a normal boyfriend would.

With a sigh of resignation, he placed his fingertips onto the stain.

… "–gonna make me sick. They aint payin' me en–"

Hale shook free from the vision of Keenan's face rubbing blood off of the floor almost as soon as he saw it.

"What did you see?!" Cass asked, hurriedly.

"Nothing yet…" Hale pressed his entire hand down on the blood.

Nothing.

He moved his palm around.

Nothing.

He concentrated, moving his nose near the opening to inhale deeply.

Nothing.

Fuck. Hale cursed to himself, pulling his hand back and staring at the floor while he thought. *Fuck fuck fuck. They scrubbed the spot down. Any trace of what was here is gone. There's nothing here.*

"Hale?" Cass spoke quietly from behind him.

"It's not working." His voice was low and defeated.

"There has to be a way," she demanded.

"I keep getting the guy who turned the place over. He wiped everything clean."

"No." Her voice tightened. "There has to be something."

"Cass, there's no blood left. It's all soaked into the wood." He stopped, eyes losing focus as he formulated a plan.

"Please, Hale," she begged. "You have to do something."

"Do you have a nail file?" He asked suddenly.

"Yes… yes." She didn't bother to question him, knowing Obie could walk in at any second. She fished through her purse, zipping open an inner pocket and pushing forward a small nail clipper with an attached file. "Here, just pull the file out, it's folded inwards."

Hale took the grooming instrument, swiveling out the file with the hooked nail pick on the end. Fishing it underneath the carpet, he grasped the tool in his hand like a dagger and jabbed it down into the wood. It took a couple tries due to the lack of momentum and dullness of the blade, but he eventually got a good purchase into the wood. He whittled the makeshift pick back and forth, wedging a small chip of wood out from the floorboard.

Hale sat back, pulling his prize out from under the carpet. It was clearly a darker red in the centimeters below the surface. Cleaning solution and brushes had not found their way as deep as the seeping liquid had during the days it had soaked in. He held it tightly, hoping it would give him something. He did not want to do what he knew was next.

Nothing came.

Sir, The General chimed in. *Decisive action and bold strokes are needed here. Do what must be done.*

"You may not want to watch this," Hale said to Cass as he swiveled the large hand of the nail clippers up.

She pressed herself against the wall near the door, hand clamped over her mouth as she watched. Phobia or no, Cass willed herself to witness Hale's divination.

He placed his left pinky finger in between the thin metal strips, pressing against them until a sizable bump of flesh protruded between the sharp edges of the nail clipper. Wasting no time to think about what came next, he inhaled sharply and squeezed the levers together.

There was no satisfying click that usually comes after clippers slice through a hard chunk of nail and slap together. The resistance given by Hale's fingertip was minute. Metal cut through the flesh easily, separating a small chunk of his finger and allowing blood to flow freely down his hand. He suppressed a whimper, trying to keep a staunch and stoic demeanor during the process for both his and Cass' benefit.

With another deep breath to steady himself, he pressed the bloody block of wood against the exposed wound in his flesh.

Hale Wandered immediately.

24

Cass' insides lurched. The sight of fresh flowing crimson sent currents of ice through her veins. Her stomach churned, threatening to seize as she watched the chunk of skin fall from Hale's fingertip. The majority of the blood flow was covered by his quick movements to press the chip of stained wood against the fresh wound. That didn't erase the initial image of the lesion oozing over his fingers. She forced herself to stand still, covering her mouth as a physical means of bolstering her determination to remain.

You can do this, Cass, she thought to herself, reinforcing her will. *This is for Dad. Anything you miss could be a link to his freedom. Watch every expression, no matter how subtle. There may be clues that Hale misses when he Wanders.*

Hale, already kneeling down at the start of the process, straightened his back and looked up. His eyes locked with an invisible being, widening in fear. His mouth pulled back into a fearful grimace, lips beginning to tremble uncontrollably. The nail clippers clattered to the ground as he flexed his fingers and brought his wrists together behind his back.

This is odd. Cass thought as drops of blood fell to the floor from Hale's fingertips. She forced her stomach into submission as it attempted to seize and went back to her thoughts. *Hale's never done this before. It's usually over by now... and he's moving a lot. Why is he moving?*

Hale's lips continued to tremble as his head and back arched back slowly. He bent like a long reed being bowed over by wind. His head tilted further, as if a force pressed on his forehead and pushed him away. His eyes were filled with terror, and incomprehensible words passed through his lips. A dark spot spread over the front of his jeans, widening with the sound of liquid hitting denim. The urine soaked through and dripped to the floor.

Tears filled both of their eyes; one of them with minor fear and shame, the other in abject terror. Hale continued gibbering incoherently as wet streaks formed across his temples and into his hair. While his face nearly pointed straight up at the ceiling, his eyes focused ahead towards the same invisible figure as before.

The memory of Hale's dripping blood faded in the sight of this new horror. Cass stopped herself from stepping forward to take him into her arms, to give him a modicum of comfort in this moment of crisis. She wanted to bestow some strength in his state of frailty, to give him confidence to come back from whatever it was he was seeing.

Oh god. A new fear crossed her face. *What if this is too much? What if the shock from what he's seeing damages him forever? What if he can't come back?*

As if in response, Hale's body convulsed. His head snapped down another inch, past its already bent state. The recoil in his body and the tension in his knees caused his frame to lift up again. Like a rag doll, his limbs and torso followed the momentum of the convulsion and rocked to the side, tumbling in slow motion to the ground. His head knocked against the floor unceremoniously, his hands still diligently held behind him. Glassy eyes remained open and unfocused, staring blankly at the open door ahead.

"Hale?!" Cass fell to her knees next to him, hands reaching out tentatively. *Oh god, oh god. What did I do to him?! Should I touch him? Should I call the paramedics? God, Hale, please wake up!*

"What the fu–" Obie's voice boomed from behind her.

Hale's body convulsed again, curling into the fetal position. His neck and jaw locked as he began vomiting violently. Remnants of breakfast and his Monument Mocha ejected from his mouth and covered the floor around Cass' feet. The brown and yellow liquid washed over the drops of blood Hale left pooling on the fake tile. His hands broke free from their invisible bonds, rocking him onto his back as he pulled his pinned limb out from under his ribs. Hale pressed his palms against his forehead as he rolled to his opposite side, vomiting again. This time the torrent splashed over the edges of the new carpet as well as more of the linoleum entryway.

"Mother fucker!" Obie reached into his belt, pulling out a handgun from under his dress shirt. "Tweaking fuck come into my neighborhood and fuck up our shit."

"He's having a seizure!" Cass sputtered. The symptoms he showed were the only thing she could match on the spot. She stood up quickly, trying to draw Obie's attention before he did something rash. A selfish portion of her mind whispered that if Hale died here, she'd never find out what he saw. "Please, he's epileptic, he needs a doctor!" Cass stood between them, self-preservation giving way to desperation.

"Back up, bitch." Obie gruffly pushed Cass to the side, slamming her into the entryway wall. "I know junkies when I see them. I knew there was something fucked up with y'all, wanting to see a goddamn murder house."

She bounced off and fell to her knees, her purse and its contents clattering to the floor.

"And you," Obie grasped Hale by the hair, holding him still as his body shivered and twitched. He snarled as he looked over the dirty and disheveled man on the floor. His eyes pulled right, and he saw the portion of carpet pulled up. "Tweaking fuck. There a fucking stash you have hidden here or some shit? You don't pull this bullshit here. You might be OD'ing, or just got some bad shit, but I promise you it will be your last time you fuck with this block!"

The cold steel barrel of Obie's pistol pressed against Hale's temple. Hale's head lazily lolled with the pressure, giving no resistance or reaction of any kind. As Obie pulled the hammer back on the gun, a clicking sound from behind him caught his attention. He risked a look back just in time for a jet of pepper spray to stream into his face and cover his eyes.

Obie yelped, jerking away instinctually to avoid the onslaught of pain. His foot planted and tried to pivot, but lost traction in the fresh pool of vomit. His shoe slipped across the linoleum, catching on Hale's legs as he toppled over onto the carpet. His hands shot up to his face as he rolled onto his back, gun still clutched tightly as he tried to rub his eyes.

Cass moved quickly, hopping over Hale and lifting her foot high over Obie. Using a small hop to help her with momentum, she brought her heel down as hard as she could. The strike connected with the back of Obie's right hand, smashing bones and crushing the gun into his face.

The gun extended up and away from Obie's bloodied face, flashing once with a boom as a bullet flew from the barrel.

Cass was lucky to have stumbled to the side after stomping down, missing the trajectory of the bullet by a few feet. Despite being untouched by the flying projectile, her ears rang from the explosion within the closed room. The sound was jarring, and nearly caused her to cower in fear.

Reinforced by necessity, she regained her balance and kicked, slamming her toes into Obie's wrist and sending the gun flying into the entryway.

The large gangster scrambled to his feet, desperately trying to gain his bearings through tear filled eyes. He held his broken hand near his chest, feebly trying to shield it from additional attacks with his forearm as his good hand wiped at his eyes.

"You fuckin' bitch!" he croaked out. "Ima fuckin' kill you."

Cass, still possessing the full range of her vision, slipped passed him quickly and dove for the gun. She tumbled over Hale, trying for a graceful landing on the ground passed the pools of vomit. She quickly realized her angle was completely wrong as her body tumbled forward and twisted her left arm under her. Still deaf from the gunshot, she felt a pop and a hot streak of agony shot up her neck and down her back. She cried out in pain, but did not stop frantically reaching for the gun with her good hand.

Obie stepped across Hale's prone and twitching form to loom over Cass. His movements were quick, but disjointed, stumbling to and fro with the obstacles in his way. He blinked quickly and rubbed his eyes, trying to regain his vision to re-enter the fray despite the loss of his full sight.

She spun the moment before he reached her, pointing the gun directly at Obie's face. "Stop!" she shrieked, hands shaking violently as she held the weapon. "Step back!"

Obie squinted and wiped at his eyes again, trying to get a lock on the fuzzy shapes threatening him. He seemed to realize his situation, and without a clear sight of Cass or his gun, he gauged his chances were better if he retreated. Holding his one good hand up, he took a slow step back over Hale.

"More!" She pushed herself to her feet, her left shoulder shooting pain down her side when she stretched it to push herself up. Cass faltered, but managed to bring herself up to a crouch. Eyes focused on Obie, she stepped directly into the pool of vomit as she reached out and nudged Hale. A flinch erupted from a fresh lance of pain from her shoulder as she shook him. "Get up. Hale! Get up!"

He whimpered to himself, small movements suggesting he was coming back to a state of coherence.

"Hale, now! It's time to leave." The quivering gun remained trained on Obie, who stood calmly with a look of contempt on his face.

"I do you a solid, and this is how you repay me?" He growled. "Fuck up my hand and spray a nigga in the eyes? Tear up this crib and steal my gun!"

"Hale," Cass ignored Obie. "Let's go."

Hale stirred, hand wiping at his face. He mumbled a few words, questioning his surroundings, and pushed himself up to his elbows.

"So that's it?" Obie lifted his head, trying to regain the air of nobility despite his crippled state. "Y'all gonna rob a nigga and leave?"

"You were going to kill him!" Cass shook Hale's shoulder as she spoke, trying to rustle Hale up.

"I wasn't gonna kill nobody," Obie barked. "But some tweakin' fool decides to get sick on my homegirl's floor, I gonna scare him til he's sober enough to walk out on his own damn feet. I ain't gonna be a crutch for his nasty ass."

Cass wasn't sure whether or not to believe him. He hadn't seemed the violent type before, aside from his initial assault on Hale. Then again, there was no way she would chance it by giving his gun back now.

"What's going on?!" Hale grumbled, eyes lazily moving from Obie to Cass as he sat up.

"We're leaving. Let's go." She tugged at his arm, gasping in pain as her shoulder protested.

Hale pushed himself up, a strand of expulsed juice dripping from his chin. Obie was right, he did look like a junkie. He may have just pulled himself from a gutter after an all night bender from his demeanor.

She couldn't blame Obie for his assumptions, then again, she couldn't condone his reactions. She did not allow her gaze to rest on Hale for long, maneuvering to keep Obie in her sights with a clear line of fire at all times.

As she stood, she pulled her purse up into her injured arm. Various trinkets and kits fell out with the rest of the clutter on the floor. She did a quick scan to ensure it was nothing essential. No ID's, cell phone, keys, or other documents that could lead anyone back to her. Just some assorted makeup and a brush.

The selfish, materialistic part of her brain chimed in again, urging her to scoop them back into her bag. It was more than what was confiscated at the airport, after all.

Now is really not the time. She chided herself.

"Where are we going?" Hale asked sluggishly as he shuffled past Cass and out the door.

"I'm going to close this." Cass fumbled with the door, curling her fingers around the edge. "You wait five minutes, and then we'll forget this happened."

"Uh huh," Obie grunted, head tilted back so he could look down at her through squinted eyes. Cass kept the firearm trained on him as she slowly pulled the door closed, watching him carefully until the door eclipsed him from view.

———————

THE PAIR moved down the pathway towards the main entrance. Cass had helped Hale down the steps, wrapping his arm around her shoulder to ensure his steps were steady. Her jacket shielded the majority of the sick that Hale had rolled through on the floor, saving her the wet feeling through her clothes. Even if her logical side hadn't taken control to guide her path to survival, the adrenaline rush would have helped her to ignore the discomfort.

Hale began to regain his bearings as he moved. He became aware of his surroundings, how he got here, and that he had obviously wet himself sometime in the recent past.

And why are my ears ringing?

A clean patch of his sleeve was used to wipe his chin and cheeks, and he forced himself to overlook the uncomfortable feeling that walking presented at the moment. While disoriented, his focus was not shifted as heavily as Cass. She had been forced into a panic and her fight or flight instinct was in control. He felt as if he was woken suddenly from a deep REM sleep. While remnants of an accelerated heartbeat and adrenaline rush lingered from his Wander, he had been winding down when Cass had pulled him to his feet.

Cass looked left and right as they moved. She had expected Obie to come flying out of the apartment seconds after they left, shouting for the help of his neighborhood friends to bring them down for their betrayal.

No such outburst came.

She knew the gunshots had been heard. She pictured a scene out of a Hollywood movie, gangsters pouring out of the apartments strapped with all manner of weapons to defend their trespassed turf. Like Butch Cassidy and the Sundance Kid, the two 'outlaws' would be gunned down in a glorious shootout with a black and white tint to the entire scene.

Some curtains had been pulled to the side, making way for curious faces to see what had happened, yet there was a distinct absence of a horde of gang bangers toting guns.

Despite the apparent lack of danger, Cass ushered Hale along the path, poorly concealing the confiscated pistol within her small jacket. Hale picked up the pace as they moved, sensing the urgency in Cass' movements and following suit.

"Are we okay?" he asked dumbly.

"Once we get to the car, we'll be fine." Cass assured herself.

They turned down the last path towards the main gate. Seeing their goal in sight, they abandoned the attempt to move inconspicuously and began to jog. A moment of quick panic set in when they saw the gate with no handle, only a keyhole to open and close the portal. Neither of the two had a key, nor lock picking skills like Obie. The moment subsided when Hale remembered their entry, reaching forward and pulling the broken gate open.

The street was clear of activity. After verifying their safety with a quick scan left and right, the pair ran into the street towards their car. It was half a block down, parked in a line of cars on the opposite side of the street. A quick sprint of less than 100 feet.

"Hey!" a voice called out.

The two spun around.

Three men walked quickly towards them. They looked as if they had come from a side street at the other end of the block, the same direction Obie had been walking from when he first approached.

"Shit, why didn't I take his phone?!" Cass cursed herself in realization.

"Hold up!" the leading man said, holding his hands out. "We jus' wanna talk."

"BACK UP!" Cass screamed, pulling Obie's gun out and pointing it at them.

"Like he said, nigga," one of the men mumbled. "She a crazy bitch."

"Go." The lead man nodded back to them.

With coordinated movements, the two in back ducked down and moved to opposite sides of the street, moving behind parked cars to cut off Cass' line of fire as they approached. The lead man stayed in the street, standing still.

"You don' know whatcha gettin' yo'sef into, girl." He faced down her gun with a fearless stare.

"Cass." Hale pressed his hand against her stomach, gently pushing her back.

"Run."

Cass panned the gun from sidewalk to sidewalk in a vain attempt to regain control over a situation far beyond her normal reality. Wasting no more time, she heeded Hale's suggestion. Turning on a heel, she bolted towards the car with Hale close in tow. A moment of clarity gave her the foresight to unlock the car en route. She pulled the keys free from her purse, and the tail lights flashed as she frantically pressed the Unlock button.

Their pursuers made quick progress towards them. The head start and panicked speed of their quarry gave Hale and Cass an edge, forcing the trio to sprint to catch up.

Hale and Cass reached the car first. Cass pulled open the driver side door as Hale jumped across the trunk and went for the passenger door.

Amidst the frenzied motion, a moment hung as Hale noticed the small boy sent to watch their car. He sat quietly on the stoop of a townhouse, hand grasping the railing idly as he watched the fleeing couple enter their vehicle. The boy gave a small, friendly wave, his expression remaining in its apathetic state. Hale managed to give a nod as he wrenched the door and slid into his seat.

The car roared to life as he slammed his door, and Cass maneuvered the car to pull them into the street. The first runner reached them, rushing up to the passenger side and launching himself at the door. Foot outstretched, he landed a heavy kick into the frame, rocking the car and sending a boom through the interior.

"Hey!" The little kid yelled feebly, standing to reprimand the attacker. "Obie said don' fuck wit da car!"

The assailant reached down, his momentum fully stopped from the collision with the car, and pulled at the handle. Hale grabbed the door as the man pulled it open, starting a tug of war as Cass maneuvered out into the street. The tight space between the fleeing car and the parked truck in front of them did not offer enough room for any open doors, and caught the window frame with the bumper of the truck. The sudden jolt helped Hale to slam the door shut and caused the thug to tumble into the bed of the immobile vehicle.

In the clear of the street, Cass floored it. Chirping the tires as they accelerated, the car jetted down the sea of asphalt, leaving the trio of men and the shouting boy safely behind.

25

Hale curled into his seat, facing out the window. Buildings and streets rolled by in silence, reflecting in his empty stare. Cass had taken mercy on him thus far. No questions. No prodding. She assumed he was in a state of misery after the episode he had just been through.

She was right.

Waking from his Wander and being thrust into a violent series of events had been a horrible experience in of itself. In addition, the Wander itself was terrifying. His throat was scratched from throwing up, though he barely remembered being sick. He was still in a daze at the time, no longer Wandering but not completely conscious. Like the experience after waking from a deep slumber. That daze was also what contributed to his careless movements, which had caused both his clothes and Cass' shoes to be spattered with his expulsions.

His pants were still wet. Optimistic thoughts prompted ideas of something being spilled on him while he was out. It was wishful thinking, Hale knew full well from the temperature and smell of the liquid when he woke that he had wet himself. He hoped the ensuing chase had been chaotic enough for Cass to have overlooked it.

He didn't know if the discomfort or embarrassment was worse. Closing his eyes to shut the world away for a few moments, he leaned towards the latter.

A sour taste lingered in his mouth. He momentarily wished for his coffee to wash the taste from his tongue. His body forced immediate regret as the association of the taste made his stomach churn, quickly removing any desire for the caffeinated beverage. The yearning for the drink was soon replaced with that of a shower; a long, hot shower where he could cleanse his body and lose himself in therapeutic steam.

He had not wanted anything with such intensity in some time.

The car made a few quick, final turns, slowing down as it entered the parking lot of the hotel and finally came to a rest.

He waited. While the car had stopped, there was no hint of motion signaling it was time to get out. He felt it was important for her to move first. He didn't want to draw her attention more than he had to. Not in the state he was in. Nothing could be worse than the embarrassment he would feel.

"Hale," she spoke quietly. "I know you are probably dying for a shower and a change of clothes right now."

You have no idea, Hale thought.

"But I need to know," she continued. "What did you see? Even if it is just a summary, something to give me some confirmation that all that was not for nothing. We can go over the details later. Just… let me know it worked."

I was wrong, there was something worse. Hale thought.

"Cass," he muttered through a raw throat. "Please, not right now."

"Hale." She gripped the wheel as if she would fly from the seat without an anchor. Her head lowered, and her voice quivered. "I need to know. Please. We've been through a lot today, and I'd rather know it was not all in vain."

"Cass," Hale moaned, curling his head farther into his chest. "I'd rather not." *Please don't make me.*

"Please, Hale." She looked over at him, a deep furrow in her brow and sadness in her eyes. "I know you're in pain, but my heart has been on fire since I found out about my dad. Just give me something, let me know you saw who did this!"

"I…" Hale trailed off.

Maybe I can just will myself to die. I can't do this.

"Hale?" An undercurrent of fear mixed in with her features. "Hale… y-you did see something then?"

"Yes." Hale's voice was a whisper.

I can't look at her. I can't watch her hope die.

"You–" She choked on the transition, taking a sharp breath to clear the way for the next words. "You saw who murdered that man?"

Unable to bring himself to talk, Hale nodded weakly.

Please don't ask–

"Did you recognize him?" Her voice vibrated.

He remained motionless.

"Hale. Hale!" She grabbed his shoulder, tugging at him gruffly. "Who did you see?"

Hale was pulled upright in the seat. He kept his chin tucked into his chest at first, though Cass' burrowing eyes and pleading words eventually demanded he turn to face her. He couldn't speak. Whether or not he was physically able, his mind refused to form the words. He instead just looked at her, his eyes tired, sad, and horrified.

"Was it the man who met with Imanu'el?" She asked, eyes lighting up. "Or Imanu'el himself? Oh god, please tell me. That would be serendipitous."

Hale's lips pursed, denying not only the hypothesis, but the optimistic viewpoint that Cass had taken.

She locked eyes with him, a frantic look creeping through her features. Her gaze darted from eye to eye, as if trying to read thoughts via his expression. A shudder rocked her frame as she felt the answer come to her. Exercising every ounce of will she had remaining, her voice steadied for one more question.

"Hale, was my Dad the one you saw?"

Hale's face remained etched in stone. He would not give words of affirmation, and the hopeless gaze in his eyes pleaded for Cass to understand. They begged her not to make him say it, and in a long moment, communicated with more emotion than his words could have hoped for.

The breath locked in Cass' lungs burst out in a scoff of denial. Her lips curled into a smile of disbelief, quickly melting back into the dread they came from. A cacophony of emotion swirled behind her eyes and bubbled under her cheeks, fighting for sovereignty over her reaction. She faltered as she turned away, returning her gaze to Hale with an inquisitive look of disbelief taking the reins again.

Let me take it back. He pleaded with his eyes. *Let me lie to you. Let me take away your fear and pain.*

"Well," she scoffed, her analysis seemingly complete. "I mean, it's not like we're even sure you Wandered into the truth. I mean, it could be a mixture of emotions and fear that culminate to–" her voice cracked, causing her to sputter out the rest of her sentence. "–a tainted memory. Like a dream."

Hale continued staring helplessly.

"Plus," She turned to face the windshield as she continued on, her voice wavering heavily as she continued to persuade herself. "You've only Wandered from blood once before. This could be completely different from what you're used to."

"Cass," Hale spoke carefully, his tone soft as if anything harsher would break her. "I am sorry, and I know this is new, but I–"

"And my dad would have told me!" she cut him off sharply, her eyes still forward. Her gaze shifted as she thought. "I know he's in prison, and his phone calls are monitored, but he would have found a way to get an uncensored message to me. He would–" Tears began falling from her eyes, raining from her cheeks to her lap. Her lips curled into a deep frown even as she tried to force herself to continue. "He would have told me."

"Cass, I'm sure he would have." Hale reached out to place his hand on her shoulder. "He probably just hasn't had an opportunity."

Her face remained an immutable mixture of disbelief and confusion. Every fiber of her being told her this was not possible. The man delivering the information must be wrong. Her intuition had guided her to this place to *free* her father, not condemn him. Wilmer Voss was the pinnacle of her existence. He was the man who raised her, taught her, and stood as a role model for the kind of person she aspired to be in life. Her disagreement with his career aside, the execution of his work had always been admirable, just, and intelligent; all qualities she had striven to replicate in her own life. He was not a monster. He was misunderstood.

Through all of these thoughts, the crushing facts crashed against the facade she had built around his image and began collapsing the mental monument to her father. The pain that accompanied the assault of debris from the crumbling shrine rose exponentially. Each second, denial lost ground, and the coldly logical portion of Cass' brain chipped away more and more of its justifications and lies. As the full weight of the truth set in, Cass felt a spike of pain seat in her stomach and jut up into her chest.

Cass howled. There were no words, just an exclamation of pain that transitioned into an incomprehensible scream, which faded into a low wail. Breath failed her, and when she stopped to take in more air, her body wracked with uncontrollable sobs. Her forehead fell against the steering wheel as she wept, tears falling freely from her squinted eyes.

———————

HALE LET the water splash against his face and lost himself in the steam.

Cass had gathered herself after bawling in the car for ten minutes. She went through several phases very quickly, lashing out at Hale at one point when he tried to console her, only to fall into his arms and desire nothing more than to be held but a few minutes later. Hale acquiesced, remaining silent for the majority of the ordeal. Consoling words were offered when appropriate, and he held her tightly when she would allow it. When she had finally gotten over the initial shock and let out as much emotion as she felt necessary, she collected herself and quietly asked if they could go up to the room.

When they walked into the hotel, they walked separately. The question arose in his mind whether she was keeping her distance due to the news she had just received, or if it was due to his disheveled appearance and clothing.

He hoped it was the latter.

Upon returning to the room, Cass gave Hale full reign to take the shower for himself, using only a washcloth and the sink to clean her face and neck before slipping into a pair of nightclothes. She nestled into the bed, hugging a pillow close to her chest while staring off in deep contemplation.

Hale took his time in the shower. Courage was not generally a problem for him. He didn't have the nerves of a frontline soldier or a Type A Executive, but he was able to handle himself in most stressful situations. He even felt he had done as well as one could be expected when Obie had attacked him outside Liberty Apartments. That said he had no desire to go out and face Cass. He knew she needed him right now. She would benefit from his comfort and support; she was a logical person and had to know this was not his fault. Shooting the messenger didn't seem her style. However, the possibility of her divvying a portion of the blame to him seemed more prevalent in her emotional state.

You're being a coward and a bad boyfriend. Hale told himself over and over. Regardless, he hid in the shower, letting the nozzle spray warm water over his head and cascade comfort down the length of his body.

After Hale reminded himself he couldn't hide in the bathroom forever, he shut off the water and grabbed a towel. The ritual of drying, grooming, and dressing in clothes not caked in bodily fluids went by in a daze. He grabbed the washcloth Cass used to clear the countertop and tossed it to the floor.

> . . . a sick, empty feeling welled up
> in Cass' stomach as she cleaned
> herself
> . . . . . . she gave a long look to the
> curtained shower, wanting to speak but
> instead retreating back to the room

Well, shit. Way to keep her waiting, Don Juan. Hale tossed the washcloth down and moved to the door. *What else is gonna kick me in the proverbial shins today?*

Hale pulled open the bathroom door and stepped into the bedroom. His movements were quiet so as not to wake Cass should she have fallen asleep. Wishful thinking, he realized. She remained on the bed, curled around a pillow hugged tightly to her chest. Her eyes were still red and puffy, though her cheeks were finally dry of tears.

He moved to turn the light on.

"Please don't," she said softly. "Can you turn the bathroom light off, too?"

Hale understood. Cass did not want to be seen in such a state of weakness. She was proud and independent, and clearly did not like others to see her when she was broken down. He turned the lights off, leaving the room illuminated by the dim glow of the city outside their window. He slipped into bed next to her, meeting her gaze as he lay his head down on his pillow.

"How are you doing?" He hoped his voice came out as supportive as he intended.

"My shoulder hurts." Her voice was hoarse.

Hale offered a sad smile. "That's not what I meant."

"I know." She sniffled and pulled the pillow closer, burying the lower half of her face in its fluffy depths.

"Do you want to talk about it?" He offered, sliding a hand around her side, being careful not to nudge her arm and risk aggravating her injury.

Cass' eyes closed as she nodded.

Hale waited a few moments, but when a more specific answer did not come, he prompted her. "Do you want to know what I saw?"

Tears threatened to break through her sealed eyelids. She nodded again.

He took in a deep breath and let it out in a slow sigh. The memories of the Wander started pulling together. Hale had to fight back the sick feeling in his stomach that accompanied them. Hale couldn't afford to be squeamish no matter the content of the images roiling in his head. Cass had sacrificed enough to bring him out here, and now that her quest had essentially been derailed, he had to ensure it at least was not in vain.

He steeled himself in preparation to regale her with the tale.

"Are you ready?"

―――――――

THE KNEELING Man looked up at Will Voss, a deep shudder forcing constant trembles through his body. A small glimmer of hope floated in the back of his mind.

I can get out of this. He won't follow through.

Despite the encouraging thoughts, his nerves refused to let up.

The zip ties around his wrists cut into his flesh as he strained against them. His first instinct had been to rip right through the bonds, as they were but small strips of plastic. This proved to be a foolish endeavor after a few minutes creating lacerations in his skin with no more freedom than he had started with.

"You realize your mistake, I hope." Will paced in front of him, a pistol hanging loosely at his side.

"Will, I–I know you're pissed." The Kneeling Man sputtered out, his lips pulling back into a fearful grimace. "You have every right to be, and I'm going to make it right. I swear!"

"That's where you're wrong." Cass' father stopped his movement directly in front of The Kneeling Man, turning to face him. The gun barrel lifted and pressed against The Kneeling Man's forehead. Will applied pressure, forcing the man to bend backwards over himself.

"I–I know, I know, I promise though, I swear!" the man gibbered as he folded back.

"You could have applied pressure a thousand ways," Will continued speaking over the man, ignoring his pleas. "All of which I would have respected and worked with. But you had to go after the one thing that I make it known is unforgivable. And then I get a panicked call from my daughter about a red SUV that damn near killed her."

The Kneeling Man continued gibbering, words coming out less and less comprehensible. Sentence structure was abandoned in its entirety. While the words themselves carried little meaning at this point, the emotion conveyed within them and his body language told volumes. His face pointed towards the ceiling, though his eyes looked down to keep locked with Will's.

Will looked down at The Kneeling Man's pants, then looked back up to his eyes. "Are you pissing yourself?"

"For fuck's sake let me go!"

"No." Will continued talking as tears streamed from The Kneeling Man's eyes. "I pride myself as a peaceful arbitrator, a Fixer that can get things done. Sure, my business is not always fair, but fair doesn't always work. I accept that. I can accept appropriate pressure being applied to swing a negotiation towards one side. What I cannot accept is a threat being held over my family."

"Nobody has to know!" The Kneeling Man shouted. "I won't tell anyone."

"Wrong again. Everyone will know."

"But... if you kill me, I can't pass on the word. It's fucking pointless!" he pleaded.

"Don't worry." Will clicked the hammer back. "I'll make sure to tell your side of things."

Will's finger depressed the trigger. The hammer snapped down. Gunpowder was ignited by a spark from the primer. Flame from the muzzle of the barrel spread out across The Kneeling Man's forehead, charring the surface of his skin. The bullet tore through the top layers of flesh, shattered the protective barrier of skull, bore a hole through his gray matter, and exploded out the other side.

The Kneeling Man's body bobbed back against the tension of his spine, recoiling up and into the waiting gun barrel. Will Voss stepped back, looking down with a mixture of vindication and regret in his eyes. The body, now limp, lolled to its right and tumbled to the ground. His head smacked against the floor, landing on the carpet and seeping blood through to the wood below.

Glassy eyes remained open and unfocused, staring blankly at the open door ahead.

26

The information set like a lead ball in Cass' gut. She didn't want to believe it, though she knew it to be true. In the past two weeks she had learned her father had lied to her, murdered someone in what appeared to be cold blood, and was imprisoned and facing a life behind bars should he be convicted. She already knew D.C. did not have a death penalty, which she was thankful for. It was little solace knowing she'd have a pane of glass between her and her father for the rest of her life.

She remained dry eyed throughout the recounting of the Wander, laying quiet and motionless for the duration. When it was over, she spoke two simple words before resuming her statuesque state.

"Thank you."

Hale had laid against the headboard, staring blankly towards the wall as he spoke. He found it easier to pull forth the memories when he focused on something inanimate. It allowed him to shut out his vision, ignore his hearing, and dampen his sense of smell. He immersed himself in the images that flooded back to him, narrating as they flowed by as if he were reading a story.

He felt queasy as the recounting came to a close, remembering the feelings immediately following the Wander. The physical disorientation had been bad enough, though the experience itself had been grueling and taken its toll. Every spike of fear resonated in Hale's blood. The begging, desperation, and terror flowed through him as if he had been the man Wilmer Voss had murdered. To experience that firsthand, to be murdered and then get up to tell the tale, it was something he couldn't fully convey in words. To transition from such a mental harrowing into a real life threatening situation was almost enough to give him a stroke.

Cass' phone vibrated noisily on the dresser. It likely would have gone through its cycle ignored had the clattering not been so annoying. She picked it up and examined the face.

Number Unknown

Cass clicked the call on and pressed the phone to her ear. "Hello?" She was irritated, and her voice made it known. Her brow furrowed as she listened to the caller. "Please try again, I can't understand you." She gave it a few more seconds before cutting back into the conversation. "Listen, whoever this is, this is a really bad time. Please try back again tomorrow."

The phone clattered back onto the nightstand, and Cass turned her attention back to Hale. She reinserted herself into the conversation. "Did you feel what he felt?"

Hale nodded, summing up the experience in one word. "Everything."

Cass pursed her lips, imagining the horror for a moment before wiggling over to snuggle him. "I'm sorry. It must have been awful."

"I'm just glad you got your answer." He wrapped an arm around her to cover the lie, pulling her close. "It would have been worse to leave without the truth, however ugly it may have been."

Cass remained silent, leaving her thoughts on the matter a mystery.

Minutes passed. They held each other in silence, attempting to comfort the other. Each trying to focus on the other's suffering in order to ignore their own. It worked. They became comfortable nestled in with one another. The weariness of the stress and the long day couldn't be held at bay any longer. As time passed, each of them found it more and more difficult to resist the urge to slumber. The inviting bliss that came from unconscious dreams was a welcome reprieve to the tribulations of their day.

Their conscious minds slowly retreated from the land of the living. The two drifted into a comfortable sleep as Hale held Cass close to him. Her left arm was cradled tenderly at her midsection, snuggling into Hale's shoulder to use him as a pillow. Dreams came quickly, and despite the turbulent day they had both endured, the images that came in their sleep were not plagued with any of the horrors they had experienced. For the moment, they had found peace with each other.

The long, peaceful silence was interrupted by clattering on the nightstand again.

The pair rustled awake, groggy and very displeased.

"Who the hell is calling this late?" Hale glanced at the clock.

1:00 AM

"It's three hours earlier in California," Cass grumbled, clearly no happier due to the fact.

"The question remains," Hale muttered.

Cass picked up her phone and examined the face again.

Number Unknown

She picked it up, irritation marring her features. "Yes?" Her voice was curt, eyebrows angled down as if she could glare at the source of her annoyance through the phone.

Hale's eyelids drooped, his body arguing that sleep was far more important than hearing one side of a phone call.

"Who is this?" Curiosity mixed with a hint of suspicion. Cass sat up in bed, bringing herself to a more alert position. "How did you get my number?"

Something prodded Hale from his subconscious. *Wake up! This is important.*

Grudgingly, his eyes fluttered open, his attention refocusing on Cass and her phone call.

"I don't understand." Her voice wavered. Suspicion had given way to concern. "What is this about?"

"Cass?" Hale asked quietly. "Is everything alright?"

"Who is this?" Cass demanded. "How do you know my father?"

Hale's eyes shot open at this, pushing himself up to sit next to Cass. He leaned in, trying to hear more.

"*Write this down,*" The voice on the other line whispered.

"One second." Cass turned on the lamp, bathing the room in light. She squinted as her eyes readjusted, her hands blindly searching the tabletop for a pen. Her vision came back to her, and she spotted the complimentary pad of paper and pen on the opposite side of the lamp. She pressed the phone against her shoulder and reached around the fixture, grabbing them both and set them in her lap. Her left hand held the pad gingerly, her shoulder threatening spikes of pain if she did any more. "Alright, I'm ready."

Hale leaned in, pressing his ear to the other side of the phone.

"Hello?" Cass said after a long pause. "Are you still there? I'm ready, what is it?"

"*We can help.*" The words came slowly and clearly, after which the line went dead.

Cass twitched. "What?! Hello?!" She pulled the phone down so she could check the screen. Upon confirming the call was ended, she tossed the device onto her pillow to free her right hand, retrieved the pen and quickly wrote down the message that she had been given.

We can help.

She stared at the words.

"Who was that?" Hale asked.

"I obviously don't know." She snapped.

"Sorry, bad question." Hale regrouped. "What did they sound like? Was there any number associated with the call? What did they say?"

Cass inhaled deeply and released the breath. "I'm sorry. I'm just… frustrated. I don't know what the hell this is all about. There was no number. When I picked up, they addressed me by first and last name, and said they were calling about my dad. The voice was low and quiet, very cloak and dagger. My questions were ignored, and he just said to 'write this down'. I got the paper, and all he said was 'we can help', then he hung up. What is that supposed to mean?"

Hale searched for connections, wracking his brain for ideas based off the little information he had on Will Voss. "Maybe it was an associate of his on the outside. Someone who owes him one, has some pull, and is interested in helping him out," Hale offered.

"Maybe, but why would they call me?" She furrowed her brow, looking at the three words neatly written on the pad in her lap. "What do I have to do with this?"

Hale went through the known facts chronologically in his mind. He knew Will was a face man and negotiator for criminals. He knew he had been locked up for the past few weeks for a murder he had committed. Furthermore, the man he murdered was killed for overstepping a boundary with Will's family.

"Cass," he spoke carefully. "Your dad killed that guy for stepping over a line, specifically for involving his family in something. I don't think it's a coincidence that you got hit by a SUV across the country and he decided to mention it when…" He trailed off. "What I mean is, I don't think it was a disgruntled ex-employee, I think that was intentional."

Cass nodded, a hint of fear creeping into her eyes.

"He told the guy he would make sure everyone knew." He paused, trying and failing to find words that would soften the blow. "What if that call was from people connected to the guy he killed?"

Her eyes fell to the floor. She calculated the possibility as she pulled her lower lip between her teeth, chewing at it idly as she thought. "I'm not sure what they'd want from me." Her voice was hopeful, attempting to dispel the possibility with optimism.

"Revenge," he said flatly. "Maybe even collateral to ensure he doesn't strike a deal."

Cass paled a little.

"Cass…" He put his arm around her. "Maybe it's time we packed up and left. I don't think there's anything else we can do here."

Her cheeks flushed, emotions conflicting with each other. This had been a mission to save her father. Now she felt as if she had only taken steps to condemn him further, as well as inadvertently lowering his image in her eyes.

"This was a good idea," he reassured her. "Your intent was pure, and you went farther than most people would have dared. I think we've found a good stopping point, though. There's nothing else we can accomplish, and from that phone call, it seems we can only damage things further."

Cass leaned into him, not wanting to admit defeat.

"For what it's worth, I'm proud of you." Hale reached up, gently stroking her hair. "And I'm sure your dad has a plan to get himself out of this, and he'll be amazed, if not a little perturbed, that you did as much as you did to help him."

Cass chuckled, smiling at the thought. Her body wanted to cry, though after the past days, she wasn't sure she had any tears left in her. She pushed the hollow feeling of loss away with the knowledge she had done everything she could. Her mind fantasized about a future where her father was released. He smiled at her, embraced her warmly and told her how much she meant to him.

She wanted that moment more than anything else.

They sat quietly for a few more minutes before Cass finally broke the silence. "I think you're right," she said calmly. "I think it is best we go back home."

"You want to enjoy the rest of the night in the hotel, or should we see if we can catch a redeye?"

"As much as I'd like to say we could pretend this was a normal getaway and enjoy our last night here in a proper manner, I don't think I have it in me right now."

"Cass," a tired smile adorned his lips. "You are insanely attractive, and I am lucky to be with you, but I think my body would revolt if you tried to seduce me right now."

She chuckled at the irony of the situation, offering a sad smirk. "This sucks."

"Yes it does," he agreed.

"Alright, let's pack up." She sat back up, looking him in the eyes. "I'll see what I can do about getting our tickets rearranged."

He gave her a smile to reinforce her decision.

The moment was interrupted by a trio of knocks at the door.

The two turned sharply towards the noise. Fear welled up between them, as the unexpected arrival compounded with the suspicions of their conversation. An uncertain look was exchanged between them as they both sat unmoving.

"What do we do?" Cass' voice betrayed a sense of rising panic.

"Stay here," Hale said calmly. "I'll check the door."

"I still have Obie's gun," she whispered.

"What?!"

"It's in my purse." She shrugged, eyes widening as the stress built. "What else was I supposed to do with it?"

"Uh, nothing. Nothing." Hale waved it off. "It's fine. Just, just don't pull it out right now. For all we know this is a room service guy going to the wrong place."

Hale stood from the bed, looking over at the door. He approached it carefully, standing as close to the wall as possible. Spy movies ran through his head, and he imagined an assassin standing out in the hallway, waiting for the shadow of a body to cover the peephole so he could shoot his target through the door. He felt ridiculous entertaining the fantasy, though self-preservation in what had been a very out of the ordinary weekend demanded he take at least some precaution.

Hale grabbed a towel, standing in the doorway between the entry hall and the bathroom. He lifted the towel up, dangling it down over the peephole.

A second trio of knocks caused Hale to jump sideways into the bathroom, dropping the towel to the ground. His heart raced at the perceived danger, and he fought to calm himself down.

Those weren't gunshots, genius. You're just being overly cautious.

A cautious soldier is a living soldier! The General reminded him.

A sacrifice without gain is a sacrifice in vain, The Poet chimed in.

Hale looked back into the bedroom, hoping Cass hadn't been watching.

She was. She eyed him with a quizzical look.

Embarrassed, he held his hands up and averted his eyes. He turned back to the door. Deciding he had exercised enough caution for the evening, Hale pushed the handle down and pulled the door open.

Standing out in the hall were two men. They were both dressed in matching black slacks, white button down shirts, and grey suit jackets. Their frames were athletic, suggesting these men knew their way around a gym. Both pairs of eyes stared at Hale with casually bored expressions.

The man on the left spoke up first. Hale associated his short, almost buzzed haircut with shaved sides with a military background of some kind.

"Hale Langston?" he asked calmly.

"Who are you?" Hale responded.

"My name is Joseph, this is Timothy."

"Call me Tim." The bald man on the right cut in. He sounded annoyed.

"Like I said," Joseph cast an equally annoyed glance at his partner before returning to Hale. "However, you are likely much less interested in us than our employer. He sent us here to collect you so the two of you could talk in person."

"Excuse me?" Hale's brow furrowed. He leaned against the door, ready to slam it at any moment.

"Allow me to extrapolate." Joseph held his hands out to signal the start of his explanation. The way he accentuated each syllable made Hale wonder if the man truly knew the meaning of the word. "You live in Long Beach, California. You travelled out here with a woman by the name of Cassandra Voss. During your visit, you have investigated leads regarding a meeting involving a man going by the alias of Imanu'el." He folded his hands comfortably at his waist. "My employer's attention has been drawn to this, and would like to speak with you in person."

What the hell? Hale's mind raced. *How did they find me? Who do they work for? How do they know all of this?* Another thought surfaced, seemingly for the sole purpose to annoy him. *Why couldn't I do this stuff as a P.I.?!*

"If I don't want to go with you?" Hale asked.

"My employer will be upset that he could not make your acquaintance formally, though unless you change your mind it will end there."

"Can I get a number I can call him and set something up?"

Both men smiled.

"No," the bald man replied smugly.

"Did you just call me?" Cass interjected, reaching over Hale's shoulder and pulling the door open more.

The two men shifted their gaze to the newcomer in the conversation. Joseph paused for a moment, giving her a quick look over before answering. "Are you Cassandra Voss?"

"Assume I am." Venom flitted through her words.

"Yes, ma'am." Joseph admitted sullenly. "I apologize for the deception. I know nothing of your father. I was simply told to use that line to get your attention."

"Why?" she snapped. "Why would you do that?"

"We knew you were here, ma'am," he replied calmly. "We just didn't know what room you were in."

"How does lying to me about my father give you our room number? And why me? Why not call him?"

"You were both asleep, ma'am," he explained. "The call caused you to turn on your light, yes?"

Cass froze. The realization that the two men had been in the parking lot during the call set in. The light had told them where their targets were staying.

"I apologize, ma'am," Joseph continued when it was apparent she was not going to respond. "I know it does not help, but I was simply following the instructions given."

"Are you enlisted?" she asked.

"No ma'am. I am a civilian."

"Who do you work for?" she barked.

"I cannot answer that, ma'am," Joseph said.

"Then I guess I'm coming along."

"I can't let you do that, ma'am. I have specific instructions to escort Mr. Langston alone."

"She comes with, or I don't go," Hale said firmly.

Joseph and Cass looked at Hale with a mixture of surprise.

"Your boss obviously put a lot of work into finding me," Hale continued. "And I already have all the info I came here for. In fact, at this point I'm more annoyed with your employer than curious, so I'm actually inclined to turn down the invite on principle. But I'll leave it in your hands. We'll either both go, or you can deliver a message that I'm not interested."

Joseph frowned. He weighed the options in this conflict, seemingly trying to figure out whether it was worthwhile to call Hale's bluff and risk his boss' ire for returning empty-handed. Either way, his pause to consider showed Hale and Cass that Hale's summons was more than just a whimsical gesture. Whoever their boss was, he clearly wanted Hale to come.

"Very well," Joseph said. "We will make room for an additional passenger."

A wave of relief washed over Hale. He wasn't quite sure what his response would have been had the two men simply agreed to the refusal and walked away.

Cass set her jaw. "One second, let me get my purse."

Hale watched her storm back towards the bed. He turned back towards Joseph and Tim, holding up a finger. "One second, I'll be right back." He closed the door, moving towards Cass.

She stripped off her sleeping clothes, tossing them into the corner as she moved to grab more appropriate garb. Her face was set in a grim determination.

"Cass…" Hale approached her carefully. "Are you okay?"

"I'm fine," she said as she moved.

"Cass, these aren't the guys that you're looking for," he assured.

"Maybe they aren't," she said dismissively as she pulled on pants.

"Cass." He grabbed her shoulders to force her to pay attention to him.

"Ow!" She jerked her left shoulder back, cradling it with her right hand. She looked up at Hale's eyes. "What?!"

"Sorry," He put his hands up, palms out. "I forgot you were hurt. I just... You know these aren't the guys your father was working with, right?"

She took a few breaths before averting her eyes. "Probably."

"This isn't your fight," he said quietly. "You helped me find this. I'm not sure how yet, but you did. This will get me my answers, the same way you got your answers. But I don't think this has anything to do with your dad."

She nodded, thinking for a few more moments before turning back to him. "You're probably right. However, you walked into a gangster's den for my answers. I'm not going to let you go into this one alone, either."

"It might be safer if one of us stayed here," he reasoned.

"Stop trying to protect me, Hale," she said firmly. "If you're right, then I will just be there to support you while you find your answers. These guys seem smart and well connected, so you could use an extra pair of eyes at your back. If you're wrong, and they are somehow responsible for my father being locked up, I deserve to be there to set things right."

Hale glanced at her purse, then back at her. "Cass, you're not wrong, but don't do anything you would regret. Don't do anything that your father wouldn't want."

Her lips pursed and her body tensed up. A primal urge rose up, demanding she strike him for being so presumptuous. Logic reined back the feeling. She realized he was speaking from the heart, and his words were the truth. She calmed herself and simply nodded. "I know. You're right."

"Okay," he said with a hopeful smile. "Let's get ready."

27

The four walked down the hallway towards the elevator. Cass and Hale held up the rear, Joseph and Tim walked quietly in the lead. They travelled quietly down to the first floor, out the lobby, and into the parking lot. Waiting for them was a large black van with no windows beyond the driver's seat. Tim approached the vehicle, opening the two back doors and stepping to the side.

Cass examined the windowless prison with padded benches and glanced nervously at Hale.

Hale stared at Joseph for an explanation.

"My employer desires to remain anonymous," Joseph stated. "This allows us to transport you to and from his location without giving away his position."

"Are you sure you're not enlisted?" Cass asked.

"Not anymore, ma'am."

"Can we follow you?" Hale asked.

Joseph furrowed his brow and frowned again. "Mr. Langston, need I repeat why these precautions are necessary?"

Hale flushed, trying not to let the embarrassment get to him. "No, never mind. This is fine." He nodded confidently to Cass and stepped into the van. He turned to help Cass in, then took a seat across from her and buckled in.

The doors slammed shut one after another. Within the minute, Joseph and Tim had taken their seats in the cab and started the vehicle. With a low rumble, the van shifted into gear, rolled out from its spot, and pulled out into the street.

Hale tried to keep track of where they were.

Left turn. Right turn. Straight for about a quarter mile. Left turn. Left turn. Straight for about half a mile. Did we just go in a circle? He looked at Cass. She seemed to be attempting the same thing he was. *Ok, we're definitely on an on-ramp now. Picking up speed… we're on a freeway. That must have been two exits, three exits tops. Another left turn. And another… another on-ramp?*

Hale came to the realization the drivers were taking no chances. Joseph and Tim did not look like the heads of their class, they knew their job and they performed it well. Even in Hale's home neighborhood he would be hopelessly lost at this point. In a foreign city, he was absolutely in the dark.

"Are they backtracking on purpose, or just lost?" Cass muttered.

"I don't think they want us to have a chance of discerning where they're going."

"They're succeeding." She sat up straight on her bench, lips pursed to show her displeasure. "There's something about retracing steps, backtracking, and all manner of actions that waste time that really annoy me. Maybe it's why I'm so good at building efficiencies in my job. Extra steps are frustrating."

"Next time I'll tell them to just sap us and wake us up with smelling salts when we arrive."

"I'll deal with the head trauma for a shorter drive."

The winding ride of circles and backtracking took about an hour in total. Hale imagined they could have made a beeline towards their destination and been there in less than twenty minutes. While Cass was more vocal in her irritation, it annoyed to him as well. He didn't fully understand the need for secrecy, and the cloak and dagger means they had taken to contact them were unnerving. Still, they had successfully attained his attention, and he was determined to see this through.

The van eventually slowed and turned down several smaller streets. It moved up a small incline onto a gravel lot, grinding slowly to a gate which noisily rolled open. As the van moved through, Cass perked up again.

"I feel dumb!" She pulled open her purse, rifling through it. "I should have thought of this an hour ago."

"What?"

"GPS," she said, pulling out her phone. "I can tell it to give me my exact location."

"Your phone is cooler than mine," Hale grumbled, though in actuality he was ecstatic she had the tool to give them some answers.

She frowned as she pushed buttons.

"What?"

"Hold on." She moved the phone around in the air. "No signal."

"No signal?"

"We're either in a dead zone, which is doubtful with my plan, or they've rigged the back of this thing to block signal." She shrugged, putting the phone gently back in her purse. "No problem. When we get out, my phone will immediately start searching, and I can check the results when I get a moment alone."

The van slowed again, and the sound of a large mechanical door sounded.

"That's a garage," Hale said with a grimace.

"Well damn." Cass zipped up her purse with a huff.

The van pulled into the garage, bumping up onto smooth concrete from the noisy gravel. The van slowed to a stop and the engine quieted as it was shut down. Gears and pulleys worked again as the thick garage door lowered and sealed shut. Once the room was secure, they heard the doors of the van opened and shut. Joseph and Tim walked with methodical steps down the length of the van, stopping in unison outside the back doors. Tim pulled the doors open while Joseph stood and looked in at the seated occupants.

"We've arrived." His voice was bored, lifeless, as if he was a tour guide for a mind numbing attraction. "Please follow us."

Hale exited first, standing in front of their two escorts until Cass got out behind him. A protective instinct crept over him. He felt the need to ensure Cass' safety, as if these men could accost them at any moment. The circumstances allowed him to argue that paranoia may be well founded.

Joseph turned and took the lead, Timothy waiting patiently to take up the rear. Hale took the opportunity to examine their surroundings.

The garage door was indeed a thick metal with no windows. The rest of the large room was solid concrete, big enough to house three cars, leaving the van with plenty of room as the only current occupant. It gave the distinct feeling of a bunker, ready to withstand charging infantry and incoming mortars. He was confident Cass would not be getting any signal on her phone from within this structure.

Joseph led the group to the back of the room where a single door awaited them. This door was metal as well, featuring no window, keyhole, or even a door handle. Joseph approached a keypad next to the door. Covering the pad with one hand and shielding it with his body, he tapped a series of digits.

Four five, six... seven eight nine, ten. Hale counted. *Jesus, a ten digit password. There goes birthdays, anniversaries, and other common possibilities.*

A loud click signaled the lock pulling out of place. The click didn't match Hale's expectations. Considering the theme of the rest of the garage, he expected something the size of a girder to be keeping the door closed. Joseph applied some pressure to the door, pushing it inward.

Hmm, wonder if they worry about fire safety, Hale joked to himself. *Can't have a rushing crowd be expected to stop and pull a door open. That's a hefty fine if they get reported.*

Hale took an intermission from his internal observation to glance down at the doorframe as he passed by. He saw no lock, no hole for the door to latch, nor a doorjamb for the door to rest against while it locked. He only saw metal plates running around the entire perimeter of the door.

"What the—"

"Magnets," Joseph spoke up, knowing the question before it was even asked.

"Magnets?" Hale asked.

"Magnets," Joseph repeated. As the quartet made their way through the door the stoic man swung the door closed.

Hale watched the door swing to the doorframe and move as if it would continue its path when a familiar loud click sounded. The door continued its movement for another quarter of an inch before pulling sharply back into place. He gawked at the show that had just been offered.

"Timothy walked through there while the magnets were on once." Joseph recalled as they walked. "The waves messed with the plate in his head. He forgot half his childhood and had to be housebroken again, it was horrible."

"Didn't make me forget your ex's address," Timothy fired back.

"You feel free to visit and re-up your syphilis subscription anytime you like," Joseph replied calmly.

Hale smirked at the banter. It reminded him of himself and Alex.

The four walked down a short hallway to a T intersection. As they approached, a single set of footsteps sounded from the hallway to the left. Hale's eyes fixated on the corner, watching to see who emerged.

Joseph moved them forward steadily and confidently, the steps not fazing him in the slightest. The owner of the footsteps arrived at the intersection seconds before the group did. Hale saw a pair of black, shiny business shoes with a dark blue canopy of slacks hanging over them. The pants and matching jacket were well made and freshly pressed, exuding wealth and confidence from the garb. A black button down shirt was complimented by a Windsor knotted length of silk with a pattern of blue stripes hanging from his neck.

The predatory smile confirmed The Suited Man's identity for Hale. This was the man he had Wandered into on two separate occasions. The man who had summoned Imanu'el across the country for god knows what purpose. The man who had brought them here tonight with an invitation that flaunted the power at his fingertips. Here he stood, smiling at his guests with an unusual expression of geniality over an undercurrent of hostility. Hale noticed The Suited Man shoot a momentary glance at Cass with a twitch of his eye.

She wasn't supposed to be here.

Hale stood staring dumbly. Cass remained at his side and slightly behind his shoulder, allowing his frame to block part of her body.

"Good evening, Mr. Langston." The Suited Man extended his hand and nodded to Hale. "And to you as well, Ms. Voss. Welcome to my humble abode."

"I wouldn't use humble as an adjective," Hale said, taking the offered hand and shaking it.

. . . "–eet you as well, Jeremiah. Right thi–" The suited
man shook Jeremiah's hand as he spoke.

That happened here. Hale shook from the Wander. He did a quick check, The Suited Man was still greeting Cass. He didn't miss anything. *Jeremiah was here within the last couple days. It couldn't have been on Saturday. Maybe today? Was Imanu'el with him? ... I think I caught a glimpse of him in the Wander... damn, I'm not sure.*

"Do you have a name?" Cass asked, her voice flat and direct. "You seem to know ours already; I would feel odd not knowing yours."

"My apologies, I'm being rude," he responded genially, right hand pressing flat against his chest as he spoke his name. "Rush. Rush Channing. And I must beg your forgiveness for the dramatic summons, however I'm sure you'll understand our need for extra layers of security in due time."

"I hope so," Hale said. He refrained from making inflammatory commentary that would color the tone of their coming conversation.

"Please follow me." An award-winning smile flashed before he turned and walked down the hallway to the right.

Hale shot a glance over to Cass to see how she was holding up. While her posture and body placement was a bit more submissive than usual, her expression was strong and determined. Sometimes, he wondered if she was more courageous than he was.

As they both turned, Timothy stopped Cass. "Ma'am, if you could please come with me."

She pulled away from him. "No, thank you."

"Ma'am," he started again. "Mr. Ch–"

"Mr. Channing can speak to both of us," Cass finished for him. "Thank you."

Timothy gave a look to Rush, who gave a simple nod back. He took a breath as if resigning himself to wasting his effort. "Very well, ma'am. My apologies for bothering you."

The pair of visitors turned and walked down the hall after Rush. The duo of militant escorts split up, one walking behind the group, the other going down the hall Rush had emerged from. The walk was short, ending at a single wooden door at the end of the hall. The portal broke the previously established theme of the structure. Thus far everything had been constructed of metal and concrete. Magnetic locks, reinforced garage doors, and modified vans designed to block cell phone signals had become the norm. Hale wondered why there was a sudden change of style.

The door opened into a small room. It was sparsely decorated, containing only a single metal table with four matching chairs, a countertop, small cabinet, full length mirror on the opposite wall, and a camera in the corner. The camera remained motionless as they entered, a small red light blinking at them as if warning that they were being watched.

Rush walked around the table, pulling a chair out for himself. He gestured to the opposite side. "Sit, please."

Cass and Hale both took seats at the table. Timothy, who had followed them into the room, closed the door and remained outside.

"So," Rush started, leaning back and crossing one leg over the other. "Where to begin? I'm sure you have a flood of questions to let loose on me, though I believe I am prepared to match you. Why don't we start with an easy one? Why did the two of you come all the way out here to D.C.?"

"To find answers," Hale responded. He hoped Cass appreciated the fruits of her teachings back at the Sandy Clam. Her evasive method of playing the question game would come in useful here. "Where are we?"

"In a secured room," Rush smiled back, smugly.

Dammit! Hale cursed internally.

"Now we can play games and verbally toss each other in circles for hours. But neither one of us wants that, do we?" Rush leaned forward, folding his hands on the table. "We both want the same thing. And I think getting to that common goal will require an ounce of trust between potential friends. What's say we take a chance, give each other some honest answers, and see if we can walk out of here better for it?"

I don't want to tip my hand just yet. Hale thought through his options. *I have no idea what they know, or why they are so interested in us... Well, in me. Plus, I have already taken a chance by–*

"I came all the way out here on blind faith," Hale verbalized his thoughts. "I think that gives me the first question."

"Fair enough," Rush threw up a hand in surrender and smiled. "Ask away."

Hale considered his options, trying to find a wording that would answer more than one question. He finally decided on, "Who are you?"

"Aside from just being Rush Channing?" he asked.

"Aside from the name, yes."

"I am the leader of a private association of like-minded and driven individuals based here in Washington D.C." His voice was direct and smooth. From his tone, he may as well been ordering pizza. "Now what are you doing out here?"

"I– uh." Hale stammered.

"Now Hale," Rush chided. "The question you asked was highly sensitive, and was answered directly. Could I have given you a watered down response?"

"Yes," Hale answered.

"Would you have known any better?"

"Well–" Hale stumbled.

"Would I still be asking you questions now even if I had been evasive?"

"Yes."

"So let's be frank with one another." The row of gleaming teeth flashed again. "Don't be evasive with me, and I will reciprocate. Agreed?"

"Uh, yes. Sorry." Hale felt as if he had been ambushed and he recognized someone better at the game than him, probably even better than Cass. He was out of his depth and he knew it.

"Good." He smiled genially. "Now, regarding your presence here?"

"Because of Imanu'el," Hale answered. His thoughts were jumbled. He felt what little control he had over the conversation had been jerked from his hands.

"And why did Imanu'el send you here?"

"No." Hale looked up at Rush. "He didn't. We, er, I, rather... Ugh." He stopped, taking a breath to center himself. "I was given reason to believe Imanu'el had been lying to us about his whereabouts this past Saturday, and that he had truly been out here when he claimed to be elsewhere."

"And why would that matter to you?" Rush folded his hands on the table and leaned forward.

"Because he was trying to recruit me into his little cult," Hale grimaced. "Because he seemed to understand things about me that no one else understood. Because I wanted to make sure the person who wanted my trust deserved it."

"All valid reasons," He nodded. "But how did you come to start looking out here?"

"I... uh." Hale stumbled. He didn't want to talk about this. It would lead to his ability to Wander, which was more than he wished to divulge.

"It's your turn to answer," Cass cut in, looking straight at Rush before turning to Hale. "It's your question. You're up."

"Thanks." He lifted his eyes to meet hers. He wished he could borrow her sharp mind for this conversation. He wrestled with questions, but only one seemed appropriate. "What does your 'association' do? What do you represent?"

"We aspire, Mr. Langston." He smiled, his tone even and pleasant. "Now what we aspire to is not something I can discuss with you as of yet, though I feel it will be made available to you within due time. I have a good feeling about you; I just need to confirm a few things first. What did you find when you came out here?"

"Nothing much." Hale admitted. "We found that you had talked to Imanu'el last Saturday, and that he had lied about where he truly was."

"And how did you find this out?" He glanced at Cass. "I'm guessing you helped him do some investigating and interrogation, am I right, beautiful?"

"It's your turn." Cass answered flatly. She fought to keep her expression even, knowing the tenseness in her jaw and suspicious narrowing of her eyes were giving her away. "How did you know about my father?"

"It was public information." He pursed his lips and shrugged. "With a couple online searches, I was able to find your name, and from that find your closest relatives. The predicament your dad found himself in came up."

"That's not public," she scowled.

"Public enough. There are databases online that anyone can access for a few dollars a search. It's the same way I found Hale for Imanu'el, actually."

"What?" Hale and Cass asked simultaneously.

"He missed his big meeting last Saturday to come out and meet me, and complained that you were the only one he didn't know how to get a hold of to make things right." Rush looked over them with a triumphant smile as he retold the events. "I found out that you had spoken a few truths about yourself during the 'orientation' Imanu'el had set up. Among them being your first name and your profession. I can tell you this with certainty, there are very few Hales who write for newspapers and online articles in the Long Beach area."

Hale shook his head. *Had I not been so careless, I'd be at home right now. Cass would probably be with me. We could have ignored all of this.*

"So you told him to gather all the Touched." Cass made it a statement of fact.

"Oddly enough, no." Rush looked genuine. "His effort to recruit his little cult is what drew my attention."

"How so?" Hale asked.

"My position takes me places. Larger cities, mostly. Los Angeles and Long

Beach were most recent on my travel itinerary."

"And you just stumbled across Imanu'el and his following?" Cass' voice betrayed her distrust.

"Not exactly," He smiled knowingly. "Serendipity did have Her part, I suppose. So tell me, what do you think about Imanu'el?"

"I think he's full of shit," Hale said bluntly.

"As you should," Rush laughed. "Randy – excuse me, 'Imanu'el', is so full of shit he stains the ground he walks on. Polygraphs overload and catch fire when he walks by. I'm not sure if that man is even capable of telling the truth."

Hale stifled a chuckle, unwilling to let Rush know that he had scored some points.

"He might have had me when I first met him, too," Rush admitted. "Fortunately I had already done my research and perused his criminal record."

"Criminal record?" they both asked in unison.

"A mile long," Rush nodded, the smug smile plastered to his face. "Mostly petty theft and possession, with a particular affinity for fraud. The man loved to work marks. It's ironic, really, if you consider his upbringing. Wealthy family, top notch schools, life laid out for him like a yellow brick road. But Mr. Randall could not resist the draw of drugs and subterfuge, and ended up getting disowned by Daddy."

"He's a con man?" Hale had not considered this long rap sheet when trying to figure out what Imanu'el had up his sleeve.

"That he is." Rush leaned forward again. "His latest venture may have worked, too. The Holy Roller thing. Especially with talent like you on his payroll, he'd have had the masses hooked in a heartbeat. Can you imagine? An evangelist who can perform true to life miracles? His congregation would be forwarding him advances on their paychecks! Granted, it would be short lived unless he could spin his checkered past appropriately, but any grifter worth his salt could do that. Hell, I could think of a few ways it could be done successfully without much effort. Not that it matters. Truth be told, I don't think he'll be pursuing it now."

"Why's that? If it's so lucrative, and he doesn't seem to have a problem with subterfuge."

"Better ventures, Mr. Langston. He was given an offer, like you will be, and he saw the wisdom in taking it rather than trying to con the religious community."

"Like I'll be?" Hale came to the sudden realization that while he was asking all the questions, it was Rush leading him down the path.

"Yes, Mr. Langston." He glanced at Cass, then back to him. "One that I very much hope you'll accept. You see, people like us have been gifted with a special talent. The talents tend to vary in their manifestation; however, I have yet to encounter one that is not truly amazing. I am also putting a significant amount of resources towards finding out why and where these abilities come from, yet the answer still eludes me. What I do know is we have an advantage over the rest of the world, and that is something I cannot ignore. We have an opportunity, Mr. Langston, and unlike many others, we have the capability to seize that opportunity."

"What opportunity is that?"

"Change," he said plainly. "We have the ability to change the world as it is today. Tell me, do you enjoy the world as it exists? Does the current order of things seem to be operating at an appropriate level of efficiency? There are starving people all over the globe, corruption in nearly every political office, discrimination, inane laws, and unjust punishments. We have people behind bars that should be leading communities, and free men wandering the street that should be on death row. Some people accept the way things are, while others rail against the system ineffectually. Wouldn't it be a cataclysmic change to see a group unite under a common banner that truly could make a difference?"

"That sounds grandiose and altruistic," Hale said, his tone expressing the question of 'what's the catch'.

"It is." Rush nodded as if to affirm it was not the whole story. "Make no mistake, the members of this organization would be well compensated for their efforts. As each one contributes truly unique talents, they should be rewarded for those exclusive services, don't you think?"

"That sounds appropriate." Hale's lips remained pursed. "But where does the money come from?"

"We have our pipelines of currency," Rush assured. "Which will only grow with our organization. Suffice to say that under our employment, you could start investing in real estate in every major city, living a life of luxury only interrupted by our call to work when your unique services were needed."

"And what tactics would be employed to achieve your goals of, well, we'll call it World Peace for now?"

"I can't give a broad generalization to paint our tactics in one color," Rush replied coolly. "We do what is appropriate for the situation."

> . . . "–ppriate for the
> situation," The voice over the phone
> said.
>
> . . . . . . "–lives of a few for
> unparalleled wealth and pow–"   Rush
> said to an unknown face.
>
> . . . . "–are tactics that have been
> tried and true since the dawning of–" Rush said
> to Joseph, placing a pistol on the table.

"–o you know about Hale?" Cass interjected.

Hale noticed her posture and tone. She had leaned forward, raising her voice a bit to draw Rush's attention. She'd noticed him Wandering and was trying to cover.

"Surely you must know something about his abilities if you're so confident he can help," she finished.

"I do," he confirmed. Rush leaned back in his seat, folding his hands in his lap and crossing one leg over another. Hale remembered this tactic in his speech classes. Crossing one's legs and taking up more space gave the image of importance, lending more subconscious weight to one's words. "Hale is an empath." He turned to Hale as he continued. "He can see truths, read minds. That is how he was led to D.C. That is how he gleaned information about Imanu'el and my meeting."

"How do you know all this?" Hale didn't bother to correct Rush's false information on his abilities.

"Through observation and reports. Plus, I have an expert on staff to help me sort through these things." He paused eyes lifting up as he considered his previous statement. "Well, as close to an expert as one can be in this field."

"I don't understand," Hale said flatly.

"He'll explain it better." Rush stood. "Let me make the introductions. Unless you had more you wanted to discuss here?"

Hale still didn't like his position. He knew very little, and trusted Rush even less. He was confident the important questions wouldn't be answered, and he wasn't even sure he knew the right questions yet. With a glance at Cass, who seemed to be mirroring his own thoughts, he stood and nodded to Rush. "Let's go meet your expert."

28

The fortress became less imposing as Hale and Cass were led through the compound. It seemed the hallways were all short, connecting a series of small, low ceilinged rooms with sparse furniture and no decorations. The building was clearly built for functionality, not for aesthetics. Wherever they were didn't have the luxury of extra space to afford its occupants more elbow room.

They moved back down the hallway where Rush had originally emerged. The next room had doors on each wall facing. The four continued straight forward through a door opposite of the way they entered. Another short hallway led them to another room whose aesthetics broke the expectations Cass and Hale had prepared.

For the first time in their visit, a room had more than just the baseline requirements for its purpose. Hale was first drawn to the difference in lighting. The dull florescent tubing that had lit the halls and previous rooms had been replaced in favor of halogen bulbs. Several fixtures were fitted in the ceiling, as well as two on opposite walls. The room was bigger, extended at least another 10-15 square feet on each side. Stacks of equipment, cabinets, files, and an examination table in the center of the room explained the need for the extra space. Cupboards lined the walls, leaving small areas of space to be filled with various medical posters, equipment containers, a full-length mirror, and a backlit surface to attach x-rays for examination.

Standing to the side of the room was a small man dressed in a button down shirt and slacks. He did not wear a tie or a coat, though the folder in his hand combined with his presence in the room gave him the immediate impression of being the local medical authority.

"Good evening, Doctor," Rush called out with a smile.

The Doctor looked up at the newcomers, an air of annoyance radiating from his pursed lips and cocked eyebrow. His brow flattened under a widow's peak of closely trimmed hair.

"Glad to see you're still here," Rush continued as they approached. "Hard at work, as always."

"Yes," The Doctor replied, unamused. "It's not as if I was called in at 1:00 in the morning for god knows what purpose. I'm ecstatic to be here." He turned to Hale and Cass and nodded, his expression clashing with an uptick of politeness in his tone. "Good evening to the both of you."

"Evening," they responded in turn.

"Now Mr. Channing," he continued, turning back to Rush. "What can I help you with?"

"Doctor Geller." Rush stood between the two parties and extended his hands out to touch both Hale and Geller's shoulders. "I wish to introduce you to Hale Langston and Cassandra Voss, visitors all the way out from California."

"There are more, then?" Geller asked. "Are we expecting any others from the sunny west coast?"

"Others?" Cass inquired, stepping out from Hale's shadow as her curiosity piqued.

"All in due time," Rush smiled, stopping her questions with a held-up hand.

"Imanu'el and Jeremiah were here." Hale turned his head towards Cass to show he was answering her, making no attempt to hide his knowledge of the information from the rest of the room.

The Doctor lifted a brow. "Were? Did they leav–"

"Thank you, Doctor Geller," Rush cut in with a smile. "I wasn't prepared to broach that subject quite yet."

"It's not like they can hide, Rush." Geller raised an eyebrow. "Unless they're good at blending in with concrete. I figured these two would run into them soon, if they haven't already."

Rush let the point go, hiding his irritation with expert practice. "Doctor Geller," he started again. "Mr. Langston was not informed of Imanu'el or Jeremiah's arrival. In fact, the last he saw or spoke of either of them was in California and had no reason to connect them to us or this place. Does that not raise a few questions in that medical brain of yours?"

Hale noted Rush's confirmation of Imanu'el's presence. He was here with Jeremiah. Hale hadn't been sure from his previous Wander, and was glad to have manipulated the answer out of Rush with his bluff.

"It does." Geller looked over Hale with an inquisitive eye. "Care to explain how you came across that information, Mr. Langston?"

"I don't really know what to call it," Hale admitted. "Imanu'el, or Randy, whatever he's calling himself, calls it being Touched. Rush here called it being an empath. I don't have a name for it. I just Wander into truth sometimes."

"Define Wander," The doctor inquired curiously.

"Ever day dream before?" Hale asked.

"Mm-hmm," Geller nodded.

"Picture that, only do it when you're interacting with something. Touch, smell, et cetera. The daydream you Wander into is someone's memories or experiences."

"Amazing," Geller said, his enthusiasm muted by scientific interest. "Can you give a demonstration?"

Not wanting to seem less capable than they hoped, Hale shook his head. The possibility of trying and failing would be embarrassing, and too telling of his limitations to those in the room. "I'd rather not do it again. I've already Wandered once in the last ten minutes, which is how I knew Imanu'el and Jeremiah were here."

"Tires you out, does it?" he hypothesized.

"Sometimes," Hale admitted. The answer was partially true.

"Interesting," Geller's eyes unfocused, drifting off into his own world to examine this new evidence in the privacy of his mind. After a few moments he returned to the real world again. "I'd love to talk to you more about this when you have time. If possible, perhaps give you a proper exam to see if we can't determine the source of your talent."

A chill ran up Hale's spine as he imagined the whining sound of a drill bit over the repeating question, 'is it safe?' He managed to conjure a nod, "Of course, maybe later."

"Good, good."

"Doctor Geller is an expert in Hematology," Rush cut in. "He was brought on for the specific purpose of keeping our staff healthy and wise. The 'wealthy' part of the holy trinity is up to us."

Hale gave a weak grin in response to Rush's smile.

"The good Doctor thinks that our abilities derive from our blood," Rush continued. "I personally do not agree with his theory, but I am also not a trained medical professional. Therefore I will be happy to let him perform his tests if he can find a way to augment or replicate our unique talents."

"You keep saying 'our' unique talents," Hale observed. "What is your ability?"

"That's unimpo—" Rush was cut off as he sidestepped Hale's question.

"If real life was a chess board, he'd be Bobby Fisher," Geller cut in.

Rush gave a menacing smile to the doctor.

"What?" Geller looked up at him. "They're here, aren't they? Might as well trust them with the truth. Maybe you'll remember this next time you drag me out of bed after midnight for an impromptu rendezvous. I get cranky without sleep."

"Thank you, Doctor." Rush continued his smile. "We'll leave you to your work."

"It was nice meeting you both." Geller nodded politely to them again, his demeanor much more calm and sincere as he turned away from his employer.

"A pleasure," Hale responded with a nod.

Rush stepped back the way they came, extending his arm out to collect Hale and Cass as he moved. "Let's adjourn back to our original room, shall we? I'd like to speak with you both some more."

"Bobby Fisher, huh?" Hale said as he started walking.

"It's a poor metaphor," Rush assured. "The Doctor is simply irritable and in the mood to spin tales to offset our conversation."

"So he's untrustworthy?" Cass asked.

"As much as any other Doctor," Rush deflected with a grin.

The group passed through the adjoining hallway and back into the room with four doors. Through their verbal repartee, a muffled voice rose almost imperceptibly behind one of the doors, followed by a sharp 'shh!' The noise caught both Cass and Hale's attention. The few steps of lead Rush had on the pair apparently put him out of earshot, as he continued moving on. They looked at each other in silence and shared a curious look before following after their host. There would be time for their questions and suspicions later.

"As you can see, we take our operation seriously, Mr. Langston." Rush gestured to the structure around them. "We spare no expense on our staff, proper equipment, and we are constantly growing. What do you think so far?"

"Why the need for so much security and secrecy?" Hale asked.

"We intend to be powerful men, Mr. Langston," Rush's voice was confident and determined. "Such individuals bring about the ire and envy of their peers. We would not want our countless hours of effort and boundless potential to be ended by thievery, vandalism, or worse, assassination."

"You really think people will come after you?" Hale said dubiously.

"Yes," His tone remained firm and confident. "Look at the President, Mr. Langston. A full staff of bodyguards working tirelessly to ensure his safety."

"But he's the President. Unless you're saying your power and popularity will rival his."

"Allow me to give some other metaphors. Movie stars, high powered CEO's, mafia bosses, drug kingpins, all individuals with varying levels of popularity, notoriety, and legality in their professions, yet all employ various measures of security to ensure their safety and continued lifestyles."

Rush walked them by the hall they originally entered through and across into the first room they had met in. Joseph, the faithful tagalong and watchdog, held the door for the other three, closing it and remaining nearby after they entered.

"Does that make more sense, Mr. Langston?" Rush asked. He moved across the room to stand in front of the wall mirror for a moment, examining himself and adjusting his tie.

"To a degree. I can understand the desire for safety, it just seems like you're preparing for a war rather than a political campaign."

"One can never be too careful, Mr. Langston." Rush turned as he finished preening, offering a smile as he sat at the table again. "Now, I would like to make you a formal offer. This is not something you should take lightly, nor is it something that can be easily walked away from, so I'd like you to think carefully before you give a response."

Hale shifted in his seat and nodded. Cass remained silent next to him, eying Rush with naked distrust.

"We'd like you to sign on with us formally," Rush continued. He leaned on the table with hands folded, closing some of the distance between Hale and himself. "You would receive a reasonable sum as a starting bonus to ensure your comfortable lifestyle was not interrupted, after which you would be paid a monthly salary, as well as bonuses when you were called in for service. As our organization grows, so will your paycheck."

"So I would essentially be on call? What would I do in the meantime?" Hale asked.

"Remain available." Rush smiled. "As long as you can be anywhere in the country within 12 hours, you may do whatever you wish."

"And what can you imagine I'd be on call for?"

"I hardly think I can predict the future with any accuracy, Mr. Langston," Rush smiled.

"You're hiring me for something." Hale pursed his lips. "You have to have something in mind."

358

"Tell me, what is the most desirable trait to possess when seeking power?"

"Excuse me?" Hale asked, thrown off by the question.

"Power," The Suited Man repeated. "What is the most desirable trait to possess when seeking power?"

Hale's eyes shifted as he thought, finally looking back up at Rush and saying, "From context, I'm going to guess intelligence."

"And why would you guess that, Mr. Langston?" Rush smiled.

"I can provide you with information that no one else is privy to. Information people won't be able to cover their tracks on, as I retrieve it via unconventional means."

Rush gave a small clap. "I couldn't have said it better myself. Information is the godsend to any organization. Resources can be shifted around, borrowed, and acquired. Talented staff can come and go. However, knowledge is the key to success for any venture. Knowing the ins and outs of your competition, the pulse of your clientele, and the general conditions of your particular market is worth more than any other commodity you can trade."

"Makes sense," Hale nodded. "Knowing what to prepare for makes you nigh unbeatable in any situation."

Rush smiled in affirmation. "I must say, you're much better at this than the last person I had this conversation with."

"How's that?"

"You speak."

"Oh," Hale chuckled. His thoughts began to race. This was something he had wanted since he was a teenager. The excitement of an investigation, uncovering clues, digging up dirty truths and exposing them; it was everything that had drawn him to being a P.I in the first place. But what of the pitfalls? He still did not have absolute control over what he saw, and there was no telling if his recent refinements on his abilities would cause the end result to be any different than his entrepreneurial career. Before, all he had to risk was his personal finances and the embarrassment of failure. What would his newly acquired employers think of a less than stellar performance?

"You didn't answer the question," Cass interjected. Her voice startled both men. Her still frame and silent demeanor had removed her from their attention. The sudden outburst jerked them out of a private moment, reminding them there was a third party to this conversation.

"How so?" Rush asked.

"Do you not have any specific jobs in mind that you would be sending Hale into?" She queried. "Would they be illegal? Dangerous? Both? After all, while he can procure information, he can't prove anything. That makes it worthless in any public or legal sense, unless you plan on applying the information in less than legal means."

"I cannot say with certainty how any procured information will be utilized, though I can say it will be put to good use for our organization."

"Do you have anything to do with my father being in prison?" She jumped to the next topic, trying to keep Rush off balance.

"No," He answered without hesitation.

Cass kept her lips pursed, staring at the man across the table from her. Hands folded in her lap, back straight and eyes boring through him, suspicion radiated from her body. Hale had been on the receiving end of those eyes, and saw them again when she'd had her doubts about Imanu'el. Both of those moment paled in comparison to the utter distrust she openly held for Rush.

"What happens to Cass in all this?" Hale asked.

"Well," Rush broke his gaze off of from the woman with hawk-like attention on him, looking back to Hale. "We don't have a formal position for her as of yet, but as a matter of good business sense, we can't simply have people walking around with our secrets without any loyalty to our organization. We are prepared to offer her something for her silence."

"Which is?" Cass asked.

"Your father," he spoke flatly, returning his gaze to her eyes. "Prison is a dangerous place, after all."

"You might want to be more specific." Cass' jaw set. Her muscles tensed as if she was ready to spring across the table.

"We have power in the legal system, of course." Rush smiled as he veiled his previous threat. "With the proper application of leverage, we could arrange for his release."

Cass remained frozen in place, hatred clouding anger, anger covering hope.

"How long do I have to decide?" Hale cut in.

Rush lingered on Cass for a moment longer before pulling his gaze back to Hale. "As long as you'd like, Mr. Langston." He held his arms out, gesturing around him. "Mi casa es su casa, as they say in your region."

"That means my house is your house." Hale furrowed his brow.

"Precisely," Rush held his hands forward again. "You understand, don't you? We obviously can't have you running off without any contractual bond to us. Whether it is employment, or simply a non-disclosure agreement, we need to have our assurances when you leave."

"But I have as long as I like to decide?"

"Of course," Rush nodded, folding his hands in his lap. "You will be boarded here for as long as you wish."

"You're taking him prisoner?"

"Both of you," Rush corrected. "But no, not prisoner. That would require us to hold you here against your will. You may choose your means of departure at any point you wish."

"Taxi. Right now," Cass responded quickly.

"Ms. Voss," Rush chuckled and stood. "Let's not be rash. If you like, I'll leave you here to discuss your options. You are more than welcome to stay here for the night if you'd like. We've prepared quarters for you just down the hall. The first room we passed through on the way to the medical bay, just take the room on the left. Should you need me, I'll be speaking with Doctor Geller."

Rush gave a last smile to the pair seated across from him. He broke his gaze away and nodded to Joseph, who opened the door and followed Rush out. As soon as the door clicked closed, the two remaining occupants of the room snapped their attention to each other.

"What do you think?" Hale said, unable to suppress a small bit of excitement from encroaching into his tone.

"I don't like it," She answered quickly.

"Why?"

"Aside from them threatening my dad?" Her jaw clenched again.

"That may have been a misunderstanding."

"Misunderstanding," she scoffed.

"They may be able to free your dad," His voice marinated in hope. He lied to himself and said the hope was all for Cass' sake, that it had nothing to do with his desire to trust Rush's words. He wanted her to believe the man on her own, and not just because it was what he wanted.

"I think this entire thing is a giant scam at best, and a criminal enterprise at worst," she said.

"Well, I didn't think it'd be entirely legal," Hale shrugged. "But I didn't think that would bother you given your family history."

He winced as he said it, realizing the inappropriateness of the comment. Unfortunately for him, the wince obscured his vision as his eyes squinted, shielding the hand arcing through the air. Cass' palm connected with his cheek, fingers slapping down with a secondary force along his jaw and cheek bones. The sound reverberated through the small room despite the small amount of force she put behind it. Small impact or no, the surprise caused Hale to jolt in his seat. The chair clattered as he rocked back, a hand shooting to his face to cover the reddening skin. Eyes wide, he stared at the woman who had just struck him.

Cass' eyes remained fierce for a few seconds, her breathing quick and heavy. After seeing the results of her work, her eyes softened and her taut lips loosened into a relaxed frown.

"I'm sorry," he spoke first. "That was out of line."

"I'm sorry," her words came out alongside his. "I shouldn't have done that."

They remained silent. Hale's eyes remained fixed on Cass, she affixed her gaze to the floor, her cheeks flushing with shame. The stress had gotten to them both, though Hale could see from her features that Cass was on the verge of cracking.

The news of her father has been a terrible burden, The Poet commented. *The weight of the revelation of her father's guilt combined with the stressful adventure to obtain it, she is in a precarious state.*

Plus, The General chimed in, *The cloak and dagger exploits of Rush and his bunker buddies aren't helping either.*

What she did was wrong, The Poet confirmed.

You could hit her back, The General suggested.

However, The Poet continued, ignoring The General's inane suggestion. *Given the circumstances, she needed to vent. The situation you both have been placed in has given her little option. Do not be too cross with her.*

"I'm sorry." Cass repeated in a meek voice, eyes transfixed to the floor.

"You've been through a lot–" Hale started.

"We both have," Cass corrected. "Yet you're not raising a hand to me."

See, The General piped up. *She was even expecting it.*

Shh, The Poet scolded.

"You've been through a lot," Hale repeated. "We'll get out of here soon, and we'll get back on track. First thing is first, we gotta decide what we're going to do."

"We?" Cass looked up.

Her eyes were watery. Hale noticed there was more than just sadness in them. She was scared. It was one of the few times Hale had seen Cass vulnerable.

"What do you mean 'we'?" Cass continued. "They want you, Hale. They want you to work for them doing god knows what, and for me to just keep quiet."

"We're in this together," Hale corrected. "I think this could be a good thing, but I don't want to walk in eyes closed. You're better at reading people than me."

"That's ironic." She gave a sardonic smile.

"Yes, it is," he grinned. "Now, tell me. What do you think? Are we going to get screwed if I say yes? Can they really do what they're claiming?"

The door burst open. Hale spun in his chair, jumping to his feet to meet the intruders.

"Yes!" Imanu'el answered. He caught the door as it flew inward, stopping it from slamming into the wall.

"What the f–" Hale stood, startled. His eyes were drawn to a fresh bloodstain on the inner forearm of Imanu'el's sleeve.

"Shhh!" Imanu'el hushed him. He held the door for Jeremiah to follow him in, peering out into the hallway to ensure no one had seen them come in before closing it behind them.

Jeremiah stood near the wall, a familiar look of confusion and fear on his face. Hale couldn't recall a time when The Gray Hooded Man had been calm and collected. He always seemed like a cat startled by a loud noise. Eyes wide, jittery motions, and nervous glances to and fro, he backed against the wall while Imanu'el spoke.

"What are you doing here?" Cass hissed.

"My friends–" Imanu'el clasped his hands, attempting to pull down his own emotions and resume his standard, collected demeanor. However, the frantic method by which he had entered the room had broken his tranquil façade, and his nerves would not let him put his mask fully back on. "I have made a terrible mistake."

"This should be interesting," Hale said, eying Imanu'el suspiciously.

"This place, these men–" He motioned back to the door. "They are evil. They are not to be trusted."

"That's rich coming from you," Cass interjected, crossing her arms.

"Why should we believe you?" Hale asked.

Imanu'el's eyes gave a nervous dart before regaining his footing. "We have a bond, Mr. Langston. We both are Touched, and we both walk a righteous path. The men here, they seek to spoil those who mean well. They seek to poison God's creation with their wicked ways."

"Cut the shit, alright, Randy?" Hale spat.

Jeremiah, who had started to rub his left temple lightly with two fingers, raised his gaze and looked back and forth between Imanu'el and Hale.

"Mr. Langston," Imanu'el started again, another nervous dart of the eyes directed Hale's attention to Jeremiah. "You have been deceived, I assure you. These men are not who they say they are. They–"

"–have something in common with you?" Hale cut him off. "I knew there was something up with you. I couldn't put my finger on it, but now things make more sense, especially after Wandering into some of your past. So how about it, Randy, you want to come clean?"

Jeremiah, despite having a look of dull pain on his face, straightened his posture and looked intently at Imanu'el.

Imanu'el stumbled, clearly caught in an internal struggle of how to proceed. "Please." His head was bowed, lifting only his eyes to meet Hale's. "Please trust me."

"We tried that once." Hale stood resolute. "You bullshitted me then, too. Just like you've been bullshitting people your whole life! A fucking con man and drug addict turned messiah? I don't buy it. Now out with it, what's really going on?"

A door somewhere nearby banged open. Rapid footfalls followed immediately after, heading their direction quickly.

Imanu'el jumped back to their door, holding the handle with both hands and wedging his foot into the base as a makeshift jam. Hale took half a step back, readying himself for an attack. Cass darted behind Hale, peering out next to his left arm.

"For fuck's sake, you have to help us!" Imanu'el said. His voice lost all remnants of its cool. His calm, collected demeanor was shattered. His polite, refined exterior gave way. Hale was reminded of a strung out face he saw when he Wandered to Imanu'el's blood. "They've been lying to us since the start! They lured me here with the threat of sending me to fucking jail, that's why I missed our first meeting!"

The door handle rattled, drawing Imanu'el's attention long enough to ensure his grip was firm before he returned his focus to Cass and Hale. Off to his side, he remained unaware of Jeremiah's devolving demeanor. What had been a face of vague pain and confusion was slowly shifting to sadness and horror.

"They offered to clear my record, to pay me, everything else you could think of under the sky," he continued hastily.

"Gentlemen?" Rush's voice came from the other side of the door. A trio of knocks accompanied his call. "Please open the door."

"I don't know how they found me," Imanu'el continued, holding the door fast. "I found out my gift less than a year ago. It was a fight, a prison brawl ending in me accidentally healing a friend when I helped him up. I've kept it pretty quiet until recently, but they found me right away! It's no secret what they want. They want all of the Touched. They've got big plans, and they want all the wild cards on their side."

"Imanu'el, you're doing something foolish, and I'd ask you to stop," Rush warned from the other side of the door. The words sounded vaguely parental, though the tone had an undercurrent of menace that threatened to sweep his listeners from their feet. This was the tone of a man used to being obeyed.

Jeremiah's eyes raced back and forth between the door and Imanu'el, a distraught look of denial flooding his features. His hand rubbed at his temple as if pain was suddenly renewed. He glanced across the room at the opposing wall and mirror, trying to focus on something before squinting against a new wave of agony.

"They contacted me right after my broadcast," Imanu'el continued. "Bought me a plane ticket and said I'd either come out and meet with them, or they'd expose me not only to my followers, but to the authorities. I didn't know what to do, so I went. We met at a coffee shop in DC and talked about power and control. Well, he talked, I just stayed quiet the whole time. They told me I'd have to give them the names and addresses of all of the Touched I fou–"

The door rocked inward, the frame cracking as a hinge bent towards them.

Imanu'el stumbled away from the impact, planting his foot on the floor to stop his fall, redirect his momentum, and slam his shoulder back into the door. A second kick landed on the other side of the door as Imanu'el rushed towards it. It flew inwards, connecting with Imanu'el's shoulder and forehead, sending him sprawling out onto the ground. Standing in the now open doorway with a fierce look of determination was Joseph. He took two steps into the room, giving a quick glance around to gauge the situation. Satisfied with his initial scan, he moved to stand over the prone form of Imanu'el.

Rush and Timothy walked in after him. Timothy moved to Jeremiah, gruffly grabbing his arm and pushing him towards Cass and Hale. Hale couldn't help but notice from the large man's lopsided walk that he was missing a shoe and a sock.

Rush took a spot between the two large men.

"They drugged us!" Imanu'el moaned. The blow to the head clearly disoriented him, and fresh blood poured freely from a gash over his eyebrow. "Asked us everything we knew about both of you. Then they told us they were taking a blood sample, but they injected so–"

With a fluid motion, a knife flashed out from Joseph's belt, arched down and slid through the opening in Imanu'el's teeth. The occupants on Hale's side of the room flinched, expecting to witness a spatter of blood and the gurgling sounds of a man choking on a blade. But the sounds didn't come.

Joseph planted himself on Imanu'el's chest, using his free hand to grip the man's jaw and keep his knife pressed between his teeth, keeping the blade buried shallow enough to avoid cutting anything deeply, however deep enough to restrict movement and make speaking very painful.

The intimidation tactic worked, and Imanu'el's frantic speech melted into quiet sobs.

Rush panned his gaze slowly across the occupants of the room. Jeremiah looked on him with a mixture of confusion and abject terror. Hale's jaw set and his head lowered, arms out to protect both Cass and the Grey Hooded Man, who both had assumed a place behind him. Cass, who was directly behind Hale's body, pressed her face into Hale's shoulder to keep the grisly visage from making her sick.

With a belabored sigh, Rush spoke. "Now this is unpleasant."

29

The world shimmered. It was a familiar state, just not one that he had experienced for some time. It was cold. He could tell from the hairs standing up on his arms, but he couldn't actually feel the chill in his blood. It was a great side effect. Warmth. Peace. Numb comfort.

Back again, eh, Rain?

Tio? Randy mumbled. Tio was the only one who ever called him Rain. He said bad luck seemed to follow him around like a dark cloud. It also covered for him slurring his actual name when they first met into something sounding like 'rain' instead of 'Randy.'

Haven't seen you in a minute, kid. Tio's voice was warm, friendly, almost paternal. He took care of his flock, making sure they were well looked after and healthy. His real name was Miguel. Tio was Spanish for Uncle, which was a role he fit well, so no one bothered with his given name.

Yeah, it's been awhile. Randy agreed, eyes lolling open. The room was out of focus. That was normal. Nothing to worry about.

So whatcha doin' back, homes? Tio said. *Thought you gave up this life.*

I did. Randy agreed lazily.

So, sup?

Missed you? Randy offered.

Nah, Tio countered. *You missed me, sure, but that's not why you came back.*

I got thirsty. Randy explained. Something resembling irritation bubbled up, threatening the bliss he swam through. He didn't want to leave. Why did Tio keep bothering him? He was ruining it.

You ain't been thirsty in some time, Tio reminded him. *Not thirsty enough to come back, at least. Come on, playa, why you here?*

Randy groaned. He didn't want to talk anymore. He just wanted to stay here. Stay in his pool of bliss. Stay in his peace and tranquility until the short high inevitably burned off. Why was Tio ruining it for him?

Think about that, playa.

Think about what? Why should he have to keep thinking about it?

Not that, homie, Tio corrected. *Think about why I'm ruining it for you.*

That's silly. Tio can't read minds.

You're right, Tio affirmed. *So why are you here?*

"Tio?" The words had substance this time. They weren't soft and ethereal as they had been moments ago.

I'm right here, kid. Tio confirmed, his voice a soft echo in Randy's ear.

"Tio," His voice was raw, a whisper. A tense, dry throat fought the words back.

Why are you here? Tio's voice repeated.

The room shifted again, taking on a more solid form. A recognizable pit formed in his stomach. He was coming down, and his body didn't appreciate the abuse he had put it through. The room was grey, colder, and cramped.

"Tio, you're not here," Randy's voice choked out.

I'm still with you, carnal. His voice began to fade away. *You always did burn off H quicker than we could sell it to you. Guess that is finally working in your favor, eh?*

"Tio…" A tear streamed down Randy's cheek. "Tio, you're dead…"

So why are you here? Tio asked again. *You ain't been with me scoring H for a minute, and you ain't on my couch chasing dragons, so where you is, Rain?*

Randy blinked his eyes. An IV hung next to his bed. He followed the hose down to a needle in his arm. A second bed next to him featured a familiar man in a grey sweatshirt and grey pants. He, too, had an IV hooked to his body.

"Jeremiah," Randy said weakly.

The IV dripped, sending more liquid down the tubes. Randy lolled his head, unable to think clearly with his system fighting the foreign substances being forced into his veins. After a minute of lazily rocking his head back and forth on the bed, he willed his hand to crawl across his body and grasp the tube taped to his arm. He breathed, summoning strength with each rising breath. After three deep inhales, he rolled to the side and pulled.

The needle popped free of his arm with a small splash of IV liquid and blood.

Minutes passed as Randy's blood quickly cleansed the toxins from his body. The feeling was akin to water swirling down a drain. Numb extremities tingled with feeling. Fuzzy edges of the bed came into focus. Churning patterns of nothing solidified. Breaths became deeper and more fulfilling.

Peace out, homie. Tio's voice faded into the back of Randy's mind.

Where am I? Randy's thoughts came into focus. *I'm in a room. A small room made of concrete with two beds and a chair. Jeremiah is here. Tio is not. He was still buried in Oak Hill cemetery in D.C. His flesh, including the slit across his throat from the rival dealer who murdered him, was long rotted away.*

"D.C.," he mumbled to himself.

D.C.! That's it! I flew into D.C. earlier today. Well, I think it was today. How long have I been out? Why am I in here?

He pushed himself up, his stomach threatening to seize as he shifted and the last of the toxins flushed from his system. He hoped there was a bathroom nearby. Leaning over, he found a similar tube hooked into Jeremiah's arm. Gently removing the tape, he extracted the needle from his arm, careful not to tear at the flesh. He searched for something to blot the wound with before realizing the obvious. Extending his own arm over Jeremiah's, his blood dripped onto the seeping puncture in Jeremiah's skin. The process began immediately, quickly mending Jeremiah's torn flesh.

The two men picked us up across from the airport in a van. We had to take a cab to get there. Why didn't they just pick us up at the terminal? What was the point? Randy slid off his bed, regaining his balance and his bearings. *They took us to a compound. We met with Rush, The Suited Man I had met with for coffee before, the one who introduced us to a doctor. What was his name? Short man. Short hair. Doctor something... Geller! Geller was his name. He examined us, then said he would draw some blood... why can't I remember anything after that?*

Jeremiah moaned incoherently.

"Jeremiah?" Randy moved to his side, shaking him softly as he whispered. "Jeremiah, wake up." Jeremiah's eyes moved from under closed lids. He gave no other response.

We must still be in the compound. Randy continued assessing the situation. *This looks like one of its rooms, just not one I've seen before. Why were we unconscious with IV's in our arms?!*

Several minutes passed before Jeremiah finally came back to the real world. He moaned and lolled, similarly to Randy's own behavior a short time ago. As he came more into focus, hands gripped his stomach and sounds of discomfort emanated from his lips. Jeremiah rolled to his side, vomiting violently onto the floor.

"Jeremiah, are you alright?" Randy asked, standing near enough to Jeremiah to comfort him.

Jeremiah breathed deeply, heaving a few more times before finally regaining control. He wiped his mouth with the sleeve of his gray sweatshirt before looking up at the man addressing him. His eyes squinted and focused.

"Imanu'el?" he said. "What is happening?"

Randy stopped, his mind reeling for a moment. The memories of Tio and the familiar haze of drugs flowing through his system had reverted him back to a place he had not visited in years. A time when he went by a different name. A name he had not chosen for himself, but rather one that had been given to him at birth.

But now, he was Imanu'el.

"Yes, Jeremiah, I am here," he adopted his cool, confident tone.

"I... I..." He held his head, steadying himself.

"We are still in Washington, Jeremiah," Imanu'el stated.

"I…" He tried to sit up, failed, and landed back on his pillow. "Oh… I remember… the doctor, he put you to sleep. I saw it."

"How?" Imanu'el queried.

"When they went to take your blood," Jeremiah coughed, making a pained face as he swallowed an acidic taste from his mouth. "They injected something instead of pulling it out. I tried to go to you, but they held me down."

"They did the same to you?"

Jeremiah nodded.

"You did everything you could, Jeremiah," Imanu'el assured him. "But now we must leave. We are likely in danger. Can you walk?"

"I… I think…" Jeremiah took a look up at Imanu'el, admiration filling his eyes. "Yes, Imanu'el. I will walk."

A low, distant rumble of machinery could be heard. Jeremiah did not hear it, as the rustle from his bedsheets was enough to muffle the sound in his own ears.

"What is that?" Imanu'el looked at the door.

Jeremiah stopped, following Imanu'el's gaze before cocking his head to listen. "The garage?" he offered. "It does not sound far."

"We must venture to it as soon as it is safe," Imanu'el declared.

A door opened and closed in the next room. Muffled voices spoke for a few minutes, followed by footsteps traveling past them. Another door opened, across from the original room with the voices. The footsteps were muffled in the second room, though after a few seconds voices could be heard again. This time closer and a bit clearer, but not enough to comprehend the conversation.

"Is that Mr. Channing?" Jeremiah asked.

"I don't know," Imanu'el answered. "I believe so."

"What do we do?!"

"We cannot trust him anymore," Imanu'el stated the obvious. "I had my concerns coming here, and even considered fleeing with you rather than accepting their invitation, but I chose poorly. I do not know what lengths they will go to in order to ensure we remain, though I imagine from our current predicament, their limitations are few. We must be prepared to defend ourselves."

"What? How?" Jeremiah's concern grew. Despite his background on the streets, he'd never been martially inclined.

Imanu'el looked around the room for anything that could be construed as a weapon. The IV stands jumped out at him first, though he imagined they would be unwieldy in these small quarters, and would likely do very little harm to their targets. And if either of the two jarheads came in to check on them, they would need something to take them down quickly, without raising any kind of alarm.

"If I were going to watch over two sleeping bodies," Imanu'el said to himself. "What would my point of weakness be?"

Jeremiah continued through his recovery, watching Imanu'el work through their problem with a mixture of fear and admiration.

Imanu'el checked his watch. "2:00 AM. If they send anyone in." He continued verbalizing his thoughts. "They will either check on us and leave, or sit here." He motioned to the plastic chair. "If they choose the latter, they will be tired, and will likely fall asleep."

He looked over the beds, examining their structure. He carefully tilted the bed on its side, going over every bar. The frames, while metal, seemed to be comprised of cheap, hollow rods; Anything but a suitable weapon. Frustrated with his lack of options, he took a deep breath and bit his tongue to prevent an outburst. His image of tranquility was important, especially to Jeremiah. The man had been saved from the streets and turned his life around due to Imanu'el, not Randy. Jeremiah devoted his existence to Imanu'el and his cause not because of who he was, but who Jeremiah thought he was.

He had to be careful to maintain that balance.

A door out in the next room opened and clicked shut. A single set of footfalls approached. "Quickly," Imanu'el hissed. "Lay back in your bed. Tape the cord to your arm. Be very still." Jeremiah followed Imanu'el's directions without hesitation. He grabbed the IV cord, affixing it to his arm with the tape that was still wrapped around the plastic, and lay back in bed as if asleep. Imanu'el pulled the pillow off his bed, removing the case quickly. He dared not tilt his bed back onto its feet, else he would notify whoever passed by that something was amiss. He could only hope now that they were not coming inside. He placed himself against the wall behind where the door would open, waiting with frozen breath.

To his dismay, the footsteps approached the room. The handle rattled as someone grabbed it, then twisted down. Light poured into the dimly lit room from the hallway as the door opened. A large figure in the doorway cast a shadow across the room, stopping a half a step inside.

"What the–" Timothy started.

Imanu'el readied himself. Timothy took another step inside, towards the overturned bed. His advance had brought him into Imanu'el's view. Jumping out from behind, Imanu'el brought the pillowcase arching down and over Timothy's head.

"Jeremiah!" Imanu'el hissed as he pulled Timothy back towards him. "Hel–"

The call was cut short by an elbow shooting back into Imanu'el's solar plexus. The wind broke from his lungs and expelled from his mouth with a wheeze. His fingers uncurled from the pillowcase involuntarily as he clutched his chest and gasped for breath.

Jeremiah rolled from his bed and leapt forward. The IV tube, still attached to his arm, drew taut and snapped away, bringing the metal stand down with a clatter. He reached Timothy just as the large man pulled the fabric away from his eyes. Though Timothy was a big man, Jeremiah was not petite. While he was neither as fit nor strong as the guard, his momentum and sheer weight overcame Timothy's strength and brought them both to the floor.

Hitting the ground with a thud, Jeremiah planted both hands on Timothy's chest, grabbing handfuls of suit material in an effort to keep him still.

Timothy exhaled sharply as the wind was forced from his lungs. The man was fit and well trained, making his recovery swift. He only took a moment to regain his bearings before swinging both arms up in a symmetric arc, landing both palms on Jeremiah's ears. A clap sounded from the impact on Jeremiah's head, and he rocked back with a yelp, holding his head in pain.

Timothy grabbed a handful of Jeremiah's hoodie, jerking him to the side to throw the man's body off of his. With a grunt, he pushed himself up, rocking to his left to support his weight on his forearm.

I swear, Tio's voice resonated in the back of Imanu'el's mind. The old story Imanu'el's former dealer had told replayed poignantly. *That crackhead fell off me like I was nothin' and started scrambling right back to his feet. I tell you what, one swift kick right here,* He put his fingers to his temple. *And it was naptime.*

Imanu'el saw an opportunity and summoned his strength back. With a swift motion, he shifted his weight and pulled his right foot back. A quick step forward launched a kick directly into Timothy's head, Imanu'el's toe planting right into the burly man's temple. The force of the kick brought the large man's upper body a few inches off the ground, after which his limp form slumped to the floor.

Imanu'el took a moment to watch the still form of Timothy, readying himself in case the burly man roused himself and re-entered the fight. After several seconds of stillness from the guard, Imanu'el allowed his eyes to leave the downed threat.

"Let us go!" Imanu'el rushed to Jeremiah's side, pulling him to his feet. "We must move in haste."

The pair quietly moved to the doorway, peering out to ensure no one else had been alerted by the struggle. The room looked familiar. It was small with four doors. Imanu'el remembered passing through this area, or one similar to it, when they had gone to meet the doctor. But he couldn't figure out which door led where, even if this was the same room he remembered. The building was a labyrinth.

A quartet of footfalls approached, accompanied by the smooth voice of Rush Channing. The noises came from the other side of the door to their left, and they seemed to be walking down a hall. If this was indeed the same room he remembered, that was their way to the garage.

"Get back inside." Imanu'el pushed on Jeremiah's chest, ushering him back into the room as he quietly closed the door.

The door opened into the next room, followed by a parade of footsteps moving past. Imanu'el gathered that they had just entered in from the hallway leading to the garage, and had just walked into the medical room. He looked at Jeremiah. "Whomever Mr. Channing has with him will likely go through the same procedure as we did. We must tie and gag this man so he does not alert the others when he arises from his slumber, after which we will make for the garage and escape."

"Imanu'el," Jeremiah spoke hesitantly. "Will we be alright?"

"Jeremiah." He stepped forward, placing his hands on each of his Zealot's cheeks. "You are among God's chosen. You assist the shepherd in protecting the flock. We will triumph here today."

Jeremiah listened to Imanu'el speak with a longing in his eyes. He leaned into the Man in White's hands, rapt in attention. When Imanu'el finished, Jeremiah remained silent for several seconds before finally nodding in affirmation. Ashamed at his own internal desires, he turned away.

From a collection of supplies within the room, Timothy's hands and feet were bound and his mouth gagged. IV tubing made up the majority of his restraints, fastening his wrists and ankles together. The pillowcase was rolled into a tube and wrapped around his head after a sock was stuffed into his mouth. The sock was, of course, donated by the unconscious guard.

"How much lon–" Jeremiah started.

"Shhh!" Imanu'el silenced him, listening.

"As you can see we take our operation seriously, Mr. Langston," Rush Channing said as the group walked by again. They were walking back the way they came.

Imanu'el's eyes widened at Jeremiah. He waited until the group had passed completely before speaking. "They're here! This explains why Mr. Channing made so many inquiries of them. They are here!"

"Is this bad?" Jeremiah asked nervously.

"No, no..." Imanu'el's eyes darted, analyzing the angles. "This is a blessing.

With their help, we can surely escape. We will speak with them and garner their assistance. Surely they will be of a similar mind."

"What do we do now?"

"We wait," Imanu'el said confidently. "If we can get them alone, we will convince them to join us. We will just have to wait for Mr. Channing to leave them with the doctor, or alone in a room. Either will work for our needs."

And so they did. Minutes passed by in silence. Each of them passed the time with their own brand of nervous behavior. Imanu'el fixed his eyes to the floor, thinking of the angles and possibilities he may have missed. Jeremiah paced back and forth, wringing his hands and mumbling to himself.

Finally the door to the next room opened again. This time only two sets of footsteps passed by. Imanu'el waited until they had opened the door to the medical room and closed it behind them before turning to Jeremiah.

"It is time. Let us move quietly."

Imanu'el opened the door as quietly as he could. The new hinges didn't squeak, which he considered a blessing. Their luck did not last long, however. The captive guard on the ground began to rouse. Muffled mumbles and groans could be heard through the makeshift gag, and it would be only a matter of time before he was fully conscious.

He moved out into the hall, beckoning Jeremiah to move with him. They closed the door quietly, traversing across the small room with delicate steps before surgically opening the next door. Just as he had hoped, it opened to the long, familiar entry hall. He knew a right turn at the bend would lead them to the garage, which meant there were two people either waiting there, or in the room directly across the hall from them.

A muffled smack was heard, causing both the white and gray clad men to jump. They paused, listening for further activity. After a short period of silence, muffled voices could be heard again.

"It is them," Imanu'el whispered to Jeremiah. "I am sure of it."

They crept down the hall, silently approaching the door. From the other side,

Hale's voice could be heard.

"Yes, it is. Now, tell me. What do you think? Are we going to get screwed if I say yes? Can they really do what they're claiming?"

Imanu'el took this opportunity to make his entrance. He opened the door and stumbled in, losing his balance as he hurriedly pushed through the door. "Yes!"

30

With a belabored sigh, Rush spoke. "Now this is unpleasant."

The room was still. Timothy waited for orders near the standing trio of Hale, Cass and Jeremiah. A fresh bruise was forming under the skin around the enforcer's left temple. That, combined with his lack of footwear, begged questions from the onlookers. Fortunately they were used to unsatisfied curiosity, as these mysteries would have to remain unsolved for the time being. Imanu'el remained on the floor, tears flowing from his eyes as he stared up at the man holding the blade of a knife in his mouth. Hale stood with his arms out, intentionally protecting Cass, and unintentionally giving Jeremiah cover as well.

"Mr. Langston," Rush's voice was calm and rich. "This is not an event we wished for you to experience during your visit."

"What the hell is going on?" Hale asked through gritted teeth. He wanted to be terrified. His body begged for him to tuck tail and flee. In spite of his natural instinct, the constant barrage of social, mental, and physical attacks he had endured in the last day prevented him from feeling anything more than seething rage.

Who the hell are these people? He asked himself. *Who do they think they are to do these kinds of things?*

They are dangerous men, Hale, The Poet answered.

Damn well organized, too, The General chimed in.

"A minor hiccup in operations, Mr. Langston," Rush explained coolly. "This man has presented a danger to our organization after entering into a contract with us. Instead of following the proper procedures to ensure his wrongs were righted, he sought to further undermine and sabotage our organization. He has attacked our personnel," Rush gestured towards Timothy, "And attempted to flee when we had an agreement that he would stay until our business was concluded."

Imanu'el squirmed on the ground, spewing out a flurry of consonants against the blade in his mouth. A yelp confirmed he moved too much, and a small amount of blood spattered up over his lips.

"Stop it!" Jeremiah shouted, hands held to his head as he tried to alleviate his own pain. "Please! You're hurting him!"

"He said they were drugged," Hale spat.

"Are you going to believe the criminal with a rap sheet littered with acts of fraud?" Rush dismissed the claim.

"He is telling the truth!" Jeremiah cut in. "Had Imanu'el not woken me up, we'd still be unconscious in that room."

"Mr. Langston," Rush continued, ignoring Jeremiah. "We will be removing these two troublemakers so you may return to your private discussion. Allow me to apologize for their interference. I assu–"

"We're done here," Hale said firmly. "I don't know what your true intentions are, but I've had enough. You're going to let us leave. Now."

"Let's not be hasty." Rush kept his tone even. Despite the chaos, his demeanor was placid and confident. "Remember what we have on the line here. Not only your own security, but for generations to come. And Ms. Voss, your father–"

"Don't!" Cass warned, remaining tucked behind Hale with her eyes pressed into his shoulder as she retorted. "That thinly veiled threat earlier was the worst thing you could have done."

"You misunderstand," Rush reassured. "I have no intent–"

"I don't believe you," Cass cut him off. "Whether you have the pull or not, I'm not letting Hale sell his soul to you for my Dad's safety."

Hale could hear the hesitation and sorrow creep in the undercurrent of Cass' voice. He could tell she wanted nothing more than for Rush to be telling the truth, and for Hale to take the deal. However, everything they'd seen had led them to believe this was an organization built on deceit and brute force. They'd both been strung along with false hope and now she was ready to oppose the figurehead of it all.

"You don't mean that." Rush either saw through her bluff, or had done enough research to make an assumption. "The idea of your father rotting in a cell for the rest of his life is abhorrent to you. Innocent or guilty, he does not belong behind bars, and you'll do everything you can to earn his freedom."

"I'm done talking to you," Cass said through gritted teeth. She then leaned up and whispered to Hale, keeping her line of sight off of the bleeding man on the floor. "My Dad told me to trust him and let him handle it. 'Don't do anything rash', he said. I didn't listen to him yesterday and look what happened. Now I'm trusting him, and I'm trusting you."

Rush sighed, turning his attention back to Hale. "And you, Mr. Langston? Are we throwing in the towel on a truly unique opportunity? Imagine the fortune that would be made available to you and your family. Imagine the life you could have with that beautiful woman. Do you really wish to throw that away over the lies of saboteurs?"

"Imanu'el is not lying!" Jeremiah shouted. His voice was strained and desperate.

"You!" Rush looked to him, his voice sharp and elevated to regain the room's attention before returning to its normal soothing octave. "You are a patsy duped into following a con artist with nothing more than a glorified parlor trick. The man you have attached yourself to is a fraud, a repeat offender who has been in and out of jail his entire life. If not for his unique talent, he'd still be on the streets scoring heroin and robbing the elderly to finance his fix.

"However, you are not lost, Mr. Higgins. Yes, we have done our research. Jeremy Higgins, born in Portland, Oregon to the upper-middle class parents Peter and Marta Higgins. Dropped out of high school after your mother died during an attempted carjacking. You turned to drugs to ease your pain, and now follow the employ of someone who committed the same type of crimes that ended your mother's life."

Jeremiah's face froze. The pain flowing through his ears and wracking his brain was matched by a newly opened pit in his chest. Rush's words had brought forth memories he had avoided for a decade. For a moment the cacophony of clashing tones of Touched receded. Images of his mother's closed casket came to the foreground, followed by his father all but abandoning him in lieu of his grief. The parallels drawn to Imanu'el were ugly and horrifying. This beautiful person couldn't possibly be like the man who tore his family apart, could he? His eyes lowered to look upon the face of the man he had fallen in love with.

The images fell into obscurity as the conflicting tones reverberated through his head again, forcing his eyes closed for several moments as he endured the pain.

"You can have a new start, Mr. Higgins," Rush continued, eyes boring into Jeremiah's. "A true start. Not the false claims this man has given you. You can get back on track to a real life." Rush turned back to Hale. "All of you can. The frontier we are ready to explore is unlike any venture ever undertaken. Together, we will change the course of history, I promise you that."

The offer sounded good. It was a dream life packaged into a contract. Hale wanted to believe it. He yearned for it to be what he was looking for. With a glance around the room, he reminded himself what was actually on the table.

Imanu'el continued to moan pitifully, blood leaking from his mouth around the blade of the knife. The image was jarring. It was something that would draw a gasp out of an audience in a theater, or perhaps a cheer if the victim was particularly villainous. In the flesh, it was nothing short of vulgar and horrifying. This was what he had to look forward to if he signed on, and it was not something that sat well with him.

"No," he said calmly.

"Come again, Mr. Langston?" Rush's jaw set.

"I appreciate your offer," Hale expanded, "though I respectfully decline."

"You understand what you are turning down?" Rush prodded.

"I understand. I just don't think I'm cut out for this type of outfit."

Rush nodded slowly. "That is unfortunate."

Before he could continue, Hale spoke again. "With my decision made, we'll be taking you up on your previous offer and will be leaving immediately." He looked down at Imanu'el. "We'll be taking them as well."

"Mr. Langston," Rush's voice arched down an octave, his tone one of warning. "You have no authority to make demands here."

"I'm not leaving these two here," Hale said flatly. "It's fairly clear where this is going, and it's not something I'm going to allow."

Sir, The General chimed in. *Exactly how are you planning on enforcing this demand?*

"We have every intention of allowing them to leave, Mr. Langston," Rush continued, his eyebrows pulling in like a hawk examining prey. "However, there are certain matters of business that need to be seen to before that happens. This is not negotiable."

"You are fine with us leaving?" Hale queried, doubt dripping from his words.

"Yes," Rush stated with a nod. "You have no contractual obligation to us, and you have a firm understanding of what we are capable of should you choose to betray the secrets you've learned here today." He glanced to Cass. "Both of you."

"Excuse me?" Cass' lips pressed together and her eyes narrowed into a piercing glare, lifting up from Hale's shoulder to lock eyes with Rush. She bore holes into The Suited Man from behind Hale. From her peripheral vision she could see the bloody figure of Imanu'el and her stomach lurched. His injury was minor, but that made no difference when her vision threatened to go dark and her stomach to heave. She kept her eyes on Rush, not letting her sight or mind focus on the wounded man.

"Ms. Voss," Rush continued, "to be as clear as possible, should you betray the truths you have learned today, we will ensure it is your father that pays for the damages done. After all, it is much easier to risk oneself than those we love. I trust this communicates how serious we are about informational security."

Cass stepped out from behind Hale. He jolted at first, thinking she was moving towards Rush. He had no desire for her to put herself in harm's way, especially when her anger was so near the surface. Realization struck after a moment. She had no intention of moving forward. She simply wanted a clear shot.

Cass raised Obie's gun up with her right arm, leveling the barrel at Rush's chest. Her left arm, clearly still tender from her injury, lifted to add a modicum of support to the weapon.

The dynamic of the room instantly shifted.

Timothy sidestepped away from Rush, widening the range Cass had to monitor to keep all three of them in her view.

Rush offered a surprised look before resuming a defensive stance with his arms held out to his sides.

Joseph pulled away, removing the knife from his captive's mouth as he pulled Imanu'el up to his feet. He spun his captive around so that they were both facing Cass, holding his prisoner between himself and the gun as a human shield. The knife slid up and against Imanu'el's neck, threatening to open his jugular should he struggle.

"You are correct," Cass affirmed. "Family is very important to me."

"I see neither of you had the foresight to search them for weapons." Despite the intended audience of his comment, Rush's eyes remained fixated on Cass.

"Now you've made a threat that I believe you can come through on," Cass continued sternly. Despite her rage and her flowing adrenaline, Hale took note of the fear creeping into her words. Her voice threatened to crack, and the gun was vibrating ever so slightly. "How am I supposed to leave with the knowledge that you are able to destroy someone I love? How can I be sure that you won't do so out of spite, or vengeance for helping ruin whatever plans you had here this weekend?"

Hale had a moment of discomfort as he drew a parallel to what caused Will Voss to pull the trigger on his victim.

"There's no need for violence, Ms. Voss," Rush stated.

"You should have considered that before you brought it forward as a legitimate tactic."

"Cass?" Hale said, tentatively reaching his hand out towards her.

"An arrangement can be reached, I assure you," Rush said calmly.

"And how do I know you'll respect any deal we strike with you?" She furrowed her brow, sidestepping away from Hale's reach. "The entirety of your organization is based on secrecy and deceit. What's to stop you from violating any agreement with impunity?"

"I'm a man of my word," Rush said with confidence.

"I'm sure you are," Cass retorted with a sneer.

"What alternative do you have?" he asked with a smug smile. "Kill me, Joseph, and Timothy? How about Doctor Geller? Will you wait for our other associates to return tomorrow so you may dispatch them as well, thereby ensuring no witnesses to your crime?"

Cass trembled.

"No." He continued smiling, hands passively held out to the sides. "You're not a killer, Cassie."

"Don't call me that," she growled through clenched teeth. That name was reserved for her father's use. The thought of this man speaking from what resembled like a paternal standpoint was unacceptable. Despite the rush of anger his comments provoked, her conviction was clearly still on shaky ground.

"My apologies, Ms. Voss," Rush said smoothly. "Now let's follow this to the logical conclusion. No one wants anyone to get hurt here. And while I do not like leaving loose ends, I can see when I have lost a battle. So here's my proposition: you and Hale leave, taking these two with you." Rush nodded to Jeremiah and Imanu'el. "Joseph and Timothy will drive the four of you back to your hotel, at which point we will all part ways. I trust everyone in here is willing to agree to simply forget about each other. Is this acceptable?"

Cass kept the wobbling gun trained on Rush, eyes darting back and forth between him, Joseph, and his bleeding captive. The adrenaline pumping in her veins prevented her from fainting at the sight of his blood, but she could feel her equilibrium shifting, and she worried about losing consciousness under the combination of stress.

Imanu'el locked her gaze with pleading eyes, silently begging that she take the offer.

"Okay," she finally agreed. "Now let them go."

"Let's show some mutual trust, shall we?" Rush extended one of his hands forward, palm down. He lowered it as he spoke. "Lower those sights, and Joseph will release Imanu'el, after which Joseph and Timothy will see you securely delivered to your destination."

> . . . "–securely delivered to your destination, then things have gone
> horribly wrong."
> . . . . . . "You will be the driver,
> you–"
> . . . . "–will handle the execution."

Hale jarred from the Wander. Content aside, he had never experienced a Wander from multiple perspectives. The first glimpse revealed a truth from Rush's perspective. The second came from Timothy. The third was from Joseph's point of view. All of them featured Rush speaking as if organizing a plan.

How did that happen? Hale wondered. *Did Rush's voice trigger a memory in all three of them, giving me access to all of their insight at once? Is that possible?*

Possibility is a grey area around you, son, The General responded.

Cass nodded and lowered her gun.

"No!" Hale barked. "He's lying!"

"What?!" Cass lifted the gun again. Her head turned for a moment before she forced herself to focus back on Rush.

"That was a signal to have us all killed," Hale warned.

"Mr. Langston," Rush gave a belabored sigh, as if suddenly burdened with an annoying inconvenience. "I am very disappointed in you."

"No more lies," Cass demanded, gun trained on Rush's chest. "Joseph, let

Imanu'el go now, or I'll show you how much alike my father and I are."

"An amusing threat," Rush balked. "However, it is hollow. You know you can still get out of here with no blood on your hands. Yes, you will have to give up these two, but you and Hale are free to go. Are you really going to pass that up for the Glimmer?"

"Glimmer?"

Rush gave into his hubris and grinned. "The Glimmer. That point in a struggle, be it physical, social, or mental, where the losing party feels they have found their out. It is the glimmer of light in a state of pure darkness, dancing just out of reach. In desperation, they reach for it. It evades them, so they begin to chase. They run, trip, stumble, stretch, but to no avail. All the while, as they put themselves into more and more vulnerable of a position, the assurance of their defeat swarms in around them without their knowledge. And the best part?" He leaned forward a little. "I control the Glimmer."

Cass readjusted her hold on the gun, trying to keep it steady with one arm supporting the weight.

"Now, Ms. Voss," Rush continued. "Take Hale, and walk out that door, and don't let us ever hear from you again."

"And if I don't?" she asked, voice wavering.

"You'll trip one last time chasing the Glimmer, and you'll finally come to realize just what cards I've been holding." Rush's voice was even, low, and menacing. His face and tone gave no indication of a bluff, but rather the sheer confidence that he was on the victorious side. "The four of you will die, and out of spite, I'll see to it that your father is convicted, and then gang raped every day until he commits suicide in his cell."

CLAP

Hale had heard gunshots before. The movies rarely did them justice, featuring loud booms fit for shotguns to handheld pistols, or reverberating explosions you could feel in your chest. In Hale's area of town, he had been near shootouts, and knew life was a subdued version of Hollywood's portrayal. That aside, the sound of a gun firing mere feet away was terrifying. To make matters worse, the room was small and built for acoustic resonance. The clap of the cartridge launching the bullet out of the barrel was amplified, causing a sharp pain to stab into the ears of everyone present.

A chip of the wall exploded out near Rush's right arm. He flinched as a small chunk of debris flew into him. The damage was minimal, as the room was made of concrete. They were all lucky the round bit into the surface instead of ricocheting off.

Rush straightened himself, hands raising to his ears as a look of pain crossed his face. He regained his composure when he deduced it was a warning shot, knowing the display of fear would only further weaken his position. He forced himself to remove his hands from his ears and pushed them out forward, showing that he was not reaching for a weapon or moving to defend himself with anything other than his voice. He spoke again, though this time his tone was not nearly as confident,

"Alright, I see that–"

CLAP CLAP

CLAP

Cass took her time aiming after failing her first attempt at firing a gun. This time, she accommodated for her lack of skill with an increase in quantity. Mathematically, she reasoned, this would give her a greater statistical probability of hitting her target.

Fortunately for her, she was right.

The first shot connected with Rush right in the breadbasket, ripping through the fabric of his suit and into his chest. The second shot flew high, as she had not yet learned to accommodate for recoil. The bullet ricocheted off the wall, shattering upon impact with the ceiling over Timothy's head. Steadying herself for a moment between her second and third shots, she readjusted her aim and fired again. This one went clean through Rush's right wrist.

The Suited Man did not fly back into the wall, nor did he jump and twist with the momentum of the bullet. Theatrics had no place here. He stumbled on his words and took a half step back as the first bullet pierced his lung. Shock took over, causing him to stand still with his mouth agape as the second and third shots rang out. The third shot pushed his arm back, tugging his body in the opposite direction as the first bullet, which had hit him slightly to the left of his sternum.

Eyes still wide and fixated on Cass, Rush's knees buckled, and The Suited Man fell to the floor.

The room erupted into motion.

Joseph's eyes were drawn to the falling form of Rush as he assessed his next moves. Imanu'el noticed the similarity of his situation to his earlier fight with Timothy. He took advantage of the moment of distraction and pulled his elbow back, slamming it into his captor's ribs. Joseph jolted from the impact, but managed to slide his left arm up and tighten his grip around Imanu'el's neck, pulling him down to force his back into an arch. Knife still in hand, he lowered the blade before wrenching it up and into Imanu'el's side. The strike did not bite. It split through clothing and put a deep scratch into his skin, though the attack left him otherwise unharmed.

Hale was reminded of the razor denting in Imanu'el's flesh back at his apartment. Something about his healing prowess gave him that extra edge of physical resilience, which at the present time was worth its weight in gold.

Imanu'el jerked, throwing his arms to his side defensively.

As if anticipating the move, Joseph swung the knife out in a semi-circle, bringing it back in with great force for a straight on piercing blow to his target's stomach. While Imanu'el's rubbery skin had deflected the initial slash, the straight on attack from the point of the blade was too much.

The knife parted through The Man in White's clothing, split through his skin and muscle, and buried into his gut. A spatter of blood spotted Joseph's hand with crimson, and the pristine white garb blossomed with a red stain.

"Drop the gun or I disembowel this little fuck." Joseph gripped the dagger, keeping it buried to the hilt in the bleeding man's gut.

Imanu'el froze, eyes lowering to the bloody mess that was his torso. He shivered, mouth opening in an attempt to scream, protest, or beg. Whatever the intention, it emanated as a mixture of soft, unintelligible sounds through shaky, staggered breaths. His hands wrapped around Joseph's, attempting to pull the knife free. A small twitch of Joseph's wrist reminded Imanu'el who was in control of the situation.

The Man in White had no trouble screaming now.

Timothy used the focus on the grappled pair to make his own move. In a fluid motion he brushed back his suit, reaching to his belt and pulling out a taser. He brought it up swiftly, leveling the device at Cass as he pulled the trigger.

"NO!" Jeremiah howled, throwing himself forward. He collided with Timothy's arms, throwing off the man's aim during the moment of truth.

Wires launched from the taser, following two electrodes that slapped into the wall and bounced off harmlessly.

Timothy dropped the taser and lowered into a hunched stance. His right arm crossed over his body, connecting with Jeremiah's solar plexus. Before the Gray Hooded Man could react to the strike, a follow up punch arched up from underneath his field of vision, catching his chin as his body attempted to double over. The crunching impact lifted the man inches off the ground, and the chips of several shattered teeth accompanied his flight.

What the hell is happening? Hale scanned the room, judging the best course of action to take. *A second ago we were all talking. Now Rush is… dead? The parallels have been realized, and the irony of the motives of her and her father's first murder are poetic. Something tells me she won't find it amusing though.*

Hale, focus, The Poet urged.

Right. Imanu'el's been stabbed. They just tried to taze Cass. Jeremiah is now missing teeth. And now Timothy is coming after–SHIT!

Hale sidestepped Timothy's incoming punch, which shot like a spear past his cheek as he moved. Hale's movement invited him to naturally lift a knee, which he then brought across Timothy's stomach in a low clothesline. The force of the blow rocked him back onto both legs. Timothy simply bent forward and clutched his gut. Going with what seemed to be the most advantageous and available attack, Hale leaned over and wrapped Timothy up in a reverse headlock. Bringing the man's head up under his armpit and staring down at his back, Hale found an opportunity to take another quick glance around the room.

Cass kept her gun trained on Joseph, who in turn firmly held Imanu'el in front of him. The Man in White was bleeding profusely from the wound in his gut, causing a steady stream of crimson to flow through his fingers as he wrapped them around Joseph's hand. Joseph was taking no chances, keeping the blade buried as a method of enforcing control over his captive.

While the gun in Cass' hand trembled and her skin tone had faded to a light shade of green, she forced herself to ignore her body's revolt and continue defending their lives.

Jeremiah wailed in agony on the floor, spitting blood and teeth into a puddle. Despite his injuries, he pushed himself to his hands and knees, valiantly attempting to re-enter the fray.

Timothy recovered, hunching down under Hale and setting his knees. To Hale's surprise, Timothy's arms wrapped around his legs and lifted Hale completely off the ground. With a sharp pivot the man slammed Hale down onto the table. Hale's death grip on Timothy's neck was the only thing preventing him from a much more brutal attack, though the impact against the table caused him to loosen it just enough for the large man to pull free.

With his restrictions removed, Timothy reared up over Hale, coming down with an overhead hammerfist into Hale's stomach. The blow caused Hale to lean forward, which Timothy took advantage of with a follow up left hook aimed for the jaw. Hale tilted his head back at the last moment, allowing the fist to whiz by his cheek.

Very Muhammad Ali of you, sir, The General commented. *Now watch for the elbow on the backswing, and then put your forehead into his nose.*

Sure enough, Timothy attempted to catch Hale with his elbow as he re-centered himself. Hale kept himself down to avoid the blow, then grasping two handfuls of suit jacket, Hale pulled himself forward. His forehead connected with Timothy's nose, but not with great force. The man was much larger than Hale, and was clearly better trained. He tucked his head and turned slightly as the blow connected, displacing the force, then returned the attack by grabbing Hale by the throat and forcing him back down on the table. He immediately followed up with a right cross, punching the prone man square in the jaw.

Hale felt a click as the burly man's fist slammed into his chin. The world flashed, and for a moment Hale thought he had been knocked out. Though out of focus, his vision came back to him quickly. Pain streaked through his shoulders and down his back from both his jaw and the back of his head where he slammed into the table. Barely a well-defined blur above him, Hale saw Timothy's fist raising for a second punch.

"NO!" Jeremiah shouted again. The single syllable declaration had become his war cry for the battle, and he used it to fuel the momentum of the chair swinging for Timothy's head. The improvised weapon connected with a thick thud and a ring of vibrating metal.

Timothy jolted forward with the force of the blow, immediately going slack and falling like a rag doll. Hale caught the body as it fell onto him, shifting his weight to roll him off the table and onto the floor.

We did it, Hale told himself in disbelief. *We're going to make it out of here.*

Well done, Hale, The Poet congratulated. *Now go see to Cass, she is likely going to go into shock once she realizes what she has done.*

Hale pushed himself up, looking over at the Mexican standoff between Joseph and Cass. *She wouldn't be here if it weren't for me*, Hale thought with a twinge of regret. *She wouldn't have been in the position where she had to choose to end someone's life had I not brought her with.*

Sir, The General cut in, *she knew damn well what she was doing, and she's a lot stronger than you give her credit for.*

True, Hale conceded. *But that doesn't mean I have to like it.*

And it is that realization that separates us from barbarians and animals, The Poet reminded.

"Cass," Hale spoke as he approached. "Are you okay?"

"I'm fine." Her voice was as steady as an earthquake. "Can we leave now, please?"

"Definitely." Hale looked up at Joseph. "Let him go and get out. Last chance."

Joseph's eyes moved back and forth between Cass and Hale, giving one look to Jeremiah before returning to Hale. Without a word, both hands loosened, allowing Imanu'el to pull away with a gasp of relief. Joseph's hands remained open and out, one covered with the false prophet's blood. His eyes remained fixated on Cass and the gun as he sidestepped towards the door.

Cass, breathing raggedly and skin paled, did not turn from the gristly sight.

"I'm going to grab Tim," he said flatly. "Then we leave, and we never saw any of this. It was just a job, I ain't got nothing against any of you."

"How many more people do you work with?" Hale asked.

"Just him and the Doc," he responded flatly. Even under fire and in a hostile situation, he maintained his composure with expert poise. "He talked a lot of shit, but this op was just getting off the ground. I'm serious, man, it was just a job. I'll grab Tim, and you'll never see us again."

"Pick up your friend and get the fuck out," Hale spat.

Joseph nodded and slowly sidestepped towards Tim, keeping his hands out and his eyes fixed on Cass.

Imanu'el looked up, pleading in his eyes. Blood poured into his hands, dripping onto his thighs to form a constellation of red stars in the white fabric. Looking between Joseph and Hale, his visage suddenly changed. Pain became surprise, and fear of his wound shifted to fear of an external threat. An unintelligible exclamation alerted the others that something was amiss.

Hale saw the reaction and followed the man's gaze to the mirror against the wall to the right of himself and Cass. Something was amiss, though he couldn't understand at first. What he saw wasn't a reflection. The body shape was wrong, as was the clothing. The firearm aimed out towards Cass was further confirmation the image he saw had nothing to do with the occupants of the room.

Familiar thick glasses adorned the man's nose, the large lenses complimenting pudgy cheeks and underlining a receding head of curly hair.

Is that...

The familiar man pulled his hand away from the mirror, which had swung out as a hidden door. His free hand moved to support the handgun pointed into the room, ensuring he was taking careful aim at his target.

Hale had no time to shout a word of warning, or to overturn the table to provide obstruction, or even to dive and push Cass out of the way. In a moment where desperation and necessity met in a titanic clash, Hale did the only thing he could.

Hale stepped in between the gunman and Cass.

31

A familiar loud clap filled the room.

He missed. Hale allowed an internal sigh of relief. The moment of relief passed quickly as Cass yelped behind him. *No, he fired a fraction of a second before I moved in the way. I was not quick enough.*

Sir, The General spoke. *This is not an ideal position. You should retreat to cover post haste.*

Do not move, Hale, The Poet urged. *This is truly righteous.*

Why are you doing this? The General queried. *He's obviously a much better shot than Cass was.*

He is doing what he feels is right, General, The Poet cooed. *He feels not only responsible for Cassandra being here, but responsible for her protection. Despite the short period of time they have shared, he is very much in love.*

The thoughts formed the undercurrent of Hale's consciousness, flowing past in half a breath. The single clap became a ruckus of applause, filling the area with repeated strikes of thunder accentuated with bright flashes. It was as if they had their own private storm.

Instinctually, Hale put his hands forward and hunched into a protective stance, though he willed himself to stay between Cass and the man.

I'm okay. Hale said, rocking back a little. *He's not as accurate as I thought.*

He attempted to release his held breath, ready to spring into action again, only to find the breath had already escaped his lungs. A moment of confusion caused him to pause. Something was out of place, and it needed to be addressed before he could move on.

A wet, bubbly feeling replaced the smooth flow of air he expected when he pulled a breath in.

He coughed, sputtered, and wavered.

I think I'm in pain.

Sir, I'm afraid you are. Look down.

Don't look down, Hale.

Hale was, by nature, a curious person.

His eyes lowered to examine what the General referenced. What he saw seemed out of place. Unreal. Incomprehensible. There were holes in his shirt, and dark splotches of red had flowered up from under the light gray material. There were three stark wounds, two of which were near his belly button; the third was over his ribs.

One. Two. Three. Hale counted slowly.

It seemed like a logical thing to do.

The clapping stopped. Hale was vaguely aware of Cass standing near him. She still had the gun, but it was in her left hand now. That seemed odd, especially since he knew she hurt that arm earlier today. He wondered if the fresh wound on her right shoulder had anything to do with her peculiar decision.

Your legs are heavy, Hale. The Poet murmured. *Why don't you sit down? You'll feel better.*

It hurts. Hale complained. *Why does it hurt now?*

You'll be fine, son. The General promised. *Do as the Dove suggests.*

Hale did.

His descent was quicker than he would have liked, though the dull pain from his impact faded quickly.

Another gurgle attempting to pass for a breath reminded him of the sharp, cold pain in his chest. It felt deep, like an icicle had been broken off in his lung.

It must not be too serious, Hale hypothesized. *It hurts, but it doesn't hurt that bad. That's promising, right?*

Son, I aint gonna lie, The General's tone was grim. *I don't think that's a good sign.*

Hale, The Poet urged. *Lay back. It's not good for you to sit up like this when you're wounded.*

Hale did.

He made a conscious effort to slow his journey to the floor this time. His abdominal muscles didn't seem to want to cooperate. Despite his efforts, his muscles' rebellion caused him to flop onto the floor as gracelessly as he had sat. His head bounced off the ground with a thud. He was grateful there was no pain to accompany it.

Cass stood over him. She was crying and shouting. One of her hands hovered over him, shaking as if she was unsure whether or not touching him would make the situation worse.

He wished she would touch him.

She didn't.

She cried, her voice pleading and distant. But she wasn't looking at him anymore. There were other people gathering. Jeremiah. Imanu'el. He remembered both of them. They were fighting about something, though he couldn't tell what about. He wished they would stop. He was comfortable. He was tired.

They were ruining it.

General, Poet. Hale said internally. *Thank you for being with me.*

Sir, it was a pleasure and an honor to serve with you.

Twon't hurt you at all; it's your time now; you just need a long sleep, child; what have you had anyhow better than sleep? The Poet recalled the Sandburg quote in a melodic tone.

And you too, Dove, The General said. *You ain't half bad.*

Though we may not have agreed, I must admit your presence will be missed.

Hale listened to them speak back and forth as old friends. It was a means of dealing with his situation that he found fitting. They were his conscience, his confidants, and his comrades. They were the dark and light of his mind, and not always in the same roles. Making them banter over opposite sides of the issue always helped put things in perspective for Hale, as it allowed him to examine a problem from both sides objectively. And now, in this moment of peril, they gave him comfort and a distraction.

The cold, numb feeling in Hale's chest began to spread. His vision, already dim, continued to fade. Violent movement could be seen above him, and voices sounded far in the distance, though none of it seemed to matter. Hale's mind was preoccupied with other things.

He thought of his parents, and tried to remember the last time he had spoken with them. Had it been months? If so, when was the last time he had actually visited? He wondered what his sister would think of Cass. He bet she'd look up to her.

He really wanted all of them to meet her.

And Ockie. The old bastard was probably waking up right now to get an early start on the week. He didn't ever want to disappoint his boss again.

Alex was probably drunk somewhere, pursuing a conquest and wondering if he should invite the Hermit out to join him. Hale wished he had called him before he left.

Then there was Commodore. The regal beast was probably sleeping on his bed right now, wondering where his loyal servant was. The insolence of the wandering slave would surely have to be addressed. Hale would take the judgmental glares from his cat gladly now, petting the feline until it ran and hid from him.

Extra tuna, too. Commodore loved tuna.

Cass was also prevalent in his mind. He wanted to be with her. Hale had always known he was different, but she was truly special. She stood amongst few people in his life whom he genuinely admired, and he desperately wanted to be somewhere, anywhere other than here, just so he could enjoy the rapture that was her company.

Through the chaos of external events, and the soft, comforting internal banter, a single pressing thought pushed its way through the haze. Its tone was clear and identifiable. It was Hale's own, true internal monologue, and it had come to express a desire greater than any other in his final moments.

I don't want to die.

32

"I'm going to grab Tim," Joseph said flatly. "Then we leave, and we never saw any of this. It was just a job, I aint got nothing against any of you."

"How many more people do you work with?" Hale asked.

"Just him and the Doc," he answered. "He talked a lot of shit, but this op was just getting off the ground. I'm serious man, it was just a job. I'll grab Tim, and you'll never see us again."

"Pick up your friend and get the fuck out," Hale spat.

Cass kept the gun trained on Joseph. At least she thought it was Joseph. Ever since she had shot Rush and Imanu'el had been stabbed, her vision had gotten hazy. Her stomach lurched and her breaths came short. Her skin caught fire with her own blood pumping through her veins, and had she not locked her legs into place, her knees would have buckled and sent her to the floor. The adrenaline of the situation was bad enough, now she had to deal with fresh blood spurting out of an open wound and a dying man on the floor.

She did her best to hide her ragged breaths and the involuntary convulsions in her hands. The fact she had already proven to be a poor shot at best was bad enough, now she had only vaguely humanoid shapes as targets. The adrenaline helped, even if it was likely the cause of her shakes. At least it kept her conscious and focused on the task at hand. Catatonia at a time like this would be inconvenient.

She forced a slow, deep breath into her lungs.

This is important, Cass. She told herself. *Life and death here. Literally. You have just killed a man, and his accomplices are not happy with you. Keep your head on your shoulders, and make sure you don't get anyone else hurt.*

Her stomach continued to churn, threatening to expel its contents on the floor at any moment. Her vision regained some of its focus. She could make out Joseph's retreating form with a modicum of detail. Imanu'el was to her left, she could see him in her peripheral vision. She averted her eyes, panning far right to put Joseph in the opposite corner of her vision. It limited her ability to see them all, though it allowed her to avoid glimpsing Imanu'el's bloody form again.

Instead, her gaze fell on Rush's body.

The hatred she had felt for the man was more intense than any other feeling she had ever felt. The manipulation and subterfuge was bad enough. She disliked people who could not sway the minds of others with truth, and instead relied on fiction to entrap them in their scheme. However, it was not his lack of morality that had driven Cass over the edge. It had been the tactic of using her father that was inexcusable. He was the one figure in her life that remained pure. Even with recent events, she believed her father would not have lied to her had the situation been different. After all, he couldn't be expected to confess his crimes with the police listening in. Therefore, he was still the same man she remembered. With that established, Wilmer Voss was not a man that could be threatened, especially as a cheap coercion tactic. Not in Cass' eyes.

Now, however, seeing his body lying still on the floor, without rage to cloud her judgment and give her justifications, a new hole opened in her stomach. Regret began to plague her, attacking her resolve and questioning her sanity.

You killed a man, Cass. How could you do that?

CLAP

She felt a push on her shoulder. Like a hard slap, but concentrated. The jolt forced a surprised yelp from her lungs, and the pistol involuntarily slipped from the fingers of her right hand. Her injured shoulder prevented her left hand from supporting the weight of the pistol at the ready, causing it to droop until her elbow rested against her stomach. She felt like an old noir detective as she held the pistol at waist height, still trained on the bad guy.

Something was wrong.

Joseph had hit the deck, dropping in a fluid motion and supporting himself in a prone position on his hands and the balls of his feet.

There were more claps, and bright flashes from her right.

The sounds are not near Imanu'el, She justified. *I can look... Dammit Hale, you're in my way.* Cass took a half step forward to peer around Hale. The section where there had once been mirror now featured a fuzzy, middle aged man. He held a pistol out, firing repeatedly.

Not taking time to analyze the situation any further, Cass hunched and pulled the gun up as far as she could, taking aim and firing.

Dammit! She cursed to herself. *Why won't my right arm reach out and help?!*

The gun fired from the hip, placing bullets in a wide array around the man, some ricocheting off the outer walls, others zooming past him and into a short hallway that was hidden behind the mirror.

I must be unsettling him, Cass reasoned. *He's not hitting me either. I'm lucky he's a bad shot, too.*

The Blurry Man finally lowered his gun, ducking away and retreating down the hall behind him. He turned a corner and scampered out of sight.

Cass breathed heavily, keeping her gun trained on the empty hallway. She didn't want him to suddenly reappear after reloading, only to renew the assault with them unawares.

Why can't I pull the trigger anymore? She asked herself. *What's wrong with me?!*

Her attention was drawn to her own hand, which was still squeezing the trigger of the pistol over and over, despite the fact its clip had been completely expended many attempts ago. The slide of the gun had locked into position, preventing the trigger from being fully depressed. She stopped, if not for the futility of the action, then to prevent her enemies from hearing that she was out of ammo.

I don't have any more bullets! If he comes back now, we'll be defenseless!

Hale fell to her side, landing squarely on the floor with little effort to break his fall. His glass eyed stare locked on her, a hint of confusion reflecting from his face.

Cass' eyes moved over him until she reached Hale's torso, spotting three fresh wounds spreading dark blossoms of blood. The lower two splotches in his gut had already connected forming a shape vaguely similar to Mickey Mouse ears across his stomach. The third in his chest had become Mickey's grim, off centered halo.

Hale gurgled as he tried to breathe, blood sputtering from his lips and dribbling down his chin. His eyes, still gazing towards Cass, were unfocused. He seemed less aware of the world around him. She reached down for him as he fell back, unable to reach him before his head thudded against the floor.

"Hale!" she cried out, falling to her knees next to him. The gun clattered from her hand as she reached forward. "Hale, can you hear me?!"

Should I lift him up? Her thoughts were frantic. *No Cass, don't be stupid. Moving him would only make it worse, and the last thing he wants right now is someone touching him. Why won't my right arm move?!*

"Jeremiah! Imanu'el!" she called over her shoulder. "Help!"

Joseph was in the midst of hefting Timothy up as she looked for assistance. The large man completely ignored the plight of the remaining persons in the room, taking his friend and breaking for the door.

Jeremiah scampered over. He had dove for cover when the shooting started. Finding no cover available, he had curled up and covered his head, seemingly counting on luck and prayer to save him. One of the two seemed to have worked.

Imanu'el remained curled on the floor half a dozen feet away. He moaned pitifully, grasping his stomach as he wailed.

"Imanu'el, PLEASE!" Cass shrieked. "Hale is dying, he needs your help!"

"Imanu'el!" Jeremiah jumped to his feet and sprung over Hale. He slid down next to his mentor, putting his arms under Imanu'el's to help him up.

"No!" Imanu'el protested, gripping the knife with both hands as if it would stab him again if he let go. "Don't move me. I need a paramedic! Please! Don't let me die!"

Jeremiah's face set with determination as a clear conflict raged behind his eyes. Without pause, he continued to pull Imanu'el to his feet. Tears brimmed in Jeremiah's eyes as Imanu'el cried out louder. He forced himself to take deliberate, advancing movements to raise them to their feet and cross the short distance to Hale.

Cass risked a looked back over her left shoulder to gauge their progress.

The wailing form of Imanu'el approached, dripping blood through his fingers and out onto the floor. His face contorted in pain, and he protested with each movement.

The image was too much.

Looking away, she saw the prone figure of Rush on the floor. He had not moved since his fall, a large pool of blood spreading out from beneath his torso and his extended wrist. His face retained the wide eyed look he had given Cass when she had pulled the trigger, though the rest of his expression was calm and serene.

She pulled her vision away, confronted by blood and death no matter where she looked. She returned her gaze to Hale. His broken form lay still beneath her. Short breaths were cut off with wet gurgles, causing his chest to jolt and seize. His breathing wheezed into more and more shallow attempts.

Unable to focus on the grisly scene any longer, Cass averted her eyes again. Moving away as far as she could from Imanu'el, Rush and Hale, she looked over her right shoulder at the mirror. A deep red stain caught her eyes before she made it. Her breaths quickened as a chill ran through her body. With a shaking hand, she reached up and gingerly touched her right shoulder.

Suddenly, as if a dammed river had finally found release, the pain flooded through her. A sharp stab akin to a white hot poker stabbed deep into her shoulder. Shockwaves of agony reverberated through her torso, across her neck, through her arms and down her legs. She allowed a small gasp of surprise mixed with anguish as she pulled her hand away.

The last thing Cass remembered before the world spun and went dark were her fingers covered in the deep crimson of her own blood.

33

Jeremiah forced himself to keep moving. In the last hour he had felt stronger emotions than he had ever thought possible. In his life, he had felt fear. Fear was a natural byproduct of his existence. Living on the streets, fighting to survive day in and day out had bred a healthy respect for fear and the motivation it could give.

But nothing compared to the fear he had felt today.

He had been nervous to come to D.C. Imanu'el had reassured him, insisting they make the trip. 'It was important,' he had asserted. Though his instincts told him to refuse, he trusted Imanu'el implicitly.

They had been introduced to very dangerous men. Rush, Dr. Geller, Joseph and Timothy. They made assurances and promises, which did nothing to abate his fear. Jeremiah had his doubts which he had not been able to tell Imanu'el. Rush was not Touched. Or if he was, he was the first Touched he had encountered without a song in his blood. This drove his suspicions even higher. But everything had moved so fast after that, and now it was too late for warnings.

Seeing Imanu'el, his mentor, his true love, be lulled into a false sense of security and forced into drug-induced slumber had opened up a new realm of terror. Being fought and forced into a similar sleep shortly after was no better. After nightmares plagued his drug addled sleep, waking up in a prison and having to fight for freedom had kept his blood curdling in fear.

Finally, being shot at had been the apex, nearly forcing him to abandon the person he held most dear and flee for his life. Had it not been for the sharp pain he had felt when the new, oscillating tone of the gunman's blood had flooded into the room and violently clashed with both Hale and Imanu'el's, he might not have had the moment of pause to consider all of his options.

But that was not what Jeremiah would do. That was Jeremy Higgins. That was the street scum that had no loyalty or direction. He had a new life, new meaning, and a hope for a new existence that was not empty and aimless, but rather filled with purity and purpose.

This made for a tragic segue into the second strong emotion he had felt: Misery.

The initial hints of Imanu'el's true self had been ignored. The man who he had come to revere was nothing less than a saint in his eyes. God's messenger. His own personal messiah. Imanu'el had delivered him from suffering and destitution and given him more than just hope.

Imanu'el had given him life.

To come to the realization that this man was no more than what he had been accused of, nothing more than a con man with an extraordinary gift, was almost too much to bear. A sinking hole had opened in Jeremiah's stomach that was eating away at him from the inside. The joy he had experienced, the rapture he envisioned… it had all been a lie. It was as if a perfect world had been building up around him, only to be toppled and scattered like a card house in a strong breeze. Had it not been for the imminent threat of death provided by Cass and the strange man from behind the mirror, Jeremiah would have walked away from this horrific place and found the nearest dealer to push himself back into oblivion. Old habits would be easily re-accustomed to, and since his new life had been a lie, why not retreat back into a familiar territory of truth?

Despite the falsified mission that had helped develop his current state of mind, Jeremiah's new resolve was strong. While the tools that had forged him had been feeble and misguided, the determination he felt had not completely waned with the revelation of their falsehoods. His will had given him the tenacity to fight and survive, not just through tonight, but through the previous months with Imanu'el. So it was this point where he had felt his third and most powerful emotion for the evening: Rage.

He fought back his anger as he had carried Imanu'el to the bleeding form of Hale. He stifled his contempt as he set the man down and pleaded with him to use his gifts. But now, as Imanu'el whined and argued, he could feel nothing be raw hatred for the individual he had once come to love.

"Imanu'el," Jeremiah tried again. "This man is dying. He is dying because you led these monsters to him. He is a good soul and a righteous man, whether or not he follows the Almighty's word. You must save him."

"Jeremiah," Imanu'el pleaded. "There is no more I can do. My blood cannot heal all wounds, and I have already lost so much. Please, I may die soon if I am not helped."

"And he *will* die if you do not." Jeremiah's voice was stern for the first time since meeting The Man in White. The claim that the blood could not heal all wounds infuriated him even more. Was Imanu'el lying about his potency to avoid helping Hale, or had he been lying about the power of his gift in the past?

"I do not even know if my blood will cure him, Jeremiah." Imanu'el grasped. "I have never healed such a wound, what if it fails? Then we may both die!"

"You've already spilt plenty of blood," Jeremiah growled through gritted teeth. "Just… spill some on him, or… something. Try!"

"Jeremiah, please!" Imanu'el rocked back, feebly reaching out and patting at Hale's wounds with bloody hands. "I can barely speak… I can't… I want to live."

"You lied to me!" Jeremiah shouted, eyes brimming with tears. "You tricked me into thinking you were some great messenger. An agent of God sent to save me and everyone else in this fucked-up world. But no, you're not a messiah. You're just another punk looking out for yourself."

Jeremiah lurched forward, leaning over Hale to grab Imanu'el by the collar. Imanu'el, while surprised, did nothing but gasp in shock, his own hands still fastened to the dagger in his belly.

"You may not believe in what you preached, but I do!" Jeremiah spat. "I believe there is a God. I believe He has sent you here for a purpose. And though it may not be to help others willingly, I will see to it that the right man survives here today, whether you wish it or not."

He stood, pulling Imanu'el to his feet with him.

"Jeremiah…" Imanu'el's eyes widened in shock. "Please, don't… remember who I am."

"I will always remember who you were, and who you should have been." Jeremiah wrapped an arm around Imanu'el's neck, pulling their temples together as they hovered over Hale's body. The deep, resonant sound of Imanu'el's blood sang in his ear. It was a peaceful, rhythmic sound that dulled the bite of the clashing songs of the Touched. The pain of being in the presence of multiple Touched at once was bearable when serenaded by Imanu'el's song, and Jeremiah allowed himself a selfish second to enjoy a final moment of peace.

Hale's song waned, weakening with every second he spent in his final moment of surety. Jeremiah acted, unwilling to let Hale wait for him any longer. With a quick motion, The Gray Hooded Man's free hand shot out and punched Imanu'el's stomach near his bleeding wound.

Imanu'el let out a sharp cry, loosening his grip on the knife at the sudden surge of pain.

Jeremiah slipped his hand down, grasping the bloody weapon protruding from Imanu'el's gut and pulling the knife free. A surge of blood poured out from the wound, sprinkling down onto Hale's prone form. To Jeremiah's dismay, he realized the spatters themselves would barely be enough to heal wounds like the small scrapes Imanu'el inflicted to demonstrate his power.

There needed to be more.

"I am sorry." Jeremiah's jaw was set with anger, his tone laden with sorrow. Tears ran freely from his eyes, and a carnal mixture of growls and sobs choked through gritted teeth. He pulled the knife back, pausing for only a moment before pushing it forward again.

"No–!" Imanu'el's protest was cut short as the blade entered his flesh again.

Jeremiah pulled back and stabbed again, piercing Imanu'el's torso for a third time. Blood poured out in rivulets, coursing onto Hale's body and soaking into his wounds. What little of his shirt that had remained its original color had been coated by this fresh source of blood, turning his entire chest into a dark river of crimson soaked cotton.

Imanu'el, unable to verbally protest, slumped against Jeremiah and sputtered. He choked on breaths, unable to draw in enough to stand, much less speak.

Jeremiah supported Imanu'el's body weight against his own, propping him up like a morbid fountain so his lifeblood would pour out onto its target. Tears ran down his cheeks and onto Imanu'el's, wetting the skin as they pressed together.

"I loved you," he cried. "I love you."

A wheeze came from Imanu'el's lips, though he could do nothing else but hang limply.

Jeremiah sniffled and wiped his eyes on his shoulder, knowing full well this was not a time for sadness. He must ensure Imanu'el's sacrifice was not in vain. He let Imanu'el's body down to the floor, moving as slowly as he could to show reverence for his fallen paramour while still keeping up the speed he needed to finish his task. Without pausing to look into Imanu'el's eyes in what were possibly his final moments, Jeremiah pulled away and stood over Hale.

Hale's body was still, torso completely covered in gore. It was a gruesome image, one that would have distracted Jeremiah had he not mentally detached himself to ensure he could complete the task at hand.

The thunderstorm of the gun battle had left Jeremiah's ears ringing. The music from the Touched had been subdued. He could hear a noticeable downshift in the octaves from both Hale and Imanu'el. Their songs were weakening, and Jeremiah knew it was an indicator that time was running out.

Jeremiah's eyes flitted left and right, trying to think of what to do. Calling on memories of medical shows he used to watch in soup kitchens, he took a hold of Hale's shirt and cut it down the center. The wet cotton provided much more resistance than he would have liked, but with a few tears and the help of the knife, the shirt was split in two.

Hale's bare chest lay exposed in the florescent lighting, the skin stained a bright red. The three bullet wounds continued to seep, though it seemed as if the two on his stomach had been at least partially healed. The bullet holes appeared smaller and less aggravated, though the wound in his chest was still gaping and leaking blood as if untouched by Imanu'el's healing powers.

Desperation crept under Jeremiah's skin.

"It's not working…" he stuttered.

Reaching down, Jeremiah grabbed Imanu'el's arm. He pulled the limb over Hale's chest, positioning the wrist directly over the wound. He dug the edge of the knife in with considerably more effort than he had expended with the point of the weapon, opening the artery. Blood leaked out once again.

Sporadic spurts spoke for Imanu'el's lowered heart rate. Despite his blood loss, a significant amount of blood still emptied over Hale's wounds. Jeremiah' placed two bloody fingers around the chest wound, acting as a funnel of sorts to ensure the most blood possible poured into the wounded man's body.

Nothing happened.

He unceremoniously dropped Imanu'el's arm and to swept excess blood from Hale's chest over the bullet hole, ensuring the healing substance touched that which truly needed it most.

"Please Lord," he whispered to himself as he pressed blood into the wound with his fingertips. "As Cain once did unto Abel, I have committed the most grievous of sins. Help me now, O' Lord, and allow this horrific act to spare one of your Touched children from a fate he does not deserve. Let not your other Touched child, misguided as he was, die in vain. Instead, let Imanu'el's sacrifice give birth to a new life here in Hale."

Hale's wounds remained as they were. Two partially healed, one completely untouched, and his song continued to fade away. Jeremiah waited, closing his eyes and praying more, appealing to the grace of God to assist him in his darkest hour. He reached out with every fiber of his being, begging for mercy for this man he barely knew. He pleaded for the safety of an individual who had shown him no kindness in any of their meetings. He believed and he knew that this selfless prayer for the betterment of mankind could not go unanswered.

After fifteen full minutes of waiting without so much as a twitch from Hale's body, there was only silence in the room. What had once been a cacophony of songs, a painful mixture between Imanu'el's dulcet tones and Hale's symphony of power, was no more.

Jeremiah quietly rose from his position and left.

34

"Ma'am, please answer the question to the best of your ability," The Officer sighed, as if the question was almost too much effort to ask. He stood with his notebook out, his lack of patience reflecting in the frown on his face. He was a portly man, obviously comfortable in his position in life as reflected in his unkempt visage. He hadn't shaved for at least a day, and while his uniform was cleaned and ironed, it looked as if it had not been upgraded to accommodate his new, fuller stature.

Cass absently stared at the ceiling. The hollow echo of her breath collided with the oxygen mask wrapped around her face, each exhale whooshed over the steady sound of her heartbeat. Her arms hurt; One from a strained tendon, which would take a few weeks in physical therapy to repair, the other from a gunshot wound that had torn several ligaments and ripped apart her rotator cuff, potentially causing permanent loss of function and feeling in the limb.

The Officer huffed as if to remind her he was still waiting.

Cass licked her lips, drawing in a slow, deep breath before forcing out words. "Can you repeat the question, please?"

Another belabored sigh preceded the question. "Please explain how you came to be on the floor of a room in which a triple homicide occurred."

Her eyes fluttered open and closed, the morphine keeping her only her vaguely aware that she was indeed awake.

"Well, you know," she began with a hoarse voice. Her words came out slow and slurred, forcing her to make a conscious effort to enunciate each syllable. "I hadn't stormed a bunker in some time, and I felt it would be a good opportunity to brush up on some old skills."

"Ma'am." The Officer's tone was one of warning.

"I was kidnapped," she said flatly. "As I said before. What more do you want from me?"

"One of the firearms was found under your unconscious body. Did you have possession of a firearm during the incident?"

"Yes." Cass knew her fingerprints were all over the weapon, and they could have performed a number of tests while she was out to verify that she had fired the gun. The question was whether they knew it was the gun that killed Rush Channing. Either way, Cass hedged her bets. "I used it in self-defense. There were three men in suits, one of which was attempting to kill my companions and I... I shot first."

"And where did you procure this firearm?" The Officer prodded.

"I stole it," Cass answered truthfully.

"From where?" Notes were scribbled across the clean sheet of paper.

"The compound. I think." She allowed her eyes to flutter. "We... it was in a locker, no... on one of the guards. I am having trouble remembering. But I am sure I took it from them at some point."

"The pistol is registered to one Theodore Palmer," The Officer stated. "He reported it stolen some three months ago during, ironically enough, an armed robbery. Can you explain your whereabouts during that time period, Ms. Voss?"

She glanced down at him, not willing to believe he was actually acting smug. After studying him for a few moments to satisfy her drug addled brain with a confirmation of his triumphant gaze, she finally said, "You do know I am visiting out here, right? I live in California, and have not been to D.C. in years."

The smug smile faded into a scowl. "Of course. I just have to consider all options."

"Then consider them." Cass' voice was a grumble. "Stop trying to force theories on the facts and let the facts speak for themselves. Take a moment and think about the plausible chain of events."

"Ma'am." It was the warning tone again. "Just cooperate and answer the questions to the best of your ability."

"Of course, Officer. Please continue." She leaned her head back, letting her eyes drift closed.

"Did you make contact with anyone during your visit here?" The Officer continued.

"Aside from Hale Langston…" She swallowed back a lump that rose quickly in her throat. "The only other person was my father. He is currently incarcerated, so I visited him."

"Do you have any other friends or family you keep in contact with in the area?"

"No." Her voice rattled as if begging him to discontinue the conversation and let it rest.

"No one at all?"

She shook her head weakly. The small gesture sent a dull arc of pain through her neck and shoulders, sprinting down to her elbow before it finally subsided. She decided not to do that again, and silently thanked the morphine for dulling what would likely have been excruciating pain.

"Do you recognize this number?" The Officer read a number to her.

"No," she admitted. "To be fair, I don't know many people's numbers. I save everything into my phone and go by name."

"That's just it, Ms. Voss," The Officer continued, his voice changing pitch as if digging for answers. "You made a call on Monday morning to a number unattached to any record in your phone. Do you remember who you called?"

"I didn't call anyone," Cass assured. "I had no reason to out here."

"I disagree," The Officer stated, flipping through his notes. "At 7:46 AM on Monday morning you made a call that lasted 5 seconds. Hardly enough to speak with someone, but perhaps it was a mistake and you meant to call them from a less traceable line?"

Cass would have furrowed her brow and adopted her inquisitive look had she not been so relaxed. Her brain attempted to process the new information, slugging through the mush that her gray matter had become under the effects of the pain killers. "What was the number again?"

The Officer repeated it.

"That's a D.C. area code," she stated.

"Yes, Ma'am." She could hear the smug grin in his voice. "Do you remember who you called now?"

"I didn't…" She trailed off, forcing her brain into action.

Think, think. She prodded herself. *Who did you call? Did you even use your phone? No… no I didn't. Not at all. Did I? … This isn't working, so let's approach this from a different angle. Where were you on Monday morning? We arrived on Sunday night. We woke up early to go to coffee. We got to the coffee shop around 7, met with the barista about half an hour later, and then left after talking for about fifteen minutes. That's around the time of the call, right? But I didn't…*

Cass' memories came crashing back in a moment of clarity.

"You might have seen my name on the rosters at UDC. I teach upper division Pysch."

His face came to her clearly now. Pudgy cheeks, a receding line of curly hair, thick glasses. He fit the motif for a professor almost perfectly. She hadn't even suspected.

"Here." He held his hand out. "Let me at least put my number in one of your phones. That way you can look me up at the University and check out my credentials before giving away any personal information. Fair?"

She gave him her phone. Willingly. She had handed him the item that had allowed him to track them down.

He smiled, punching in keys as he continued talking. "It's so rare these days to find good talent, you know?" He pressed a few more keys before pausing. "Would you mind if I put this under my first and last, Nicholas Lyman? Some students prefer Professor Lyman, but I think that is rather formal in cases like this."

He was stalling. Cass realized. Her breath caught in her throat as she replayed the image in her mind. *He had dialed a familiar number, something he could check later, and he stalled us in conversation while it connected.*

"I come here so often, I'm surprised we haven't run into each other before!"

Cass began putting things together, piecing together the most probable truth. *Was he telling the truth? Did he really just happen upon us because we visited a coffee shop that he frequented? Rush brought Imanu'el there for their meeting, maybe he was using it as a meeting spot. It makes sense. He wouldn't risk the cell phone trick if he already had the means to follow us.*

"Ms. Voss," The Officer said. From his tone, it was not the first time he had attempted to regain her attention.

"I'm sorry," she mumbled. "My head is not all here right now. What did you say?"

"I said, who did you call?"

"I saw an ad for a student taxi service," she murmured. "We didn't want to walk all the way back to our car in the cold. After a couple rings Hale said 'screw it, let's just tough it out.' He was always worried about money." Cass smiled to herself at the half truth.

"That number was not for a taxi service."

"Oh?" Her face, nor voice could muster an attempt at surprise. Fortunately, all of her expressions were muted due to her state.

"It was a pre-paid cell phone. One of those you can buy at stores and use until they run out of minutes. Commonly used by people for emergencies who can't afford a normal cell phone, or for individuals who don't want their identities tracked by their contact info. Do you know anyone like that, Ms. Voss?"

"Yes," she said flatly. "But if I was calling one of those people, do you really think I would do so on my phone, and only let the call go for five seconds?"

"Alright, then can you describe the faces of your kidnappers, or perhaps why the anonymous caller who led us to you had details of what was going on inside that compound?"

Cass, eyes still closed, let her mouth pull down into a frown.

"I honestly can't say."

"You can't say the descriptions of the men who kidnapped you?" The Officer's tone expressed his distrust and disdain.

"No," she retorted. "I can't say why the caller knew so much. I can tell you about Joseph and Timothy, who lured us out of the hotel with promises of disclosing information about my father. You can probably get their faces from the hotel security footage. I can tell you about Rush Channing, the man we met with. I can also tell you about Dr. Geller, the physician they had on staff."

"This sounds a little too fantastic to me," The Officer glowered at her.

"You're probably right," she agreed. "I actually hollowed out a, what did you say it was, self-storage facility? Yes, I arrived four days ago, built a bunker using a storage facility as a front, and shot myself and my boyfriend–" Her sarcasm died as her voice cracked. The sarcastic itch that burned to be satisfied on the snide officer faded quickly, remorse and sadness welling up in its place.

The memory of Hale's smiling face beamed at her. His lips moved to form comforting words that complimented his endearing expression, though his voice was muted.

Through closed eyes, tears pushed forth and streaked down her temples and into her hair.

———

THE PUDGY Faced Man walked down the street. His long wool coat covered a black hoodie, which he pulled up over his head. His head hung low, allowing fabric to block onlookers' views of his profile. He liked remaining anonymous. Staying behind the scenes allowed him to work with near impunity, removing distractions and giving him the ability to retreat to the shadows should his plans go awry. While failure was unexpected with his particular talents, it was still possible for variables to cause chaos he could not prepare for.

He had recently learned this all too well.

The loss of his compound set him back at least two years. The remodeling was not difficult. It was reasonably cheap given the circumstances, though it had been time intensive and difficult to find the right workers. Specifically, workers who would not care about anything but a paycheck, and could be assured in their silence after the job was done.

The front itself had not been cheap. The old, rotting storage facility had been a perfect location. Unfortunately, even with its placement outside city limits and away from most communities, the business was costly. His investors had put in a good deal of capital to ensure the land was placed in his hands.

Silver linings, he thought to himself. *One of the investors is dead, and the other one thought you were someone else... specifically the aforementioned dead investor. This removes all of your current debts, giving you a fresh start.*

The Pudgy Faced Man liked fronts. Businesses masking true inner workings, faces projecting images that fit his purpose. Pawns on a chessboard, made to be used and sacrificed for whatever strategy he was executing at the present.

Rush had been a loss. On the board of life, Rush had been the King to his Knight. Versatile. Capable. Loyal... to a point. The Pudgy Faced Man knew all too well Rush's limitations. He knew Rush's weakness was money and control, and when the day came that he no longer needed The Pudgy Faced Man's counsel to ensure his power base, Rush would have betrayed him. It wouldn't be the first time he'd seen an attempt to become the real power on the throne instead of the figurehead taking direction from his shadowy master. No, Rush would not have been a long term asset... though he definitely had more potential than what he put out.

Also, like any good King on the board, he acted as the primary target for his opposition. With the King toppled, the Knight could maneuver to another army.

At least the money he put in has no more strings, the Pudgy Faced Man thought. *I still have a little nest egg from his investment even if I did lose the compound. This was a loss, and though his services will be missed, even his contributions as my face can be replaced.*

The Pudgy Faced Man stomped up a staircase, boots thumping against the rotting wood. A frustrated scowl crossed his features as he remembered some of Rush's less-than-advantageous gambles.

Why the coffee shop? He grumbled internally. *We use that for our internal meetings, not for meetings with the potentials. Giving them the location of my favorite java house does nothing but give them a potential connection. Why risk that? Then again, it did lead to me bumping into Hale and Cassandra... as disastrous as that ended up being.*

He allowed himself an internal chuckle. *Dr. Lyman. Doctor 'Lie Man'... puns really do tickle me.*

The humorous moment of reprieve didn't last.

I should have waited. He kicked himself. *Randy, or Imanu'el, whatever he was calling himself, said he knew where Hale lived. I could have sent Joseph and Timothy out to collect him in California in a week and excluded the troublemaking woman all together. Granted, retrieving him in California could have several issues, especially if Hale had refused the invitation. Besides, I got greedy. I saw a surefire angle with my Sight in Cassandra. She had a weakness: her father. With that leverage, I could bend her any way I wanted. I have always liked surefire options, this one just had unexpected consequences.*

He thought back to their meeting.

"Again, sorry to interrupt, I was just curious what curriculum this case study came from. I'm very interested in following up with you to hear your results," he smiled eagerly. *"What are you hoping to find?"*

   ... Wilmer Voss stood in a cell, the guard had
      arrived to lead him out
         ...... The judge pounded a gavel, booming
         'Innocent' to the courtroom
.... Cass picked up a gun with two fingers covered by
a handkerchief, excitedly bagging the evidence to

exonerate her father

He had been so sure of the results of the brief interaction he did not bother to risk a second meeting to secure his findings. That decision had cost him two years and a competent staff.

The Pudgy Faced Man walked down the outside corridor, moving towards his client's apartment. The morning air caused his breath to come out in puffs of steam, and put a thin sheen of freezing condensation on the lenses of his thick glasses.

Geller had to open his mouth, the overconfident ass that he is. His weakness is definitely discretion, which can be murderous in this line of work. However, his potential for research and discovery is incomparable to any other doctor I have found, so in my mind, the risk was worth taking, and will be worth taking again should I reach out to employ him once more. This time, I will limit his interaction with those who do not absolutely need to associate with him.

The information Geller spilled about Imanu'el did not help settle Hale's mind, and Rush's gamble to appeal to Hale's greed was ill advised. I had told Rush what Hale's leverage was: the girl! Well, the girl and the promise of valued work. The boy had a strong desire to be useful. Regardless, the girl had been a strong influence on him. While he had his own opinions, he would swing with her views. I had Seen it! Then, instead of attempting to salvage the situation, Rush threatened Cassandra's father... how abhorrently stupid. The greatest power of the world at my fingertips, and my plans are unfurled by the arrogance of a cocky Faceman. I shouldn't be surprised, it was his hubris. It is what made him so useful, and in the end, so detrimental.

A rapid pair of knocks alerted the occupants of the apartment that he had arrived. He breathed steadily, readying himself for the coming meeting.

Two years of preparation. Four capable recruits lost... well, one dead, two thugs MIA, and a fourth who has retreated to his private practice. Geller may still be salvageable. I'll have to weigh the benefit of cutting him loose and keeping the

funds Geller had donated without strings. After all, Geller thought that Rush was
the man with the power, not me. We've never even met. Well, not under a real
name, and certainly not under memorable circumstances.

The door opened. A short Latino man stood in the dimly lit room.

"Orale, Counselor," he mumbled in greeting, wiping his eyes. "You said you
was comin' by early, but fuck, this is early early, homes."

"My apologies, Mr. Vasquez," the Pudgy Faced Counselor smiled. "I know
you cherish your sleep, but we are on a tight timetable."

"Come in, man. And call me Augustus, that Mr. Vasquez shit bothers me."

"Of course," The Pudgy Faced Man smiled, and entered as directed.

The small apartment was well furnished, featuring a strong oak table and
leather sofas. A large LCD TV was mounted on the wall, several game consoles
populating a table below it. Flanking each side of the entertainment center were
shelves of movies, games, and various accessories to the myriad of electronic
components.

"You're doing well for yourself," The Pudgy Face Man observed.

"What can I say?" Augustus shambled over to the table. "The community
has been good to me. Charitable donations and all."

"Don't let your parole officer find out about those charitable donations." The
Pudgy Faced Man examined the rows of DVD's as he spoke. "He might think
you're dealing again."

"Fuck that piece of shit," Augustus spat, animation flaring up from his
previously tired demeanor. "That cocksucker is tryin' to sell me a year's worth of
solid reviews for twenty G's. Corrupt mother fucker."

"Isn't that a deal for you? Impunity for 365 days sounds like it would give
you an opportunity to thrive." The Pudgy Faced Man pulled down a DVD copy of
The Usual Suspects. "Mind if I borrow this?"

"It's a deal if the counter offer ain't to send me to jail if I don't pay. It's a
fuckin' shakedown, that's what it is." Augustus leaned back, glancing at the DVD
in his lawyer's hand. "Yeah man, take it."

"Thanks, I love this movie." The Pudgy Faced Man put the movie in his pocket and turned to his client. "Augustus, do you remember that inmate you told me about? The one you used to sell heroin to?"

"Which one, man?"

"The special one."

"Oh, that carnal," Augustus leaned forward, holding out his hand to display a scar across his finger. "The one who did this, right?"

"The same."

"How could I forget, man?" Augustus poked at the scar. "It's like rubber, aint that shit weird? We both damn near get shivved and barely fight the vatos off, right? Randy gets his palm cut open, I get shanked in the side, they almost got my kidney, and get my pinky near shaved off. My homies get there just in time to pull the vatos off us, and Randy, the stupid fucker, grabs my cut up hand to lift me off the ground. I almost decked him it hurt so bad... but then the shit just goes numb. I thought I lost my damn finger man! Thought he pulled it right off! But nah, there it was. I look down and the scar is already forming. I thought I was seeing shit, but when I woke up in the infirmary, there it was, all healed. How crazy is that shit?"

"Crazy, no doubt," The Pudgy Faced Man said with a sardonic smile. "And why didn't you keep him around after that? Seems like an interesting friend to have."

"I tol' you, man, he got released before I got out of medical. Homey kept sayin' he was going to head out West or something. Had friends in Long Beach he was gonna hook up with and start some new gig."

"What do your associates think about the story?"

"Pshh, man, they think I belong in a straitjacket." Augustus waved him off. "I stopped telling people about it months ago 'cause they were starting to think I lost it in the pen."

"How many people did you share it with?" The Pudgy Faced Man asked curiously.

"Shit, five, maybe six?" Augustus shrugged. "We had our meeting the next day, so I told you. All hopped up on meds and lying in a bed, that story sounded like a good thing to tell to my lawyer, right? I'm lucky you didn't drop me right there. Then I told a couple more of ese's in my cell block, but none of those vatos believed me. I just wrote it off and called it a day, man. Speaking of which, a bunch of my homies have been calling you, leaving messages and shit. You too busy to show up in court anymore?"

"I've been busy with personal issues." The Pudgy Faced Man smiled again. "So tell me, what would it take to get you to tell this story to others again?"

> . . . Rolls of cash were placed in Augustus's
> hand
> . . . . . scantily clad women rubbed against him
> . . . . a gun pressed against his forehead

The flood of images kept coming, giving dozens of scenarios in which Augustus would spill his secrets. It was not even a question to The Pudgy Faced Man. He could See it.

He'll crack. And when they come looking, he'll lead them to me.

"Pshh," Augustus scoffed again, answering with words well after The Pudgy Faced Man had received his answers. "I ain't telling that story again. It's bad for business."

"Of course." He smiled supportively, pulling a folded up bundle of papers from his coat. "Well, I just need you to sign some papers to conclude our business, after which you can forget about me until you need a face in court... again."

Augustus took the papers and set them on the table. "Yeah, no offense, man, but I hope I don't see you for a long time."

"I'm sure you'll find an arrangement that keeps you out of the law's hands, Mr. Vasquez."

"Yeah, no doubt." Augustus began to sign.

"Put the 8th."

"Ain't it the 9th ?"

"Yes, but if you put the 9th , I'm required to bill you for another day." The Pudgy Faced Man smiled. "Consider it a parting gift, my final trip here is free of charge."

"Shit, I ain't think a lawyer ever done nothin' for me for free," Augustus scoffed, putting yesterday's date next to his name. "Gracias, carnal."

"My pleasure." The Pudgy Faced Man took the paperwork proving the last time he saw his client was a day earlier and put it in his inner coat pocket. As he did so, his eyes glanced up over Augustus' head. "Where did you get that painting?"

Augustus turned around, looking up at the patch of wall that had drawn his lawyer's attention.

The Pudgy Faced Man, hand already in his coat, withdrew a pistol. He took a half step back to avoid spray, aimed at the back of Augustus' head, and pulled the trigger. The shot was muffled by the silencer, the metal clack of the hammer and sliding bar adding to the effect. Even so, the sound could easily be mistaken for a chair sliding into the wall, or a pan slapping against the oven.

Blood splattered across the table and wall, exploding forth from the exit wound in Augustus' cheek. The Latino man rocked away from the bullet, swaying while his dead weight found a comfortable direction to fall. Fortunately for The Pudgy Faced Man, his target's body slumped onto the table and came to a rest.

"Thank you, Mr. Vasquez," The Pudgy Faced Man said to the corpse. "That will be all. Now, if you don't mind, I am going to pillage your home for whatever cash and drug holdings you have stashed away, as right now my business is in need of extra funding."

He didn't revel in the death of his client, but it was a necessary step to achieve the thing he craved. The journey to power would be long, arduous, and full of danger. The Pudgy Faced Man welcomed the challenge with a smile.

About the Author

Sean Mooney started Mad Moon Rackets in 2002. He spent two years writing, editing, commissioning illustrators, and finally publishing his first game in 2004.

Made Men – Welcome to the Family, a Tabletop Roleplaying Game, did a few small print runs, was featured at the last Gen Con So Cal, and then at Gen Con Indy in 2005.

Attention shifted to writing One Shot Larps after the fact, and Tomorrow Dies Today was born. TDT was written and playtested several times as a fun side venture, but ended up on the back burner.

Sean also began writing Touched, with a mantra of "2K a day!" to get a manuscript fully written. After putting 135K words to paper, the manuscript did what many others do and gathered electronic dust.

With life getting busier, creative projects got pushed to the side.

The mantra of 'I'll do it later' was constant, but upon turning 35, Sean realized 'later' was 'now'.

Mad Moon Rackets is back in business, with a rebrand to Mooney Bin Entertainment in 2019. Sean is actively writing, with several new projects on the horizon. It is Sean's mission through Mooney Bin Entertainment to entertain its readers and players.

Visit us Online!

www.MooneyBinEntertainment.com

www.facebook.com/MooneyBinEntertainment